Praise for
the New York Times bestselling
Belador series

ROGUE BELADOR

"When it comes to urban fantasy stories, Dianna Love is a master." ~~A. Richards, Always Reviewing

"This adventure win or lose is going to change things for Evalle and her friends. Brava Ms. Love for another fantastic ride." ~~ In My Humble Opinion

"It was worth every day of waiting." ~~ J. Cazares, Amazon

"As always, Dianna Love delivers another sensational story that will blow your mind," ~~ Barb, The Reading Café

"Keep them coming and I will keep reading. Thank you for another awesome adventure." ~~ Candi, Amazon

WITCHLOCK

"Fans of Rachel Caine's Weather Warden series will enjoy this series. I surely do." ~~D. Antonio, In My Humble Opinion

"Every scene in WITCHLOCK is absolutely spellbinding...This

remarkable author repeatedly leaves you wondering if there truly are happenings on earth of which we are not aware..." ~~Amelia, SingleTitles.com

"I LOVE THESE BOOKS! I wait impatiently for every book to come out and have never been disappointed." ~~Elizabeth, Reader

DEMON STORM

"..non-stop tense action, filled with twists, betrayals, danger, and a beautiful sensual romance. As always with Dianna Love, I was on the edge of my seat, unable to pull myself away." ~~Barb, The Reading Cafe

"There is so much action in this book I feel like I've burned calories just reading it." ~~D Antonio, Goodreads

"...I have to thank Dianna for keeping this series true to the wonderful world, witty dialogue and compelling characters that I have loved since the first book." ~~Chris, Goodreads

RISE OF THE GRYPHON

"...It's been a very long time since I've felt this passionate about getting the next installment in a series. Even J. K. Rowling's Harry Potter books. It's a story you don't want to end and when it does, you can't help but scream out 'No! NO THEY DID NOT JUST DO THIS TO ME!! NO!!!!'" ~~Bryonna Nobles, Demons, Dreams and Dragon Wings

"...shocking developments and a whopper of an ending... and I may have exclaimed aloud more than once...Bottom line: I really kind of loved it." ~~Jen, Amazon Top 500 Reviewer

THE CURSE

ALTERANT

BLOOD TRINITY

"BLOOD TRINITY is an ingenious urban fantasy with imaginative magical scenarios, characters who grab your every thought and more than a few unpredictable turns ... The meticulous storyline of Book One in the Belador series will enthrall you during every compellingly entertaining scene."
~~Amelia Richard, Single Titles

"BLOOD TRINITY is a fantastic start to a new Urban Fantasy series. The VIPER organization and the world built ... are intriguing, but the characters populating that world are irresistible. I am finding it difficult to wait for the next book to find out what happens next in their lives." ~~Diana Trodahl, Fresh Fiction

"BLOOD TRINITY is without a doubt one of the best books I've read this year... a tale that shows just how awesome urban fantasy really can be, particularly as the genre is flooded with so many choices. Brilliantly done and highly recommended." ~~ Debbie, CK2s Kwips & Kritiques

DRAGON KING
of TREOIR

THE BELADOR SERIES

BOOK 8

NEW YORK TIMES BESTSELLING AUTHOR

DIANNA LOVE

Cover Design and Interior format by The Killion Group
http://thekilliongroupinc.com

The Belador series is an ongoing story line, and this is the reading order:

Blood Trinity
Alterant
The Curse
Rise Of The Gryphon
Demon Storm
Witchlock
Rogue Belador
Dragon King Of Treoir
*Midnight Kiss Goodbye (Belador novella in Dead After
Dark anthology; timeline is concurrent with Blood Trinity)
*Tristan's Escape (Belador novella occurs between
Witchlock and Rogue Belador timelines)
*Firebound (novella of how Evalle found Feenix – free at
www.AuthorDiannaLove.com)

Dedication

This book is for readers who share the love of urban fantasy with me. Thank you for joining my world of Beladors.

CHAPTER 1

The underworld realm of Anwynn

Two thousand years of paying for one mistake.

Two thousand years of pain, every minute of every day.

Lorwerth cursed his thirty-one-year-old body that would not age and could be healed so easily. He begged for death with each breath. Today would be different.

I should be leading a powerful army against my enemies, but instead ...

"The Koovl!" Stomp.

"The Koovl!" Stomp.

All at once, his world spun back into focus. He lost his grip on that place in his mind where he traveled to escape reality.

A loud crack from the forty-foot whip rent the air above his head. Fire danced along the strands, throwing shards of sparkling light across this cavernous den of misery.

None of it touched him.

This time.

Prisoners cheered on *Y Cwfl,* The Koovl.

Lorwerth's naked backside and legs had been flayed to pieces, left raw and burning. He tensed, waiting for that next hit, but the bastard flogging him, *Y Cwfl,* toyed with each prisoner, reaching for emotional abuse as much as physical.

Lorwerth bit down hard, focusing only on the end.

It would come today.

Prisoners of Anwynn shouted their favorite chant, calling *Y Cwfl's* name and stomping.

Death would not come. No blessing of eternal sleep for the

damned. Not in Anwynn, land of the dead, ruled by the Celtic god Arawn.

Pain fed Arawn's power. The more his minions suffered, the stronger Arawn and his enforcers, like *Y Cwfl,* became.

No more. This ended today.

Lorwerth had a plan.

"The Koovl!" Stomp.

"The Koovl!" Stomp.

Lorwerth's knees quivered.

His body would have sagged if not for his outstretched arms held up by woven iron rope. Spikes along the binding dug into his wrists.

Stinking sweat poured into his eyes. His hair stuck to his head and neck. His back lay in raw agony from a whip split into five lengths, each strip hot as burning coal spun into leather.

The Koovl had paused in striking him.

If Lorwerth's heart gave out, which it had many times, The Koovl would call his master to bring Lorwerth back to life. They'd dump him in his hole, a circular space ten feet across, and leave him until he'd healed enough to start the vicious cycle over.

Torture came in many forms.

Like waiting for the unknown.

Every time he regained consciousness after healing, he waited in terror for what would come next. It changed constantly, from beatings to perversion to flogging to losing body parts that were later regrown.

Through it all, his mind refused to give way to insanity.

That left him only one choice—force The Koovl to destroy his body beyond the point Arawn could heal it.

Lorwerth had seen The Koovl make that mistake once before, three or four hundred years ago. Arawn had meted out his punishment. Lorwerth shuddered at that memory, even though he should be smiling.

"The Koovl!" Stomp.

"The Koovl!" Stomp.

He smelled his death. So close. He would have his victory today.

Now was the time to take control.

Lorwerth allowed a groan to slip from his cracked lips.

Cheers went up around the room until The Koovl shouted, "What say you, *llwfrgi?*"

Being called a coward shouldn't bother Lorwerth, not after all this time. But he'd been a feared warrior in his day. An eternity ago. No person would have dared call him such a name back then and expect to live.

He should never have given *Y Cwfl* that weapon to use against him.

The first time The Koovl had called him a coward, Lorwerth had foolishly attacked Anwynn's enforcer. The Koovl had never let him forget his mistake.

"*Llwfrgi?* Have you nothing to say for your worthless self?"

Remaining silent would lead to being whipped at least three more times. As Lorwerth's breaths came slower, The Koovl would watch for the moment he could call in Arawn to heal the prisoner.

To succeed at forcing The Koovl to lose control and lash Lorwerth without stopping until the enforcer cut his body in half, Lorwerth had to push The Koovl beyond all reason.

He drew in a deep breath to show that he had plenty of life left in him. A lie.

The whip slapped the air back and forth as The Koovl warmed up for another attack.

Lorwerth mentally prepared himself and yelled, "We are men and will always be men. The Koovl wears a robe to hide that he is a eunuch. That is why he is Arawn's bitch."

All the shouting stopped in a flurry of gasps.

Lorwerth would like to see The Koovl's face. Actually, everyone would like to see the enforcer's face. That wasn't happening since it was hidden deep inside a hood.

Rage ripped from The Koovl in a long, feral roar, the sound of a beast threatening to destroy everything in his path.

That's what Lorwerth wanted. The Koovl completely out of control.

The whipped cracked through the air above Lorwerth with so much power his ears felt as if they'd burst.

That had been a prelude, a taunt meant to drive terror through every corner of a man's brain. It worked. But that would be The

Koovl's last win over Lorwerth.

He panted fast, gritting his teeth and fisting his hands, ready for that final strike. The one that would rip his body in too many pieces to repair. He shook with anticipation.

Air whistled sharply.

"Cease!" thundered from the only person capable of interrupting *Y Cwfl* and stopping his strike in midair.

Arawn.

Silence swept the room.

"No!" Lorwerth screamed. *"No, no, no!"*

Candlewicks burst into flame, sending a red glow over the cavernous room.

Please, no. Not now, with Lorwerth poised to draw his last breath. Tears ran down his face. How could they have known that stopping at this moment inflicted more agony than at any time in the past? He closed his eyes, no longer able to face what came next.

Lorwerth's bindings vanished.

He dropped hard onto his feet and went to his knees, burning them on the hot stones. Struggling, he wobbled his way back up to stand on bare feet he could no longer feel. Blood streamed along his back and legs, sizzling when it hit the stones. Blisters bubbled and the smell of burned flesh clogged his nose. His head spun. His eyes blurred, then everything came back into focus.

So close, if only he could lose consciousness.

Just give me that.

The damned in this treacherous underworld stomped and cackled. They howled at him with joy.

But he stood with his hands free.

Or was he hallucinating?

Something was off, even for Anwynn. Never had he returned to his hole while able to stand.

Turning to face his persecutors, Lorwerth expected to see Arawn. The ruler was not in sight.

Only the ten-foot nightmare of Lorwerth's world stood in the center of the room. Two searing red orbs peered out from inside his hood.

Where was the master? Had Lorwerth only imagined the interruption?

What was going on?

Lorwerth's heart thumped slower and slower. The Koovl stood there, power so strong radiating from him that tendrils of red smoke drifted off of his robe.

Lorwerth dropped his head and closed his mind. The Koovl would rip his chest and genitals apart now, a reminder that anything could be worse. For the millionth time, Lorwerth pleaded to every god he'd known before landing in this dung pit, offering his soul, anything he could in exchange for relief.

No one heard him here.

His head spun. He recognized the blessed end of consciousness. *Thank you.* Sweet darkness swallowed him. A reprieve? Not possible.

Time passed. Bloody nightmares kept him company.

"Wake up," a voice close by ordered, dragging Lorwerth back from oblivion.

He cursed at being roused already. His eyelids fluttered, struggling to open, then giving up the battle.

Why should he open them?

"Get up, Lorwerth."

That wasn't *Y Cwfl*. The Koovl had a voice that would raise hair on a corpse.

The master never spoke, not to Lorwerth.

So who was it?

Opening one eye, he squinted at a blurry figure. No matter how long he looked, the tall shape would not come into focus.

"I do not have time to waste, Lorwerth. If you do not rise soon, I will find another."

In all these years, no one had come to see him.

This wasn't a place to visit. This was an eternal destination of suffering, and no one risked setting foot here voluntarily.

But unless he was imagining it, he had a visitor.

Sliding his hands next to his shoulders, Lorwerth pushed up on trembling arms. He kept forcing his naked body to move until he stood at his full height of over six feet.

He'd had a commanding profile at one time. He'd been considered a handsome warrior with coal black hair. A man who should be ruling—

Excruciating pain stabbed his heart at all he'd lost.

Some things were far worse than any physical torture. He forced those thoughts back. Memories of a golden life that had been snatched away.

Now standing, he stared at the stranger. The person's shape remained out of focus. Blinking his eyes didn't help.

Lorwerth asked, "Who ... who are you?"

"I'm the only person who matters in your world from now on. I'm taking you out of here."

Shock stole his breath. His lungs cried for air. He clutched his chest, sure that his heart would fail again.

Leave here?

Then reality crashed in. This could be nothing more than an evil game being played by his keepers. The kind of evil that The Koovl would enjoy inflicting, but this was too subtle for the enforcer.

And why now?

Weary to the soles of his blistered feet, Lorwerth wiped his face and scrubbed at his eyes, pausing to peer again at the figure, whose shape wavered.

Foolish man that he was, a tiny flame of hope forced Lorwerth to inquire, "What do you want?"

"To give you your freedom, Lorwerth. For you to live in the current day human world, which has changed much in two millennia."

His hope died just as quickly.

Who would come here to free him?

"Of course you want to do that," Lorwerth muttered, mentally preparing for this new phase of torture. He'd been whipped, but hadn't been bludgeoned in a while.

Why couldn't they just pound his body?

"I am not toying with you," the blurry person said. "You made an error in judgment once. I've traded a favor as payment for your mistake."

Payment?

What had the last two thousand years been? He knew how long he'd been here only because The Koovl enjoyed informing the prisoners every time a year, decade or century passed.

Still, what if this offer was real? What if this figure told the truth? Just who was this person? A man? A woman?

Would that matter?

No.

Lorwerth knew better than to allow hope to take root, but his curiosity, dormant for so long, flickered to life now. If nothing else, he'd find out what trick hid beneath the surface of this offer. "If you take me from here, you would then own me."

"This is true, Lorwerth."

"What depravity will *you* foist upon me?"

"None. I am not here seeking entertainment. I need a warrior. Someone who can lead soldiers. You do recall how to be one, don't you?"

This could not be real.

Lorwerth reached a hand to pinch his side. *Ouch.* He was definitely awake. Had one of his many prayers to different gods been answered?

Which god was behind this?

Would that matter? No.

Finally, Lorwerth said, "I will lead an army of demons if you take me out of here, feed me and clothe me."

"Your soldiers will be far more than demons. You will have what you need to accomplish your duty."

Lorwerth's heart tumbled over. Was this really happening? He licked his chapped lips. "I . . . I will need time to return to fighting condition."

"You will regain the same face, body and skill you possessed the day you were sent here. You will retain the ability to heal yourself and I will gift you with a power for defending yourself. You will be revered among your men. You have but to swear that you will perform any task I require."

Lorwerth made a scoffing sound. As if there was anything he wouldn't do at this point? "Name your first task so that I may get started."

"I want the Treoir dragon brought to me."

Treoir? Dizziness swept him momentarily. "The dragon-shifter? Do you mean *Daegan* Treoir? He is alive and free of TÅµr Medb?"

"Yes," his new benefactor confirmed. "Is there a problem or do we have a deal?"

Lorwerth had been sent here because of the Treoirs. "We have a deal, my lord. I will serve you forever and perform any task you request just for the chance to bring that dragon to his knees."

"I can see I've made a wise investment in you."

He would have freedom and vengeance. For the first time in many centuries, Lorwerth smiled.

CHAPTER 2

Present day - East of San Diego, California

Reese Ó Rinn checked her rearview mirror one more time for two headlights closing in on her, two bright dots bouncing with the hard pace she kept on this dirt road.

Time to back off her speed so they could catch her.

Winding up out here in the middle of nowhere east of San Diego late at night and alone wasn't the action of a rational human being, but then she'd never been accused of being rational.

Or human.

At twenty-nine, she was stuck firmly between human and screwed.

Yep. Those two motorcycle demons were gaining on her.

That wasn't an exaggeration or a slur on bikers. She literally had a pair of *jötnar* demons hot on her tail.

She'd killed her share of demons during the ten years since losing her powers.

But this was the first time she'd been chased by *jötnars*.

Very likely to be her last.

She had one hope of beating them tonight, but not much faith in her idea working. Her next-door neighbor Donella, who was five years older than Reese, would admonish her negative thinking and offer the old motivational saying to make lemonade when life handed you lemons.

Hey, I'm a positive thinker. When I get handed lemons, I say slice those suckers and pop open the tequila.

It was all about perspective.

As for tonight? No positive way to spin having two demons hell-bent to turn her into their Friday night recharge station.

She'd caught the pair in her neighborhood about to attack an old woman who couldn't see the demonic appearance beneath human-looking exteriors. Just two clean-cut, twenty-something males trying to convince a lonely old woman to share a meal with them.

If Reese hadn't come along, the human authorities would've found her body in an alley or maybe a roll-off garbage container.

Not exactly her entire body. Her organs would be gone and she'd have a terrorized look stuck on her sweet face.

Drawing the threat away from the woman had required Reese to expose her own internal energy, which demons craved like crack.

Now an hour outside of San Diego into the foothills, she could face those two without worrying about humans being involved.

Killing demons had turned into an art form for her after she'd had her powers bound. For her own good, no less.

Bound. Yeah, right. She had a better word. Stolen.

She'd been left with no supernatural fighting abilities, but she still carried massive internal energy. In simple terms, she'd become a homing beacon for all kinds of demonic nasties. Sure, she actively hunted them in her spare time, but she'd never go looking for *jötnars*, because they hunted in pairs.

They shouldn't even be on this continent.

Demons wanted the energy pulsing inside her, but it wasn't as if she broadcast where she lived. Just the opposite. She kept that pulsing current hidden behind a corset created primarily of silver chains. It wouldn't completely mask the rhythmic bursts, but it dulled the pulse. Demons had to be very close to notice.

She couldn't risk a throwdown with humans around. When the *jötnars* showed up, she'd pulled off the shield in a bathroom, tossed it into her jeep and walked within a hundred feet of the deadly duo.

Their heads had snapped toward her in tandem. Grandma forgotten.

No camera could capture their true appearance, with black

eyes, chalky-white skin, tall ears, shark-like teeth, and a horn curving back over the top of each head. As they'd stared at her, their eyes had boiled red with excitement.

Now, nothing short of a ten-story building dropping out of the sky onto them would stop the chase.

She looked up. No tornadoes in sight.

Ten years of fighting with only human ability had motivated her to be deadly with any weapon at hand. She was, which meant she'd become too confident. So much so, that she'd made the stupid mistake of gaining possessions she didn't want to lose—a dog, a place she considered home and neighbors who treated her like a friend.

She had no business wanting a life with humans. A being like her didn't deserve to share their world. If she couldn't even keep her own neighborhood safe, then she shouldn't be anywhere she put innocent people at risk.

Overconfidence in her skills and a weak moment of loneliness had led to this day.

The game of cat and mouse was now well outside of the city, but she knew this area. She'd hiked here before.

She hoped that advantage would weigh in her favor.

Probably not. Her kickboxing instructor, Wiley, would admonish her to never go into a fight expecting to lose.

She'd think on that, if she didn't hyperventilate first.

Of course, Wiley thought she'd be using all those ninja fighting moves on humans.

Her bare-bones Jeep Wrangler bounced along the rutted road, blowing up a dust cloud behind her. Her headlights stared into a void of black.

Time to look for the place to make her stand.

Local residents and outdoor enthusiasts drove up Minnewawa Truck Trail to Doghouse Junction during the day so they could hike to the summit and take in a view of Lower Otay Reservoir. She'd seen that beautiful view during one of her reconnaissance trips in preparation for a worst-case scenario.

Like tonight.

She gave her mirror a last check.

Those two must suck at driving motorcycles. They were falling back. Hey, maybe they sucked at fighting, too.

Keep telling yourself that.

At one time, she'd had the kind of raw power that meant a fair match. Back when she'd been whole.

Just a faded memory now.

Her damp hands clamped the wheel. If they got her down, they'd siphon off her energy and leave her to die slowly and painfully. Not a comforting scenario, but she'd known this day would come. She'd gotten too relaxed and started believing she could live out her life among humans.

She'd even made plans for her thirtieth birthday—an occasion human women focused on so heavily.

She'd likely never see a cake with candles, but these two behind her were not harming another person if Reese had anything to say about it.

Oh the irony. She was a regular battery pack for demons, but could she tap that power and save her own butt?

No. Not after an asshat took her powers away a decade back and left her stranded in the human realm. He'd told her she had to earn them back.

That giant ego hadn't shared any tips.

Just said go do it.

She'd done everything she could for the first two years in hopes he was noticing. Since then, she'd given up waiting for him to summon her. Years of waiting and not a peep.

Just another male who had screwed her along the way. The first one ...

She slapped the steering wheel and yelled, *"Screw all of you men!"*

Including those two imposters behind her ... who were catching up.

Her pushy conscience pointed out that she'd passed ten perfectly suitable battle locations.

"Okay, okay. Maybe I am stalling," she muttered. She hoped her conscience didn't follow her into the afterlife.

Damn thing had gotten her into more trouble than it was worth. Now it seemed determined to hurry her toward that afterlife.

She spotted a place up ahead. Digging for some backbone, she got her speed just right then let off on the accelerator, pulled the hand brake and wrenched the steering wheel, going into the steps for a controlled spin.

Time slowed as her headlights swept around to face the two motorcycles tearing up the road. She heard every loud heartbeat pumping blood and adrenaline through her. For those few seconds when she was living in a moment all her own, she watched the world turn with her.

All too quickly, time sucked backed to high speed.

Damn good spin, if she did say so herself. The stunt pro who'd taught her would have given her a high five.

She pulled out of it, slammed hard on her brakes and killed the engine along with the lights. Yanking on night vision goggles, she grabbed her gear and slipped into the dust cloud still swirling.

The high-pitched sound of sport bikes wound down as the demons pulled up fifty feet away and parked. In the next second, the bikes were quiet and their lights switched off.

They would have overtaken a human by now. Their hesitation meant they had no idea what she could do.

The energy she'd been born with warmed her chest, generating power when anything preternatural got within about thirty feet.

She moved twenty steps away from the Jeep and stood next to a pinyon bush that reached her waist. This terrain offered little in the way of tall cover to hide behind, but hiding wasn't part of her offensive plan.

She'd come prepared with an uber-short, Saiga semi-automatic twelve-gauge shotgun and a homicidal attitude for facing demons bent on stealing her essence.

Full disclosure. She was packing double-ought buck shells full of silver shot and a custom-made short sword sporting a blade also inlaid with silver. A silver bullet wouldn't kill a *jötnar* demon, but that metal was as close to their kryptonite as it got.

On the other hand, cut off a head and it wouldn't grow back.

Movement to her right caught her eye. That would mean the other one stalked her from the left.

"I can make this fast and easy on you," the demon coming in from her right said, his rough voice hitching a ride on a dead wind. All he had to do was slice one of his poisonous claws across any part of her body and she was done.

In less than an hour, she'd be paralyzed and easily accessible.

She said nothing in reply, just stood there as if she hadn't heard him. Without turning to the right, she could see him easing closer to her, then pausing to stare.

Not answering the demon threw him off his game.

Not hitting them with a blast of power would too, until they realized she had no supernatural weapons.

She held the shotgun angled across her body, ready for anything, and cut her eyes to the left. His partner came into view, climbing uphill from a shallow gulley.

The one on her right spit out something in Latin she couldn't decipher, then leaped at her.

Reese dove away from the bush, twisting to fire off a round that ripped into his shoulder. He jerked in mid flight and landed on the ground with his arm flopping.

Her pulse jackhammered. She sucked in a deep breath, rolling up to her knees and turning.

The other demon raced in howling.

She swung the muzzle upward as he dove forward.

Her aim was true this time.

The tight pattern of shot entered through his eye and blew out part of his head, knocking him sideways with the point-blank impact. He still managed to catch her with a claw as he flew by. The razor-sharp nail tore a gash in her upper arm the length of her hand.

Burning pain almost blinded her.

Shit. She wouldn't have long. Her body urged her to lie down and curl in on herself, but that wouldn't stop the pain. Besides, they had to siphon off her energy while she still lived. *Not happening.*

The second demon she'd blasted got to his feet and walked in a circle, holding his head. He made gargling noises. Was he trying to heal himself?

Unfortunately, it took more than blowing away a serious chunk of gray matter to kill a *jötnar.*

Blood seeped into her shirt. *Hurry.* She didn't have much time and one of the bastards was still on the ground.

Had to be playing possum.

She pushed up and stepped slowly around the pinyon bush.

When she got close, the demon rolled away. She fired two rounds that popped chunks from his side and thigh, but that didn't keep him down.

He jumped up and ran into the black night.

Huh.

Why had one run off? That was not how she'd planned this. Both of them should be coming toward her so she'd know where they were. She needed to reload while she still could. Chills shook her body. Hands trembling, she grabbed a full twelve-round magazine from the carrier on her belt, released the old magazine and shoved the new one in place.

The second demon still stomped around. *Jötnars* were practically zombies, mindless butchering machines. But even a demon missing part of its head couldn't function fully. She'd planned to kill this one after she'd cut the head off the first one.

Why'd they have to screw up a good plan?

Her vision blurred and the gash in her arm felt on fire. *Don't quit now.* She blinked and turned, lifting her shotgun. She pulled the trigger to blow out the demon's knee from behind.

He jerked, fell face down then rolled over, screeching and kicking his good leg around.

She walked over and shot each shoulder, disabling his arms, which shuddered as he writhed on the ground. Her skin felt like ice snakes crawled all over her. Sweat ran down her face and pooled at her neck. She reached over her shoulder and withdrew her sword. With one swift move, she came straight down, slicing his head off.

His body stopped moving.

One piece of shit down.

His body began to wither.

She booted his disgusting head twenty yards into the dark.

"Field goal, bitch. You lose." Turning slowly, she sheathed the short sword and waited for the other one. Where was he?

Then she heard it. In the distance, footsteps pounded toward her, fast and hard.

She focused her hearing ... he was coming from her left.

All at once, the sound stopped.

What was he ...

Movement above jerked her gaze up.

Airborne demon incoming, fifteen feet off the ground. He flipped and turned his feet down, intending to land on her.

She lurched backwards to avoid being crushed and ripped off two shots as she fell.

The first round went wide.

Her second one hit right between his legs, striking his jewels. Neutering one of them would make this the field trip of the week.

He landed hard and rolled over howling, clutching his crotch.

"Regenerate that while I cut your head off, you bag of shit," she muttered, getting to her feet again and stumbling forward. The ground moved. Hard to look badass when light headed. *Hold on*, she told herself.

She saw a double image of the demon writhing on the ground.

He lifted a rock the size of a football and flipped it at her. She wasn't quick enough. The stone missile struck hard, breaking her right forearm.

There went her trigger hand. The shotgun swung loose on its sling.

Sounding like a rabid beast, the bastard twisted around, making guttural sounds that raised the hair on her arms. He came at her on all fours.

She swiped up the shotgun with her left hand, scrambling backwards.

He crawled faster, then stood, lifting his hands and snarling.

She braced for the recoil against a one-handed grip, but the demon hit her with a kick to the abdomen. Shoving the shotgun forward, she unloaded her last seven rounds at his face on her way down.

He stopped at her feet, towering over her.

The top of his head and most of his face had been chewed away. *Thank you double-ought buck.*

He wobbled, hands flailing blindly, then fell.

Could he have fallen backwards and spared her?

Hell, no.

His body smacked down on her. He raked his claws wildly along the sides of her body.

The pain. Oh, the gods, she hurt.

Screaming didn't slow him down.

The bastard laughed.

Bad mistake. She hated to lose. Thanks to one last burst of adrenaline, she fought her way out from under him and shoved him off. With her last magazine spent, the shotgun was no longer of use. She dropped it to the ground to lighten her load, because she'd need what little strength she had left to kill this demon. Reaching a shaky hand for the hilt, she grabbed her sword and chopped at the arm still trying to gouge her.

Her broken arm erupted in white-hot pain with every movement, but the agony ripping through her body kept her from passing out.

Tears burned her cheeks.

She damaged one of his arms enough to scoot away. The energy churning in her chest built to a crescendo of noise in her ears.

She sucked in a breath and made it to her feet, hunched over, with her broken arm tucked. This last cut had to be good. She was out of second chances. *Story of my life.*

Swinging with all she had, she chopped across his neck.

He went still.

The energy calmed down. The demons she'd fought normally turned to dust. Not these. Why not?

She looked in the direction of her Jeep. Too far away. No point in attempting to reach it.

Even if she lived long enough to make it back to her apartment, she wouldn't survive the poison flooding her system. She'd just scare her neighbors and her dog.

Weaving, she took two steps and dropped to her knees, then fell backwards, staring up at the stars now out in view. Blood trickled from her mouth. Every breath rattled and wheezed ... sounded like a crow cawing.

She blinked. No. That wasn't right. She listened.

It *was* a crow.

Another crow joined the first one. Then another and another.

"Dammit, do not tell me ... the last thing I hear ... will be the sound of crows."

A tear drizzled down her face. Her sweet mutt would mourn her death even if no one else did. Well, her neighbors might miss her, and they'd take care of her dog. The sitter would not abandon him.

They loved Gibbons. She'd named her dog that because his furry beard reminded her of the guy in ZZ Top. More tears spilled down the side of her face. She'd never been a pussy when it came to getting hurt, but ... this time her heart hurt.

Gibbons was the first pet she'd ever had. Would he understand when she didn't come home? That she'd abandoned him to prevent risking a demon from following her home and harming her loyal sidekick?

Her muscles tightened up. Here came the paralysis.

The stars overhead turned into a swirling blur of motion.

Her heartbeat slowed to a thump ... thump ... thump.

A bird landed on her chest.

Big freaking crow. Raven. Whatever.

She hissed, "Get. Off."

It stepped around on her chest. The other birds circled closer and closer until they flew so fast they sent a beam of light down.

Of course, the damn crow would get the spotlight when it was *her* death.

Something else hit her chest. If it was crow poop she was going to do her best to come back as the biggest flying predator ever known. But she doubted beings like her were sent back to live again.

She'd probably turn into dust and—

The crow walked toward her belly button and dragged something up her shirt until it touched bare skin on her chest.

She forced her head up, but only made it an inch, just enough to see a disk two inches across. Not bird poop.

Her inner energy started buzzing again, but this time it sent tendrils sizzling through her chest to touch the disk. She could feel the minute her energy connected with it.

The disk sparkled a bright gold.

Her energy. Was it back under her control? Could she use it to heal?

Evidently not, since the paralysis was continuing to spread through her body. Colors flashed through her aching head and light sparked in her vision.

The big crow on her chest walked up close to her chin and stared into her eyes.

She grumbled, "What?"

It spoke in a throaty voice, "You have been summoned."

Yáahl.

Spent and hurting, Reese dropped her head back, giving up. "Just kill me now and be done with it."

CHAPTER 3

Downtown Atlanta, Georgia

Walking briskly along Piedmont Avenue in downtown Atlanta, Quinn countered Evalle's argument before she could take it further. "No. If Isak's black ops group gets involved we'll have a greater risk of collateral damage in a confrontation. I want to find out who's killing the Medb as much as you do, but this is strictly a preternatural issue. We don't need humans involved."

Yeah, the irony of patrolling these streets late on a Friday night to protect his people's deadliest enemy wasn't lost on Quinn. A blinking time-and-temperature sign in front of a bank contradicted him. It was actually closer to one Saturday morning.

As the current Belador Maistir over North America, he had no choice but to guard the damned murdering Medb witches and warlocks until he found out who was trying to set up the Beladors.

"Isak is not your average human." Evalle paused to swig her water. She raked a hand over her face, shoving loose, black hairs from her ponytail off her damp skin. Wet from one-hundred-percent humidity.

Rain slickers kept most of it off, but Quinn had been in it so long his clothes stayed wet anyway.

All day and night. Strange weather for this early in the year.

Steady rain had fallen nonstop for four days, keeping everyone perpetually drenched. The only good news was that the constant rain had apparently brought a warm front with it. Temps in the upper seventies were much nicer than the cold and snow they'd had only days earlier. Warm spells were not that unusual for Atlanta in January, but still ... this weather was flat out peculiar. And muggy as hell.

He was actually starting to miss the cold, since it had come along with some sunshine.

Evalle asked, "Why are you being so unreasonable about Isak?"

Was he?

She might have a point.

Even more telling was that she questioned his judgment, which she'd have never done at one time. At just short of six feet tall, Evalle had always been strong on the outside, and she was no longer a woman who accepted the status quo.

Not since meeting Storm, her Skinwalker mate.

Quinn couldn't be happier for her.

Still, Evalle and Tzader had tiptoed around him for weeks. His two best friends had been supportive and understanding of his loss. He knew they wanted to keep him from sinking deeper into a bottomless hole of guilt, but it was his own doing. He owed them for being true friends. Neither had judged him when he'd carried the body of a Medb priestess, a powerful enemy, out of Treoir. He'd taken Kizira to Atlanta and buried her there, instead of burning her body as he should have.

Now he couldn't.

Not before the Tribunal meeting.

But Evalle deserved better than his brittle attitude.

Quinn explained, "Isak may not intend to create a problem, but we don't even know who is behind these deaths. With every finger pointing at the Beladors, I don't need Isak adding to the death toll accidentally. I know he's your friend and he's been a Belador ally in recent times, but we can't have him in the middle of this. Until we know for sure who or what we're hunting, I'm not taking any chances."

If he didn't uncover evidence to prove who was behind this insanity, and stop them, the Beladors and the Medb coven would go to war. They'd danced close to it on more than one occasion, but with a new leader in charge of the Beladors and their former goddess, Macha, gone, anything could set off a massacre.

There'd been supernatural skirmishes around Atlanta in the

last four days, but nothing that couldn't be explained away to humans as gang problems.

Hiding an all-out war between preternaturals from humans, who were presently oblivious to the powerful beings living among them, wouldn't be possible.

Evalle yanked off the dark sunglasses that shielded her glowing green eyes and wiped them with the tail of her soggy T-shirt. She consulted her watch again, and slapped her leg. "Where's that blasted witch? She said she'd be here after midnight. I should have made her be more specific."

"Adrianna? Is that why you're checking your watch?"

"Yes. I told her I was headed over here to walk this section of Piedmont with you. She agreed to meet me before I went on patrol. I wanted her walking with me tonight, because I'm thinking with her Witchlock ability she might pick up on something we're missing. All three killings have been in the area most densely populated by Belador families, where the Medb have also been infiltrating. That's not a coincidence."

That was why Quinn had patrols specifically in or near Midtown. "Good thinking. I thought you were waiting on a call from Storm?"

Evalle's face softened at the mention of her mate. "He texted a little while ago and said he was still tracking. If I don't see Adrianna before we reach Midtown, I'll text her when I split off from you for my patrol. How many agents do we have in that area tonight?"

"Me, you, and Devon are the only Beladors. Casper is helping us. And Adrianna, if she shows."

Evalle lifted her face to him, shock evident and lips flattened into a line. "That's all? I knew we were shorthanded, but what the heck?"

"I felt it was necessary. The best way to confirm that Beladors aren't behind this is to lock down everyone and watch Midtown for any new attack. Trey is staying home to coordinate telepathic communication for us, as usual. If someone besides the three of us is out here, then it's an unauthorized Belador. If another attack happens, I want to be able to prove without question that it's not one of ours at fault."

She grumbled, "This rain is driving me batshit crazy. I wish it would dump all at one time and be done with it. I hate this freaking drizzle. Let's take the side roads. We'll get there faster at hyperspeed and no one's going to see us this late at night with the rain."

"Good point."

She took off and Quinn fell into step with her, fully appreciating her frustrated tone. Weather aside, he'd been one tight wad of irritation since teleporting out of that blasted Tribunal meeting with a deadline hanging over his head.

Taking long strides at the speed of a human running, Evalle asked, "About Isak—"

Quinn growled at her. "Hell, Evalle, I'm not arguing just to be contrary. What if he walks up on a fray between preternaturals and the good guys get blown to smithereens?"

"Isak will be sure before he shoots anyone or anything."

Quinn wasn't as convinced, but he let it go. "We've had zero usable intel other than the single fact that Medb witches and warlocks are being tortured, then killed. The only power residue we've found is too much like Belador to deny. I've racked my brain to figure out how someone could be planting that residue. The simple answer is that either a Belador is aiding the killer, or we have a vigilante. We're lucky the Medb don't keep track of their people any better than they do or VIPER would be in the middle of this by now."

"I almost feel sorry for the Medb. Almost." She cut her gaze at him, her eyes filled with concern. "How soon before you have to report this?"

"I should have informed VIPER already, but the coalition turned its back on us when we were losing our powers." Damn coalition. The whole point was to police preternaturals and protect humans. When the Belador power base had been damaged months ago, leaving Beladors vulnerable to Medb attacks, VIPER hadn't lifted a finger to help.

Quinn shook his head. "As Maistir, the Beladors are my first responsibility. We need to find answers first, or any Belador fingered by the Medb would be dragged in to face a Tribunal. If the killer is one of ours, we'll handle it then tell VIPER. That's why, until then, the fewer people involved—humans especially—the better."

She squeezed water from her ponytail that had been slapping her back. "I hear you, but here's the bottom line on Isak. We're not going to be able to keep him out of this anyhow. Wouldn't you rather we know what he's doing and utilize his resources? We need as many friendly feet prowling Atlanta as we can get right now. It's getting tougher to keep our world hidden from humans, Quinn. We need to develop some human allies."

"True. If it turns out to be a Belador at fault in this, it could be the tipping point that exposes all of us ..." He sighed, not wanting to give voice to the chaos and bloodshed that would follow.

"Have you heard anything from Trey recently?" she asked, jumping topics.

"Not a word in the past three hours." They all depended on Trey to keep communication flowing between Quinn and other Beladors during a mission. Trey's telepathic reach was unmatched, making him mission central.

"Did you convince Devon to use his cell phone tonight?"

Quinn grunted. "Finally. He knows there's no room for ego in the middle of all this. He wasn't happy about admitting his telepathy sucks, but he did."

Just like I suck at being Maistir. Tzader had been a far better one for many years, but he deserved the break he was currently enjoying with Brina.

Tzader had entrusted Quinn with the position while he was gone and what had Quinn done? Pissed off the powerful Medb queen and now they might have a vigilante Belador on the loose.

Evalle waved her hand at some thought. "Our real friends are standing with us ... if Adrianna would get a move on and show up. That's another reason Isak is going to be underfoot."

"Why? With the exception of you, he hates nonhumans."

She let a scoffing sound slide out. "He seems to have taken an interest in Adrianna."

"Really? A witch?" Although calling Adrianna just a witch was an understatement now that she controlled the ancient power known as Witchlock.

"Yep, but she's not making it easy for him." Whatever thought had prompted that comment drew an evil smile on Evalle's face.

"What if one of our people kills Isak or someone on his team,

Evalle? Collateral damage works both ways."

"First of all, we're bound by an oath that penalizes the Belador and everyone in his or her family if we break it by killing when unprovoked. Number two—"

Quinn interrupted. "We gave our vows to Macha. We're no longer responsible to the goddess now that Daegan booted her off of Treoir Island. We have yet to find out what he wants. He hasn't shown his face in the human realm." That rubbed Quinn. He still hadn't gotten over the shock of learning that Macha was gone. Not that he wasn't glad after hearing the whole story about Daegan, their new dragon king, but where *was* their new leader?

Quinn had been informed of the regime shift just after he'd left a Tribunal meeting, dazed over what had occurred. He'd been given a deadline to deliver Kizira's body to Queen Maeve less than two days from now.

Then Evalle had informed him that the dragon throne, which Tzader, Evalle, Storm, Tristan and their resident Sterling Witch, Adrianna, had snuck into TÅμr Medb to steal, had turned out to be an actual dragon ... once Adrianna broke a curse Queen Maeve had used to imprison him.

Daegan was actually the two-thousand-year-old Treoir ancestor of their Belador queen, Brina.

Her uncle, to be specific.

Evalle cleared a big water puddle and kept going. "As I was saying, I also pointed out the risks to Isak when I tried to keep him out of this, Quinn."

"Really?"

She turned a sour look on him. "I'm *not* so hardheaded that I wouldn't try to first talk Isak out of joining this fight. I don't want any of my friends harmed, but Isak said he and his team were soldiers. They're human, but they train to fight nonhuman predators. He was doing that when I met him. He even offered us access to his extensive intelligence network, which right now might be far more useful than Nightstalkers. Including Grady."

Evalle meant her favorite informant who generally produced the best intel. He was a ghoul she'd named after Grady Hospital in downtown Atlanta, where he hung around.

"Just think on it," she said, lifting her watch and muttering something ugly about an irritating, pint-sized diva. "I'm gonna split off and head to my patrol. You want to touch base near daylight?"

Evalle had a deadly reaction to the sun, a side effect of her strange mashup of DNA that marked her as an Alterant, a genetic mess of both Belador and Medb. She might possess a screwed-up mix of blood from both sides, but her heart belonged to the Beladors.

"Let's meet at your place right after daylight," Quinn suggested. "Maybe we can sort through intel with Storm." Quinn couldn't keep putting off what he had to tell her and Tzader. He added, "Even if Daegan is coming to the human world at some point, I think it's time to bring Tzader here at least for a briefing."

Quinn, where are you? Trey McCree's voice shouted telepathically in his head so loudly, Quinn slapped his hands over his ears. Like that would help?

Trey understood his telepathic power and normally took care not to explode someone's ears with the sound.

Quinn held up a hand for Evalle to let her know he was communicating with someone telepathically. He replied to Trey, *I'm with Evalle on my way to Midtown. What's wrong?*

Devon Fortier called and he sounded bad, but that could just be his faulty telepathy. I only got his location and two words—Belador and attack—before he went dark. I can't reach him by phone either. He's not far, but I have no one to watch over my family. I'm not leaving them unprotected. With three warlock deaths, this could be a trap by the Medb to get us to leave our homes.

Quinn's neck muscles tightened.

Devon wouldn't have tried telepathy if he hadn't been in dire straits. Quinn said, *Stay where you are, Trey. Give me Devon's location.*

Trey gave him directions.

Rain started pouring down now, like impatient fingers tapping at Quinn to do something.

"What's going on, Quinn?" Evalle's body language changed from exasperated to attack mode in an instant. "My empathic ability is nothing like Storm's, but I can feel your stress." She whipped her head around, searching the area. "Who's in danger?"

He shouted, "Follow me," over the clamor of rain on every surface. With little chance of being seen by humans, Quinn headed back to the main road for a direct route to Midtown. He sped up even faster than the pace they'd set earlier, but Evalle had no trouble hanging with him.

If someone did notice, all they'd see in this flood would be two blurs sliding through the night.

Quinn repeated what Trey had told him.

Evalle had the stride of a gazelle. She asked, "Devon was patrolling Midtown?"

"No. He was supposed to be in an area two miles away. He might have followed someone, or something, and got made."

"Trey's not coming out here, is he?"

"No and I don't want him to leave two women and a baby alone." Quinn kept seeing the body of a female victim in his mind. A human who had happened into this mess. That was one image he'd like to unsee. Human police activity had hampered Storm's and Lucien's ability to process the preternatural parts of the crime scenes. One Belador within the Atlanta Police Department had been aiding those two in allowing as much access as possible.

Evalle nodded. "Trey's wife and sister-in-law might be badass witches, but I agree. The Medb are going to demand retribution for these killings once they find out about them. Any time now I expect them to use it as an excuse to start attacking our people. I wouldn't have left the twins or Feenix alone at our place if not for the ward Storm put around our building."

She and Storm had opened their doors to a pair of eighteen-year-old male witches. They also had a room for Lanna, Quinn's teenage cousin, but she was at another location recovering from a brutal attack by a mage, who was now dead. Good thing, or Quinn would rip him apart by hand. Mother Mattie, an elderly white witch, and her Fae half sister were watching over Lanna for him.

What was he going to do about Lanna before he left for the Tribunal meeting? He didn't want to leave the girl without telling her what he had in mind, but neither did he want to upset her. He couldn't deal with that right now, but he had to make plans and do it soon.

When they reached 10th Street where it ran through Midtown, he took a right turn, sweeping a thorough look over Piedmont Park as it flew past on his left. A large part of the area's residences were perched along the streets fingering away on his right, tucked in close the way homes had been built in the late 1800s.

If the world functioned as it should, lightning would strike the killer and rid neighborhoods like this—and the universe—of a blight. No such luck, though. Rain now hammered every hard surface. No lightning accompanied it, which was bizarre. Even the weather stations were trying to figure out what had descended on metropolitan Atlanta.

He glanced at Evalle, someone as close to him as the sister he'd never had. He hadn't protected Kizira, but he would not lose Evalle.

"Stick close and don't take any chances, Evalle. I know you can handle yourself, but let me deal with whatever we find."

She flipped a hand at him in a "yeah, sure" reply. "Fine, but let's try not to kill our suspect."

"That's what I'd normally tell you," he pointed out.

"Hey, I don't have the ability to scramble their minds like you do."

"That's not what I do with mind lock."

"You've been on edge more lately, which I understand." She sent him a quick smile loaded with caring. "I'm only saying don't unleash any more badass than necessary just because you want to keep me out of the battle."

Damn, she had a point, which he hated to admit. "I shall do my best to contain any homicidal tendencies."

"Welcome back, Mr. Sarcastic," she quipped, still striding hard. "Just sayin'. If we can find out who really is behind the attacks tonight, we can get out of this blasted weather."

He nodded, once again realizing how much she'd matured in the past year. She had the ability to be a leader even if she didn't want to lead.

His gaze swept the area. With the exception of a single light glowing in a window here and there, most houses were dark. Residents were in for the night.

They slept, secure in their homes with no idea that a deadly killer moved through their area. Until this threat was put down, no one—human or otherwise—would be safe.

As a Belador, Quinn had inherited kinetic power and telepathic ability from his powerful ancestors, but he'd been born with an extra gift.

He had the rare ability to mind lock with any living being—at least as far as he knew—powerful or otherwise. With great power came great responsibility, which to him meant not pushing into a mind uninvited unless lives were on the line.

Entering the mind of someone from the preternatural world came with its own set of risks.

Evalle slowed before they reached the area Trey had told Quinn about. She stared straight ahead. Quinn recognized that as her being involved in a telepathic conversation.

She snapped her head around to him. "I just got word from Trey. A human relative of our people contacted Trey saying she heard strange noises in a neighbor's yard much further down."

Quinn frowned. "Why didn't Trey call me?"

"That's the area where I'm supposed to be patrolling in a half hour. He figured I was either there or headed that way. We have more Belador families down there. I'm going to check it out."

Shit. "Go, but don't engage with anyone. I'll hunt for Devon. Call me if you find anything and wait for me to back you up. Right now, we don't know what we're up against."

"Got it, *Dad*." She palmed her dagger from where it hung in a sheath at her hip and took off.

He kept a steady stride, hanging a right to enter a cozy neighborhood with nicely tended yards.

So safe looking.

Where was Devon? Quinn sent out a telepathic call, but Trey would be doing the same. If Trey couldn't reach Devon, no one could.

Rain battered the hood of his slicker when he walked through a break in the gnarly oaks along this route. Even the winter-bare limbs knocked off some of the relentless downpour.

A telepathic voice lunged into his mind. *Evalle here. Have you found anything?*

No. Why?

I picked up an unusual energy as I started up this last street. The energy made a weird humming sound, like a really low vibration from a thousand bees flying in formation. I was crouched, hiding between vehicles, when that buzzing sensation rolled over my arms. It's definitely not of the human world. I'm following it the best I can, but I think it's heading your way. Any sign of Devon?

Not yet. Quinn would love to have the ability to teleport at this moment. He'd zap over to be with Evalle, but since he didn't possess that gift he warned her, *If you meet up with Devon, don't link with him. I don't want to risk both of you being taken out with one hit.*

When Beladors linked, if one died they all died.

Evalle sent back, *Understood.*

Quinn called to Trey, *Any word from Devon?*

No, and that's insane. I can reach people in another country and he was only a few streets away from my house when I heard from him. I feel like shit for not being out there with you.

Don't beat yourself up, Trey. I'd have made the same decision in your shoes, plus we need you where you are to coordinate for all of us more than we need you out here.

I guess, Trey said, not sounding convinced. *You have any idea what we're up against?*

Not yet. I've covered the street you indicated for Devon's last location, but I've found nothing. I'm heading to meet Evalle. She's checking out that disturbance in someone's yard and a strange buzzing noise. It might be entirely unrelated, but it's more than we've had all night.

After a brief pause, Trey added, *I just hung up from talking to Lucien by cell phone. He's been through all the crime scenes with Storm and so far they have nothing new to share that's connected besides ...*

A Belador power residue, Quinn supplied, wishing for better news.

Right, Trey said, continuing. *But we have so many Belador warriors on police forces that I don't see it as a smoking gun. I want to hang these killings on the Medb. If it's one of our own ... shit, that would suck.*

Agreed. Quinn raced back up the street he'd just covered,

headed for Evalle. He remembered something he'd wanted to tell Trey. *Evalle was looking for Adrianna. Find the Sterling witch and Casper. Tell them everything and send them to meet me at the location you gave Evalle.*

Copy that. Here's hoping you don't find another young woman.

Bile ran up Quinn's throat at the reminder of the seventeen-year-old human victim found dead alongside a warlock at the second crime scene. Evidently she'd come by the neighborhood selling magazines and had ended up in the wrong place at the wrong time.

She had been someone's daughter.

Blood soaking a flowery scarf decorated Quinn's dreams now. His skin chilled at the reminder that he had a young daughter of his own. A thirteen-year-old girl he hoped was safe because no one knew where she'd been hidden. Not even him.

Kizira trusted him to keep their daughter safe.

He'd met Kizira when he'd been a young man patrolling the hills of Slovakia. Unaware who she was, he'd spent two weeks with her, and on the last day found out he'd fallen in love with a high priestess of the Medb coven.

The last time he'd seen Kizira, she'd died in his arms after saving him from a gryphon attack during a battle between the Beladors and the Medb. With her final breath, she told him of a child they'd created long ago. She begged him to find their daughter and protect her, but the light in her eyes had dimmed before she could tell him where to look for Phoedra.

Quinn ... tell Evalle not to ...

That had been Devon's voice in his head.

Quinn shouted back, *Devon! Where are you? What's going on?*

Not a sound. Son of a bitch. Adrenaline raced through Quinn. His heart played a drum solo on his chest wall. What the hell? He called out telepathically, *Evalle, stop wherever you are and wait for me.*

Silence answered him.

Evalle? Evalle? His mind roared, *Eee-valle!*

Not a peep in reply.

CHAPTER 4

Haida Gwaii Islands, British Columbia

Reese curled into herself, pleading for the end.

Dying shouldn't take so long.

The whirlwind noise slowed until Reese could hear each labored breath she fought for. And every time she breathed, the cuts ached more.

She opened her eyes, peeking to see if she'd landed in the realm ruled by the raven god of the Pacific Northwest Haida tribe. Her mother's people, at one time, before they'd shunned her.

Reese had grown up hearing about Yáahl, but she'd never known anyone who had met him ... until she'd been desperate for a place to hide. Ten years ago, she'd turned to a Haida wise woman who told her she had only one chance of staying alive. The woman had called upon the raven god.

That was the first time Reese had traveled through the whirl of space and time to this realm.

A place no human could find or happen upon.

Twilight darkness dusted lush grass that stretched across a small clearing to a lake. A waterfall poured into the lake, gently rippling it toward a giant boulder in the middle. No animal sounds. No wind sounds. She looked up into nothing but a hazy mist.

Yáahl's domain.

Where was the raven?

Normally, it was cold at this altitude, especially in winter. She shivered, but that was more about the demon poison than the temperature. Yáahl controlled his environment. The air was only borderline chilly even though his realm was on top of a mountain—one of the Mosquito Mountain peaks on an island off the western coast of Canada.

No sense of time in this place.

If she spent the equivalent of a week here and returned to the human world, it *might* still be Friday night, one second later than she'd left.

If, if, if. She was dying. Time, life and death depended upon what that giant, winged ego running this place decided.

Pain lashed through her. Damn, she wished she had the strength to stand up and yell her head off.

Instead she whispered, "Hate you," on every miserable exhale and closed her eyes.

Damp, warm air descended, dragging her from sleep.

When she woke this time, she was in a sitting position. The moisture she'd felt was a fog that had formed an arch over the space like an ethereal dome. It shed enough light for a soft glow. Now that she could see further, she noted tall evergreens surrounding the meadow.

She held her broken arm over her chest. She hadn't died, but neither had she healed. The gashes down her side leaked blood and smelled of demon poison. Her cuts were still raw.

Why had the raven god brought her here?

And why now?

Ten long, miserable years she'd waited to hear something. Anything.

If he'd intended to return her powers, he could have done so at any point. Once she'd decided the raven wasn't *ever* going to return them, she'd made the best of her life.

That day she'd broken the first rule of survival, which was to form no attachments.

Two years ago she'd given up all hope and decided to pretend she was human. Two years to grow attached to a dog and the people living around her. Two years she refused to regret.

She'd known better, but after so much time alone, she'd let her guard down. If she was going to admit her shortcomings, the truth was she'd been lonely, dammit.

A crow cawed loudly.

Reese jerked from her wandering thoughts and hissed at the pain.

That freaking bird sounded like it was laughing.

The increasing warmth hugged her body, but that wouldn't save her. She had no choice but to sit and wait for the elements to take her if the demon poison didn't finish her first.

Who had sent the *jötnar* demons, anyway? She knew little about *jötnars* beyond the basic stats she'd studied. Appearance, powers, skills, vulnerabilities. But demons generally answered to someone. What were they doing in California?

And why hadn't they turned into dust?

They were Scandinavian demons that lived to torture and kill humans when they weren't draining some preternatural being's essence. But the fact that they'd shown up so far from their territory and in *her* neighborhood—that was a little too coincidental for her liking.

They'd clawed her. But if she was sitting here, holding her arm, she was no longer paralyzed. Why not? She still didn't have her powers or she'd be healing herself. Had Yáahl put her body in some holding pattern so he could berate her as she died?

That would be like him, to stretch out the pain of her last hour.

Above her, the dome began to brighten.

Air swirled and warmed even more.

A large shadow crossed overhead, swooping back and forth, a massive crow the size of a human. It glided down to the giant rock in the center of the lake, which changed from a plain old rough-cut boulder to a pearl-white platform that glowed.

Energy swept through the secluded area, leaving a six-and-a-half-foot man dressed in a black tunic and pants. His sharp cheeks, teak-colored skin, blunt nose, and straight, black hair apparently hadn't changed in thousands of years. He still had the small, dark eyes of the indigenous Haida tribes who had once ruled this land.

His stern mouth might as well be carved of stone.

Reese had yet to see him smile. "Hey, *Yáahl.*"

Every time she said his name, she felt like a Paula Deen wannabe shouting, "Hey, y'all!"

His voice carried the distance between them with little effort. "Welcome, xahlk'uts'. How have you been?"

Reese huffed at his ridiculous attempt to be sociable. "I am *not* a porcupine and I'm pretty sure you know I'm dying, or I was when you sent your minions to get me."

Angling his head to the side, he mimicked human movements and stared as if concentrating. "No, I believe that name suits you well. I have never met another whose hackles rise so quickly as yours over trifling issues."

Did that mean he hadn't screwed up someone else's life the way he had hers, to the point of survival being a trifling issue? Let him say whatever he wanted and be done with it.

She didn't care anymore.

It'd be nice, though, if he'd get to the point.

Reese crossed her arms. Actually, she wrapped her good arm over her bad one, careful not to jar it, and gritted her teeth against the sharp pain of jostling her broken bone. No point in worrying about social manners, not now when she'd lost everything. Now would be the time to say what she wanted.

Cocking her chin up at him, she said, "Not a word from you for over a decade and *now* you want to talk?"

"A decade is not such a great amount of time when you have lived as long as I have."

Yeah, just you and Methuselah. "Sorry if I sound cranky, but you may want to move this along before I expire." Licking lips covered with the metallic taste of her own blood, she managed to squeeze out some sarcasm. "To what do I owe this unexpected honor?"

"Is your life so busy you do not have time for me? If so, please go. Do not stay on my account." He waved his hand in dismissal.

"Sure. I'll just jog down the mountain with a broken arm and blood pouring from my wounds. Not to mention demon poison flooding my body." She panted, wondering what was taking her body so long to quit.

She'd waited a bazillion hours to hear from Yáahl. Maybe popping off would piss him off enough to take her out of her misery.

"What gives, Yáahl? You get a new pair of boots and needed

someone to kick? Is that why you finally remembered I was still around?"

He pinched the bridge of his nose, sighed, and asked, "Don't you want your powers returned?"

Reese froze. She'd begged and pleaded the last time they'd faced each other.

Yáahl had refused her pleas.

Furious beyond any sanity, Reese had spewed a string of curses at him and swore she'd never beg for anything again.

Not from him.

Funny how years of living without what she most wanted and facing her own mortality could make her eat those words.

Yeah, she'd crawl through crushed glass naked and with her arm broken if that was what it took to feel whole again. Then she'd be able to heal herself *and* protect the energy inside her from demons.

She'd come close to being a power supper for two *jötnar* demons tonight, and it had been terrifying. They weren't the only ones who wanted what she had.

Trying to sound calm, Reese said, "Of course I want my powers." She waited, her heart jumping in anticipation.

She watched for a sign, something to let her know he was going to make good on the offer.

He said nothing.

She should have known it wouldn't be easy with him. A ripple of suspicion raced along her neck. *Don't be a bitch. Don't be a bitch. Don't be a ...* "Out of curiosity, why are you giving them back to me now?"

"I have not said I will return your powers."

He crushed her hope without even blinking. The fragile hold Reese had on her temper snapped. "*What?* You just ... argh! You called me here just to screw with me?"

"I summoned you to discuss a task I want you to perform."

Had existing since before the dinosaurs finally fried his brain?

She gritted her teeth and asked, "Really? What can I possibly do for you, oh *mighty spirit*?"

"That mouth will be the death of you."

"With any luck I'll bite it before I have to hear all my flaws marched out again."

As if he hadn't noticed her bleeding out, he said, "I want you to bring me someone."

Her half-baked mind woke up.

He wanted something? For real?

Then he had to be willing to barter, right? "What about my powers?"

"That's not what we are discussing at the moment."

Reese fisted her good hand and swallowed the bile climbing her throat. She struggled to keep her temper beaten into submission, because no one won an argument with the raven.

On the other hand, this might be her last chance to speak freely. "Why should I do anything for you?"

He asked, "Have you forgotten that you owe me a favor? I gave you sanctuary when you came to me asking for aid."

Reese didn't even try to smother a bitter chuckle that ended in a cough. But the sharp pain in her chest came from a broken heart. "Yeah, well, so much for being given sanctuary. You let my baby die."

"I offered you protection, and that's what you and your child received." He spoke in that know-it-all tone that had driven her crazy when she'd been under said protection. He continued, "Those who wished to harm you were unable to find you. I do not interfere with the normal laws of life and death."

That did nothing to soothe the ache in her chest that never went away. The pain of holding her baby who'd never taken his first breath. People said time would soften the loss.

Not true.

Now was not the moment to indulge in grief. It wouldn't bring her child or her powers back. Ten years was a long time to dodge preternaturals and hide in the human realm.

She'd fought well but lost that game in the mountains outside of San Diego tonight.

But she refused to be brought all the way here and forced to listen timidly to Yáahl. "Let me get this straight. It's clearly okay for *me* to interfere in someone *else's* life on your behalf, but not the other way around. That baby was all I had. He didn't deserve to die. You have a lot of freaking power. You *chose* not to intervene. You could have ... given him to someone else, as long as he lived. He shouldn't have been cursed because I was his mother."

"Stop wallowing in guilt. And stop blaming the world for your troubles. The death of that child was not on your shoulders."

Reese's laugh grew meaner by the second. "Yes, it was. I blame *you* for not saving an innocent child, but the lion's share of fault was mine. I was told that no baby could survive in my womb. I shouldn't have dismissed it. I should have been more careful about getting pregnant."

"You were only nineteen and raised in a tribe that shied away from the modern world. You were naïve."

His gentle words threatened to crack her armor.

Reese stared off into the distance, trying her best to not relive that time in college, when she'd fallen for a man five years older who had used her. If she were entirely honest, she'd admit that the silly young woman she'd been had thought she could defy the curse on her family.

Live and learn.

No attachments. No family. No babies.

Forcing the grief back into that dark space where her heart had once thrived, she said, "You're the Haida raven. When you met me, you had to have known what would happen. You knew my family had been cursed when my mother was raped by ... that *thing*. Everyone in our tribe knew. When I came to you heavy with my son, you should have told me *then* that he would not survive, not even in your sanctuary."

That was the rub.

Reese felt that the raven could have prepared her for the loss. If he had, she would have stepped off a cliff and left this world to join the next one with her baby so he wouldn't have been alone.

She accused, "You knew what I was. You could have taken my life instead of his, found him a home, and saved a lot of misery. No one would have missed me." She blinked back tears.

The raven would not see her cry.

Yáahl argued softly, "How many times must I tell you that all who come to me are treated the same, regardless of who or what they are? It is not my place to interfere with anyone's fate. I can only do all within my power to protect those I agree to shield until it is time for them to meet their destiny."

Oh, I get it. My baby's destiny was to live for nine months in my womb and be stillborn? Whatever.

Drained physically from blood loss and fighting the pain, Reese flipped her hand in a "never mind" motion. "Let's get back to business. I'm thinking there has to be more to this meeting than you expecting me to go hunting someone down with nothing more than my charming personality. Am I wrong to assume you're going to heal me?"

"I cannot do that. You must heal yourself ... both inside and out."

Reese started laughing. She closed her lips tight or the hysteria would take over.

Damn her curiosity, she wanted to know what he was up to so she forced herself to get a grip and stay on track. "Let's play your game. What makes you think this person will even come back with me if I do find him or her?"

"The dead do not argue."

A body? She struggled to breathe without coughing. It hurt so much. "You're sure this person is dead?" Reese qualified.

"Yes."

There had to be a catch. "Where exactly *is* this body?"

"In your human realm."

"That is *not* my realm. I don't even like humans." Lie. She cared about her neighbors. And her dog. Gibbons was better company than most humans.

Ignoring Reese's protest, the raven said, "Two energies are moving toward this body. They must not be allowed to take possession of it."

"Who's after it? Demons?" That would be funny. *Not.*

"Worse. One of the energies is family."

Did she really give a flying fig who was after what? Not even.

She wanted her gifts returned. If he expected her to do anything, he'd have to heal her or give back her powers. She still threw the bullshit flag on his inability to heal someone, but she wasn't using that argument. Not if he thought she needed her powers to heal.

There was another upside to her accepting the deal. If she brought him the body, this task should wipe out her debt to Yáahl.

Double benefit, because she was not doing anything for free. Except dying.

She asked, "Let's say we make a deal. What do you have for *usable* information on how to find this body?"

"I have had a vision that the body is sealed inside a tomb above ground on your continent."

Don't even waste your breath explaining that America is not your continent. "That's it, *Yáahl?* You gotta narrow it down a little more than that if you expect me to find a body in the next century. Is it male or female? What about the person's name? Big town? Small town? Cold weather? What?" She couldn't feel her legs. She *could* feel the poison still slithering down her limbs.

It should have locked up her lungs and suffocated her by now.

"This body is a female." He looked up for a moment, closed his eyes, nodded to himself then opened his eyes. "She is in a large city that claims a history of rebuilding from the ashes of a war long past, something about rising like a great phoenix. I do have a name."

But he wasn't giving it up yet.

Reese thought back over the history she'd helped her neighbor study. Civil War? "Atlanta? As in Georgia?"

"That is possible. You will find out."

"*Atlanta?*" she shouted. "You expect me to go back there?"

"The father of your child is no longer in that location."

"Father? No. He was nothing more than a lying sperm donor." The minute she'd told him she was pregnant, the man she'd thought hung the moon had decided it was time to share the news that he was married and wanted no part of a child.

He'd given her money for an abortion.

She hadn't gotten pregnant intentionally, but she would not destroy a precious child. She'd used the funds to travel across country to an old wise woman in her mother's tribe, who'd sent Reese to Yáahl. When Reese explained she was not a member of the tribe—because Reese had turned her back on them for shunning her mother—the woman assured her Yáahl would not refuse her sanctuary.

Looking up at the fog dome, she recalled that first visit with the raven and muttered a curse.

A plant leaf swatted her across the shoulders.

"*Ow!*" She rubbed the skin with her good hand. "I'm in pain here." That gained her no response. "Okay, okay. I'll go find your body if I live long enough. Before I do that, I'll need a day to get my house in order since I don't know how long this will take and we still have to discuss compensation."

"Everything living or otherwise in your home will be safe while you are gone. Your dog sitter believes you are on a business trip and will continue to care for your animal during your absence."

"Don't mess with my dog or my dog sitter," Reese snapped. "Good ones are hard to find." He had better stay out of Reese's life back in San Diego.

That was not part of this deal.

"I harm none. You know that," he said, shrugging, which looked odd on someone so powerful.

"Debatable," she countered, but arguing with Yáahl would only be an exercise in futility. "Fine. As long as my dog is safe and fed, I'll go find this body and bring it back if we can reach an agreement." Now was the moment of truth. "You can't expect me to do that unless I'm healed."

Yáahl pointed a hand at her.

A crow swooped low and dropped a necklace on her lap.

She lifted the black leather thong to look at the round pendant, which was larger than a silver dollar. It appeared to be onyx with a raven carved on one side and a sun and moon on the opposite side.

Was this the disk the crow had used to teleport her here? "What is this?"

"Put it on."

She studied the pendant. "Is that carving supposed to be you? Not sure they got your good side. Oh, wait. You don't have one. My bad."

"Put. It. On," he replied in a terse voice that made her smile.

She slipped it over her head, hissing at jostling her injured arm.

The minute the medallion dropped inside her shirt and settled against her skin, her body relaxed for the first time since getting slashed by the demons. Every aching muscle and bone eased. She was so exhausted, she leaned back against a tree and closed her eyes, feeling wounds close and the power wash away poison burning everywhere inside her.

Her broken arm shifted.

She lifted her head and looked down to see the bone knit itself back together beneath the skin. It was as if she'd been hit by a truckload of feel good.

"Wow, that was ... thank you." She meant it and repeated, "Thank you for healing me. Sorry if sounded unappreciative, but I was a hurtin' unit when I got here. Okay, we've got a deal as soon as you hit me with all my powers then I'll get rolling." She stretched, enjoying the rush of strength, then pushed to her feet.

"You are confused. You will not receive your powers unless you are successful in your task."

"You expect me to pull this off with no powers? If I'm looking for someone for you, I'm thinking there's a good chance they're probably supernatural. Am I right?"

"Yes, this person was quite powerful when she lived."

Shoving her hands to her hips, Reese leaned forward, pissed off all over again. "And you don't think I need my powers when I go poking around in the preternatural world? I don't even know what I'll be up against."

"You've proven capable of surviving in the human world for a decade without them. You're a clever woman. You'll figure it out."

"Oh, thanks for the backhanded compliment." Reese stomped back and forth, trying to think this through. He'd healed her, so she had a chance to still get her powers. In fact, he said she'd get them when she completed her mission and returned.

Not when but *if*.

Running her hands through windblown brown curls that needed a shampoo after that trip through the desert, she turned to Yáahl. "Are you going to give me anything? Magic wand, crystal ball, rabbit's foot ... ?"

"You call yourself an investigative photographer, so go investigate."

Anger flooded Reese's chest. She hadn't expected simple, but neither would she believe Yáahl really expected her to succeed with no powers.

This was insane even for him.

What were her options?

None. Now that she felt alive again, he knew she'd do anything for her powers. He would be right.

She took a couple of slow breaths that felt so much better than before, and decided to test how important it was for Yáahl to get his hands on this body.

He didn't do necromancy.

She knew that much about him, so why did he want a body?

It was time to find out how much negotiating room she had. "What if I refuse this task?"

Things turned so quiet, Reese wondered if Yáahl was withdrawing. Her heart beat crazy loud in her ears.

Finally, he said, "Refuse me now and this will be our last communication. If you allow that body to fall into the wrong hands, you will never feel your powers again."

"What? Are you kidding me?" Reese shouted and grabbed her hair. Her mind raced to find a way to make him see reason. Not possible so she went with mouthing off again, which at least made her feel better.

"What did I ever do to you? This is crap. When you bound my powers, you said I had to learn how to live. I admit that I was, uhm, a bit self destructive, but I've proven that now I'm not. I've done pretty freaking good in San Diego and I haven't asked anything of you." Mainly because she wouldn't have been able to find him. He had to summon her.

He stared quietly, offering nothing in return.

"How can you do that to me, Yáahl? I was born with those powers. They're mine." She hated the pleading sound in her voice, but everything she wanted was so close, yet beyond her reach.

He answered, "I have taken nothing. I explained to you before that they are merely dormant. No one should possess a gift if they intend to misuse it. I am giving you a chance to prove that you have learned to make wise choices."

And that's when it finally sank in.

Yáahl had to have been keeping up with Reese to know how she'd been making a living. He'd let her battle two demons, allowing her to almost die during that attack. He knew how much she wanted freedom from living as a powerless human hunted by demons.

Knew she'd be desperate.

He'd been right about one thing.

From the minute Reese had been dumped into the human world, she'd had to be fast on her feet and even quicker at learning how to carve out some kind of life.

"You should know one more thing, Reese."

There was more? "What?"

"Demons are still searching for you in San Diego. That is your doing, not mine. Word of your demon hunting has traveled far. That is what brought those *jötnar* demons to you. They were drawn by the challenge of a demon huntress. I am shielding those you care for from the demons. They will remain under my protection until you give me a reason to withdraw it. Do not fail me."

She'd screwed up royally, but her jaw dropped at his threat. "You should protect them because they're innocent in all this."

"They have not come to me to ask for my help. I am offering it freely now while you perform this task for me."

A task was picking up milk at the store, not stealing a body.

This was the moment to grow a pair of lady balls to beat him at his own game. First she had one more worry. "Speaking of the *jötnars*, why didn't they turn to dust?"

"I merely delayed their decomposition until I was sure no others followed you, but they're bodies are now ash."

No DNA left in case someone found them. Reese got down to business. "I'll need a name to hunt for someone in this world. Who died?"

"The body is that of Kizira."

"The Medb priestess?"

"Correct."

Reese kept up with preternatural activity by surfing the dark internet sites. She'd thought the story was a bogus rumor spread by Beladors since a Medb priestess should be fairly indestructible. "She's really dead?"

"Quite."

Hell. This is a suicide mission. Who messed with the Medb coven and survived? The only people worse than them were on Reese's paternal side. How had Yáahl gotten involved with the

Medb? What purpose did he have for that body?

All good questions. Not any he would answer.

Reese rubbed her gritty eyes and blew out a deep breath.

If the raven wanted Kizira's body so much, he might be willing to make one concession.

"I'll go find Kizira and bring her body to you, but to do that, and in so little time I should add, you're gonna have to give me my powers at least while I'm gone."

His sigh ruffled the surface of the lake. "Do you ever ask for anything, Reese?"

She tapped her chin. "Let me think about that." Dropping her hand, she said, "No. The last time I did, I ended up indebted to you."

"Very well, you may access one power at a time by calling it up while touching the medallion ... *if* it deems your request worthy. You may also return with the body by touching the medallion and asking to be sent to this meadow. There is a limit to the power accessible through the medallion, and it will cease to function if all chance of acquiring the body is lost."

"How much power will I—"

Yáahl never slowed in giving his instructions. "Prepare to receive your power and travel to the city in my vision. It is the early hours of Saturday there. You should appreciate this information and that I am sending you there to save you time." He lifted both hands, fingers pointing at Reese.

Now? She held her hands up in defense. "Wait. What about money, my weapons, a phone—"

Reese blinked out of the forest and tumbled head over heels through a whirlwind of energy. Her body bounced against swirling walls that shot sizzling friction over her skin.

She landed on her butt. "Ouch, dammit." Rain showered down on her face and body, soaking her clothes.

Yáahl couldn't have given her a raincoat, dumped her under an overhang or inside an empty building? At least it was fairly warm, which seemed odd for Atlanta in January.

She got to her feet and looked around, trying to get her bearings.

Energy inside of her sizzled an alert.

That was bad. Really bad.

CHAPTER 5

Atlanta, Georgia

Reese held still as rain pelted her in the dark. After midnight in Atlanta.

If *Yáahl* hadn't fed her a bunch of crap. She didn't even have a watch.

She listened, waiting for the attack.

Wouldn't it be just like Yáahl to drop her in a nest of demons? Where were they? Her energy vibrated, warning her of at least one demon nearby, but she didn't see him.

That was new.

When had any demon ever hesitated to come running for an energy- meal-to-go?

The air buzzed, and she could hear a humming a little ways off. Was something flying in this crappy weather? Dogs barked down the street. She melted into the available shadows. The humming sound had come from the end of the street, maybe half a mile away where it looked like this road connected with a bigger one.

Nothing stirred in what she recognized as an older section of Atlanta, but where, exactly, was she? A smattering of small to midsize cars parked for the night hugged curbs on both sides, but no one was out and about.

She couldn't blame them. She'd like to be home with Gibbons on a rainy night like this.

Buzzing increased, and the humming grew louder. Was it coming toward her? The sound died down as if moving away, but... No, it was coming back again.

What in the world was going on in Atlanta these days?

She hadn't heard anything about this out on the West Coast, even though she kept up with preternatural news.

Down the street near the entrance to this area, a tall figure appeared suddenly. A male wearing dark coveralls. He was running full speed in her direction as if he'd teleported into the middle of a road race.

Had he opened a bolt-hole?

She had no experience with bolt-holes, but understood they existed.

"Get back here!" an invisible person shouted.

This was getting stranger by the minute. Was someone yelling at this guy from the other side of the bolt-hole? Was that even possible?

The guy kept running. He couldn't have seen her hiding here, but her energy vibrated more the closer he came. Was he ...

He lifted his head, revealing two bright red orbs for eyes.

Shit. Shit. Shit.

She yanked out the medallion with her left hand and lifted her right, calling her energy to her fingers.

Nothing happened.

Footsteps were slapping the wet pavement, as loud as gunshots now.

"You will pay for this if you lied to me, Yáahl." She hadn't done this in ten years. *Calm down and focus.* Feeling inside for her power, she pushed it to expand. Her chest warmed in a way it hadn't in a long time, but not fast enough. That demon would be here in seconds.

"Come on," she whispered, frantic for anything. Contact would be in ten seconds.

Nine.

Eight.

Heat rolled through her arm and spread to her fingers. Not there yet.

Six.

Five.

Four.

Power hit her hand so hard she thought her fingers might

explode. She jumped away from the tree she'd hidden behind and fisted her hand, hitting him an upper cut to the jaw as his sickle-like claws reached for her.

She hit him so hard his head flew back ten feet, dragging his body with it.

Oh, yeah, baby. I'm back. She stomped over to where he was trying to get up. She booted him in the chest. He hit a fire hydrant, but thankfully didn't break it. She checked all around. No lights on. No humans to interfere.

He made coughing sounds as he reached his feet again. Blood ran down his head from where it must have cracked on the hydrant. He swiped blood from his mouth, turned those unholy eyes on her, and smiled.

His voice sounded like he'd been chewing on rusty nails. "I would have made it fast. Now, I'll take my time draining you just so I can hear you scream."

"Sorry, I didn't get that. I don't speak bullshit."

He stopped and crooked his head, confused.

She noticed the buzzing had vanished. "Did you open a bolt-hole?"

He answered with his own question. "What are you?"

"Besides in a bad mood?"

Whatever confusion he'd suffered must have cleared up. He leaped at her and she hoped her power didn't fail her this time. She slapped her hands together with the medallion between them and sent a bolt of energy at him that blew a hole through his chest.

It knocked her on her ass, but he dropped to the ground, smacking it face first.

Nice.

His body turned into gray dust and made a *pfft* sound when it shot up and dissipated. Now *that* was how it oughta happen.

Gotta love easy clean up.

That demon had just *appeared* in the middle of the the street. She had to choose a direction. Turning around to head away from this street sounded like a good plan.

Reese considered her next move as she covered new ground. "I have nowhere to stay. No money and now I have to spend the night wet because you didn't even give me an umbrella. Thanks,

Yáahl."

The rain started falling even harder.

Water ran along the street, rushing toward the drains.

She'd heard about Nightstalkers in this area who traded information for a handshake with a powerful being, but she wasn't sure her babysitter medallion would deem that a *worthy* use of her powers.

Probably better to avoid the ghouls since they held no allegiance, sharing intel with anyone. That meant they'd tell a Belador she was in the city, which would get her pulled into VIPER. They'd ask too many questions.

She'd lived off the preternatural radar for the past ten years and wanted no part of that coalition. They were the equivalent of Big Brother in the supernatural world. A person like her would have to choose sides in a conflict.

She would not be pushed into joining anybody's side in any supernatural fight.

All she had to do was find one body.

She'd do it, too. That little taste of her powers hadn't been enough. Yáahl would have to make good on his offer, because she had every intention of collecting.

At the end of the street, she turned left. There were few streetlights, so darkness shrouded much of the area.

Just the way she liked it.

Without access to Nightstalkers, she had to get to the dark net that might have information on Kizira's burial. That meant finding a device with internet capabilities. A mobile phone would work, but she hated a thief so stealing one was out. Once she reached the main roads, she might be able to convince some sympathetic soul to loan her their phone. She'd give them a down-on-her-luck story, which wouldn't take much effort.

Two more streets down, she looked back to the right.

No buzzing. Maybe she could zip up this street to the main road and get out of this neighborhood.

This area reminded her of Midtown. If it was, she'd head for somewhere like the Flying Biscuit near Piedmont Park. That had been one of her favorite places to eat. Nice people. Someone would help her out.

Halfway up the street, she picked up that buzzing sound again.

Energy in her chest revved up. This time, she anticipated a demon, but where was it?

What was this place? Preternatural central?

Well, hello. Atlanta *was* the headquarters for VIPER and the Beladors in North America.

She moved to stand by another tree. Not that it kept her out of sight last time, but at least she had something at her back.

Now that she knew to watch for something to emerge from the buzzing, she grasped the medallion where it dangled from the leather cord tied around her neck. The minute she concentrated on the humming sound, she could see the air wobble and undulate. Like looking through wavy glass, she could see through to the other side, just not clearly.

Barking cranked up again at a house on her right.

A movement close by pulled Reese's gaze to a woman who hurried out of her house with an umbrella in one hand and the leash to a big, lumbering mutt in the other.

She missed Gibbons. That goofy dog would love all this rain.

The odd vibrating noise got louder and seemed to rise above her head. Was it spreading?

Reese waited, gauging when the cloud of buzzing would reach the woman. Was another demon hidden in it?

She tightened her grip on the medallion and called up a shield to prevent a demon from sensing her power, which would work great until she needed her hands free to defend herself. But if she could avoid a battle, all the better.

Shouting broke out in the middle of the street, but no one was there.

The woman with the umbrella turned toward the noise. Then she was sucked off her feet and yanked by some invisible tether to the middle of the street, where she vanished.

The umbrella fell to the ground.

Her dog went crazy barking at the street.

Reese sighed. She dropped her shield. If a demon had the woman, Reese couldn't stand by and allow that death.

A demon appeared out of the air just like the last one and fell backwards from where the strange vibrating noise had parked in the street.

All at once, the buzzing quieted and four men appeared. They were holding the woman and looking up as if they'd been caught with their pants down.

The demon was on his feet. Red eyes glowed in Reese's direction.

"I could have stayed in San Diego if I wanted to fight demons all night." She gripped the medallion, ready to put it to use again.

CHAPTER 6

Quinn made a mad dash through another Midtown street, hunting for Evalle.

A dark figure at the other end cut a path through the rain, heading straight for him.

Whoever it was had already spotted Quinn, so he kept moving forward, ready to battle.

This part of the city had a substantial Belador population of warriors Quinn could normally call out at a moment's notice. But he would not put any more of his people in danger tonight.

Dull light from a street lamp outlined the hulking shape walking with a determined stride. He toted a weapon that had been built to destroy nonhumans.

Quinn stopped. "What are you doing here, Isak?"

The black ops soldier flipped up his monocular, leaving only the whites of his eyes showing in a face covered with black camo paint. "We got a report of trouble in this area. Turned out to be a breakin. Nothing paranormal."

Quinn had no time to waste debating on what to do about Isak. Evalle had a point. No argument would deter this man.

Instead, Quinn said, "Evalle encountered a strange energy. She *was* east of us, four streets away. I lost telepathic contact with her. I've been running every street on my way there to avoid missing her if she's headed this way."

"Let's go." Isak turned to his side, waiting.

Hello clusterfuck. Quinn didn't care. Isak could join him if he could keep up. Quinn took off, hearing a string of Isak's curses in his wake. Heavy-footed splashing followed, surprising Quinn at just how fast Isak could move that much body mass.

Quinn sent a telepathic message to Trey, telling him what was going on and finished with, *Let me know if anyone gets eyes on Evalle or Devon.*

Will do. Then Trey added, *Adrianna and Casper should be intercepting you, Evalle, or both of you pretty soon.*

I'll keep you posted.

Taking a hard right into the neighborhood where Evalle should be, Quinn searched the darkness for any sign of her. A movement at the end of the dark street caught his eye. He ran toward it to find Devon struggling to get up.

Hoisting Devon to his feet none too gently, Quinn growled, "What happened to you? Where's Evalle?"

Devon shook his head, spraying water like a wet dog, and stepped back from Quinn. He lifted a hand. "Give me a minute to shut up Trey so I can talk to you."

"We don't have a minute," Quinn shouted. "Tell Trey you're with me and start talking."

Devon wiped water off his face. "I was following an energy field—"

"Was it buzzing?"

"Yes."

Quinn confirmed, "Evalle sent me a message about it. She's tracking it."

Devon shook his head. "She may *think* she is, but I'm pretty sure it's letting her track it and probably dragging her into a trap. I thought I was tracking it, too, but whatever is in that energy field is sentient. When I snuck up to see if I could figure out what was going on, it literally threw me against a tree, but I heard voices."

"Sentient? Or is it a cloaking device for beings and they attacked you?"

"I have no idea. Just telling you what I noticed. I didn't have a chance to see anyone before I smacked a tree hard enough to knock me out." Devon rubbed the back of his head.

What the hell were they up against?

"Did you see Evalle at any point?" Quinn asked.

"No. I caught a snippet of her telepathy, but couldn't make sense of it."

"She was heading back toward me," Quinn muttered. "Dammit. I've tried calling her and Trey is trying, but—"

"The minute you get close to that buzzing, it blocks any telepathy. I doubt even Trey could project if he was caught up in it."

That could be one hell of a cloaking device. Quinn hoped Adrianna could determine what was going on with it.

Isak jogged up to them, holding his demon blaster across his chest, and with his monocular back in place.

Quinn asked, "Are any of your men out here?"

"Just me. I've got teams waiting at different spots around the inner city to come the minute I call." Isak reached into a pocket on his cargo pants and pulled out two comm units, shoving them at Quinn and Devon. "These are tuned for your sensitive hearing. We can't work as a unit if we're blind to everyone's position."

He designated Quinn as Delta One and Devon as Delta Two.

Devon said, "What's your handle?"

"Alpha One," Isak replied in a tone that indicated it should have been obvious and wasn't up for discussion.

Quinn rolled his eyes. He didn't give a rat's ass what they called each other. He'd wear an aluminum foil hat right now if it meant finding Evalle.

In spite of Isak's self-appointed leadership, Quinn started issuing orders, sending Isak in one direction to the main roads and ordering Devon to sit tight.

Isak gave Quinn a quelling look, but to his credit he moved out.

How were they going to find Evalle?

In these older neighborhoods around Midtown, some of the streets were a grid pattern, but not all. There were areas where a street might stop then pick up at an offset point. Then there were curves thrown in just to keep it interesting.

As soon as Isak left, Quinn explained to Devon, "You're going to wait here until I get four streets down in that direction." He pointed away from the park. "When I get there, we're both going to walk east, mirroring each other for as long as we can. We pause to check in when we reach the same cross street. If you can't hear me or I can't hear you telepathically, then we head toward the person we can't hear. By process of elimination, we might find that energy field."

This would be a great time to have Evalle's mate on the team. Storm had more than one way to find her quickly, but he was still following a scent trail from one of the crime scenes.

Storm was a possessive bastard who would dismember anyone who harmed Evalle.

He'd have to stand in line behind Quinn if anything happened to her tonight.

Quinn blew down the street to his start point and told Devon to start walking at normal human speed. He shouted out telepathically to Evalle again.

Every silent moment that followed twisted him into one big, frustrated knot.

After vaulting over a wooden fence separating small yards, he made it to the next street over. Dogs howled nearby, maybe one more street down. He could take off at super speed again, but he feared missing sight of Evalle by moving too quickly if she was trying to slip through the shadows.

He headed toward the chorus of dog howls, which took him deeper into the neighborhood.

Isak's sharp voice shot into Quinn's ear. He yanked out the comm and could still hear him. Apparently Isak wasn't quite up to speed on just *how* sensitive a Belador's hearing could be. "I'm at the end of the park near Monroe. I'm heading back."

Devon replied with, "Copy that."

Quinn had made it three streets when he received no reply from his telepathic call to Devon.

He turned left, heading for where Devon should be.

A figure that matched Evalle's size and movements rushed across the street two blocks ahead.

Got her. Relief shook the lead out of his feet and he shot forward, only to see her vanish again. *Dammit!*

He shouted telepathically. *Evalle! Eee-valle!*

When he closed in on where he thought she'd been, a man in a black coveralls appeared a hundred feet away in the middle of the street as if he'd just teleported in. Except that he was falling backwards.

Then four more men immediately appeared, all huddled around something.

Had *they* just teleported here?

Or ... had that buzzing cloud been a cloaking device after all, which failed for some reason?

Between Quinn and those men, yet another person entered the mix, but this one had stepped from beside a tree. A woman. She was average size and had a head of curly light-brown hair.

Evalle's voice shouted in Quinn's head, telling him the street she was on where men were appearing and for him to meet her.

I hear you, Evalle. I see the men, but not you.

You'll see me. I'm on my way to kick some butt then we'll interrogate them.

Everything happened at the same moment.

The guy in the black coveralls jumped up, red eyes glowing. Bloody hell. A demon. The woman from behind the tree headed for the demon and certain death.

The demon charged her.

Quinn rushed to close the distance behind her and shouted, *"Get down!"*

She swung around, wide-eyed, and dropped as he hit the demon with heavy kinetic power.

That strike sent the demon flying into the four men, breaking up the pile better than a bowling strike. One of the men grabbed a woman who had evidently been what they'd huddled around, slung her over his shoulder and took off running toward Piedmont Park.

Ignoring the human bystander on the ground, whom Quinn would deal with once the threat was handled, he kept moving forward with his hands out, using his power to pin the demon to the wet pavement.

The woman he'd just saved cursed a blue streak and raced past Quinn in the direction of the guy carrying the other woman. Definitely nuts, but Devon should intercept her since he was on the park end of the street.

The incessant rain had increased to a downpour now, harder than it had been all day.

There was Evalle on the opposite side of this bunch from Quinn, and now battling two men. But where was the last of their foursome?

Those two ganged up on her to lift her, both using kinetics to toss her over their heads at Quinn.

He had no choice but to release the demon. Quinn angled his power up to catch Evalle, who was flipping head over bottom through the air.

She'd probably land like a damn cat, but he couldn't risk that she'd hit on her head and crack it like an egg.

He slowed her descent.

She turned at the last minute, hitting feet first. She called out, "Thanks."

They both turned to find the demon and the three men gone. Devon was shaking his head, walking toward them. "I tried to stop the guy carrying a woman, but he and a buddy ganged up on me. I can't believe the power they hit me with."

Quinn asked, "Did you see another woman running behind them?"

Devon shook his head. "Sorry. Guess it's getting hit twice in a short time. I was addled for a bit."

Evalle stomped the ground. "How are they using that much kinetic power against us? I know others have kinetic ability, but I can't think of another group that fights like we do. That was crazy."

Quinn had many short words to describe it, but crazy would work for now. "Are you okay, Evalle?"

"I'm good." She straightened her cockeyed sunglasses and slapped her head. "I heard voices before those men started appearing out of thin air—"

Isak's voice blasted through Quinn's comm set again. "I hear screaming coming from Piedmont Park." Then Isak gave Quinn his location and asked, "Where are you?"

Quinn paused and caught the sound. He acknowledged, "I hear it, too. We're closer than you and going to the park now." He tore away through a wall of rain.

"Me, too," Evalle yelled. She and Devon were doing a hard sprint with Quinn.

When they crossed the highway, the only car in sight was too far away for the headlights to touch them.

Adrianna and Casper were coming in from the left.

Quinn gave hand signals, everyone keeping quiet as they slowed to a fast walk. For once the miserable rain was covering their footsteps.

Red eyes flashed in the dark fifty yards away.

That damn demon.

Quinn motioned for Evalle and Devon to spread out so they could watch each other's backs. Adrianna followed suit with her and Casper teaming up.

His team spread out just as a scream started again then was cut off in midstream.

Damn. Had they killed one of those women? Or both?

Quinn rushed in to find that crazy, curly-haired woman fighting the demon. The female who had been carried off was on the ground, not moving. The demon dove at the curly-haired woman. Quinn prepared to strike the demon with kinetics, but the woman lashed out with a whip of energy that shot from her right-hand fingers.

A blue-white streak burned a hole through the demon's head right before he landed on her.

She was not human.

Quinn grabbed the demon off her and had to yank because the demon's claw had snagged on a cord. Quinn tugged and something that looked like a black coin hit his foot. He flipped it off into the mud.

In two steps, he ended up with a handful of gray dust as the demon decomposed.

"Who are you?" Evalle demanded.

Quinn spun around to see if the demon-killing woman was still alive.

She raked a hand over her out-of-control curls and got to her feet. She replied to Evalle, "That depends."

"On what?" Evalle asked.

"On if it's any of your business. The answer is, no, it's not."

Adrianna was squatted down checking the body on the ground. She called over. "Medb witch. Dead. Broken neck. It didn't have time to maul her."

Devon and Casper walked up. Devon said, "We found nothing. I'm going to keep scouting around."

Quinn gave him a curt nod of confirmation and Devon took off. Now it was time to take this cocky woman down a notch. "You should tell us your name and what you were doing out here."

She snorted a laugh. "That's not going to happen. I walked up on that woman being attacked and tried to help her. End of discussion."

Hardly. He asked, "What type of being are you?"

"Wow, you're going all Barbara Walters on me. If you were a vegetable what kind would *you* be?"

She had powers. She was being evasive and she had a smart mouth. Not a wise combination when outnumbered by nonhumans.

She was also toned as if she worked hard to be in fighting shape. No delicate flower, even if she did have heart-shaped lips and smooth skin.

He grimaced. Not a description he'd share in a mission report.

He gave her one more chance. "Are you registered with VIPER? And before you give me lip, you should know that I'm the Maistir over the North American Beladors. I can take you in and keep you there indefinitely."

Light colored eyes—blue?—locked with his.

Hers narrowed. "Are you always a surly bastard? Really, who killed your dog?"

Evalle glanced at him, her gaze searching his face for a reaction.

Yes, he was a surly bastard, but he hadn't lost a dog. It had been a woman. He stopped short of yelling that at this crazy person—whatever she was. He had more control than that, which he showed by calmly telling her, "You'll need to come with us until we can confirm why you're in Atlanta."

"I'm going to warn you one time to leave me alone," she said in the cool voice of someone who knew she could back up her words.

He suffered a moment of admiration for this woman who stood her ground in spite of being surrounded by preternatural beings. That mental slip irritated him, which caused him to double down on the steel in his voice.

"I'll give you fair warning as well. Threaten anyone here again and you'll regret it. We're investigating Medb murders in this area. You're not going anywhere until I get answers."

That should have put an unholy fear in her.

Not even.

Fury lit her gaze. She took two steps back. "I don't want to hurt any of you, but I'm leaving now. If anyone tries to stop me, I *will* hurt you."

With that said, she extended her right hand as she patted her left hand around her open collar. Her face registered shock.

Evalle and Quinn reacted just as fast, pushing up a wall of kinetic power to stop her strike.

In the microsecond it took for all of that to happen, Adrianna spit out two words and the stranger doubled over and fell to her knees, then flat out on the ground.

Casper had stood by during all of it, because he had unusual gifts but not like a Belador or Adrianna. He looked at Adrianna. "Damn, that's hot."

She gave him a wry glance and one of her almost smiles.

Isak came striding up and took in everything.

Quinn followed Isak's gaze to where a white glow the size of a tennis ball spun in Adrianna's palm. That was just a tiny example of the mighty Witchlock power.

Evalle asked, "How long will she be out?"

Adrianna's mouth twisted with regret. "I'm not sure. That was something new I've been practicing with Witchlock. I'm relatively sure it won't kill her though."

Evalle said, "I hope not. We need to know what she knows."

Based on what Evalle had told Quinn about Isak and Adrianna having a relationship, Quinn expected Adrianna to fill Isak in, but she ignored him.

Evalle must have noticed. Her gaze ping-ponged between the pair then she told Isak what had happened.

He said, "Wish I'd been here. I could have stunned her instead."

Adrianna argued, "By the time you could have done that, she would have cut you in half with the power from her little finger."

"Never happen," he said in a dismissive tone.

Evalle walked out from between them to pull Quinn aside and whisper, "We have to talk about those men in the energy field. I heard one of them."

"What'd he say?"

"He was trying to get the demon back in place and telling one of the others to grab the Medb."

Quinn thought back. "I didn't hear him say anything."

She started to explain more, but he halted her with his hand when Devon's voice came into Quinn's mind.

I'm over by the bridge. The four men from the energy field are here and nothing is buzzing. We should be able to take them.

You mean Park Drive Bridge? No water flowed beneath the bridge. Only urban art donated by nameless crafters who'd decorated a hangout spot for teens.

That's the one, Devon confirmed.

Adrenaline rushed through Quinn at the chance to get his hands on these men, but his gut warned him something was very off with all of this. That he should pull his people back and keep them safe.

What would Tzader have done in his shoes when Tzader was Maistir?

His friend would have told his gut to shut the hell up and trust the skills of his people. Beladors were powerful beings who backed down from no fight, not even one against an unknown enemy that had outmaneuvered them already.

Yeah, this sucked.

Quinn told Devon, *Stay close but don't engage. We're coming after them.*

CHAPTER 7

Quinn wanted everyone moving out immediately, but without alerting the prey. He explained, "Devon found the four men over near the bridge. Evalle and Adrianna pair up. I'll leave Casper to cuff our captive and keep an eye on her."

Evalle nodded. "Isak can put his gun on stun."

"That'll work." Before heading out, Quinn made one thing clear to everyone. "We need one of these men alive for any chance of uncovering who is driving all this."

Everyone nodded and fell in with Quinn, who led the way.

As they neared the thirty-foot-tall underpass covered in graffiti, Evalle and Adrianna split off to the right. They would circle wide, cross the bridge and come in from the opposite side to cut off any escape. Quinn didn't think these men were teleporting, but that buzzing energy field had made them virtually invisible.

Devon spoke through the comm gear, telling Quinn and Isak that two of the men had departed to the east of the area and he was following.

Isak confirmed the message and said he'd join Devon, then the soldier peeled off to Quinn's left.

Quinn eased through the sparse trees near the bridge and paused when he heard low voices arguing. One voice said, "How're we going to explain that we lost both fucking demons?"

"We'll just tell him they went crazy. He's the one who said the demons were dependable. That's his problem."

Quinn salivated at the hope of finding out who they were referencing as *him*. Had to be the man in control.

"Demons have *never* been dependable."

"You can tell that to—"

Quinn held his breath for the name. He eased forward until he could see the two men, one in profile, one from behind. He was tempted to dive into one of their heads and yank out the information. But his code of honor would not allow it. That would be like committing mental rape.

The men stopped talking suddenly.

A shout over to the left snatched his attention.

The two men he'd been listening to turned and moved out of view toward the sound. Were Devon and Casper engaged with the enemy? Quinn had taken a step that way when a blast of power caught him by surprise and shoved his body up against a tree.

He was pinned five feet off the ground. He tried shoving his own kinetics back at whatever was holding him, but damn, the power they were using was startling.

Both men walked back into view side-by-side with arms raised.

Quinn struggled to catch his breath against the pressure crushing his chest.

He called up all his kinetic power, shaking as he tried to shove it between their power and his chest. Not happening. He couldn't breathe. In another thirty seconds, he'd black out and be at their mercy.

He had no choice now but to use mind lock.

Diving into the mind of the man on the right, Quinn came up against a fierce shield that shoved him back. He gritted his teeth and pushed a load of power, forcing his way past the shield.

The attacker on the right dropped his arms and grabbed his head.

His buddy, still pinning Quinn against the tree, shouted, "What are you doing, Sergio? That shit hurts. Kill him before he kills us."

Quinn could breathe again, barely. He continued the pressure on Sergio's head, and Sergio dropped to his knees, but the shield began attacking Quinn's mind, stabbing his head with sharp needles of pain. He clenched his teeth, straining to funnel all his power into one brutal shove to break through, but those shields were like trying to drive a toothpick through steel.

The guy still forcing kinetics at Quinn spewed a string of words in a language Quinn had never heard.

Sergio rocked back and forth, clawing at his head.

Pressure on Quinn's chest was no longer gaining power, but neither was it letting up completely.

Evalle ran up, using her kinetic power to knock aside the guy still standing. That broke Quinn free. He dropped to his feet, but he was still connected to Sergio's head. Quinn had sensed something that he refused to believe.

Adrianna shouted, "What are you doing, Quinn? Your nose is bleeding."

Evalle yanked on Quinn's shoulder. "Get out of his head, *Quinn!*"

Quinn saw the fire erupt in the man's mind a second before he broke the connection and pulled out. He slumped to the ground, wheezing for air. His head would feel better if he'd shoved it into a blender on high speed.

Sergio howled, beating his fists against his head and whimpering, "You lied. You lied. You ... "

His mouth frothed, then his eyes rolled up. His head burst into flames. In seconds, the fire engulfed his body.

The other guy had fallen six feet away from him, but his body erupted in flames, too.

Quinn made the mental jump as to why, but he didn't want to accept it.

Rain falling in a steady downpour did nothing to slow the fires or stop the bodies from turning into a thick layer of black ashes in less than a minute.

Adrianna asked, "What happened?"

"It was them or me," Quinn explained, wiping his nose on his wet shirt. He wasn't sure if that explanation was for anyone but himself. "I used my mind lock on ... *them* ... trying to break their kinetic hold on me. I couldn't get through their shields. The best I can guess, the attempted breach of their mental shields set off an involuntary suicidal reaction."

Evalle watched him, but she didn't call him out by asking how he'd been in both minds. He'd never entered two minds at one time and frankly doubted he could, but he was not admitting what he'd just discovered.

Not yet.

Adrianna mused, "That's an incredible spell, if it has the power to destroy them if their minds are breached. Do you want to hunt down the other two or start on cleanup?"

"Let's clean this up. Devon and Isak went after the other two, but I'll call them back in."

Quinn spoke softly into his comm unit, telling the men they needed to fall back and regroup. He directed them to join Casper who was guarding their only witness from tonight. Devon confirmed.

Adrianna lifted her hands over the first blackened spot. "Do you have any use for the ashes?"

"I know you don't do necromancy and I would not ask that of you, but do you have any contacts who could simply give us a read of what type of beings these men were?"

"No one I'm speaking to."

"Understood, and I would never ask *that* of you, either."

"Thank you." Adrianna spoke over each body. As she did, the black ash swirled then vanished into the air.

On the way back to where Casper stood watch over the unknown woman, Evalle slowed her steps.

Quinn figured out what she was doing and pulled back to give them room to speak privately.

Evalle kept her voice down. "We didn't finish talking. I don't think you got what I was saying. When I was close to the energy field the first time, I heard a guy talking telepathically to the others."

Quinn hadn't understood before, but he did now. He nodded, allowing her to keep talking.

She sounded as if she was trying to convince herself when she said, "I shouldn't have been able to hear someone who was not Belador, and I shouldn't have been able to hear a conversation not directed at me. But ... I don't know. Maybe that buzzing energy caused it, but then those two shoved me up in the air. Right before they did, one of them shouted to link." A sick look climbed over her face. "Quinn, they can't be ... I just don't believe it, but ..." She couldn't finish what had to be an impossible thought for her.

But Quinn had seen something in Sergio's mind that shook him more than all that had happened. He'd recognized the power as the kind he'd seen his whole life.

Add that to the kinetic strikes, Evalle hearing the telepathy, plus the men linking their powers, and it all added up. Telepathy had to be what Devon had also meant when he recounted hearing the men.

He admitted, "Those two I fought were linked as well."

She walked along, silent, no doubt considering the ramifications of what they'd discovered. She admitted, "I didn't think you'd ever mind locked with two people."

Quinn swallowed hard, unable to fathom any other explanation. Those men working with a demon were Beladors.

He felt physically ill. Sure, he'd considered the possibility, but for *one* vigilante hunting justice, not a team and not someone who would turn his power on another Belador.

This had nothing to do with justice.

It was cold-blooded killing. Murderers.

Evalle went back to sorting out her thoughts, reaching the same conclusion. "This isn't a vigilante. For a group killing like this, someone has to be behind it."

"I had the same thought." Quinn said, "We have to figure out who created that energy field."

Evalle covered her face. "What if ..." She lowered her hand, exposing the disappointment that powered her words. "What if Macha is doing this to show the Beladors they're making a mistake by following Daegan?"

"That's possible, but—"

"It isn't Macha's style," Evalle argued against her own point. "I'd expect a goddess with her power to vaporize hundreds at one time and make a statement."

"Maybe in the past, but she needs followers. If she can convince enough Beladors to follow her before they align with Daegan, then we're looking at—"

"War. Daegan said a war was coming, but I never dreamed it would be Belador against Belador. Is this the start of it?"

"I hope not." Quinn had an even bigger problem now. How could he take Kizira's body and run if the Beladors were facing a war? He'd planned to wrap up this investigation, then find

Tzader to inform him and Evalle at the same time that he had to disappear forever with Kizira to protect the identity of his child. Quinn had stayed as Maistir as long as possible, but he'd put the Beladors at greater risk if he hid the body and stuck around.

He'd put Phoedra at risk if he didn't get her mother's body safely hidden.

That left him with only one option. He'd get Tzader to convince Daegan to declare Quinn an enemy of the Beladors once Quinn left.

He still had a little time left. He would not give up hope of finding a way to protect everyone he cared for, but he'd prepare Tzader, Evalle and Daegan before he made a final move.

When he reached Casper and the unconscious woman again, Quinn asked, "Has she stirred?"

"Nope."

Evalle looked around as Isak approached. "Where's Devon?"

"Those two guys we followed were just walking along and all of a sudden they took off, like with your kind of speed."

Evalle met Quinn's gaze with a hopeless look, but didn't comment, which allowed Isak to finish explaining. "Devon said he'd meet us back here, then he left so fast I couldn't tell you which way he went after the first ten feet."

Quinn said, "Devon won't engage without contacting me."

"Right," Evalle agreed then returned her attention to the unconscious woman. "We don't have any prisoners and she showed up out of nowhere. I say we hold onto her until we have a chance to interrogate her."

"Agreed," Isak and Quinn said at the same time.

Adrianna lifted an eyebrow at them. "Where do we take her?"

Isak offered, "We can take her to my interrogation room."

"No." Quinn caught himself. An image of waterboarding came to mind. He wouldn't treat her like a criminal. Yet. But he definitely wanted answers, and quick. Who was she? *What* was she? That power was unlike anything he'd seen before.

Was her presence tonight coincidental?

Not in his world.

She'd been here for a reason and she was going nowhere until he flushed it out.

Since Evalle trusted Isak and there was no time to segregate this group, Quinn made one thing clear. "I want this contained as a Belador issue. That means we need to keep it from VIPER."

Evalle was quick to agree. "Absolutely. I have no doubt that Daegan will deal with the guilty."

"Who's Daegan?" Isak asked. He asked the witch, "Do you know?"

Adrianna drew a dainty breath and said, "Yes, but it is not my information to share."

"What the hell, Adrianna?"

She rounded on him. "Don't give me attitude when I have no idea how you'll handle information on nonhumans. My knowledge of Daegan came from a classified mission. You do know what that means, right?"

Quinn looked to Evalle, who had a put-upon look. She said, "Isak?"

He whipped his head at her. "What?"

"Daegan now rules the Beladors, but he has not made any formal announcement or met with VIPER. We're trying to give him time to get situated. He spent the last two thousand years locked up in Táur Medb, cursed into the shape of a dragon throne. Once we learned he was there, several of us launched an unauthorized rescue mission and now he's our leader. I'm telling you because I trust you not to share this with anyone, not even your teams, until Daegan makes his plans known within the non-human community."

"Nice to know *someone* trusts me."

Adrianna sniffed at his comment, trying to look annoyed, but Quinn thought he saw hurt before she covered it with her usual in-control mask.

Casper said, "I only know about it because Quinn asked me to join you tonight and he explained this was an off-the-books mission. But I get it. If VIPER gets involved, the Beladors will be suspected of every infraction against the Medb."

Isak said, "I thought that was SOP for these two groups."

"It is," Evalle replied. "The difference is that instead of leaving policing our group up to us, VIPER might take it another step and drag Beladors into Tribunals, where determining guilt isn't as important as expedient judgment. As an example, if a deity asked a Belador whether they'd ever wanted to harm or kill a Medb and he or she said yes, that could prove guilt even if they had committed no crime."

"Damn."

"Exactly."

Quinn's gaze went to the woman on the ground. She'd curled up, soaked to the bone, and had started shivering. It wasn't cold out here. Was she having a reaction to the Witchlock power?

Great. Now he was feeling guilty about someone who had threatened to attack them. He was ready to get moving. "Can we take her to your place, Evalle? It's close."

She gave the woman a quick perusal. "Sure. She's contained."

Isak shrugged. "That works for me."

Quinn hadn't said the soldier could join them, but Isak was now part of this.

Devon came running up to them, face flushed and eyes hinting he had something important to say. Thankfully, he spoke telepathically. *Quinn, I've figured out something. I know you aren't going to believe this, but those men were ...*

Quinn watched pain cross Devon's face as he hesitated to deliver the bad news that Quinn already knew.

Devon finished, *I don't want to accuse our people, but we need to talk with only Beladors present.*

Quinn told him, *Evalle and I have come to the same conclusion I believe you have reached. As much as I trust this group, I don't want to share everything we know with non-Beladors.*

I hear you. When I followed those two men after I sent Isak back, I found out what they were after before they split up. I tried to hang with them, but they're actually faster than me.

What'd you find out?

They've been torturing the witches and warlocks to find someone who could open a tomb.

A tomb. His blood turned to ice.

Quinn felt his blood pressure bottom out, which had to be why Evalle gave him a worried look. Her empathic gift might not match Storm's, but it was clearly functioning.

Quinn forced his brain to override his emotions. He had to act, not react.

It couldn't be.

Queen Maeve wouldn't have been killing her own people to get to Kizira's body, would she? Why do that when she knew where Quinn had buried the body, *and* expected to receive it in less than two days? Plus, she had the power to compel her own people. Why would she kill them to get what she wanted?

That made no sense, but hell, he had no idea what she'd do.

Quinn ran back over what Devon had said. They weren't just looking to *open* that tomb. The person employing those demons was also generating enough power to create that force field, and make those warriors self-destruct against their will.

They wanted Kizira's body.

Meeting Evalle's questioning gaze, Quinn asked, "Can you clean this up without me and get that woman to your place?"

"Sure. What's going on?"

"I've got to go somewhere before I meet you there. I'll be right behind you."

She hesitated and sent him a telepathic message. *Is everything okay, Quinn?*

I'll know how to answer that when I see you at your building.

Got it. Speaking out loud, Evalle replied to him as if they hadn't spoken telepathically. "We'll be at my place in twenty minutes if nothing else happens, like humans deciding to come out and dance in the rain."

The humans had to be as sick of the rain as the rest of them. Creeks were overflowing around the city and flooding had caused nonstop problems.

"Thanks." Quinn turned to Isak and Adrianna. "Thank you, too, for helping tonight."

Then Quinn keyed the button on a small transmitter he carried and started walking quickly toward 10th Street, taking the sidewalk in the direction of the interstate. He'd made it two blocks when a Lexus SUV pulled up along the curb. He climbed into the rear seat where a towel and scotch waited for him.

"Where to, boss?"

"Oakland Cemetery."

Quinn dried his hair and slugged back two shots of single malt scotch during the ten-minute drive to the historic cemetery near downtown.

Not waiting for his door to be opened, Quinn climbed out and refused the umbrella offered to him. "I'll only be a minute."

"Yes, sir."

With no humans around and having the cover of darkness, Quinn raced away at hyperspeed to reach Kizira's tomb.

CHAPTER 8

With daylight coming in less than a half hour, Evalle strode into the building that never failed to brighten her mood.

This was home for her and Storm. The next floor up housed apartments currently in use by the twin boys, and Lanna, once she returned. The third floor had been dedicated as a play space for her sweet pet gargoyle. She and Storm had made the top two floors their home.

Her wise mate had dedicated this street level space for offices. A large part of it was already usable, but some space had been left unfinished until they took a tenant.

They had a functioning conference room plus two furnished offices, one of which was Storm's and the other he'd designated as Evalle's.

She had no idea what to do with an office, so she mostly visited his when she wanted to distract her mate.

Leading the way from the garage that could easily park ten vehicles, she walked into the conference room and pointed at a sofa Storm had installed for her and Feenix. Her sweet gargoyle enjoyed NASCAR. Even though Feenix had his own television in his play space upstairs, Storm had also installed a large flat-screen unit on the wall at the other end of the conference room for times when Feenix joined them down here.

Isak followed Evalle, carrying their still-unconscious captive.

Casper and Devon stayed behind to patrol the Midtown neighborhoods and Piedmont Park until daylight. No Medb attacks had happened during the day, which allowed the Beladors on patrol a chance to rest. So far.

Isak deposited the woman on the soft leather.

Adrianna entered next.

Evalle had caught Trey up on the way here and assured him Quinn would share more as soon as they knew more.

They'd all grabbed towels in the garage to dry off, but Evalle went down the hall to a bathroom and returned with a stack of hand towels she plopped on the conference table.

Isak lifted one and ran it over his head, which was no longer covered by his NVG gear. He asked Adrianna, "Any guesses on what she is?"

This was the first time Adrianna had been given a chance to look at the woman in decent lighting.

She shook her head. "No. I could feel the energy inside her when I put my hands on her, but I don't know what it is. Which is strange."

Evalle walked to the mini-fridge and grabbed bottles of water she passed around to everyone. There was a certain irony in being dehydrated after spending hours in a downpour.

She slaked her thirst and pointed her bottle at Adrianna. "What do you mean by strange?"

Isak chuckled. "Good point when strange is the operative word around you people."

Adrianna had been about to reply, but she paused in that careful and controlled way she had. She cocked her head at Isak.

Evalle took one look at the witch and backed up.

Standing too close to a pissed off woman who held the power of Witchlock in the palm of her hand, literally, could be a deadly mistake.

"I'm not sure what is more insulting," Adrianna began, turning her words on Isak. "Your comment about us being strange as if all humans are so *normal* or the way you said *you people.*"

Isak held up his hands. "I wasn't saying strange is bad, just that it's ... already unusual."

Adrianna studied Isak. His hair should have stood up from that much intense witch focus, but the human didn't know Adrianna as well as some of them did.

Evalle smothered a laugh.

When she'd first met Isak, he'd been toting his standard

demon blaster and had made it abundantly clear to her there was no place in his world for anything not human.

That was before he discovered *Evalle* was not human.

He'd chased her for a bit, and had seemed fairly serious at the time. But that was before Evalle made it clear she only had eyes for Storm. Isak met Adrianna around the same time. Those two had mixed like oil and water. Isak's attention to Evalle had been nothing compared to what he'd turned on the little witch now glaring at him.

Evalle had thought Isak possessed better survival skills until he started to speak again. Evalle shook her head at him and warned, "Put the shovel down while you're almost ahead."

Did Isak take the hint? No. When in doubt, men had their own standard "go to" reaction.

Isak crossed his arms and put on his intimidating look, which had zero effect on Adrianna. She muttered, "Never mind."

Dismissing him, Adrianna finished her thought on their captive. "To answer your question, that woman's energy felt strong, but as though it were wrapped in a protective casing. I couldn't reach it."

Evalle asked, "Not even with Witchlock?"

"I didn't try with that. I'm still working through the learning curve on the power. Unless it's a critical situation, I'm trying to use it only when I feel relatively certain I'm not going to have a backlash, blow something up or ... kill someone."

They all looked at the unconscious woman. Evalle said, "She's breathing, but her skin is losing color."

"Her arm was very hot when I touched it," Adrianna said.

Evalle grabbed a hand towel off the table. The room had a wet bar, but she stepped over to soak the towel with colder water from the water cooler. She placed the folded rag on the woman's head.

When she stood up, she caught Isak smirking at her. "What?"

"Nothing. That's ... very Florence Nightingale of you."

"Aren't you in enough trouble without pissing me off, too?"

He gave her an arrogant male grin. That bear had better watch himself. Evalle blew off his arrogance, but Adrianna would turn him into a bug and drop him in a frog pond.

Adrianna walked over and put her hand on the woman's

cheek. "Still hot. Worse, actually. I could try my majik on her again, but if she's having a reaction to it, another shot might kill her."

~

Reese stayed perfectly still, keeping her eyes closed and her breathing shallow, as if she was still out cold. She wished she were. Yáahl had said the medallion could heal her. He'd failed to say the pendant would take its time doing so.

Evidently it hadn't healed *all* of her *jötnar* wounds, and the flush of having her power back had masked a gash in her side that had decided to continue bleeding.

And the *jötnar* poison was still running through her body.

Who were these people?

Why were they acting concerned after that witch had tried to kill her at Piedmont Park?

Reese had finally figured out her location after chasing down the guy, a Belador it seemed, with the female Medb. When had Beladors turned bad? And teamed up with demons? She'd only gone after the guy carrying the woman because she'd thought it was a human she'd be saving from a demon.

She couldn't believe she'd risked her life for a Medb witch. They valued no one's life. That stupid action had landed her in the middle of a Medb-Belador mess.

Oh, and to put the cherry on her day, she'd been caught by a Belador Maistir.

Quinn.

Yeah, this had jumped straight from bad to sucking beyond belief. In spite of Yáahl's annoying habit of finding the best way to make her life miserable, she would've thought he'd drop her somewhere close to the body if he really wanted her to keep it away from the Medb.

So where *was* Kizira's body? And how was Reese going to escape this group without her power?

Biting pain spread through her abdomen. She forced herself not to curl into herself and groan. If she could get out of here soon and find the medallion, she could still stop the poison. But from the way her body felt, she might have an hour or two, and that was only because she had less poison in her now.

The medallion had come off while she was fighting that demon. Talk about poor strategic planning on Yáahl's part. How was she supposed to fight with one hand on the medallion? She had to get back to Piedmont Park before someone either picked it up as a found gift or threw it away.

Without that, she had no power to fight anyone nonhuman and no way to teleport the body back to Yáahl.

Her toes felt numb. Not good. If that persisted, they might turn black and fall off soon.

"You'd get answers faster at my place," the one called Isak said.

Reese had names for each one. She'd regained consciousness when they'd parked in this building. The way Evalle had given instructions to everyone and played hostess had to mean she owned the building.

They'd dropped Reese on the sofa with her head positioned so that she could see a fuzzy image of the door at this end of the room if she barely moved her eyelashes.

Evalle pulled out her mobile phone. "I'm going to find out how far away Storm is. I'm thinking he'll know what to do."

A tone sounded on a small display panel by the door. Reese risked opening her eyes just a tiny slit, which allowed her to see Evalle smile, then put her phone away without using it.

Evalle said, "That might be Storm."

Who the hell was this Storm? Had to be Evalle's boyfriend, or husband, the way she smiled. Reese checked out Evalle's left hand. No ring.

The energy in Reese's chest came to life in a big way and added to her misery.

What the ...

"I'm here ..." a male voice called from the hallway.

Just as he got to the door and swung inside, Reese came alive. She rolled off the sofa and to her feet, wobbling into a run.

Isak stopped her.

Storm roared, "What the hell is *that* doing inside my wards?"

That's who they were waiting for? Reese tried to squeeze between Isak and the wall.

She shouted, "Get him out of here." Pain rushed through all

parts of her body. The energy and poison were having a party.

Evalle grabbed his arm. "Whoa, honey."

"Let go, Evalle."

"We think she's sick."

Truth. Bile rushed up in Reese's throat. She couldn't stop the shakes. This was no different than staking a lamb for a sacrificial offering.

Storm's eyes went bright red. "Not a problem. I'm going to kill her."

Heat baked Reese's brain or she'd have had something snappy to throw back at him.

Isak stepped forward, blocking Storm. "Back off, dude. She's unarmed."

Reese silently cheered for the super-sized human.

Shoving his face up at Isak, Storm warned, "Get out of my way or I'll toss you through that wall."

That must have been possible, because Evalle raced over and wedged her hand between them, pushing the men apart.

It looked as if moving a building over a foot would have been easier. She stepped fully in front of the demon. "Storm, what's wrong? Don't get upset with them. I brought her in here."

What was the relationship between Evalle and that demon?

Storm had been shaking with fury, but when he turned his eyes from Reese to Evalle, his faced calmed.

He went from angry to confused. "Do you *not* know what she is?"

"No, we were all wondering so if you do, tell us."

Reese spoke up in a raspy voice. "What exactly do you think I am, *demon*?"

They all turned to her.

Storm's hard stare returned, but his eyes were golden now. "I know what you are, *demon*."

"Heh. I guess it's true about takes one to know one." Lame, but she wasn't at her best.

Storm's red headlights glowed hot again.

Taking potshots at a demon while she had no powers and was cuffed might land her the Stupid Award Of The Year.

Reese said, "Okay, everyone calm down. I am *not* a demon."

"I can sense your energy, but ... " Storm argued, but he

frowned as he did. "You're telling the truth."

How would he know if she lied or not? She explained, "I *am* a demon magnet, though, which means I have demon blood in my ancestry. Demons turn rabid around me, because of the energy inside me. I don't harm others and can't help my ancestry. When I have my powers, I kill demons like the one I killed at the park." She stared at Storm when she said, "Although, I am impressed that this one maintains such good control."

Adrianna sucked in a breath at that and Evalle's face crinkled with a look of "oh, shit."

Storm said in a tight, but even, voice, "Move, Isak. I'd like to address her one-on-one."

Isak must have been tired of battling everyone. He said, "You know what? It's not a human. She's all yours."

The traitor left Reese standing alone, leaning against the wall for support, with sweat soaking her shirt that *had* almost finally dried.

"It? You called her an *it*?" Adrianna said in a tone that warned Isak he had hit on a sore topic.

Storm saved Isak by walking up to Reese and yanking everyone's attention to the imminent bloodbath. Why had they kept her alive if they were going to let a demon kill her?

When Storm stood only a foot away from her, Reese's energy lashed at her insides, burning her along with the poison. She'd never spent this much time so close to a demon.

Not and both of them still be alive.

Her knees banged together from her body weakening and she hated it. Hated to ever feel vulnerable.

But she was not backing down. "What are you waiting for?" she taunted him.

Storm smiled and she wondered if that was the face he showed prey right before they were slaughtered. He put his hand on her stomach.

She jerked at the rush of energy that flooded toward him. Done with him toying with her, she snarled, "It calls to you, doesn't it? Demons live for a chance at this kind of power. You want it, don't you?"

For some demented reason, she wanted to prove he wasn't stronger than she was. That he couldn't hold out against the pull of her energy.

At this point, she'd help him to gouge out the damn energy. It throbbed with hot zaps of pain through her chest.

Storm's jaw flexed. He studied her intently as if trying to decide something, then he whispered words that sounded like the Haida speech pattern, but she didn't understand the language.

Reese gasped for air and slid down to the floor. Her knees had given out. She looked up at him. "What did you do?"

He arched an eyebrow at her. "Based on you being the one cuffed, you're the one expected to answer questions. Not me."

The pain in her chest receded, not all the way, but on a one-to-ten scale, it was down to a six after Reese had just suffered ten thousand. She wrapped one arm across her waist—an effort with flex cuffs on her wrists—and stretched her fingers to the gash in her side.

Yep, still there.

Evalle let out a rush of air that sounded relieved. She stepped up next to Storm but looked down at Reese. "You looked perfectly healthy when you were fighting in the park. Are you having a reaction to Adrianna's power?"

Reese considered lying just to make them all feel guilty, but she didn't have the energy to play games. "No."

"Why are you sick now and you weren't then?"

"I had on a protective disk that someone tore off my neck." She searched the faces for a sign that someone had it. No one seemed to know what she was talking about.

"What's your name?" Evalle asked.

"Reese." She clamped her lips shut and groaned. "Sorry for the short visit, but I got hit with a load of poison earlier from fighting a pair of *jötnar* demons. Since I doubt I'll last much longer, I'm done answering questions."

Adrianna came over. "I'll see what I can do."

Reese shook her head. "You can't fix this. Ask him." She nodded in Storm's direction.

They turned to Storm, who still looked as though he hadn't made up his mind not to solve her problem by removing her head from her body. In another fifteen minutes she'd be begging him to do just that.

CHAPTER 9

Evalle considered Reese's condition and Storm's anger. She put her hand on his arm.

Her mate lost his demon glare when he turned to her and waited to see what she'd ask of him now. Clearly, bringing a demonically influenced person into their home had not gone over well. She couldn't fix this now, not with an audience.

She squeezed his arm and said, "We need to talk to her. It's very important. I'll explain it all as soon as I can, but I told Quinn I'd keep her safe until he gets here. Can you do anything?"

The furious glint slid away and Storm's warm brown eyes returned. He brushed his hand over her hair. "Maybe. Let me see."

He moved out of Evalle's grasp and sighed when he took in the pitiful sight of their captive. Addressing Reese, he said in an even tone. "I will help you if you swear on your life not to harm me or what's mine."

Reese struggled to look up and forced out, "Yes, but—"

He produced a knife and leaned down.

Eyes terrified, Reese clamped her lips shut and followed his every move.

He sliced through the flex cuffs then stood up.

She rubbed her wrists, now wary as she kept him in view.

Storm held both of his hands over her and lifted his head. He spoke in a tongue that Evalle had heard before, but not often.

It took a moment before she realized he was speaking Ashaninka. He'd been born part Ashaninka and part Navajo, but he'd gotten his demon blood from his South American roots.

Well, damn. She hated for him to tap that side to help anyone, but interrupting him right now might do greater harm to Reese.

Tonight's private conversation just got more conflicted.

As he spoke, the lights in the room quivered and the air turned brittle cold. Storm's voice had a sharp, nasal tone but was filled with respect.

To Evalle it sounded as if he were calling upon his ancestors to do him a favor.

Hair on her arms stood up.

Adrianna's white-blonde locks lifted off her shoulders.

Isak wore a horrified expression, but kept his gaze locked on Reese, unable to look away.

Reese grabbed at her chest. She made garbled noises as if something inside her struggled to get out.

Evalle kept track of Isak to be sure he wouldn't pull out a demon blaster and use it. His eyes couldn't get any rounder.

Adrianna, on the other hand, watched Storm with intense fascination. The kind of attention a student would give a master, which was quite a compliment considering Adrianna was the baddest witch in the east these days.

Maybe in any direction.

Reese's eyes turned white. Her body lifted up in the air, arms hanging loose and head dropped back.

Black smoke curled up from her open mouth. It continued to feed out in a silky tendril, then rolled into a dark ball that smelled sick and nasty.

Her body shook, but slowly her form shifted upright until she stood flatfooted. She gasped for air then bent over, hands on her knees and coughed, sucking in one deep breath after another.

Storm kept his eyes shut, but turned his face toward the black cloud floating over Reese.

He shoved his hands into the dark mess.

No! Evalle reached for him, but before she could grab Storm to pull him back, the cloud exploded into microscopic crystals that sucked into themselves and sizzled out of existence.

She grabbed his face, turning his head to her. "Storm, are you okay?"

He opened his eyes. The red glow died down and returned to

his normal brown eyes. He blinked and all sign of demon was gone. "I'm fine."

She held his face. "Don't ever do that again, okay?"

He kissed her, murmuring, "Then don't bring a demon home again."

"It wasn't intentional."

Reese argued, "I'm not a—"

Ignoring Reese, Storm spoke over her, suggesting, "How about next time you treat something unknown like it might be a rabid animal and lock it in a cage until I get here?"

She dropped her hands. He was still angry, though keeping it hidden from the others. She knew it came from him thinking she'd been at risk, but he also knew she killed demons for a living.

Just to let him know she wasn't fooled, her lips twitched and she shrugged. "I don't see a cage, do you?"

"I'll build one."

"You do that."

He sighed. "Ever the hellion."

Adrianna interrupted. "She's stable again. She might make it this time now that you got the poison out of her."

Evalle leaned in, pausing right before she kissed Storm lightly to say, "Thank you."

He sighed again, the sound of a man in love who knew he could not win this fight. "You're welcome." He turned the quick kiss into one he put his stamp on that told everyone in the world that Evalle was his.

He added in a whisper next to her ear. "Let's wrap this up. I have plans for you."

When he pulled back, she quipped, "Then don't piss me off again."

"I'll work on that, sweetheart."

Even angry, he had the ability to send her heart somersaulting with his endearment.

"You two done making up?" Isak asked, not the least bit happy.

Storm turned around, putting a protective arm over Evalle's shoulders, and she let him.

Isak grunted out a derogatory scoffing noise.

Adrianna had caught the whole exchange. She told Isak, "You could take a few tips." Then she walked over to wash her hands.

Evalle didn't need her empathic gift to know that Storm was enjoying a smug moment.

The security monitor on the wall made a soft ding. She started to go check.

Storm kept her in place. "That's Quinn. I gave him and Tzader codes for entering and set the ward to allow them to come in."

Adrianna stepped back over and teased, "What about me?"

"I have a code for you, too, but I need you physically here to set the ward."

He'd clearly surprised her. "Okay, thanks."

Isak said, "That will be handy."

Storm replied, "For them. You, on the other hand, can only come inside when invited."

Evalle slid a look at Adrianna, whose smirk said she enjoyed the exchange, which only pushed Isak's irritation level up another notch.

Those two needed to stop circling each other and find a room.

"I got here as soon as I could," Quinn said, striding into the room. He nodded at Storm then asked, "Has anyone gotten anything out of that woman yet?"

Adrianna chuckled. "Storm did, but the only one it helped was her. She was loaded with demon poison."

Reese stepped forward and told him, "*That woman* has a name. I realize it may strain your alpha egos, but try to show a little respect and talk to me as if I have a mind."

Evalle wanted to dislike Reese because of catching her in the middle of tonight's mess and because of Storm having to tap his demon blood to help her, but she had spunk. A fighter. Evalle certainly couldn't disparage the woman for having mixed blood. She knew well enough how it felt to be shunned because of prejudice. Of all the people in the room, Evalle might be the only one who saw beneath the woman's bravado to the fear.

Storm's empathic side had to be alerted, but he may have been too pissed off at first to sense Reese fully. The confusion trickling into his expression probably meant he was finally taking a deeper look at Reese.

Reese might be earning a bit of sympathy. Or so Evalle thought until she caught the dark thoughts simmering in Quinn's eyes.

He didn't look a bit sympathetic.

She spoke to him telepathically. *What's wrong, Quinn?*

Let's deal with this woman first. Then he asked the room, "Nothing useful, huh?"

Storm and Adrianna gave Evalle odd looks, searching for an explanation. They knew Quinn well enough to catch that something was off.

Isak didn't.

Evalle would have to ask Isak to leave or they'd be forced to dance around what they could say.

Isak's phone buzzed. He lifted it and read the monitor. "I need to go." He put his phone away and told Adrianna, "I'll call you later."

"Why?"

Evalle almost spewed the water she'd just slugged back.

Not the least bit put off, Isak walked over to Adrianna. Standing toe to toe with her, he said, "To talk about having dinner."

"Why?"

Storm watched with amusement lighting his gaze. Quinn seemed close to snapping at everyone, but Evalle had enlightened Quinn about these two. Quinn liked Adrianna, which was probably why he allowed the witch a moment.

Sounding perturbed now, Isak stared down at Adrianna. "Because I want to share a meal with you. Why is that difficult to understand?"

She gave him a dainty shrug. "I'm a strange person. Not even a person. I'm a nonhuman, based on the definition you use, so why would you want to have dinner with such a being?" She paused and added with emphasis, "An *it*."

Isak muttered under his breath.

Evalle caught something about a woman turning him into a lunatic.

Storm hugged Evalle. He might not like Isak, but she caught a touch of sympathy rolling off Storm. Storm had gone through a lot to win Evalle's trust. She figured he could empathize, even with Isak, when a woman was making a man crazy.

Leaning down, Isak said, "I'll call. You'll answer. We'll discuss this later." Then he picked her up, kissed her hard, dropped her back down and walked out.

It took Adrianna a second to realize what he'd done and yell, "Hold your breath waiting on that."

His booming laughter answered her.

Quinn started rubbing his head.

Evalle took pity on him. She asked Storm, "Did you get your bar stocked?"

"It's *our* bar and the answer is yes." He started for the bar built into the wall. "Two fingers of Boodles, Quinn?"

"Absolutely."

"Tea for you, Adrianna?"

"I can get it. I found it earlier when I opened the wrong cabinet."

"What do you want, Reese?" Evalle arched an eyebrow at the woman, warning her she had few friends in this room. In other words, don't mouth off at a potential ally.

Reese must have taken the hint, because she politely requested a soft drink.

Once they all had something in hand and had pulled chairs into a half circle to face Reese, Quinn asked Storm, "What can you tell me first?"

"She has demonic energy—"

Reese gave him a frown then told Quinn, "I clarified that I'm not a demon, but a demon magnet. Big difference."

Quinn looked to Storm with a question in his gaze.

Storm held his hands out. "She's telling the truth."

Reese scoffed. "You keep saying things like that. What are you? A human lie detector?"

No one said a word, waiting for Storm. He smiled at her and said, "That's exactly what I am." Then he told Quinn, "Next question."

Evalle said, "I didn't even think to explain about Storm and lying."

Quinn said, "Why should you? It doesn't matter ... if she plans to tell the truth."

Reese's gaze jumped from person to person until she finally

accepted what he'd told her, looking more worried than she had when she'd obviously thought Storm was going to drain her, kill her or both.

CHAPTER 10

A human lie detector? *Screw me.*

Reese had no idea such a thing existed. Considering she was sitting in a room with Beladors, a demon guy and a witch, she shouldn't be overly surprised.

Not just Beladors. No, she'd opened door number three and had gotten their leader for this part of the world.

That Quinn had a dark attitude. If he didn't look ready to fight the world at any moment, she'd call him attractive. Nothing fit with him. He had a British accent but a face that reminded her of the Russian ancestors in her screwed-up bloodline.

Quinn would be the hardest puzzle in the room to crack.

None of these people were making sense to her. The witch had knocked her out, then had been willing to heal her. The human guy, Isak, hadn't turned his scary weapon they called a demon blaster on her.

Evalle had been cautious around her, but Reese picked up positive vibes from the young woman.

The oddest thing to accept? Storm. He was a demon, but he'd healed her. Granted, he'd dialed back his anger for Evalle, but still ... a demon.

"Reese?"

She'd lost track of the last thing said. "What, Quinn?"

His head pulled back at being called by his name.

She said, "That is your name, right?" Going from one side of the half circle to the other, she called out each one. "You're Adrianna, a witch with a lot of mojo. You're Storm and we both know what you are." She gave him a snippy smile that he ignored. "You're Evalle, a Belador who I assume is the demon's main squeeze."

Storm growled at her.

Evalle said, "You really aren't much for keeping things calm are you?"

"Calm is boring." Then Reese turned to badass Quinn. Storm was hot. No question about it. She'd give the demon that, but Quinn had a presence about him that spoke of power and leadership. He wasn't a man who took orders from anyone.

He was the one person in this room who could destroy her by handing her over to VIPER.

She cocked her head at him. "You're Quinn, the Maistir. See? I paid attention when you were reading me the riot act in the park."

Adrianna picked up the questioning. "Evalle brought up a good point earlier while you were still out of it. How were you fighting that demon if you were so sick? I'm not questioning whether your illness was real. We all saw what Storm pulled out of you. What did you mean about a disk protecting you?"

"I had a talisman that had started healing me, but I lost it in the fight at the park."

"What kind of talisman?" Evalle asked.

"A black medallion that looks like an oversized silver dollar."

"Do you need that to use your powers?"

What was the point in trying to lie in front of Storm?

Reese said, "Yes." She took in their faces. Quinn hadn't been here last time. "Anyone happen to see a disk dangling from a cord necklace?"

"Stick to answering the questions, not asking them," Quinn said, shutting down her inquiry.

She drew in a slow breath and waited. This was not going to go well if she got pressed for more details. She couldn't tell them why she was in Atlanta or she'd blow her best chance at gaining that body.

Quinn started in. "Were you with those men who attacked the Medb witch tonight?"

She gave him an offended look. "Of course not."

He checked Storm, who nodded that she'd told the truth.

"Then who are you and where are you from?"

She decided to test Storm. "Like I said, my name is Reese, I live in California and I'm thirty."

"Name and California are true. Your age is a lie."

Damn. He was good. "Correct. I'm not quite thirty."

"Testing me?"

She shrugged. "Just want to know if I'm being played or not."

His eyes smiled in confidence. Evidently, she'd amused the lie detector.

Her interrogator started up again. Quinn asked, "What's your last name?"

"Sorry. I'm not sharing that or where I specifically live. I have no idea who you people are or what you're after. I will not expose my family and friends to unknown preternaturals." She looked at Storm, daring him to question that.

He didn't.

Her last name must not have been a big issue for Quinn, who asked, "What do you do in California?"

"Photographer." No records of her as photographer existed. She used a third party and a pseudonym for selling her photos.

"Do you know why those men were looking for the body of a Medb priestess?"

She almost blew her next answer by hesitating. She covered it by arranging her face to look confused. "No." Storm kept his eyes on her and showed no reaction. Clearly, her answer passed as truth. She had no idea what was up with that group who appeared out of nowhere and needed to avoid them if they ran with demons.

"So you're definitely not helping those men in any way?"

"No." Truth. She was only helping herself on this trip. She hurried to get ahead of a question she couldn't answer honestly. "Why would anyone be hunting the body of a Medb? If it's in this realm, I'd expect it to be burned and scattered with salt."

She started to push it further, but she glanced over at Quinn and got sidetracked by the grief in his eyes. The pain in them called to her, spoke to the silent voice inside her. When he caught her looking too closely at him, his countenance turned stony. That, she also recognized.

How often had she shielded herself behind a cold exterior to hide what went on inside?

A dead Medb priestess could only be Kizira.

The darknet had erupted about her death, blasting out conspiracies about who had killed someone most would believe possessed no vulnerability. Until her talk with Yáahl, Reese had dismissed the stories as propaganda.

Yáahl believed the body was in a tomb and Reese would stack a heavy bet on anything he believed. He expected Reese to find said body, then keep it from the Medb as a minimum. Who had buried a dead priestess in a tomb in the human realm?

If not for the history of hate between the Medb and Beladors, she'd take Quinn's intense questions, stacked up beside that grief he was working so hard to hide, to mean he might have buried it.

That wasn't even logical.

But she did realize one thing. She'd found a lead on Kizira's body. It burned her to admit it, but maybe Yáahl's timing and location for where he'd dumped her hadn't been so off, after all.

Huh.

With the demon poison out of her system, Reese was back in business. She settled into the sofa, prepared to hang in here long enough to find out where Kizira had been buried.

Then she'd escape.

Quinn went and ruined her good mood. "Are you aligned with VIPER, Reese? Before you answer that, let me remind you that besides Storm's ability to call you on a lie, I am in direct contact with them daily."

"No, I'm only visiting. I know VIPER requires anyone who stays longer than three days to register with them. I'll be gone before that." Hopefully.

"What are you doing in Atlanta?"

There it was. The question that would hang her. She hedged, "I'm here doing a favor for someone."

"That's not good enough," Quinn countered.

Things were about to get real.

Out of the blue, Quinn lifted his finger in a signal to hold everything for a minute as he stared into nothing.

If Reese had to make an educated guess based on what she knew about Beladors, she'd say he was having a telepathic communication.

When his eyes focused again, he said to the other three,

"Tzader says a meeting has been called. We need to go now."

Saved by the bell, so to speak.

Reese said, "If that's the case, I need to get going myself." She'd leave, then double back to watch for someone out of this group to follow."

Quinn stood. "You aren't going anywhere."

"Are you kidding me?" Reese jumped to her feet. "I was minding my own business and got sucked into your fight. I saved lives by killing that demon. I have a personal reason for being here." She eyed Storm quickly, but that was as much the truth as anything else.

He didn't seem a hundred percent sure about what she'd said, but neither did he throw the bullshit flag on her.

So why was he studying her so closely?

Shoot. She'd said she had a personal reason for being here.

She tilted her chin at a take-no-crap angle. "As I was saying, I have a personal reason for being here. To tell you more would be to break a confidence and expose details about something that I can't share."

Storm asked, "Does this confidence you hold have anything to do with us?"

That was a tough one, but she reasoned that she didn't know how they were associated with her task and replied, "I don't see any reason it would."

That earned her a frown from Storm.

What did that mean? Undecided again?

"You have no reason to hold me," she argued.

Everyone looked at Quinn who said, "But we *are* holding you."

She considered several insults and dumped them, going with, "What happened to southern hospitality?"

Storm pointed out, "I didn't kill you."

"That leaves me all warm and fuzzy."

Evalle offered, "Why don't you spend the night here and give your body a chance to finish healing?"

Reese wanted to snap back at her that she had things to do, but two things happened. She realized that if she stayed close to these people, she might find the body even more quickly. The other reason she changed her tune?

The incredulous look on Storm's face at Evalle's invitation.

Reese sweetened her voice just to tweak the demon's nose. "That would be so kind of you. Thank you."

Adrianna said, "I don't think you did yourself any favors with that sappy tone, Reese."

Storm had a cat-that-caught-the-mouse gleam in his eyes now. "You have no use of your powers without your medallion?"

"Nooo." She dragged it out just to let him know he got on her nerves as much as she got on his.

"Truth," he told everyone. "Keeping you here tonight might just be a good idea. I've got the perfect place for you."

What the hell did that mean?

CHAPTER 11

Tristan groaned as his booted feet touched the solid ground of Treoir Island and the spinning colors of teleportation dissolved. He'd kept his eyes shut until the end or his vision would be out of kilter when he opened them.

With a peek, he sighed, glad to be back in one piece even if he'd had to give up his Friday night to come back early with news.

Twilight softened the edges of everything. The day-night thing never translated the same way here as in the human world.

That last teleport to and from Atlanta had been erratic, but he'd landed right on target. Spread out in front of him were the bluffs that overlooked a turbulent Irish Sea rolling and crashing against Treoir's rocky shoreline two hundred feet down.

He'd stopped first at the castle, but had earned a little reprieve before giving his report when Daegan hadn't been available. He planned to spend it gliding over the island in his gryphon form, clearing his head.

A shrill screech pierced the air.

He covered his ears.

Trees crashed against each other in the forest behind him.

Just five minutes of peace. Was that too much to ask? He turned just as something slammed across his back, knocking him off his feet. His body shot forward.

He had no time to use kinetics to break his fall, so he shoved his hands out instead. That didn't stop him from hitting the ground hard. His face and hands plowed up tall grass. There were no giants on Treoir that he knew of, but damn if that hadn't felt like being hit by a mega baseball bat belonging to one.

When the ringing in his ears cleared, he heard furious flapping and stomping too close for comfort.

Tristan spit out dirt. Fucking gryphons were at it again.

The ground shuddered with heavy pounding headed his way.

He flipped over fast, prepared for an attack.

A pair of ten-foot-tall gryphons battling each other crashed out of the woods.

That meant a tail as thick as his thigh had swatted him.

The closest beast to Tristan flapped up and down in an exaggerated backwards hop.

Shit! Tristan rolled again to his right and barely missed getting his head crushed under a monster paw.

His nostrils stung with the stench of fresh blood and singed feathers.

What the hell had happened since he'd left the pack this morning?

The tangled-up gryphons crashed into a tree, which didn't slow them down a bit. They kept right on beating their huge wings and lunging at each other with sharp beaks that gouged bloody gashes. With the head and wings of an eagle stuck on a lion's body, they had plenty of ways to rip each other apart.

Son of a bitch. *Can't I just get one break?*

Tristan recognized the black feathers intermixed with bright red ones.

That would be dickhead Ixxter.

The silver-gray-feathered gryphon with a gold head was no mystery either. Bernie could be just as dangerous as any of the other seven on this mystical island.

But in human form, Bernie was a skinny little guy who never gave Tristan grief and always stepped up to do anything asked of him.

Ixxter, on the other hand, was a vile man in any form, who made life here a misery and enjoyed exerting his power over all the other gryphons who stayed on Treoir.

All except Tristan.

I might need to revise that if I have to tangle with that beast right now.

Ixxter couldn't win a fight if Tristan had a chance to return to full power, but after the round trip teleporting from this realm hidden in the Irish Sea to the human world, and back, he was spent.

Teleporting hadn't been a natural power for Tristan to begin with, and using it sucked his energy faster than anything else.

Shoving up to his feet, Tristan knocked weeds out of his hair and spit out dirt. Maybe he'd get lucky and those two idiots would wind down.

Nope. Bernie and Ixxter kept battling as if he weren't present.

Whatever had that pair pissed off was nothing compared to Tristan's frame of mind right now.

None of them could speak in gryphon form. Tristan opened his mind to shout at them telepathically. *Stop fighting right now or I'll kick both of your asses.*

Heh. When in doubt, make empty threats.

Ixxter shouted back loud enough to make Tristan's head vibrate. *I'm sick of this little prick's bullshit. He thinks that golden head makes him special, but he's no different than the rest of us.*

Bernie complained, *It's Ixxter's fault ...*

Ixxter took advantage of Bernie's distraction and flew at the smaller gryphon, but Bernie hadn't survived this long by being slow. He ducked his head and dove under Ixxter's chest, taking out Ixxter's legs. That turned into a new round of wing beating, claw slashing and beak snapping.

Remind me again why I agreed to deal with the gryphons while Evalle was gone? Tristan silently asked himself. He wiped his hands over his face, trying to wash away the fatigue from weeks of this crap. All the gryphons tipped the scales at around two tons, but Ixxter had another two hundred pounds on Bernie.

The real difference between the pair was that Bernie hated fighting and Ixxter lived for stomping anyone's butt.

Tristan understood needing to blow off steam.

Hell, he could fuel a locomotive with all the steam he needed to release. Getting laid would help, but that wasn't going to happen in this place and the only woman he wanted was human. Mac had been gone during his last visit to the human world or he'd have carved out some time with her.

Screeching reached an ear-bleeding decibel.

He should kinetically shove those two knuckleheads into the thick trees surrounding this normally peaceful clearing, but being a quart low on power had him hesitating.

Best to not risk exposing a weakness, which would happen if his kinetics failed to knock Ixxter off his feet.

Ixxter broke free of Bernie's claws, which had been gripping Ixxter's chest. The larger gryphon backed away, flapped up in the air and flew at a wobbling Bernie.

Ixxter hit his mark, then tucked his wing, rolled and gained his feet. He jumped on Bernie, bouncing up and down.

That fucking Ixxter would crush Bernie one bone at a time if Tristan didn't stop him.

Tristan ripped his shirt off and shed his jeans, then called up his gryphon form, forcing the change fast.

Damn that hurt.

He groaned at the pain when muscles stretched and pulled. Bones extended and his back split on each side as two wings burst from his body, which was now the color of a thundercloud. Blue and black feathers sheathed his wings.

He shook out the kinks and pains, feeling spent as a battery with only a surface charge.

These gryphons had been stuck here too long and by no choice of their own. They needed a chance to return to the human world and feel like real people again.

All except Ixxter.

He needed to feel Tristan's foot shoved up his ass.

Bernie whimpered and tucked his wings, trying to protect his body. Ixxter kicked the balled-up gryphon.

Fully shifted, Tristan cracked his neck.

Their resident bully-gryphon needed to be reminded who was in charge.

Tristan sent a challenge telepathically. *Ready to take on someone your own size, Ixxter?*

Ixxter swung around, feathers puffed. Hatred burned in his eagle eyes. In human form, they all had glowing green eyes, something they shared from their Alterant heritage. Just a bunch of bastard half-breed Beladors, but in a battle they were the baddest of the bad. Ixxter fluttered his red-and-black feathers, puffing up his wings and body even further.

Tristan said, *Nice trick. I'm so impressed. I'd clap if I could. Fuck you, Tristan.*

I have standards. Not unless you buy me dinner first.

Ixxter's razor-sharp beak could snap off a human head, but he'd have to work harder to cut off Tristan's eagle head. Ixxter's chest feathers blazed fire red then blended into dark brownish-black skin with translucent scales on his lower half. He stood on tree-trunk legs bulging with muscle. His thick tail swatted Bernie.

What a bastard.

Tristan opened his stance. *What's the matter, Ixxter? Change your mind? Or is it true that when bullies face a real threat the truth comes out? They're just spineless dweebs with short dicks? I know the short part is right, what about your spine?*

With a sliver of luck, Ixxter would let this go and give Tristan a couple hours to rebuild some of his strength. But if Ixxter still wanted a throwdown, Tristan would accommodate him and not be the only one walking away bloody.

A noise ground out of Ixxter's throat, then the gryphon's harsh voice scraped across Tristan's mind. *You're not our leader.*

Technically correct.

The most powerful gryphon led the pack and that would be Evalle Kincaid, who was currently in the human world with a team hunting a serial killer. He'd hate to be in her shoes, tracking some unknown threat, and not be able to shift into gryphon form in the human realm.

Maybe their new leader, Daegan, would fix that rule.

Tristan might be tired of flying around Treoir as part of the island security some days, but he liked the freedom to change forms whenever he chose.

And he believed Daegan meant it when he said the gryphons didn't need anyone's permission to be free.

Ixxter huffed and scratched the ground.

Tristan wasn't the true gryphon leader, but he couldn't stand by and allow that ego-bloated bastard to unleash his frustration on poor Bernie.

Ixxter stalked forward slowly with his wings hunched.

The last time this gryphon had started a fight that Tristan interrupted, Ixxter had moved in the same manner, acting as if he was heading over to fight.

But in the end, Ixxter had passed Tristan and kept going another twenty feet before taking flight.

Tristan didn't trust Ixxter one bit.

He watched for any movement that might televise Ixxter's intention to take a cheap shot.

When Ixxter came shoulder to shoulder with Tristan, he paused, giving Tristan a hard, eagle-eyed stare.

Really? Now they had to play a stare down game?

Ixxter snorted and continued toward the edge of the bluffs, picking up speed to take flight. It was that or fall to the cliffs below.

Tristan let out a long breath.

Pain still spiked through his muscles from shifting so quickly, especially when he was physically drained, but his joint aches were worth ending a conflict without bloodshed this time.

The sound of wings flapping behind him confirmed Ixxter's departure.

Good riddance.

Now Tristan could focus on the gryphon still curled up on the ground. *Are you hurt, Bernie?*

I'll be okay, Bernie mumbled as he struggled to his feet.

What the hell were you two fighting over?

It wasn't my fault, Tristan. Ixxter started talking trash—

Dammit, Bernie. I told you to not let him bait you.

I know, Bernie said, stretching his wings and shaking his head. He turned to face Tristan and his bright green eagle eyes rounded in panic. *Tristan! Wa-watch out!*

Tristan turned as Ixxter dive-bombed him at full speed, knocking Tristan backwards and sending him cartwheeling.

When his paws found the ground, Tristan clawed to stop and pushed up, flapping hard to catch his balance.

Ixxter whipped around in midair and came right back, ramming Tristan sideways and drawing a bloody line along Tristan's wing.

The guy was crazy.

Bernie's voice burst through Tristan's thoughts, *I'll distract him so you can get away.*

Tristan shouted, *No. Stay back or you'll get in my way.*

He shut out everything but the whooshing sound of Ixxter's wide wingspan as the gryphon worked his way back again.

Adrenaline rushed through Tristan in a surge of energy. He quivered with fury and called up the Alterant beast that lived inside him. They had all started life as Alterants, a mix of Belador and Medb blood. That beast had been his alter-form prior to evolving all the way into a gryphon. His beast energy could still boost his ability to heal.

But nobody knew his entire ability, not even him.

While stuck in a jungle prison, he'd been given a witch highball that allowed him to beef up even faster. Muscle beneath his feathers and the scales covering his body began pumping up, bulging and rippling.

Shifting back later was going to suck, but Tristan had to survive long enough to worry about the agony of returning to human form.

Ixxter had not stayed on Treoir out of loyalty to anyone. No, this had been the only sanctuary of a sort.

His gritty voice slapped the inside of Tristan's head. *I've had it with that sniveling twerp and your bullshit. I've waited long enough to get off this fucking island and you should have made that happen by now.*

Tristan replied, *Everything is not about you, dickhead. If you'd stop causing trouble I could spend more time getting all of you off the island for a break.*

I don't want a break. When I leave, I'm not coming back. Ixxter came in fast, front claws ready to flay Tristan the minute he slid in for a landing.

Tristan kept his wings wrapped around his body and whispered to himself, *Wait for it ...*

Ixxter's body dropped to twenty feet off the ground, fifteen, ten ...

Tristan opened his wings and showed Ixxter what a gryphon jacked up on witch juice looked like.

Ixxter's bright eyes widened, but his momentum drove him forward and his arrogance rode shotgun.

Tristan released an unearthly battle cry and flapped up in the air just high enough to use his sharp lion claws. He raked Ixxter's chest over and over, driving the crazed gryphon back.

Tristan's plan had been damned good.

It would have worked, too, if Ixxter hadn't twisted away and caught one of Tristan's hind legs with his beak, dragging them both to the ground.

Tristan clenched his beak to keep from screaming at the white-hot pain shooting up his leg every time Ixxter yanked, ripping muscle.

Any strategy went out the window right then.

Tristan fell back on what he'd learned as a street fighter, which was to do whatever it took to survive.

He should kill Ixxter and rid the world of one more homicidal maniac, but dying would only make Ixxter more powerful. The gryphons regenerated up to three times due to the way the Alterant-gryphons had evolved.

That was some fucked up genetic coding, and they'd all gone through one death. Some, like Evalle, had been through three, the maximum number before death was final.

Killing Ixxter and bringing him back more powerful was not happening.

But breaking every bone in his body was on the table and would slow him down while the bully healed.

Tristan jabbed a claw at Ixxter's eye, gouging the orb and forcing Ixxter to release his beak's hold on Tristan's thigh.

Finally.

Hurting like a mother from one end to the other, Tristan shook it off and leveraged what energy he had to get up on his legs. He ignored the urge to hop around and spare his damaged leg. He could heal it, but he wouldn't do that yet and risk taking his attention off his opponent.

Ixxter sidestepped, weaving and shaking his head.

Bernie had been standing off to the left and made a move toward Ixxter as if he still planned to help.

Tristan glanced over and ordered, *No, Bernie!*

Ixxter took advantage of Tristan's divided attention in that split second and raced forward, flapping at the same time. As he lifted up, claws dug into Tristan's wings, yanking him off his feet. Ixxter dragged him backwards toward the bluff.

The sound of water crashing against jagged boulders below warned Tristan not to go over backwards.

But he had no way to wrench his body when he couldn't get his backpedaling feet beneath him. The chance of flipping a body as big as a truck and catching air in time to avoid being crushed on the rocks was laughable.

Teleporting would not happen. He was too spent to use it again and had no idea if it would even work normally in gryphon form.

At the last second before the ground fell away, Tristan lunged up and caught Ixxter's wing with his beak, clamping down to hold on.

Ixxter released a screech of pain that sounded like metal being twisted.

They shot past the drop off with Ixxter flapping one wing and attacking Tristan with his beak to free his other wing.

A buffeting wind flipped their position, putting Tristan on top.

When he saw water beneath him, he released Ixxter and focused every ounce of power he had into flapping his wings.

But flying worked best when gravity didn't have a head start.

Tristan burned muscles whipping his giant wings and strained to slow his body from screaming toward the rocks.

Ixxter did a sideways roll and opened his wings wide.

Expecting a rogue updraft?

It would be close but ... that damned black-and-red body glided away from one pile of boulders, giving Tristan hope that he could also catch an updraft.

But Ixxter's wingspan proved too wide to pass through an opening between two tall outcroppings. The wind drove him toward them.

His right wing whacked the rocks. Ixxter spun around and hit the water in an explosion of feathers and spray. He flipped end over end, and landed with one massive splash.

Tristan prepared for the same wreck as he headed downward and spread his wings to catch any air. He forced his body to bank to avoid those two outcroppings.

If he didn't bank hard enough, he'd be caught in the same situation that had gotten Ixxter.

If Tristan didn't catch some updraft, he still risked dragging his body across the top of tall, jagged rocks below. They'd rip his chest open.

That would suck, but he'd rather have his wings, which meant use of his arms once he shifted back to human form.

If all that happened before he drowned.

CHAPTER 12

Saltwater bashed the boulders straight ahead, bathing the serrated edges in foam.

Tristan fought the force of falling at hyperspeed and wrenched his wings harder to catch air. This was not going to work. He prepared for a bloody collision with the boulders waiting to tear into him.

His world condensed to microseconds.

A wind buffeted him. He wobbled. The wind caught beneath his wings and forced him up and further right. He zipped past the boulders, close enough that he cleared them only by sucking his chest in and keeping his feet tucked. He went up and up.

Damn. That was a rush and a half.

Yeah, enjoying that made him certifiable.

Surviving the near-impact had shot his attention. It took a moment to realize he was still flying up, but slowing. He'd stall next if he didn't start flapping his wings.

He swept around, now a half mile out from the rocks, and had to admit that even with all his sniping at Evalle about being stuck here patrolling, he did love flying.

Guess I'll have to save Ixxter's miserable hide.

Tristan circled, searching the churning water where Ixxter had disappeared.

The gryphon had managed to get up on the rocks and was drying out his wings.

Good. That icy bath should cool off Ixxter's temper, plus the bully would be down there a bit while he called up his power to heal anything broken.

Tristan lowered his legs as he came in for a landing at the bluff.

Bernie had returned to human form and was in the process of pulling on his ripped T-shirt and ragged jeans, which he must have found in the woods.

Tristan sucked it up and grunted as he shifted back to his human shape, which took much longer than it should have. He was done with changing for a while. Doing it one more time right away would be damn near impossible. That damn Ixxter had ruined Tristan's plan for a relaxing flight.

Once he got through groaning and panting with the effort, Tristan dressed and walked over to Bernie, who looked ashamed.

Bernie swatted a handful of red-brown hair off his face and his shoulders drooped. "I'm sorry about causing trouble, Tristan, but Ixxter said ... stuff he shouldn't have."

"What could be worth getting stomped to death?"

Bernie's eyes flared with fury. "He called Petrina names and said she was sleeping with all the guards. I'm gonna kill him."

Fuck. Tristan wished he hadn't shifted back already or he'd kick Ixxter's ass again.

Petrina was Tristan's foster sister and Ixxter knew everything he said about Petrina was a lie. If Petrina found out, she'd go after Ixxter. Petrina was deadly as a gryphon, but Tristan would not allow Ixxter to put one mark on her.

Tristan scrubbed his face with his hands and dropped them to his sides. "You do realize Ixxter said all that just to goad you into a fight, don't you, Bernie?"

"I know," he mumbled glumly. "I hate that guy."

"He's not winning Pack Member Of The Year, that's for sure."

Bernie looked up with panic. "You didn't kill him, did you?"

Tristan walked back to the edge to check on the jerk. "Hell no. I'm not giving him any edge over us."

Ixxter was no longer sitting on the rocks.

Had he gone back to the gryphon camp?

The sound of wings beating furiously and heading his way gave Tristan his answer when he looked down the coastline.

Ixxter had flown below the bluff and was coming back.

Oh, hell.

Tristan couldn't shift again. He strolled back to give himself some room to work. Standing by the edge wouldn't work out as well this time.

Bernie started trembling. "What are we going to do?"

"You stay back. I've got this." Good to know Tristan had not lost the ability to lie through his teeth. He cut his eyes at Bernie and cringed at the hero worship staring back.

Ixxter slowed and set his wings to land, taking a couple steps and towering over Bernie and Tristan. A gleam of victory flashed in his green eyes.

Tristan had to suffer through Ixxter laughing telepathically. Sometimes it would be nice to turn off his inner hearing.

Ixxter stepped forward, taking his time. If an eagle's beak could smile, it sure looked like Ixxter was grinning. He dipped his head to eye level with Tristan and said mind to mind, *If I bite off your head, you won't regenerate.*

True. Cutting off the head of a supernatural being was generally a good way to ensure death no matter what.

Tristan shrugged. Did Ixxter really think he'd beg? He sent back what might be his last words. *If I do regenerate, I'm coming after you and I will not leave enough parts to fit back together.*

Ixxter hesitated as if considering that possibility, but must have realized how tiny a chance Tristan had of surviving, because Ixxter lifted his head and screeched in triumph.

The blowhard was rubbing it in before he killed Tristan.

Bernie whispered a shaky, "T-Tristan?"

Tristan kept his attention on Ixxter, waiting to the last second to make a defensive move. He'd probably still end up ripped apart, but he was not going down without a fight.

Ixxter arched his neck, bringing his head back down to Tristan and stretching his beak wide.

Another set of wings flapped and the gryphon froze.

I'd think twice about biting off more than you can chew, Ixxter, Daegan's voice said, booming in Tristan's mind. That meant everyone present had heard it.

Ixxter jerked around and sidestepped.

A fifteen-foot-tall dragon with leathery skin covered in red scales and giant, bat-like wings swept in, landing hard enough to shake the ground.

Daegan looked like a red mountain with wings next to Ixxter.

"Shit," Bernie muttered.

That about summed it up. Tristan said, "Good to see you, Daegan."

The dragon cocked his head at Tristan and spoke out loud in a clear voice, which the gryphons couldn't do. "You would have seen me sooner, had you teleported to the castle first, Tristan."

Tristan gave him a nod of deference. It was good to be friendly with the dragon king of Treoir.

Ixxter's lower beak dropped open.

Tristan had informed the pack about Daegan and that he could speak in dragon form, but Ixxter must have thought Tristan had been exaggerating.

"I did stop by the castle," Tristan said with a wry grin. "But you were detained in a private conversation with one of the guards." Daegan had met a female guard who had been more than willing to become an inside guard.

Tristan had no idea if anything had happened and he sure as hell wasn't judging. Not when that dragon had spent two thousand years imprisoned as a throne in the realm of their enemy.

But something told Tristan that while Daegan might enjoy charming the women, he would be careful about allowing any of the guards into his bed.

Daegan chuffed out a puff of smoke and Ixxter drew back as if the dragon had unleashed fire. "In that case, you were wise not to disturb me, Tristan." When Daegan's silver, reptilian eyes turned to Ixxter, all humor fled. "You *are* known as Ixxter, correct?"

Ixxter bobbed his head up and down.

"You have been given the opportunity to remain here where you're safe from the Medb warlocks hunting for all Alterants. Have you decided you no longer wish to remain on Treoir?"

That surprised Ixxter, who had been complaining constantly that it was time for him to have a visit in the human world.

Tristan hadn't known Daegan long, but he knew enough to catch the note of decision in Daegan's voice. The dragon stepped around Ixxter, eyeing him with a predatory look. "I hear you're unhappy. You are not being forced to stay, nor are you expected to return should you leave."

Ixxter was worse than a barking dog pulling hard against the end of his chain. Unclip the chain and some dogs froze, unwilling to follow through on the threat of attack.

That gryphon had griped constantly about wanting to leave, but Tristan didn't believe Ixxter expected to be given a one-way ticket, no matter how much he pretended that's what he wanted.

"What will it be, Ixxter?" Daegan demanded. "I will not tolerate any of my gryphons or my Beladors being harmed."

And that was the real question.

Would Ixxter declare himself entirely free of Treoir rule, or admit that he wanted to remain a member of the pack?

Ixxter must have answered Daegan telepathically because the gryphon moved his wings as someone would use their hands while trying to explain.

Daegan angled his monstrous dragon head to one side, then back the other way, concentrating.

When Ixxter stilled, his gaze went to the ground, no longer pumped with arrogance.

"Go change into your human form and get dressed, Ixxter. Come to the castle and I'll teleport you. I will give you one week to make your decision about whether to return ... or not."

Ixxter nodded his head and took two steps then leaped into the air and flew out over the water, banked wide, then soared over them toward the gryphon village they'd created.

Bernie had done his best to become invisible once Daegan arrived. When the dragon's head dropped down to eye level with Bernie, Tristan worried the guy would embarrass himself and need a change of clothes.

Daegan's voiced gentled. "I would ask you to take on a responsibility."

All color fled Bernie's face. "O... kay."

"You agree before I've told you what I require?" Evidently Daegan found that humorous.

"Y-yes ... uh, sir. King. Dragon."

Tristan rolled his eyes. "Bernie, he's not going to eat you or torch you. You met Daegan back the first day he was here."

Bernie turned to Tristan. "He was on top of a mountain talking to us in our minds, not right freaking in front of me."

That Bernie could still snap at Tristan was a good sign.

Daegan snorted and a cloud of smoke smothered Bernie, who swatted it away, coughing. "Ugh ... stop it."

Lifting up to his full fifteen-foot height, Daegan said, "I want you to oversee the gryphon village and keep me informed of any issues. I don't want the gryphons fighting each other. We have battles coming and we need to be strong."

The smoke dispersed. Bernie pulled his shoulders back. "Yes ... *dragon*?" he squeaked, unsure.

"It's Daegan to those of you who belong to my guard."

"Oh, wow, I mean thank you, uh, Daegan."

"Now, go to the castle and inform them of anything the gryphons need that we've overlooked."

What a way to win over the rest of the pack.

The more Tristan was around Daegan, the more the dragon grew on him, which was saying something. At one time, Tristan had vowed to kill everyone involved with Treoir, including the Beladors, but that was due to his being unfairly imprisoned for four years.

"Absolutely," Bernie said, nodding like a bobble doll. "The pack does need a few things and—"

"Bernie," Tristan said, cutting him off before Bernie got on Daegan's nerves after he'd been given a promotion. "I think he wants you to go to the castle immediately."

"Oh, right. Okay, I'm gone." Bernie hurried away, disappearing into the woods where a trail led to the castle grounds.

Once Bernie was out of hearing range, Tristan crossed his arms and looked up at Daegan. "That was a great idea. He needs to develop confidence, which would not ever happen with Ixxter around. I'm glad that prick is leaving, but things are getting tense back in Atlanta, so you may want to send him somewhere else."

"Will he cause trouble?"

"Probably. The biggest problem may be that he'll shift. We were all forbidden from doing that in the human world, but to be honest ... " Tristan opened his arms. "I have no idea what the rules are now that you've taken over Treoir."

Greatest smack down ever when Daegan showed up and ordered Macha off *his* island four days ago.

"The only rules that count are my rules," Daegan clarified.

"Agreed, but no one *knows* your rules. I'm also talking about rules for when we're in the human world."

"That's no different. Anyone who is loyal to my rule will do as I say there as well if they want my protection."

This was going to get testy, because Tristan was no mediator. "I see your point, Daegan, but you haven't spent any time in the human world in two thousand years except for when we dragged you around Georgia in the shape of a chair."

"Throne."

"Semantics." Tristan went back to his original point. "The Beladors have been part of the VIPER coalition for longer than I've been around. What do you plan to do about that? I have no idea how the Belador leadership worked with VIPER and the Tribunals, but I'm thinking we can't ignore them."

"I heard about the coalition and the Tribunals over the years while I was imprisoned in TÅµr Medb."

"But you aren't actually familiar with how things work in places like Atlanta, right?"

The dragon made a grumbling sound and a flame curled from his snout.

Note to self. Don't point out shortcomings to a dragon.

Tristan said, "I don't see any big issue, but you have to decide if we're going to stay with the coalition or not."

"Why would we?"

Laughing, Tristan said, "I couldn't give two shits about staying with them, but Evalle is always trying to get me to see the other side of things. She's the one to talk politics with, but basically if we pull out of VIPER then we become an enemy of the state. If we stay, we're subject to the rule of the Tribunal. That's all I know."

"I am subject to *no* one's rule."

See? Evalle needed to be here explaining. "I agree, Daegan. I'm just telling you what I know of VIPER and the Tribunal. With a trio of three gods and/or goddesses on a Tribunal at any given time, that's a lot of nuclear power to piss off."

"I will consider this. Now, about this Ixxter. I'm going to teleport him to Atlanta—"

Hadn't Tristan just said that was a bad idea?

"—and I'm sending you, too. You and Evalle should be able to deal with Ixxter if he becomes a problem."

Shit. This sucked. Tristan didn't hide his irritation. "Why send him *there*?"

"I warned a war is coming, but I'm in no hurry to put our warriors at risk. However, someone may be setting us up to be the ones who start the war. We have Beladors and their human families to protect."

Tristan nodded even though he couldn't see where Daegan was going with this. He said, "When I left, Evalle was out with the teams patrolling residential areas with the heaviest populations of Beladors and Medb. I'm still not following you about why to send Ixxter. Has something happened?"

Daegan lifted his head and stared at the water. "Yes, Tzader just learned there was a new attack in Atlanta, but this time Quinn's task force interrupted it and killed two men."

"That's good news, right?"

"Not necessarily. Quinn believes the two men they killed were Beladors."

"Hold everything," Tristan said, unfolding his arms. "Our people are committing the murders?" When had he started thinking of Beladors as *his* people?

Oh yes. The minute Daegan stepped in to run things and told the gryphons they were free to come and go.

Daegan swung his big dragon head around and looked down at Tristan. "Someone is recruiting our warriors. I'm going to assume they're offering something of value and targeting those who are not happy with my being in charge, since I haven't gone to meet with our forces yet."

"Do you plan to do that?"

"Eventually, but not until you have time to scout Ixxter."

Tristan put it all together at once. "You're sending Ixxter out as bait and you want me to follow him to see if he flips to the other side?"

"He's a logical choice. If he's loyal to us, he'll find Quinn, you or Evalle to inform on anyone attempting to solicit his allegiance. If he fails to do so, then he will have put himself in a compromising position." Daegan's silver eyes narrowed. "It will be Ixxter's choice, but as bait he'll have only one chance to survive."

Tristan hoped that didn't end with the bait's shadow dying, too.

Daegan stretched his wings. "I'll be at the castle soon. While I'm gone, you should warn Ixxter not to complain about any delay in my teleporting him to Atlanta. Also, go find Tzader."

"Okay, what am I telling him?"

"We must protect Beladors and their families. Tell him when I return I want to meet to discuss a plan. Have Brina teleport Evalle, Storm, Adrianna and Quinn to the castle."

Before Tristan could get pissed over being left out of Daegan's inner circle, Daegan added, "If they arrive before I return, you start the meeting."

"Me?"

Daegan's head swung down to Tristan's eye level. "Yes, you. I want my closest advisors there, the people I know I can trust to speak the truth. You have earned your place at my table and your advice will always be welcome. Don't ever doubt that."

Guess that's what a big slice of humble pie tasted like. Tristan said, "Got it."

Appearing satisfied with that answer, Daegan lifted his head and drew in a deep breath, expanding his chest then exhaling slowly.

Tristan waited to see if Daegan would take flight, wanting to ask him something that might put a kink in their working relationship. With the exception of sleeping a handful of hours, Daegan had been flying every minute since Tristan first gave him a tour of the island.

Their new leader was not flying for the hell of it any more.

The dragon was hunting something.

Tristan risked Daegan's wrath by asking, "You want some help?"

Daegan had been staring out to sea and turned to him. "Help with what?"

"Finding whatever you've been hunting for since you flew over the island the first time."

They had a moment of studying each other, then the dragon turned around, swishing his big tail behind him so quickly that Tristan had to jump back out of the way.

Guess that's all the answer I'll get, Tristan mused silently to himself.

Daegan spread his wings and with a couple of hops, he took to the air.

Tristan watched as Daegan flew with a grace not one of the gryphons had, not even Tristan.

The red dragon circled, light rippling across his scales with each sweep of his wings. As his massive shape passed overhead, Daegan's voice came into Tristan's mind.

Do not let me hear that question spoken aloud again. Ever.

The underlying threat in those words ended any other speculation on Tristan's part. At least any he'd let slip past his tongue.

What could be so important to Daegan that he wanted it kept *that* secret?

CHAPTER 13

Treoir Island

Quinn paced the room where Evalle, Storm and Tristan waited for Daegan, their new leader whom Quinn had yet to even meet. He wished he had come to this spectacular castle to visit his friends and not to bring bad news to a dragon he knew little about. With Saturday half gone back home and the Tribunal deadline rushing at him, he had to make the most of this time in Treoir.

This could very well be his last visit.

Tzader came strolling in holding Brina's elbow, which was more for Tzader than Brina. The woman might be pregnant, but she could teleport if she started to fall. They made quite a pair. She had red hair falling to her waist, sharp green eyes, and pale skin that hailed to her Celtic genes. A beauty with a backbone of steel, who was the perfect match for his friend. Tzader appeared African in descent, but he'd once told Quinn that his family tree went back to the time of the black Celts and the Picts.

All that muscle bulk reminded Quinn of the Spartan warriors.

Tzader might be a bit overprotective, but he'd waited a long time to hold Brina's elbow.

All the anger eating at Quinn died down at the sight of those two. Tzader was the brother Quinn had never had, just as Evalle was a surrogate sister.

Quinn found a certain peace in seeing Tzader finally with the woman he loved after years of Tzader standing on the opposite side of a ward from her. He and Brina had committed themselves to each other at a young age and were, at last, sharing the life they'd dreamed.

Quinn and Kizira had also met when they were young, but any parallel between the two relationships ended at that point. He and Kizira had burned hot and fast over the two weeks they'd spent together.

She hadn't informed him she was a Medb until the day she left.

That had been thirteen years ago.

More than once over the years, Quinn had believed he'd moved on. Then she would show up and he'd want her as much as he had the first time. He'd dismissed it as lust, determined to do his duty as a Belador, but the day she died ... nothing had been clear in his mind since then.

Over the last year, his feelings for her had been turned inside out and upside down as the Belador-Medb conflict had escalated beyond the normal hatred. The fact that he and Kizira had met for the last time during a bloody battle wasn't lost on him.

Watching her die had put him in conflict with himself. He knew the stages of grief, but he seemed to be stuck on anger.

Why couldn't he get past that point?

How could he be angry with a woman who had sacrificed her life for him?

Because she never trusted you. That's what cut so deeply. She'd never trusted him enough to tell him the truth about her situation and give him a chance to help her. She'd never trusted him with the truth about their child during thirteen years.

Why not? Had Kizira thought he'd refuse to protect their child?

Or had she worried he would keep Phoedra from Kizira?

No, he couldn't believe that about Kizira. Yes, she'd been a Medb priestess, but how could he fault her for decisions made while in an impossible situation? He wasn't sure he could have pulled off hiding a child the way Kizira had from a ruthless Medb queen who compelled her at every point.

This internal argument is pointless.

Quinn's head had been a battleground of its own making for too long and it had to stop before he put others in jeopardy.

He was tired of his agonizing mental and emotional

confusion. He just wanted to look in the mirror and respect that man again.

Brina came over to him. "I'm happy to see you, Quinn."

He opened his arms and hugged her, truly thrilled for Brina and Tzader. "Not as happy as I am to see you healthy and safe. Congratulations on the baby."

"Thank you." She stepped back smiling, a good look on her after she'd sacrificed what she wanted for so long to protect her people.

"It's good to be feelin' like a free person again," Brina said, her voice full of the smile on her face.

Tzader stepped up next to her and Quinn wondered if his friend realized he'd been hovering. He didn't blame him. Quinn would do the same in his shoes.

He asked Tzader, "What about you, Z? How are you doing?"

Tzader stroked his hand over Brina's hair and pulled her to his side. "I try to be happy for what we have now and not think about how long Macha kept us apart, and how close we came to never being together."

Evalle strolled over with Storm close behind. The place was full of overprotective males and the women who loved them.

Quinn's gaze flicked to Tristan. *I'm not the only solo male standing around like a fifth wheel.*

Tristan tilted his head at Quinn, a reserved greeting from their normally outspoken and cranky Alterant.

Evalle asked Tzader, "What's the plan for fixing this mess with our Beladors?"

"I don't know."

"What's Daegan saying?"

"Today will be the first time I've seen him since you left."

Quinn asked, "Does Daegan know everything that's going on? I don't mean to question his position, but our warriors don't even know he exists yet unless Macha has told someone, which I doubt or we'd have heard. They need to at least be informed as to whom they now answer and what he expects of them. Does anyone know? For example, will Daegan stand behind an individual in a crisis? Will he go to a Tribunal meeting if necessary?"

Quinn's concerns would have more impact once this group

realized he could no longer be Maistir.

Tzader said, "I have no doubt that Daegan has a plan for our people and that he's going to support them, but I'll admit I don't know more because I've been distracted for a few days." His gaze went to Brina, who actually blushed. Tzader winked at her then told Quinn, "Ask Tristan. He's spent the most time with Daegan. He's the one who asked Brina to bring all of you in for this meeting."

Everyone in the circle turned to Tristan.

Quinn asked, "So you've spent time with Daegan?"

Tristan's glowing, Alterant-green gaze took in all of them before he slowly nodded. "Yes." He lifted a shoulder, brushing it off as no big deal.

Something more was going on with Tristan. Quinn asked, "Has your role here changed?"

"Not really. It helps that I can teleport between here and the human world. I brought Evalle's last update to Daegan, but that was before tonight's patrol. I know he heard telepathically from Tzader, but anything else you all have from tonight is new."

Quinn said, "It sounds as though you might know him best at this point. What else can you share?"

Tristan maintained his distance and indifferent attitude. "Nothing much. I probably see Daegan more because he likes to fly the island."

Evalle shook her head. "Why are you being that way, Tristan?"

He held his arms out. "Now what have I done?"

"Nothing, but Quinn hasn't even met Daegan. Quinn covered our butts by keeping Queen Maeve and Cathbad at a Tribunal meeting to give us time to rescue Daegan so he could cure Brina. All Quinn's asking for is a little insight, your opinion of Daegan now that our new leader has had a chance to settle in."

Tristan cocked his head at Evalle. "You've met him. What do *you* think of Daegan?"

"I'm pretty sure I speak for everyone else when I say we're ready to stand beside him, even if it means going to war." She looked to Storm, Tzader and Brina, who all nodded in agreement.

Tristan shoved his hands in his pockets and moved closer to the group. "Here's what I think. I believe Daegan will protect everyone who supports him. I think he'll wade into battle neck deep and I have a feeling he's not the least bit intimidated over facing a Tribunal."

Quinn said, "That sounds—"

"But," Tristan continued, without slowing to let Quinn speak. "Daegan spent two thousand years imprisoned and has his own agenda. He's going to do things his way and on his schedule, which may not suit all of us all the time. In fact, it may not suit any of us a lot of the time, but I respect him and trust his decisions as being honorable. He's someone I will stand beside."

Quinn tried to reconcile this version of Tristan with the one who had put Evalle on the hot seat on more than one occasion. Tristan of the past would have smarted off by now and pissed off everyone who questioned him.

What had brought on this change in an Alterant who had been on the wrong side of a battle with the Beladors the first time Quinn met him?

Evalle raised her eyebrows in surprise, but quipped, "I can live with that. Sounds like you're his new spokesman."

"No," Tristan snapped. "I don't speak for him, I'm—"

"Doing an exceptional job, Tristan," boomed from the entrance. "But you're wrong about him being my spokesman."

Quinn swung toward that deep voice to find a man strolling into the room whose size hailed back to the days of Viking marauders. Daegan wasn't a person so much as a presence. Evalle had described the medieval attire the dragon king had worn after shifting from dragon to human, which was the image Quinn had expected.

But their new leader must have gotten some clothing tips since then. He wore jeans and a dark T-shirt that pulled tight over his broad shoulders and fell loose at the waist. His forearms appeared capable of swinging Thor's hammer. But it was his eyes that said he would not only lead the way into battle, but succeed in killing every enemy he met.

Nothing like the flashy look Macha had maintained when she'd ruled here. Quinn liked the change.

Evalle seemed miffed at Daegan's announcement. "Why can't Tristan be your spokesman?"

Tristan growled, "Evalle."

Storm slashed a warning glare at Tristan, who ignored him.

Daegan strolled up to the group and crossed his arms. "You should take care with your tone around Evalle, Tristan. Her mate is offended."

Tristan smirked.

Evalle must not have seen the interaction. She sent Storm a censuring look.

Storm said, "What?"

"Nothing."

Chuckling, Tristan said, "Oh, yeah. Daegan, *nothing* from a female is still code for big trouble. I'm guessing that hasn't changed in two thousand years."

Storm muttered, "You have to leave here sometime, Alterant."

Appearing amused by all the posturing, Daegan announced, "To answer your question, Evalle, I would not be pleased with Tristan as my spokesman."

Evalle gave Daegan a pissy look that fazed him as much as water on a duck's back.

Tristan said nothing, but Quinn could see the way Daegan's remark had cut the young man.

Was Daegan capable of leading warriors in this era?

Daegan explained to Tristan, "Anyone can be a spokesman. I expect far more from you. I *will* call upon you to speak on my behalf at times, but you are my *Rí Dtús*."

Evalle asked, "What is ... what do you mean by re-*duce*?"

Daegan sighed. "Your Irish is sorely lacking."

"Highly likely since I don't speak the language," she retorted with an arched eyebrow.

Brina spoke up. "Daegan is sayin' ree then doos. It means Tristan is the king's first."

"Aye. That is correct. Tristan will be in charge of all the royal guards on this island and will head up my Council of Seven."

While Tristan stood there dumbfounded, Quinn asked, "Who is on this council?"

Daegan finally acknowledged that he had a new member in the room. He extended his hand. "I take it you're Quinn."

"Yes." Quinn clasped his hand. The moment he did, he felt the power flowing through Daegan. It reminded him of a dangerous volcano, capable of erupting at any second and unleashing a power that could rearrange a continent. "It's an honor to meet you."

"And you." Daegan folded his arms again. "The seven are those of you standing here now, and that irritatin' witch."

"Adrianna?" Evalle supplied with a grin. "Tzader said she was invited, but she couldn't make it. She asked me to pass along the message that if you want her to visit in the future to give her more notice."

"Just as I said, irritatin'," Daegan groused. "I'll be discussin' her responsibilities with her when we meet again."

Evalle murmured, "I want to be there for that."

Daegan sent her a wry look, but returned his attention to Quinn. "I believe you have concerns about our warriors."

That had been a diplomatic way to broach Quinn's issues. Quinn began, "Yes. They don't know you exist, for one thing, so none of them have any idea what you stand for or what is expected of them."

"Understandable."

How was that reply helpful? Quinn pressed on. "I can appreciate how unrealistic it is to expect you to meet with all of them, but—"

"Oh, but I do intend to meet with every one of them," Daegan countered.

"What?" Quinn's sentiment echoed around the room.

"I can't expect men and women to put their lives at risk and to blindly follow someone they neither know nor trust." Daegan paused in his explanation. "Why are we standin' here?"

Tristan asked, "Is that a trick question?"

In reply, Daegan waved them back. "Give me room." He lifted his hands and motioned as if he were directing an invisible symphony. When he lowered his hands, he murmured soft words and a round table with eight chairs appeared in the center of the room. Each chair had a different name engraved on the tall wooden back, and the seats were of soft deerskin.

The top of the table was at first a wood finish with bronze accents, but when Daegan placed his hand on the surface and barked out words Quinn didn't recognize as Irish or any other language, Cyrillic symbols began appearing on the surface just inset from the edge.

The six-inch-tall, gold letters ran all the way around the perimeter of the table, creating a completed border when the last gold stroke touched the first one.

Rubbing his hands together, Daegan pulled the largest chair away from the table.

Quinn noted the dragon image inlaid on the chair back in place of a name.

Daegan said, "Take your seats."

Tristan's chair had been placed directly to Daegan's right. Tristan hesitated for a moment, then took his place of honor.

Quinn had never seen the young Alterant so humbled, or respected. Daegan just might turn out to be the leader they needed after all.

The sad part was that as much as Quinn would like to observe the changes that were surely coming, he would not have that chance. He had no choice in his future.

Brina sat on Daegan's left, then Tzader, Evalle, Storm, Quinn, Adrianna's empty seat and finally Tristan. Tall, frosted mugs appeared in front of Daegan and Tzader that Quinn would bet was beer.

Tzader leaned across the table and whispered to Quinn, "I'll explain the mega beer mug later."

Daegan waved a hand at the others. "Just ask for what you wish to drink and it will appear in front of you." As drinks began showing up, Daegan explained, "Also, everything said at this table is protected as long as I'm sitting here. The only way those conversations will be shared is if someone repeats our words after stepping away."

Quinn had no doubt that everyone seated understood that unless Daegan gave them leave to share anything discussed, to do so without permission equaled treason.

Fair enough. There was no other way to build trust than to offer it, which Daegan had just done.

With everyone now ready, Daegan said, "I do expect loyalty from all of our warriors once they've been informed of having a new leader, and even while they wait until I have a chance to meet with them, which will take me a few months. I sit here a free person, able to assume control of all that belongs to me, only because of the sacrifices each of you made while aiding my escape." He glanced at Quinn. "I'm not yet clear on this Tribunal group I've been hearin' about, but your efforts there were explained to me, and the degree to which you put yourself at risk."

Quinn nodded, but his esteemed position was not going to last long. He might be gone before the beer in those mugs.

Daegan added, "I've said before that we have a war coming. I would prefer to avoid havin' our people in danger and exposing supernatural beings to the humans, but the time may come when that is no longer our choice to make. We must protect our people from threats we can see, and those we do not. We must watch for traitors among our own people. I trust each of you, but our enemies will only grow in number now that I'm free again. Queen Maeve made a huge mistake in allowin' me to live when she had a chance to kill me in her realm."

Tzader raised a finger and brought up a point. "We all understand that you're immortal, but how vulnerable are you to an attack? I ask so that we'll know how to protect your back."

Daegan sat back and Tristan sent him an interesting look. One that Quinn could only interpret as Tristan waiting to see if Daegan would share something Quinn believed Tristan already knew.

The dragon king said, "Any living being can be killed. It's more difficult to kill an immortal, than a mortal, but each of us has an Achilles heel. I have no intention of sharing mine, even with you. A warrior should never show a weakness, but it's important that you know one thing. It is almost impossible to kill me in this realm and a few others, but I am more at risk in the realm of an unfriendly deity, such as in TÅµr Medb."

Quinn's mind clicked together the pieces. "What about in a Tribunal meeting? It's held in another realm with a mix of three gods and/or goddesses."

"I would be in a vulnerable position in that realm if the three deities joined forces against me."

Tristan piped up. "You shouldn't go then. Macha rarely went to the meetings. She stuck Brina with it."

Tzader swung a dark look on Tristan. "Brina is *not* going to a Tribunal meeting, especially not while she's expecting."

Brina took offense. "I'm capable of doin' my duty, Tzader."

His face and voice eased when he turned to Brina. "I know, *muirnin*, but the last time you went there they held your holographic image captive. I'm done watching people try to harm you."

"I wasn't suggesting she go," Tristan made clear.

Daegan cleared his throat, drawing everyone's attention. "Brina?"

"Yes?"

"You'll not be leavin' this island while you're carryin'. Before you start squawkin' at me, I'm not treatin' you as a female whose only use is breedin'. You and I hold a great responsibility for our people, but you are the only one who can carry the next generation. It's important that you put your health first and remain protected while you're expectin'."

She sighed. "I understand. I just don't want to be put on a shelf. I spent four years *protected* and I'm tired of feelin' weak."

"You won't be treated as a fragile trinket and you are not weak. Treoirs are a mighty clan. I need your sharp mind for strategic planning."

Once again, Quinn found himself impressed with Daegan.

Evalle interjected, "I'm glad to see you've given Tristan a position of authority." She smiled at Tristan's surprised look. "But what about Tzader?"

"I'll do whatever is expected of me, Evalle," Tzader replied. "I also agree with the position he gave Tristan."

Quinn expected Daegan to react negatively to being questioned by anyone, but the dragon king's face revealed nothing. Still, Evalle had brought up a valid point.

Where did everyone fall in Daegan's power structure?

Daegan lifted a hand, silencing everyone. "I can see you all have questions. As a leader, all responsibility falls to my shoulders. I will not always explain every action I take, but I will share what I can or what I feel you need to know. I am not demoting Tzader or anyone else, but we must look to the future with a new frame of mind. Macha ruled through intimidating her followers by threatening death if they broke her rules. I will not hesitate to take a life if that is the right decision, but I will not have people followin' me out of fear. Strength breeds loyalty. I want no warriors who do not willingly join us. Those who do will step into battle alongside me, because I lead from the front."

With a slow, pointed look at each person around the table, Daegan said, "You have already proven far more loyal than those I trusted in my past. I observed much over the years I was captive, but I am not entirely familiar with the modern human world, or all of the changes in our own world yet. I need each of you to do your part, to be my eyes, ears and advisor. You are all even more important to the cause of our people than you were before I returned to this island." He looked at Brina. "That includes you, niece. You will one day come and go at your pleasure, but for the good of all right now you must keep yourself and your babe safe. The less attention we have to focus on you, the more we have for the battles we'll face."

Brina frowned. "I know what you're sayin' and I agree."

"Now, tell me what the devil is going on in the human world," Daegan demanded.

Evalle said, "You know some of it, but—"

Quinn spoke up. "Forgive me for the interruption, Evalle, but I have information no one else has and it's imperative that I inform Daegan immediately."

She lifted her shoulders. "Floor's yours."

"Thank you." Quinn met Daegan's questioning gaze and said, "You are correct in thinking we're headed for a battle, perhaps even a war. I fear I have only escalated this situation when I made a grave error by holding onto a body I should have burned."

Daegan squinted at him. "Is this about Kizira, the Medb priestess who died here?"

"Yes."

Tzader leaned up. "Hold up a minute, Quinn." He shifted his attention to Daegan. "You know about the attack by TÅμr Medb on Treoir, right?"

"Of course."

"Kizira saved Quinn's life during that battle."

Daegan said, "I saw the replay of that on the scrying wall in Queen Maeve's chambers before you pulled me out of her realm."

Evalle jumped in. "But what you don't know is that Kizira and I had a plan to save Treoir. She ... " Evalle paused to look at

Quinn, who swallowed and nodded, giving her permission, so she said, "Kizira loved Quinn deeply and was working against us only when the queen compelled her. She died when she stepped in front of a gryphon, who was *also* compelled, that attacked Quinn. As soon as Kizira died, we were released from the compulsion spell. Kizira's death saved Belador lives and is the reason Tristan and I, plus the other gryphons, are here now."

Daegan said nothing for a moment. "Queen Maeve does not understand why Kizira died in that way or why Quinn was holding her as she died, but the queen does know that Kizira has been buried in a tomb. The queen is on a mission to find her. Prior to Tzader and his team bashing the wall during my escape, the scrying wall had already revealed a corruption of some sort when she and Cathbad tried to access the Medb history on it. She could not hear what Kizira was saying to Quinn as she died." Daegan asked Quinn, "What was she telling you?"

Quinn considered the consequences of his answer, but said, "She shared something personal that I must protect from that queen and her followers with my life."

"If that was the case, why didn't you burn the body?"

Because he hadn't been ready to give her up and foolishly thought he could protect her body long enough to allow their daughter a chance to grieve the loss of her mother.

Evalle reached across Storm and tapped Quinn's arm. When he turned to her, she said, "The only ones at this table who don't know are Brina, Tristan and Daegan. Tzader and I trust them. I think you should, too. We'll all help."

"You're right." Quinn patted her hand, then gave up the truth. "Kizira and I met when we were barely adults. The circumstances were such that I had no idea of her true identity. I stepped in to protect her and ended up wounded so badly I was close to death. She healed me and we spent ... some time together. I had no idea that we created a child during that time until thirteen years later when Kizira told me as she died."

Daegan stared at him a moment then angled his head, looking as if he couldn't believe what he heard. "Are you saying there's a child out there with your powerful Belador blood and that of a Medb priestess?"

"Exactly."

"Where is this child?"

"That's the problem. I don't know. I am prepared to withdraw from the Beladors—"

Evalle gasped. "No."

Tzader gave a stern, "*Quinn!*"

But Quinn continued. "By keeping her body, I have put the Beladors, as well as my child, at great risk. The killings in Atlanta are not random. They're tied to Kizira's body. Medb warlocks and witches are being tortured by people who are after her body. I know you've heard a preliminary report sent to Tzader. I did not recognize the suspects, but based on my team's experience in Atlanta just before dawn, we believe there is no explanation other than that the killers *are* Beladors."

Tristan asked, "What if Queen Maeve has cooked up some spell to make it look like they're Beladors?"

Quinn shook his head. "If you met one of them in battle, you wouldn't think it was merely a spell."

Daegan said, "It's not Queen Maeve. She would simply compel her people for information and if she used Noirre majik, it would be evident." He turned to Storm, "Correct?"

"Yes. There's no hint of Noirre at the crime scenes, but there's always a residue of Belador power."

Quinn gave Storm a nod of thanks and said, "I had hoped it was only a lone Belador turned vigilante for some personal reason, but I never considered that a group of our people would be committing these crimes. I probably still wouldn't if I hadn't been there in person. Evalle, Devon Fortier and I faced attackers who used kinetics, telepathy and linking powers like we do. But the smoking gun was revealed when I had to enter the mind of one man who was trying to kill me. He and his partner had linked their powers and were using them to crush me against a tree. When the guy whose mind I entered died, so did the second man."

"You did *what* to their minds?" Daegan asked.

Quinn quickly explained his mind lock ability.

"That's an impressive gift," Daegan said, then rolled his hand in a sign for Quinn to continue.

"I didn't have an opportunity to retrieve anything of value, because from what I could tell, someone had placed a spell on the attacker that triggered immediate death upon having his mental shields breached."

"You almost didn't pull out in time," Evalle muttered.

"True, but my point is that the moment I entered his mind, I encountered the familiar essence. I've never seen anything like it except in those born a Belador descendant."

Evalle confirmed, "They had kinetic ability that rivaled ours. They're also generating some kind of cloaking cloud that buzzes. It interrupts normal telepathy, and it sometimes makes private telepathic messages available to others. When I got close, I heard voices inside the buzzing cloud. Devon heard their telepathic conversation before the energy field broke apart, which means we have to be careful about who we speak to telepathically. I would know any of you, but in a battle we could be tricked by imposters, or they could eavesdrop on our strategies and plans."

Tristan said, "Who *are* these people? Beladors from another continent?"

"I can't answer that, because we have no image to show other Maistirs who could identify them for us," Quinn admitted. "The chilling part is that they had no issue with killing both Beladors and Medb alike."

Tzader rubbed a hand over his bald head, a habit he had when he was working out a problem. "I'd think missing Belador warriors would have been reported."

Daegan's brow creased in deep thought. "Quinn, you said these people are after Kizira's body?"

"Yes. Devon heard them talking about it."

"You didn't tell me," Evalle accused, sounding hurt.

"I didn't want to say anything until I knew more and we had too many people around at times." Like Isak, who was not within Quinn's circle of trusted confidantes. "I figured I'd tell everyone at the same time, but we first needed to find out whether our captive had any involvement."

"I got you," Evalle said, nodding that she understood he was referencing Reese.

It was time for Quinn to tell them all that he'd learned, but Daegan had been leaned back, looking up at the high ceiling.

The dragon king clearly had something on his mind. He brought his chin down and worry stretched through his face. "We have to find out who is behind turning Beladors against their own people and we must stop them from locating Kizira's body."

Brina asked, "Why?"

Quinn supplied the answer. "Because someone can use necromancy to unlock the secrets that Kizira hid, Noirre spells and more."

Daegan said, "That would be a deadly result, but that is not the sole reason we must keep her body away from everyone."

Now Quinn was as confused as the rest of the group appeared. He had to protect his daughter. But Daegan should be concerned only with how this affected Beladors.

Quinn said, "I don't understand."

"You wouldn't without having lived as long as I have," Daegan replied. "How old would your child be?"

"Twelve."

Daegan put a hand to his forehead, squeezing his head then dropping his hand to the table. "Putting aside that we have Beladors hunting Kizira's body for some unknown person, Queen Maeve wants the body to withdraw every drop of information she can about what transpired prior to her reincarnating as the current queen of TÅµr Medb. But the minute she discovers Kizira had a child who still lives, the queen will unleash all her resources to locate that child."

Tristan snorted. "Are you trying to say that crazy queen wants to play grandmother?"

"No. In Queen Maeve's hands, a child of powerful Medb and Belador blood would become a weapon capable of wiping out Beladors systematically and completely. That's before you consider whether this child inherits Quinn's mind lock gift. Allowing her to fall into Queen Maeve's hands would be like handing her a weapon much like those nuclear bombs humans created, but with the ability to target only her enemy. That would not stop her from wiping out humans and nonhumans alike if they didn't fit her plan for ruling the world."

Mouths dropped around the table.

Quinn clapped a hand over his eyes and murmured, "What have I done?"

Instead of ordering Quinn to a dungeon or worse, Daegan segued into strategic planning. "We can't bury the body on this

island. The land would reject it, but we can take it to a proper
location to—"

Quinn looked up and stopped him. "No, we can't."

Daegan finally lost his calm, which is what Quinn had been
expecting sooner. The dragon king stood. "I would not condemn
a man who made a mistake born of grief, but I will *not* allow you
to put every Belador life in jeopardy for the same reason."

"You don't understand." Quinn rose to his feet. "I would do
anything I can to prevent someone from finding my child and I
would definitely do anything to protect my Belador brethren, but
there's a problem with your plan."

"You haven't heard it all. How can you know it won't work?"

"Because you're suggesting we burn the body and spread the
ashes with salt."

"Aye."

"I went by the cemetery on my way to meet up with Evalle
before coming here. The tomb I buried Kizira in is gone. As of
tonight, the killers aren't hunting the body. They're looking for
someone who can open the tomb I sealed it in. There's nothing
but an empty space where it stood. I don't know who has
Kizira's body."

CHAPTER 14

Daegan dropped into his seat, sweeping a look at his newly formed council of advisors. This would be a hell of a first task for this group. His mind raced through all the potential thieves who might have stolen Kizira's body.

Thumping the table, Daegan said, "Queen Maeve is the obvious choice, but not the logical, which leaves us where?"

"What about Macha?" Evalle asked. "Could she be building her own Belador army to battle you?"

"She's a valid candidate, but Macha is not one to get her hands dirty. She requires followers to do her work. She would have had to organize a team in just four days. It's not impossible, but a bit improbable. Unlike Queen Maeve, Macha plans and takes her time to be sure she'll succeed if she's going to crush someone."

"Wow, you do know her."

Better than you can ever imagine. "That doesn't mean she's not on our list of people potentially behind this, but if she is responsible, she's found a powerful ally to do her bidding. Either Maeve or Macha could be doing this, or it could be a different enemy."

Quinn appeared to be waiting to speak again. Daegan nodded at Quinn, who continued, "We must assume a preternatural stole the tomb, as doing so required great power. Queen Maeve knows I'm the one who placed the body inside, but someone else may or may not know. Queen Maeve and Cathbad would certainly have enough sense to not attempt teleporting inside a tomb I sealed, though they may have compelled one of their followers to try. If someone other than the Medb has tried, they've *also* figured out they can't teleport in. At this point, any nonhuman with enough power to move the tomb would *now* be expecting a deadly repercussion when an attempt is made to open it."

"You have this tomb rigged in some way?" Daegan asked, respecting this Quinn's ability more every minute.

Tzader snorted. "My man Quinn? I wouldn't try to break into anything he wanted kept hidden. You booby-trapped it, didn't you, Quinn?"

"Yes. Whoever took the tomb paid a price just by separating the structure from the land. I did not ward the outside against immortals, simply because a ward would have acted like a neon sign to our kind, announcing that the tomb contained something of value. The spell around the base was meant as a first warning and deterrent to someone the level of a Medb witch or warlock."

"How much of a deterrent could it have been for them to go ahead and steal the damn thing?" Tristan scoffed.

Quinn said, "The first use of majik to dislodge the base would have destroyed someone's eyes, past the point of blinding them. There would be no orbs left in the sockets."

Everyone flinched.

"At that point, whoever attempted to then break the spell would have had to use significant power to separate that tomb from the land. I had an identical tomb built to replace the original historical one I happened to know was empty. The one I had built was bonded to the land with the spell. Taking it from the land was akin to ripping a limb away from a body. Everyone involved in extracting it would have felt pain as though they'd had their own limb ripped off. Those of lesser power may have, in fact, lost limbs."

Daegan sized up Quinn. Though he was sorely disappointed the man had held onto an immortal witch's body, he could tell the decision had not been an easy one to make and one reason might have been to save something a person of dark powers could use for locating his child. That would not be honorable, but Daegan wouldn't criticize the man since Daegan would do that, or worse, to find his kin.

Tristan had grown more serious throughout the meeting. "What happens when they do try to open the tomb?"

Quinn shook his head. "If someone cracks the outer wall, they'll suffer a power lash that would cause the equivalent of a severe headache for a preternatural. But to actually open that tomb for access would be quite deadly. Even if they *could*, which they can't, they would die in the process. I'm the only one who can open it safely. If someone did manage to survive opening it, they'd have to break a ward placed on the body by someone half as old as Daegan. If the ward is broken, the body will erupt into flames."

"No worries then, right?" Tristan asked, addressing everyone with that comment.

Evalle asked Tristan, "If you wanted that body and went to the trouble to take the tomb, realizing that you couldn't open it, what would you do?"

Tristan's forehead creased. "Shit."

"Exactly. You'd take something or someone and hold it hostage to trade for opening the tomb."

Daegan stood. He needed his council to prioritize the problems. "First, what will happen if we tell this VIPER and Tribunal bunch the truth, that we believe someone has turned a number of our warriors against us? What will they do, Evalle?"

"They won't believe us. The Tribunal has dealt with conflicts between the Medb and Beladors for too many years, and those have been escalating lately. The deities have gotten short-tempered and go for the simplest answer that demands as little time on their part as possible."

Brina offered, "We wouldn't be havin' these escalatin' problems if the Tribunal had not accepted Queen Maeve and Cathbad the Druid into the coalition. We've been fighting each other nonstop since VIPER allowed Medb warlocks and witches to enter the human world to infiltrate our communities. You probably know about that since you were in Táur Medb when that decree was passed, Daegan."

Nodding that he did, Daegan said, "That was a stupid mistake on VIPER's part."

"Agreed," Evalle said, picking up the thread. "It's an ongoing situation that is only getting worse. The minute we hint that a Belador might be behind these killings, the Medb will take advantage of that and point fingers at us over every infraction.

Then VIPER will drag our people in to face Tribunals where justice is not always served."

Daegan pondered this. "Power residue is the only evidence of Beladors at the killing locations?"

"Yes," Storm said. "When I picked up Belador scents at each one, I hoped it meant your people had been on the human police investigations, but the areas where I found the scents bothered me. I picked up a demon scent near each one, which didn't appear connected until I heard about tonight's attack." He held his hands open in resignation. "Unfortunately, if I was forced to testify at a Tribunal, I'd have to say the Belador scent was at every crime scene."

Brina snapped her fingers. "About those demons. Tzader told me one was with the group you stopped tonight. Why would they have demons if they can kill with the ability of a Belador?"

Evalle studied the table a moment, then said, "I don't know. That's a good question we need to answer. We also need to find out how they're powering their cloaking device. Adrianna didn't mention whether she noticed anything, but we cut our meeting short to come to Treoir. I'll ask her about that."

Tzader pointed out, "Whether or not the Medb are behind the attacks in the southeast, if the only evidence is Belador power residue, we can't hide that if they bring in another tracker. If that happens, VIPER will start bringing in our people anyhow. We're pretty much damned if we do and damned if we don't, and that means we're on our own with this and need to get answers yesterday."

"It's unacceptable for our people to be persecuted." Daegan held up saying more when Quinn spoke.

"While in the cemetery, I found a Nightstalker and shook hands for intel."

"Nightstalker?" Daegan glanced around the table. He'd missed much during his time imprisoned. "I heard the term used in TÅμr Medb, but have no idea what it is."

Tristan explained, "We have ghoul informants in the human world who have no loyalty to any group. If someone with power shakes hands with them, they'll share intel on the preternatural world and in exchange they receive ten minutes of corporeal form."

"What do they do while in solid form?"

"Drink rotgut, usually. They're homeless people who died during weather disasters."

Interesting. Daegan returned everyone's attention to the intel. "Go on, Quinn."

"I just recalled something the Nightstalker said, which didn't register at the time because the only information he'd been able to share was that two people had visited Kizira's tomb earlier in the day and they wore hooded robes."

Tristan quipped, "That could be anyone. It's like saying someone drove a white pickup truck."

"Exactly," Quinn agreed. "The Nightstalker hadn't been around the tomb during the theft. I was distracted, trying to figure out if Queen Maeve was behind this so I didn't pay close attention when he said, 'they want Alterants.' Thinking back now, he may have meant those two in the hooded robes who visited the tomb. The thing is that no human would have gone near the tomb, because of the repellent I put around the outside."

Evalle sent a pointed glance at Storm as she said, "Before everyone gets lathered up about these people hunting Alterants, I am not going into hiding. I'll be sure to work with a partner."

Storm only grunted, clearly not happy about her being at risk, but it was obvious that Evalle would not tolerate being left out. Daegan felt more and more certain that he'd chosen well with this circle of warriors as advisors.

He asked Tristan, "Have you informed them of your new assignment?"

"No."

"Why not?"

"I share nothing that you say without your permission."

Damn good answer. Daegan said, "This may help bring us answers sooner. You may share our strategy now."

Tristan explained about the plan to send Ixxter to Atlanta soon, and that Tristan would tail him. Ixxter would be a prime candidate to draw attention as a Belador and as an Alterant, especially one who wanted out of the gryphon pack.

Evalle leaned forward. "Is he bait for them to take or bait to draw them out or what?"

"We're thinking they'll go the easier route and try to recruit him first, before they try to grab him. It's easier to control someone who holds a grudge against his own people. If they do flip him to their side, I can discover who is behind this *and* determine whether Ixxter is going to be loyal or not."

Tzader asked, "Do I detect a large amount of doubt?"

"Yes."

Evalle said, "Ixxter's a hothead, but he's been stuck here a long time. I wouldn't judge him based on the past few months."

"Why not?" Tristan sat forward. "He's not the only person who has been stuck here for months, but he's the troublemaker, and the most belligerent of the gryphon pack. He'll have a chance to show his true colors. He's either with us or against us."

"Point taken."

"Speaking of the gryphons," Daegan said, butting in. "You've both done your best by them and I understand Evalle took the lead position when she killed one of the others."

"Not just one of the others," Storm said, pride rolling through his words. "She killed the baddest one in the pack at that time."

He placed his hand over hers on the table.

She smiled at her mate and explained to Daegan, "It was situational. Not by choice. When the Alterants were forced to evolve into gryphons in TÅμr Medb, they had to be mortally wounded to complete the process. That's when we were informed we could regenerate up to three times."

"I recall parts of that time."

"Well, I'm done. I used up my third regeneration here on Treoir when I won the battle against a gryphon trying to kill Brina. Tristan, on the other hand, is still good for two, which means that if he does have to regenerate, he'll only get stronger each time."

Daegan hid his amusement. The woman was determined that Tristan receive his due, and now Daegan understood where she was going with that line of thought. "I'm glad to know that, Evalle, because as part of Tristan's responsibility as *Rí Dtús* he will rule the gryphons unless you're unwilling to cede your position."

Tristan stared, obviously unable to speak.

That allowed Evalle enough time to say, "It's his. I'm all for him leading the pack."

"Good. We have a lot of work to do." Daegan directed his next comments to Storm and Evalle. "Storm, I'd like you to visit the cemetery and see if you can stir up any scent or power signature."

"I'll do that," Storm answered.

"Excellent. Evalle, you continue investigating and back up Tristan when he requests it."

Evalle grinned. "No problem."

Storm growled softly.

Daegan said, "Tristan will let you know when he needs backup tracking Ixxter in case nothing happens in the first day. None of you will be useful if you run yourselves into the ground, so be wise about resting even for short periods and sharing the load. If this eventually leads to war, it will not be a sprint but a marathon."

"Got it," Tristan acknowledged, still glowering at Evalle.

She tried to mollify Tristan with, "It only makes sense for you to lead the gryphon pack with me gone so much."

Storm's lips twitched. He found Tristan's reaction amusing? Must be history there of some sort.

Daegan had to get everyone moving so he could take care of his own problem. "Quinn, you will take the lead on locating that tomb. You know all the players. Are ghouls your only resource for now?"

"No, I have my own network of intelligence gatherers as well."

Evalle offered, "We have Isak Nyght's resources, too."

Daegan frowned. "Who is he?"

Quinn shot Evalle a warning look that had no effect on her answering Daegan. "Isak is one of the few humans who know we exist. He's a black ops soldier with a team trained to fight nonhumans and an intelligence network that rivals the human national security groups. His people know how to find our kind sometimes."

Quinn argued, "He also specifically targets nonhumans who he believes don't belong in his world."

"He doesn't hate Beladors. He's helped us before and he'll help again, especially when it comes to using his demon blasters," she argued.

Daegan ended the discussion. "Find out what this human with the demon blaster requires for payment and use him."

"Will do."

Evalle added, "We also have a female witness from the fight tonight."

"A human?"

Quinn answered, "No, but we're not sure what she is yet. She carries an energy she says is a demon magnet. Her appearance at the scene made no sense. Our people were there, the killers were there, then our witness showed up out of the blue and killed the demon. She doesn't fit anywhere in all of this yet, and claims she just happened upon the conflict. We were called here before we could finish the interrogation, but Storm has her contained."

"Can you use that mind lock on her?" Daegan noted the hesitation on Quinn's part.

Quinn said, "I don't unless the situation is dire, but Storm is our walking lie detector."

Daegan turned to Storm with new respect. "That's a handy gift to have."

Storm answered with a subtle lift of one eyebrow.

Daegan told Quinn, "I'll leave it up to you to decide how to extract information." Moving on, Daegan said, "When we find out who has the tomb, we're going after it. And as soon as we know who is using Beladors as puppets, we're going to cut those strings."

Tzader spoke up. "What am I doing?"

Quinn interjected, "Unfortunately, the position of Maistir is open again, Z. I'm thinking he'll need you to take over. I'm sorry for not giving you more time with Brina."

"Where do you think you're going?" Tzader asked.

Pushing his gaze from Tzader, around the table to each of his friends, then to Daegan, Quinn said, "While I was buying time for our people to pull you out of Táur Medb, I was given an unexpected order. When Queen Maeve and Cathbad showed up in the Tribunal meeting, Maeve demanded Kizira's body. The Tribunal agreed and gave me a deadline."

Evalle snapped, "By what right? Kizira hated them."

"I know, but they called *Dlí Fola*, known as Blood Law, which allows the leaders in war to claim bodies of their family members. It held up. The Tribunal expects me to appear with Kizira's body intact to hand over to the queen. I was given five days, which will run out by four in the morning tomorrow."

"Unbelievable," Evalle muttered. "When were you going to tell us?"

"I'd actually planned to tie up our problems in Atlanta, tell all of you to declare me an enemy of the Beladors, then vanish with her body before the Tribunal."

"Oh, Quinn ... I'd hurt you if you did that." She gave him a sad smile.

"That's not happening," Daegan declared, drawing everyone's gaze his way. "Which means Tzader will have plenty of time with Brina, because he's not leaving the island while she's pregnant."

Tzader didn't even try to hide his shock. "Don't get me wrong, because I'm here for her no matter what and I hate giving up any time I can share with Brina, but you need someone with my experience helping with this mess."

"I do," Daegan agreed. "But I will be the one leaving the island before you do. Even with all the work our people are doing to shore up our defenses, the Medb have gotten onto this island before."

"That shouldn't happen again since Kizira was the only Medb who had the coordinates and she's dead," Evalle said.

"But her body is not secure."

"Oh, yeah. There's another reason we have to find that body."

Daegan told Quinn, "You have not been relieved of your duties as Maistir. No one has the authority to make that change but me. Understood?"

"If that's what you wish," Quinn said in a guarded tone.

"It is. Evalle, Storm and Quinn, prepare to return to Atlanta."

Once Daegan had teleported them back, he turned to Tzader. "I need to know Brina is guarded at all times. Other than me, there is no better person to watch over Treoir and Brina, than you."

Tzader stood and pulled her chair back. "I hear you, and seeing it from your point of view, I agree."

Brina muttered, "It would be nice if everyone stopped fawnin' over me. I'm not a bairn." She ruined her protest by yawning.

"Time to rest, *muirnin*," Tzader said, kissing her head and excusing them.

With everyone gone except Tristan and Daegan, Tristan sat back with his hands clasped on the table.

Daegan sighed. "What is botherin' you?"

"I haven't known you long, but I've known you long enough to realize you're worried about something and it's nothing we discussed at this table today. Not entirely. If I'm going to be your right-hand man, which by the way I'm not sure I'm the best choice for, but ... seems I'm it for now. I can't be much help to you if you don't trust me."

"First of all, you are not it for *now*. You are it, period. Second, I do trust you. It's just that ..."

"What, Daegan?" Tristan leaned forward, putting his hands flat on the table. "You said any conversation at this table is protected. What are you trying to fix by yourself?"

Gaining trust only happens when it is given in return. Daegan leaned in. "I'm hunting the body of my sister who originally lived here. She wears a ring that carries the protection of a god. The ring is visible only to another Treoir and can be removed only by someone with Treoir blood. Once I have it on, it will protect my descendants as long as they are on this island. It will also shield me to some degree if I end up having to enter another realm that is hostile to me. Not guaranteed to keep me alive, but I would be stronger. I must be able to protect my family, my people and myself."

"You're sure Brina doesn't have it?"

"Yes. It would have shielded her from the Noirre majik attack, but I did ask if she had any of her mother's jewelry, just to be sure. She showed me a necklace, that's all."

"If no one can see the ring or steal it, that means we have to find your sister's body." Tristan glanced up. "That's why you're flying so much."

"Exactly. If I have to enter the Tribunal realm, Queen Maeve will know I'm at my weakest there. There is much I don't know about this new era, the politics and the players. If she gives those deities reason to kill me and they choose to, I will not be able to stop them."

"Damn. That's screwed up."

"I would die today if that would protect Brina and her family for the future, but my death will only put them at more risk. Now you know why I'm preparing for war."

"Queen Maeve and Macha know you're most vulnerable right now."

"That is it. In their shoes, I would gather my army and attack. It won't be as straightforward as marching on a city, as it was in my day, but this will be war just the same."

Tristan sat up and fisted his hands. "Send Ixxter wherever he wants to go in Atlanta, then I'll teleport a few minutes after him so I can follow. He won't trust us not to spy on him right off the bat, but once he gets comfortable, he'll be cocky. I'll come back as soon as I figure out where he stands. Do you want any of the gryphons to help you hunt? Other than Evalle, I have two I'd trust with my life. One of them is my sister."

Daegan had a made a good choice in Tristan. "I would take you up on it, but they can't find what I'm after. I'm the only one who can recognize the power that rises from her body. It's subtle, but I can sense it."

"Good luck."

They'd all need more than luck if Kizira's body was not found before the Tribunal meeting.

CHAPTER 15

Lorwerth took stock of the camp he'd established as a headquarters for his mission. They were close enough to Atlanta for his men to make runs, but far enough away, in North Georgia, that security was simple.

After instructing a unit of his men to execute a security sweep of the perimeter, he stepped over to a wooded area near the camp. Any of his men still in the camp would think he was taking care of personal needs.

A blurry image wavered into view, though never entirely into focus. This was the person he'd raze the entire continent for, if asked. Cloaked in a gray robe with a hood so deep no face could be seen, Lorwerth's benefactor had revealed nothing about himself.

No age. No family. No preternatural political ties.

He had only indicated to address him as *my lord.*

That was fine by Lorwerth, who quickly got to the point. "I've had three teams in the city. They've each killed a Medb witch or warlock, my lord."

"What Beladors have they encountered?"

"None until early this morning. They battled with a Maistir called Quinn, an Alterant known as Evalle, a Belador warrior called Devon, a warrior called Casper who did not show his powers, and a witch of unknown origin, but not Medb. Oddly they had a human with them, military type."

"Did your men capture the Alterant?"

"No. The Beladors killed two of our team members. There was another female they couldn't identify, and she killed our demons. They seemed attracted to her."

"A shame they did not bring the Alterant, but they'll have another opportunity."

Lorwerth waited during the pause. He'd come to understand that his benefactor wanted only information he requested, no unnecessary talking.

"What of the dragon king, Lorwerth?"

"No sign of him, my lord."

"Then we must move to the next step at nightfall. Are your men ready?"

"Yes." That one word should convey the faith Lorwerth had in his men and his ability to lead them.

"Very well. Protect the tomb I brought you."

"With my life, my lord."

CHAPTER 16

Reese tried to envision anyone with worse luck than hers.

Nobody came to mind.

She'd been sitting here for what felt like two or three hours, watching a two-foot-tall gargoyle named Feenix fly around the room. He chased a colorful plastic whirligig that flew whenever he tossed it in the air.

Someone had placed a spell on it.

This entire floor was his playroom and Storm had made it very clear that if anything happened to Feenix, no one could save Reese from him or Evalle.

That was right before he stuck her in this corner on a chair and warded an enclosure. She'd figured out Yáahl was correct about this being Saturday. By now it was probably noonish. If she had her powers, she'd give breaking that ward a try, but she didn't.

The whirligig lost speed as it usually did after two minutes and fell down inside her corner.

Feenix came flying down and landed six feet away. He stared at his toy then at her, looking perplexed.

She smiled at him and he smiled back.

This had potential. "I'm Reese."

"I know. Thorm told me. You Reethe."

That lisp was too cute, but he had ignored her until now. She had to stay serious to figure out how to escape. "I would love to play with you."

Feenix started clapping and chortling as he walked in a circle. "Play, play, play!"

Now we're making progress. Reese said, "I'm stuck over here. I can't play unless I get out of this corner."

Feenix stopped clapping and frowned at her.

She was losing his attention and asked, "Do you know how to get me out of here?" Granted it was a long shot, but she couldn't risk sitting here if he had a way to break the ward.

In the preternatural world, anything was possible.

Feenix waddled over to a bright yellow beanbag, one of three different-colored ones in the room. He picked up a stuffed alligator, hugged it to him and sat down, still frowning.

Oh, no. What if she'd upset Feenix? He was clearly Evalle's pet from the way those two had hugged before Evalle left.

Reese had to fix this fast. Evalle had been her only ally and the one person who had kept Storm at bay. "Tell you what. Never mind about getting me out of here. Tell me what games you like to play."

The little gargoyle let out a fat sigh and jumped up, waddling back over to her. He sat down and pointed at his toes. "One, two, three, four ... "

That went on for the next fifteen minutes. She finally realized the majority of his vocabulary came down to a handful of words and numbers up to twelve. He was very proud of eleven and twelve.

When he stopped, his eyes focused on the whirligig. Well, hell. Just because she was miserable didn't mean he had to be. She tossed it to him, but the thing didn't fly.

It landed in front of him. His eyes lit up. He grabbed it and threw it in the air. Before he abandoned his alligator to take off after it, he turned and said, "Thank you, Reethe."

What a sweet gargoyle.

She hadn't gotten to hear her baby talk or watch him play. Her eyes burned at the loss and she shook it off. She stood up, pushing her hands against the invisible wall. Not budging.

"Who are you?"

She jumped at the question, then did a double take at the matched set of young men who walked in. With an extra look, she could tell a slight difference between them. One had a devil-may-care look in his eyes and the other's gaze held a suspicious glint.

"I'm Reese. And you are?"

The devil-in-the-making said, "I'm Kardos, the fun guy. The sourpuss here is Kellman."

Kellman gave his brother a put-upon glare.

Feenix had been at the end of the huge room. He shouted, "Kellman! Kardoth!"

Kellman could smile after all.

Feenix flew at him like a cannonball, but slowed down to land in Kellman's open arms. The little guy was chortling like mad again.

That meant Reese was off the hot seat for upsetting him.

Feenix asked Kellman, "Play?"

"Not right now, buddy. Kardos and I have to go see Kit."

"Kit? What ith kit?"

"That's a lady we know. I'll tell you about her later."

Feenix leaned out to see Kardos. "Where you go?"

Kardos reached over and patted his head. "Camping. We'll be back in five days."

"Fun?"

"Yeah, we think it'll be fun. We'll be out in the woods doing ... stuff. I don't really know. Kellman got us sucked into doing it."

"Kardos, give it up. You wanted to go the minute you heard the sun was shining in the mountains."

"True. I'm waterlogged."

Sounding confused, Feenix asked, "What fun? NATHCAR?"

"No NASCAR. We won't have a television."

That perplexed Feenix. "Peetha?"

"No pizza. No way to cook it."

"Take me. I cook." Feenix pointed his mouth up and shot out a burst of flame.

Reese jumped.

The guys were laughing. Kellman said, "We should take you. We wouldn't have to build a fire, but Evalle would be so sad if you went with us."

"Oh." Feenix put one fat little digit on his lip. "I thay here."

"That's what we thought."

A buzzer sounded.

Kellman said, "Okay, Feenix. That's our ride at the front door.

See you when we get back." He lifted Feenix into the air and the gargoyle flapped his bat-like wings.

Reese panicked. "Wait?"

Kellman asked, "Why?"

"I really need to get out of here. I said I'd wait for everyone to return, but I've got an appointment and I need to know how to leave the building."

Kardos eyed the ten feet between them. "Can you walk to the door?"

No. "Uh, I got myself stuck in this corner somehow. I was up here visiting and bam, just got stuck."

The brothers exchanged a loaded look. Kellman said, "If you're stuck there, Storm put you there, which means no one here will lift a finger to free you even if we could and we can't."

"No, that's not what happened—"

Kardos laughed out loud. "Don't try lying around Storm. If you can't convince me, you have no chance around him."

With that they left with Kellman asking, "Did you leave Evalle and Storm the note?"

"Yes. It's on our kitchen counter. Stop being so anal."

There went the first people she'd seen who *might* have helped her find her medallion if she'd actually planned a strategy instead of sitting here silently griping.

Reese shook her head at that idea. Even if she'd been ready, it never would've happened. Not with this tight-knit group. She needed that medallion for any hope of escaping.

Slumping down on the chair, she was ready to scream, but Feenix was happy again so she just grumbled under her breath.

Twenty minutes later, she heard voices.

Footsteps came upstairs. Storm walked in, took stock of Feenix first, who had been playing at the far end of the room. The gargoyle called out, "Thorm!"

Storm said, "Hi Feenix. You okay?"

"Yeth." Feenix returned to whatever had been entertaining him.

That one word must have confirmed that Reese had behaved, because Storm didn't inquire further. He walked over, cleared the ward and said, "Let's go downstairs."

Her energy churned, but nothing like before. If she made a run for it, she doubted even Evalle could stop Storm from taking her down.

Miserable demon. She followed him back to the conference room where he handed her off to Quinn, saying, "She's all yours, buddy. Evalle hasn't slept in almost twenty-four hours. We're going to eat, grab some rest, and I'll be in touch tonight once I check the cemetery."

"That works. Thank you."

Storm walked out of the room. Evalle's voice joined his. Reese listened as their voices drifted upstairs along with their footsteps.

When she brought her gaze to Quinn's, he said, "None of us are convinced that you're here by accident. Now is the time to come clean. I don't need Storm here to determine whether you're telling the truth. If you don't convince me otherwise, I'm handing you over to VIPER to put in lockup while we figure out what to do about these killings."

That put her heart in her throat.

She couldn't negotiate from a point of weakness. That meant she needed something to trade him. She took a stab, saying, "Whether you believe me or not, I'm not aligned with those people you fought in Midtown and Piedmont Park. This seems to be a big issue between the Beladors and the Medb. If they're looking for Kizira's body and you know where it is, why don't you tell them and solve the problem?"

Even better, tell her and solve all *her* problems.

"No one knows where it is. The body has been stolen."

Did the news ever get better? She considered all that had transpired and asked, "Are you looking for the body?"

"Yes."

"If I could help you find it, would that buy my freedom?"

His stern face lost its rigid edges. "What do you mean by help? Can you locate it?"

"Depends on if I can touch somewhere that the body has been. I have a gift of vision." It wasn't as simple as that and her remote viewing gift had flaws, but why complicate a negotiation with negativity?

If he was trying to hide his surge of interest, he failed. Everything about him had stayed calm, but his eyes filled with hope.

Not that she wanted to crush that hope or ruin her chance for freedom, but she had to qualify one thing. "Remember when everyone wanted to know how I killed the demon and I said my powers were tied to a medallion I lost? I can tap my gift if your people can find it, but they have to hurry because the medallion has a shelf life." She wasn't sure that was true, but time was absolutely of the freaking essence for her.

Quinn's forehead smoothed when he relaxed. He reached in his pocket and withdrew a cord with her medallion dangling from it. "I'll give you one chance to prove that you're telling the truth."

CHAPTER 17

The realm of TÅμr Medb

Maeve studied the water flowing over her decimated scrying wall. The rare gems of all sizes and colors still sparkled.

All that failed to hold her attention when her gaze kept being drawn to the huge blackened area and holes where only shards of the largest gems poked out at odd angles.

That arrogant dragon had *destroyed* her scrying wall.

Not her wall. She had better taste.

That idiot Flaevynn, the woman who had reigned as queen in Táur Medb until Maeve reincarnated, had created the garish wall.

Thankfully, Maeve's return had forced Flaevynn to blink out of existence.

Lights from hundreds of candles in her private chamber struck the jewels that remained, creating a brilliant glow on the gaudy display. Certainly not a structure Maeve would have created, but that wall had held information from the six hundred and sixty-six years of the last queen's existence, which Maeve needed now more than ever.

A swish of sound behind her announced the doors to her chamber opening.

She looked over her shoulder as Cathbad the Druid strolled in with a consoling look on his handsome face.

He said, "There you are, darling. I've given you space to come to terms with your loss. It's time we talked."

"Talk?" She swirled around, her feet floating inches above the floor. "My wall is destroyed and my throne was stolen. They.

Stole. My. Throne!" Her gaze went to the empty spot where her dragon throne had sat for two thousand years. She was not finished with Daegan.

Not by a long shot.

"Yes," Cathbad said, continuing toward her. He lifted a hand to her cheek. "I know the anger you carry and I wish to share your burden, but that won't happen until you're ready to look forward instead of behind."

She hissed and spun up into the air.

Energy flashed away from her in fiery red lightning bolts, striking everywhere. Candles melted from the burst of heat. Stones on the scrying wall exploded. The walls of her chamber shook and groaned from her anger.

Staring down at Cathbad from high above him, she snarled, "Do not lecture me on when to let go of my anger, druid."

Unfazed by her show of might, Cathbad smiled. "Ah, but you mistake my words, love. I am not telling you to let go o' your anger, but to channel it so that you may receive your pound of flesh."

Floating back to eye level with Cathbad, Maeve said, "A pound of flesh will not satisfy my hunger for vengeance. Daegan owes me for the rest of his life."

Cathbad lifted his hands in supplication. "Do not shout at me. I did try to encourage you to kill him when you could have in this tower. He was at your mercy in this realm."

"Kill him? That would be too simple a payment for his debt. Most of the two thousand years he spent as a throne passed while you and I slept. I barely got to enjoy any of it. I had practically no time to watch him suffer. He dared to betray me then tried to kill me. No, he will be my throne again, but it will be far worse this time."

Heaving a sigh, Cathbad relented. "Very well. Let's get busy figuring out how to accomplish that."

"I want more than just having him back. So much more."

Cathbad gave her a measuring look. "I can't wait to find out what's churning in that beautiful head of yours, Maeve. I'm just glad I'm not on the receivin' end."

She didn't acknowledge that one way or the other. No one was safe from her wrath until she had her hands on Daegan again.

When the silence dragged out too long, Cathbad took to pacing. "We'll need a way to ambush him for any hope of catching him unaware in the human world."

"I can't go after him there. He'll be waiting for a chance to kill me."

Spinning on his heel, Cathbad said, "That's not so easy to do. But killing *him* will be just as difficult, from what I recall of dragons."

"That's not what I have in mind for him."

"Now, Maeve, we may only get one shot at the bastard, and if that's the case, you do want to destroy him, don't ya?"

"No!" she roared, shaking the entire room again, but much worse this time.

"Maeve, calm down. You don't want a repeat of—"

Her head warped out of shape and she grew six feet taller. Red, black and silver flashed around. She screamed, her throat burning from the sound. "I will have him back! That dragon will not be allowed to live, or die, only exist. Here!" Her eyes burned liquid red.

She lifted her fists and shoved them down as if hammering a table. Power exploded from her, blasting Cathbad fifty feet away to where his body slammed the wall. He hung there a moment, groaning, then slid to the floor.

Her heart thundered in her chest. She wanted to burn everything in sight. She could do it, too. Wreck this tower. She would—

"Maeve, darling, you ... you must control yourself or you will lose this battle." Cathbad walked slowly back across the room, dusting himself off and straightening his shirt.

She grabbed her head. It throbbed from the power overload. Glaring at him, she demanded, "What are you saying, druid?"

"That you can't face an enemy as deadly as Daegan and be out of control," he replied with more steel in his voice this time. "You want to win, then you must hold your power in a tight fist until we need it unleashed. I don't know what is causing this reaction, but you've done this twice in two days. I can't protect your back if you allow him to goad you and leave yourself at his mercy."

He was right, damn him.

She'd lost control once before, right after she'd returned from a Tribunal meeting to find her private space ransacked and her dragon throne gone.

Her reaction had been three times as bad then, killing two of her guards, but that was natural culling if they couldn't hold up to a strike.

Outside this realm, she would be vulnerable, but even more so if she lost track of where she was at any moment, which would allow Daegan the perfect chance to attack. She might die from an overload of her own power.

But she needed to kill someone, needed to watch blood flow.

The only thing protecting Cathbad was the blood deal they'd made to protect each other while they were waiting to be reincarnated in current day. And there was the fact that he was also stronger in this realm.

He could take that hit and walk away.

He might not be so fortunate if this had happened in the human realm. Then where would she be without him? Who would watch her back?

Shrinking back to her normal size, she shook off the remnants of anger that clung to her and took a steadying breath. She would make Daegan regret escaping this room.

When Maeve's throat cooled to where she could speak in a normal voice again, she told Cathbad, "Daegan might win a battle, but he will lose the war and there will be one ruler."

Pinching his chin in a thoughtful pose, Cathbad nodded. "Now you sound like the woman I made a pact with to rule the human world."

She never agreed to share that rule. Cathbad could remain, so long as he was of value to her. "You said you came to talk. What is your idea?"

"We need to find out what is going on in the human world. What has happened now that Daegan is there."

"*If* he's there," she amended.

"Where else would he be?"

"Treoir Island."

"You think Macha would welcome him to the island?"

"No." Maeve laughed. "No more than I would in her shoes,

but he has the right as the first son of King Gruffyn to take Treoir back from Macha *if* he managed to get into that realm *and* to break my curse."

"I did not know he could claim the island at this point. When did you plan to tell me this?" Cathbad's grin dissolved into a foreboding expression.

"When you needed to know." She shrugged. "Stop looking at me that way. I have not betrayed you."

He spoke softly with a chilling edge. "No, you told me you needed help creating a prophecy that would create gryphons who possessed Belador and Medb blood in this era. I did my part and there are now Alterants evolving into gryphons. You told me you wanted a partner who would sleep for thousands of years with you and reincarnate when the gryphons rose and the prophecy was fulfilled. I agreed. You told me you wanted to conquer Treoir Island and take control of that power, but you never mentioned that Daegan could take the island simply by right of birth."

"Well, now you know. What's your point?"

He didn't answer at first, just stared so hard he should be driving holes through her chest. "Time and again, you refused to kill that bloody dragon and now he's more powerful than ever if he's on Treoir. We could have killed him, and then the only thing between us and conquering Treoir would have been Macha."

"She's not much easier to kill than Daegan."

Cathbad's fury boiled over. He shoved his arms up in the air and opened his mouth, spewing out a black, swirling cloud that wrapped the room and shrouded Maeve. Her skin crawled at the feel of it, but she wouldn't blink while he showed his power.

Demonic wraiths shot back and forth through the room.

Five of them surrounded Maeve, gaping mouths filled with pointy teeth ready to rip into her.

His power did give her pause, but he'd be a fool to harm her in her own realm.

"Call down your dogs, Cathbad."

He still stared up and his arms remained extended. The shrieking went up a notch.

She had the uncomfortable thought that she might have

pushed him too far this time.

But he would never see her sweat.

"Call them down or you breach our agreement," she warned.

Seconds stretched. The wraiths snapped their jaws, moving closer to her.

Cathbad jerked his arms down and shouted a word as old as time. The wraiths sucked backwards into a miniature tornado that spun itself into dust and dissolved into a smoky cloud.

"Are you through?" she asked, sounding more bored than anything.

Smoothing his hands over his perfect hair first, he straightened his sport coat and said, "You need me, Maeve. Don't ever forget it."

She seethed. "I need no one. We have an agreement. If you no longer wish to uphold your end, say so, but do not ever assume that I need anything or anyone."

Confidence purred in his voice this time. "Ah, but you do. You think I don't have a few secrets of my own?"

"I'm sure you do."

He started toward the door, which meant passing her. He slowed next to her and whispered, "You've unleashed a dragon who can kill a deity if he finds a mate."

"I doubt he finds another dragon in this day and age."

"Oh, are you so sure about that?"

She turned to Cathbad and realized she was close enough to enjoy his sculptured mouth, if she hadn't been so angry. "Are you telling me you know of another dragon?"

"I'm not telling you anything. Just as I'm not saying that I may know how to kill Daegan. Think about that when you go down to collect Kizira's body."

"Me? I can't go somewhere he might have the upper hand."

"Then you should think about that before you play games with me, Maeve. One of us has to collect the body when Quinn delivers it, or the Beladors may call foul and default. You have no scrying wall. You need Kizira's body to get your answers."

CHAPTER 18

As a leader, Daegan rocked in Evalle's book if for no other reason than making her life easier by teleporting her and Storm to arrive *inside* their building in the middle of the day.

Too bad Daegan couldn't snap his fingers and make this a happy Saturday afternoon like most couples were enjoying.

She followed Storm up to their residence on the top floors, which were far above the conference room she had no desire to visit right now. Not after having a conflict with Storm over Reese.

He'd checked on Feenix, handed Reese over to Quinn and called a time-out for them. She hated the brittle silence between them, but appreciated that Storm would never lose his temper in front of her friends.

Sure, he'd wanted to kill Reese at one point, but that was a natural reaction to someone he'd thought was a demon.

There'd been a time when he'd kept his anger locked down and avoided pushing her. She didn't want him to hold back.

Not that she wanted him to be angry with her, but she'd come a long way in this relationship and would not backslide. Both of them needed to vent at times and both of them deserved to have their say. They were a pair of strong personalities. Storm had pushed her to be honest with him at every turn.

She wanted his honesty as well.

He opened the door and held it for her. Always a gentleman when it came to her.

She took two steps in and turned. He closed the door with a click then leaned back against it with his arms crossed.

She crossed hers. "You might as well get it off your chest. You've been stewing since you walked in and found Reese in the conference room."

He looked down. "Reese?" He lifted his gaze back to hers and the fury was banked, churning and ready to escape.

"That's her name."

"You say her name as if she's a new neighbor. You don't even know what she is, but you still brought her here."

"You're still mad about me bringing her here?"

"Bingo."

She could never talk without being in motion, so she started pacing back and forth. "I had Quinn, Adrianna and Isak with me. Between the four of us I'm fairly certain we could take her down if that had been necessary. But it wasn't. She was unconscious and sick."

"You don't know that she was truly dying. You didn't know enough about who she is or what she is to realize whether you were being gamed."

The fact that his words rang true didn't help.

Now she felt foolish and she liked feeling that way about as much as feeling weak. Not at all.

When in doubt, she went on offense. "What are you saying? I don't have a say in who comes here without your permission?"

He stood up and dropped his arms. "No. That's not ... you're turning my words around."

"I just need this clarified that you're saying I can't decide who comes and goes unless I clear it through you first."

"Of course you can, Evalle. I'm not saying that, I'm just ... " He paused long enough to curse in one of his many languages. Then he drew a breath, but his face still had 'pissed off' written all over it. "Just stop bringing in unknown beings. That's all I'm asking. Promise me that."

Calling her Evalle was never a positive sign. It was the same as saying he was close to the end of his patience.

She stopped pacing. "How can I promise what I'll do in the future when I have no idea what tomorrow brings? I don't work a normal job. I'm around strange things all the time and I'm not letting something die that isn't trying to harm me. I did think this through first." Counting off on her fingers, she said, "I couldn't

take her to a human hospital and I couldn't take her to healers in
VIPER headquarters with Sen there and ... wait a minute." She
took a step toward him. "What did you mean by *keep bringing in
unknown beings*? What other time are you talking about?"

Storm muttered to himself, but she heard, "Might as well get
this done now." His tone came out slow and calm as if trying to
explain to someone who might react badly. "You brought Oskar
here. In fact, you had no idea what he was capable of and you
drove around alone with him in my car, Evalle."

Sweet little Oskar?

He was a witch's familiar the size of a small dog and he
hadn't been the least bit dangerous. Well, not to Evalle. She
probably should have let it go, but she felt like she'd failed a
simple test as his mate.

With no better defense, she grumbled, "I'll get your truck
detailed."

Storm crushed the keys in his hand and let the debris fall to
the floor. His voice was low and furious. "I don't want the damn
truck detailed."

Dishes in the cabinets started rattling.

Evalle lifted her hands. "Then what do you want? If I say I'm
not going to do something then I won't break my word to you.
But just know that if we hadn't ended up here, plan B was Isak's
interrogation room. Are you saying we should have taken her
there?"

"No!"

Energy raced through her veins. She had to stop or she'd shift
into a gryphon right here. Not that anyone would know but she'd
probably take out the ceiling and half the next level.

Storm stood there, saying nothing.

She knew that look. He was giving her time to calm down.
Well, that wasn't happening.

"What. Do. You. Want. Storm?" she strode over to him.

He grabbed her shoulders and his hands shook with the energy
rocking him. He wouldn't hurt her, she knew this, but he was
furious.

His chest expanded and contracted with shuddering breaths.
When he finally spoke, his words came out hoarse. "I want to
know you're safe. I built this for you so that you would have a

place where you know nothing can harm you. I want to know that if I'm not here, you'll be just as safe when you're home alone." The worry behind his anger peeked out from his gaze.

He eased his grip and moved a trembling hand to stroke her hair. "I hated the entire time you lived under that building of Quinn's. I spent days upon days worrying about you. I knew that the day might come when you take on a monster you might not defeat. I have never been so happy as having you here with me."

Her heart squeezed at the mix of love and fear in his voice. Her eyes watered.

Storm feared nothing, except losing her.

She felt the same way about him. In his shoes, she'd probably react even worse.

There were no hard and firm rules for the world they lived in beyond survival being the top priority, which gave even more weight to his words. She'd been caught up in the moment and would have done the same thing in the past when she lived in the underground apartment.

But she lived here with Storm, Feenix, the twins and Lanna, once Quinn's cousin returned. Evalle would not intentionally put any of them at risk.

She and Storm had worked through his overprotectiveness. Since then, he'd been true to his word to give her space to perform her job.

Now she had to do her part as his mate.

He deserved better than to worry about their home.

Before she could speak, he added, "I might have overreacted since that woman doesn't appear to be a threat. But the minute I walked in and sensed demon energy, the next thing I saw was you too close to her. She could have touched you before I got to you."

She hugged him. "I do get what you're saying and I'm sorry. I love our home. I love that it is a safe haven. Living here with you is more than I ever dreamed. You're right. I don't always think before jumping into things."

He squeezed her and chuckled. "Understatement."

She pinched him and he kissed her on the head. She said, "I won't bring anyone, or anything, here again that I don't know for sure is safe."

"Thank you." His voice was now back to the deep tone that soothed her. "But don't get me wrong, sweetheart. This is your home as much as mine, for you to share with your friends ... except Isak."

She smiled. Storm didn't mean that, but he was no longer thinking about Reese.

Storm's hands wrapped her waist. He picked her up and sat her on the counter, pulling open her shirt so fast buttons flew all over the kitchen.

"That's one of my BDUs," she tried to protest, but it died on her breath when he popped the snap on her bra. He covered one breast with his mouth and he filled his hand with the other.

Heat pooled between her legs as he moved those amazing hands to yank her jeans off. His teeth scraped her sensitive nipple, now hard and begging for more.

She gripped his hair, pulling it out of the leather thong so the black silk washed over his shoulders.

He covered the other breast with his mouth. He kissed and bit until she shook with need. Her body levitated off the counter.

He pressed on her thighs, bringing her back down and dropped to his knees, kissing the skin along the inside of her legs. Then his lips moved closer to her heat.

Her voice went up a notch. "Now. I need you now."

His whispered, "Not yet," dragged a groan from her when he spread her legs and nuzzled her heat.

Then he licked her. Again.

She dug her nails into his shoulders, clinging to him, to the man who had given her so much more than a safe home. He'd shown her how to live and to feel.

His tongue tortured her, teasing, and almost there, but not yet. Two fingers pushed inside her and she clamped the edge of the counter to hold herself down.

He sucked her hard, shoving her up to that peak ... then over, free falling. She called his name to the heavens. When she fell back to the earth, there he was holding her to him. She wrapped her legs around him, fully expecting him to be naked.

He didn't disappoint her. Ever.

With an easy move, he lifted her then brought her down as he slid home, groaning at the feel. Somewhere along the way he'd slipped a condom in place. Good thing, because she'd lost the ability to form a rational thought. Muscles bunched and moved on his back as he slowly eased in and out.

He moved his lips to her mouth, kissing her as if he'd never get another chance at her. Every minute with Storm was like that. He made her feel as if nothing mattered more in his world at any moment than her. Every part of her wanted his touch. He made love to her mouth and her body, taking his sweet time at each spot he touched.

She'd been physically exhausted only moments ago, but Storm woke up every nerve in her body again. How he could make her ready to beg so soon after that last orgasm was one of life's little mysteries she didn't care to unravel.

But now she wanted more of what he was giving her.

"Faster," she ordered.

"No." His kissed her slowly, in a seductive way that promised he could do this for hours.

For her.

She loved this man beyond comprehension.

He pulled out and pushed up hard. She clutched him to her, gasping, waiting, ready.

Still, he rained kisses along her face and neck, taking measured moves out and in. His body tightened at the effort of holding back, but he'd pause then keep moving.

Until she whispered, "Please. Now. Come with me."

"Anything for you." He made good on his words then by picking up his pace. His power wrapped around her, holding back until she tightened around him and cried out. He followed close behind, driving harder into her over and over, then the feel of his release sizzled over her.

She draped her arms over his shoulders. Her legs hung loose over his powerful arms.

The kitchen smelled of damp bodies and sex.

She smiled against his shoulder. "Love you."

He leaned her back until he could see her face. His voice had a sex-roughened edge. "I love you more."

"You must. Anyone else wouldn't survive your anger."

He looked chagrined. "I'm sorry I yelled at you."

Evalle smiled. "I'm not."

That confused him. "Why?"

"It means you know I can hold my own with you as your mate. There was a time where you'd have thought twice about it. We don't live in a simple world and I'm not the easiest person to live with—"

"Says who?"

"Says me."

"I don't agree."

She huffed out a laugh. "You're not objective."

"Not when it comes to you."

"Well, you had a point. I heard it. We can't grow together unless we put everything on the table when we disagree. Besides, the make-up sex was worth it."

Storm laughed and hoisted her up, then he threw her over his shoulder and walked off.

She asked, "Hey, where are you going?"

Storm had his hand on her bare bottom. "To fight in the shower. Then we'll have wet make-up sex."

Evalle laughed only until his hand moved to a more interesting spot.

CHAPTER 19

Quinn led the way through Oakland Cemetery, which normally had tourist traffic on a late Saturday afternoon, even in the winter. But the temperature felt like spring. If not for the rain that had yet to let up, this cemetery would be crowded. He'd passed a few people with umbrellas and cameras, but that had been closer to the entrance. No one was back here.

Reese walked alongside him, wearing a rain poncho he'd gotten her on the way.

Before rushing here to find the tomb missing early this morning, Quinn hadn't been to Oakland Cemetery since placing Kizira here.

He'd stayed away to keep her safe from discovery.

Major fail. He'd planned on never coming back until he'd found their daughter, which seemed further out of reach every minute.

"What is it about cemeteries that fascinates people?" Reese wondered aloud.

"Oakland has been here since the mid 1800s. It's filled with families. There are seventy thousand graves."

"That's not what I'm talking about. I understand when people visit to be with a loved one they lost and I get that some people hunt ancestors through death records, but the rest apparently are just sightseeing."

"True. I've heard some say they enjoy the peace in a cemetery." He couldn't recall when he'd had a simple conversation like this with anyone. His world was filled with preternatural politics, conflicts and just plain everyday headaches involving the Beladors.

"What do you want with the body, Quinn?"

"What?" He blinked at her, surprised by her question.

Reese glanced up, holding her own with her stride. Rain drizzled from the ball cap he'd given her. She lifted the hem of the poncho and wiped her face with the sleeve of the Atlanta Braves hoodie he'd also bought for her. It was a bit too large, but the convenience store hadn't offered much and her thin T-shirt had been wrecked by the demons. She must be from a warmer part of California, because she had definitely not come to Atlanta dressed for any kind of winter.

Storm had reacted to the demonic energy inside Reese, but Quinn didn't sense a threat from her.

Why not?

She lifted her eyebrows in question.

What had she asked? Why he wanted the body. Like he would share that with her? He said, "It doesn't matter what I plan to do with the body."

"It might."

"I thought we had an agreement. You'll help me find the body, then I give you back the medallion. You do what I say, when I say, and it will go easier for everyone."

She muttered something that included the word "dickhead" then ducked her head and shook it off. Looking up, she said, "I do want my medallion back. It's critical that you return it to me. I only asked about her body because I don't care for necromancy."

She'd surprised him with her concern over someone abusing Kizira's body. He hesitated over what to say, but he couldn't tell Reese any more than he had about all this. He said, "I don't intend to perform necromancy on the body."

"I see."

No, she didn't, but that was fine by Quinn. "You said you were a photographer in California. What kind?"

She looked everywhere as if watching for something or someone. "The kind that gets paid for her work. Where is this plot?"

There was the sharp mouth again.

Quinn looked up. They were almost there. "Turn left at the next opportunity."

She did, and paused at a child's grave. The headstone showed the baby had the same day for both birth and death in 1927.

"Is something wrong, Reese?"

Realizing she'd been caught looking at the grave, she said, "No. Where to now?"

"Straight ahead." But he'd put his finger on what he'd sensed about her. Reese had an inherent sadness that clung to her like a second skin. She came across as combative and argumentative, but those might be her emotional defense shields.

When he reached the empty space where the tomb should have been, there was no one nearby, which meant the spell he'd put around it was still pushing humans away, even with the private mausoleum missing.

The empty rectangular plot now stood out, with so many massive memorial sculptures and headstones crowded around. They had the scenic backdrop of the Atlanta skyline.

Reese stopped in front of the plot, hands on her hips, staring. "Has anyone noticed it missing?"

"Humans wouldn't."

She nodded, clearly catching that this had been shielded with a spell or ward.

Letting out a long sigh, she said, "I need to put my hands down there. I'll tell you when I feel something."

"What happens then?"

"If I catch a little luck, I'll travel remotely to wherever the tomb is and tell you what I see."

"What if you aren't lucky?"

"I might travel to the inside of the tomb where the body is and that would tell us nothing unless someone has gotten inside."

"I seriously doubt that."

"Why?"

"This is taking longer than I'd expected," Quinn said. "I thought you were in a hurry to get your medallion back."

"Fine. Whatever. I need a moment to see if I can feel anything. Once I have a good spot, then I'll need to touch my medallion." She dropped to her knees and looked around.

"What are you looking for?" he asked, full of suspicion.

"Súile marbh demons."

"Why?"

"That's what I killed this morning, so I'm just keeping an eye out for more. Or pretty much any demon."

But she'd known the specific demon. "What do you know about súile marbh demons?"

"Not much. They're like killing robots. They do whatever they're created to do."

That could be said about most demons. He dismissed it and the possibility of a demon in the cemetery. That didn't mean they couldn't enter, but he had a feeling the thousands of spirits still residing here might make that difficult. He told her, "I'll watch for demons. You do your thing."

"And don't stare at me," she ordered.

She was a bossy thing. "I'm not about to turn my back and allow you to disappear."

"I'm not going anywhere without my medallion." She'd said that as though he were clueless that the pendant was her lifeline.

"Very well. Get busy. I'll keep an eye out."

His mobile phone buzzed. He stepped under a tree to block some of the rain so he could read the text message. Devon had sent an update.

He finished replying to the text and heard a scuffling sound, then, "Quinn!"

He swung around to find a man dragging her off. Her face had turned deep red from being strangled.

Quinn shoved the phone in his pocket as he rushed over, yelling, "Drop her now!"

The human face that lifted to him had black eyes. It blinked and the eyes were red. *Demon.* Bloody hell. And he'd blown off her concern.

It sent a blast of power at Quinn, slapping his head to the side.

Quinn sidestepped, caught his balance, and turned to the pair. He hated to enter the mind of a demon, but if he used kinetics, the demon might kill Reese before Quinn could stop it. Using mind lock was the quickest way to free Reese, who was fighting for all she was worth but turning blue.

He powered up and shoved inside the demon's head. The screeching noise that hit him sounded like bad feedback at a rock concert turned up a hundred decibels.

Walking forward at a steady pace, Quinn held onto the nasty

mind. Swimming in a sewer would be more pleasant. He pushed harder into the frenetic noise and found a place to latch onto its mind. He sent a burst of power through the connection that rocked the demon back.

Reese now hung limp in the creature's arms.

Finally it lost its grip, snarling at the pain Quinn was causing.

That's when Reese came alive.

She shot upright and shoved her booted foot back to slam the demon's knee. It was enough to knock the demon off his feet and for her to break loose. She turned to fight him.

Quinn wanted to strangle her himself.

Didn't she realize that now was the time to run away from that thing? If she'd back off, Quinn could use his kinetics and get out of its head. Quinn hit the demon with a solid mental punch that buckled its knees.

Taking advantage of the demon's weakened state, Reese showed off some serious kickboxing skills with her next hits.

Quinn released the demon that had now turned into a quivering mass on the ground. That creature could regenerate, though, so Quinn smashed a double-fisted kinetic hit down on its head. The body stopped jerking. In the next minute, it became gray dust that swirled into a miniature tornado and vanished into the air.

Reese turned to Quinn with a smile that showed the woman she kept hidden. An attractive one, when you got past the angry glare and churlish attitude. But Quinn recognized an adrenaline high when he saw one.

How many times had she fought demons?

Reese rubbed her neck where she had red welts appearing on her skin. "I wasn't sure you'd turn around in time."

She stopped, frowning as she glanced around her with a question in her gaze, then shook it off and started toward him again.

Another demonic being, dressed as a human, but with the same black eyes, dove out from behind a headstone taller than Quinn.

Reese spun, but too late, and got hit broadside, the impact knocking her to the ground.

She and the demon rolled away in a flurry of punches and

kicks.

Quinn hit the demon with a kinetic blast, but the thing dragged Reese along when it slid thirty feet away. She never stopped punching the demon and slamming its head backwards, but the demon slashed at her with sickle-shaped claws as long as Quinn's fingers.

Quinn yanked out two triquetras, specialized, razor-sharp throwing stars formed into the shape of the triangular Belador symbol.

The demon's jaws opened to rip flesh from Reese's neck.

Quinn sent the blades flying for the demon's throat. They bit flesh and cut straight across. The demon froze. His head fell to the side, barely attached, and his body flopped down.

Just like the first demon, the body immediately turned into a gray dust and spiraled away.

Quinn got to Reese and dropped to his knees. He slid his arm behind her and lifted her into a sitting position. "Reese, are you okay?"

She had two gashes across her neck. She tried to speak. The only word that came out was, "Medallion."

He fished out the medallion and she gripped it like a lifeline. Slowly the bleeding stopped and the skin closed up, healing over, but leaving puffy red marks.

She lowered her hand. The rain washed red streaks of blood down her fingers. She caught her breath. "That's better."

"Why did it heal you to a point and stop? You still have two wounds on your neck that are barely closed."

Her gaze dropped down and away. "Majikal healing is not exactly a perfect science."

He agreed, but she was not telling him the whole truth. When he pulled the medallion away, she snarled, "That's mine, dammit."

"Why do you need the medallion to activate your powers?"

She stonewalled with a flat expression.

He suggested, "You could help yourself by telling the truth on occasion."

"You could help yourself by pulling your head out of your ass and knocking off the power Gestapo act," she grumbled. Running her hands through her golden-brown hair, she tossed curls everywhere and huffed out a breath. "Listen, this hasn't been the best of days for me. I'm trying to work with you, but you're screwing up my schedule."

"I only want to understand why you don't have your powers."

"Someone turned them dormant. Before you ask, no, I'm not telling you who. That's my business."

He couldn't argue with that and in spite of a constant swirl of suspicion around this woman, he sympathized with the crazy way their world functioned. Someone more powerful than she was clearly held something over her head.

Quinn said, "I have an unusual ability called mind lock. Our powers are controlled by the mind. Would you like me to slip inside and see if I can figure out how to unbind your powers?"

"Oh, hell no!"

Why hadn't she healed from the demon attack that happened before they'd met her in Midtown? Why did her healing powers only work to a point now?

He couldn't help her *and* watch for demons, which he now realized were a significant threat, even here. Spying a mausoleum fifteen by twenty feet that he could stand up in, he said, "We need to move."

"Where?" She leaned forward, making the move to stand up, but Quinn hooked his hands under her arms and lifted her to her feet with ease. She wasn't tiny, but she was shorter than Quinn, and she didn't weigh a lot. She could stand to put on a few pounds, in his opinion.

Jumping away as if his touch had burned her, she turned a scowl on him that deterred the giving of any such opinion.

Using his kinetics, he opened the mausoleum. "Over there. I'll give you the medallion then you can heal yourself before the demon poison harms you."

While dusting her pants, she eyed him with a look that questioned why he would help her. The effort to tidy up was wasted since the poncho had been shredded, and she now had blood splatter on her sweatshirt.

Talking to herself as she followed him into the mausoleum, she complained, "I wanted to never see this city again. If I ever get out of here, I plan to stay gone for more than ten years next time." She sniffed and wrinkled her nose. "This day just gets better and better."

The interior did smell of mildew and death. But at least they were out of the rain.

He pushed the door almost shut, close enough to slam it if need be, but leaving a slit of ambient light filtering in. He asked, "Why are you—"

Reese arched her back and stretched up onto her toes, head thrown back and a guttural sound coming out of her.

Quinn cursed and yanked the medallion out of his pocket, shoving it into her hand. "You've got your powers. Fix yourself."

For the second time in as many minutes, he'd witnessed crippling attacks on her body. How did she survive this constant battle with demons? Who had put her powers out of reach, dependent on a piece of jewelry that could be so easily taken?

She had a white-knuckled grip on the medallion.

Her bowed body trembled, straining as the majik tried to work.

She lifted the fist that gripped the medallion, mumbling, "Damn ... you ... all."

Her powers clearly weren't working.

Quinn hesitated to put his hands on her, unsure if he'd do more damage than good. "You have to let me help you, Reese."

"No. You're a ... head doctor. My head's ... fine."

"That's debatable if you're turning down help. And I'm not a bloody doctor."

"Then you can't—"

He put his hands on her head.

Reese gritted out, "Don't!"

Quinn kept his hands there. He could feel the power rushing inside her. "Why don't you want my help?"

"My energy ... might attack you."

"If that's the only reason, I'll take my chances." He firmed his grip and drew energy through his arms to his fingers. "I'm going into the pain and healing center of your brain only. I'm not invading your personal ... "

Her body was stretched so tightly, he expected muscles to start snapping. She screamed, "Then do it!"

CHAPTER 20

Reese's body lifted four feet off the ground, turning horizontal until her stomach faced the cobwebs inside the mausoleum.

Why wouldn't the medallion let her tap her powers?

What the hell, Yáahl?

She felt the minute Quinn pushed inside her mind and panicked at the intrusion.

Then the poison twisted her spine.

His energy moved to the center of healing in her mind. She could feel the spot, but not tap it. Pain shot in every direction.

Quinn was talking to her. "Stay with me. The poison should be localized, but it seems to be spreading through your system."

She couldn't even complain about getting crappy updates.

His energy rushed from path to path, pausing at one moment, then moving on.

What had he seen?

He'd given his word that he wouldn't snoop, but he was a man. What man had ever made good on his word to her?

None.

But as his energy moved around searching for the poison, she realized he wasn't being invasive.

A healer would do this differently, but he'd told her he wasn't a doctor ... apparently he wasn't a healer either.

He muttered, "Have to get the poison in one spot then I can ... "

"Wh ... what?"

"I told you I'm not a healer. I can't stop the poison from doing damage."

She was screwed.

"But I can pull it into me and kill it in my system."

"Are you ... "   She groaned. "*Crazy?* No!"

"Too late."

She felt the change. She could actually feel the poison moving through her to her chest where he placed his hand over her heart.

What if it killed him?

Quinn grunted and cursed, then his hold relaxed. "How are you?"

She'd been so worried about him, she hadn't realized the poison was no longer trying to kill her.

Her body sagged.

He caught her before she hit the ground.

She looked up at him. The grimace said he was uncomfortable. "Are you okay?"

"Yes, it's like bad heartburn, but that will go away."

"Where did you learn to do that?"

He finally lowered his gaze to her. "Draw demon poison out of a body?"

"Yes."

"I didn't. That was an experiment."

"You idiot!" she yelled at him. "You could have died from that."

"I didn't."

Holding her against him, he turned around, looking. When he found what he wanted, he stepped over to sit on a narrow ledge with her still in his arms.

She should push him away. Get out of his lap. Definitely. She'd do that in just a minute.

But it felt so good to be held. It felt even better being held by a man with such a nicely built body. Powerful, yes, but Quinn had a certain refined air about him. Might be the British accent, but she didn't think so.

His face was calm. That was the other reason she couldn't move yet. He'd seemed angry and tense since she met him, but right this minute his face held a peaceful expression.

What was going on in that powerful mind of his?

She tried to hold her eyes open, but they closed, and for the first time in a long time she slept.

Quinn couldn't look down at the woman cradled in his arms.
What's wrong with me?

Reese was just a woman who had been injured. But the last woman he'd held had died in his arms.

He waited for the pain to swamp him.

It didn't. There was only a dull ache at the reminder.

Odd.

Always, the pain hung like a thick fog around him, threatening to sweep in and choke him at any opportunity. It sucked for that to have become his normal.

He'd had to fight constantly to stay in the present, to keep from giving in to the devastated war zone his soul had become.

As always, the pain was there, but ...

Something felt different.

For this moment, he experienced a peacefulness he hadn't felt in so long. Why? Had the demon poison he'd taken from Reese dulled his senses?

Doubtful. It had taken far more than demon poison to affect his mind and emotions in the past.

He fingered his power at the door and it opened another inch, offering a breath of air and a clear view of anyone coming.

He stared out at the downpour and the soggy cemetery, fully alert and present in this moment. Rain tapped on the mausoleum and the headstones surrounding it. No demons or wars existed in this moment, only him and ... the warm woman cradled against him.

What had happened to Reese? He'd glimpsed damage in her mind that had been there for many years. Long enough that she should have healed emotionally. Why hadn't she?

Who am I to wonder?

He'd been to powerful monks who had helped him repair his mind more than once. They'd tried to help him after Kizira died, but they'd told him it was not his mind that needed healing, but his heart.

They might be right in theory, but why should his heart heal when Kizira's never would?

He'd stuffed his emotions into a deep hole so he could function when Tzader and his tribe needed him.

Why did having Reese in his arms stir up all those emotions he'd shoved out of the way?

I'm a Maistir. I can handle holding a woman in a professional context.

He was doing just fine with that until Reese curled toward him, clutching his body and murmuring, "Missed this."

Those words struck a tender note. Finally looking down at the contentment in a face that had, up until now, worn a scowl as default, he knew without any question that she had not been held this way in a long time.

When was the last time he'd had a chance to hold someone in a quiet moment?

If holding Reese brought her peace even for this short time, he could do it and ignore the dark gremlins climbing around in his head.

This strange woman had exploded into his world and stirred things inside him. Forced him to question things.

One minute he was angry over Kizira's lack of trust and the next he cursed himself for not deserving that trust.

His mind had been a wasteland since losing Kizira. He should have protected her and he'd spent hours asking himself why he hadn't. What man deserved a woman if he couldn't keep her safe?

The truth was that he'd never deserved her love.

He didn't deserve anyone's love, and dreaded the moment he had to face his daughter and explain why she'd never see her mother again. But even that fear would not stop him from finding her and keeping her safe.

Reese mumbled again and snuggled even closer.

When she opened her eyes and smiled up at him, it was like looking into sunshine.

That lasted two seconds.

She realized where she was and shoved off his lap.

He grunted when an elbow almost unmanned him. *"Good goddess! Careful!"*

"What the hell?" She backed up a step.

"Not the appreciation I was expecting," he groused, getting to his feet. Her look of repulsion took care of his momentary insanity.

For a moment, Reese seemed at a loss, then literally shook her head, muttering, "Can't go there." Her gaze jumped all over the place. "What are we doing in here? Where are the demons?"

"They turned into ash after I killed them. I brought you in here so you could heal where I could better protect you from an attack."

She cast a wary glance around, like a cornered animal. She ran her fingers through her wild hair and asked, "Did you do something to, uh, heal me?"

"Yes, but before you go ballistic on me, I did not touch anything in your mind except the area that called up your healing. I pulled the poison out, so you shouldn't have any residual problems."

"That's right. I remember."

She'd lost her ball cap in the attack, and now kept moving her hands over her face and hair, flustered. Then she finally, grudgingly, said, "Thank you."

Quinn caught himself before laughing at her. She was an odd mix. "You're welcome. Why are demons hunting you if you're a demon?"

"I never said I was a demon. In fact, I've said several times now that I'm *not* one."

"I stand corrected, but what about—"

She held up her hand. "You writing a book on me? If so, leave out that chapter and call it a mystery."

"You're a regular comedienne."

"I don't find any of this funny, starting with you holding my medallion hostage when I did nothing to harm any of your people. You suspect me of being involved with those men and that demon. I am not and therefore I shouldn't be treated like a criminal."

He hated that she had a point, but every instinct he had warned him to trust his suspicions, and not her.

She crossed her arms. "Do you want me to look for the missing tomb or not? If you do, I need my medallion back."

Give up the only hold he had over her? Not a chance.

If she wanted to be all business, that worked for Quinn. It

helped tamp down his ridiculous and unprofessional need to protect her. She'd offered to help him locate the tomb in exchange for the medallion. If, after giving him information, he decided she'd done her part and proven no threat to anyone, then he'd hand it over.

Quinn lifted the leather thong with the medallion from his pocket.

Her eyes lit up.

He doused that excitement when he said, "You can touch it, but it stays in my possession."

"Why? I'll be right in front of you."

"That's just it. I'm not sure you won't *disappear* right in front of me. Other than your admission to having demon blood in your ancestry, we still don't know what you are, what you're capable of or why you were in the middle of a fight with those men this morning. Want to enlighten me some more?"

Her face locked down tight, sharing nothing. She spun around, then walked out of the mausoleum into a mild shower preventing anything from drying out.

He closed the entrance to the small building and followed her over to the empty plot.

Stepping into the center, she sat on the wet ground with crossed legs and ordered, "Hold the medallion where I can touch it."

Quinn moved closer, and held the medallion out in front of her. Would she tell him the truth if she found the tomb?

He reminded her, "You don't get this back until I can see or put my hands on the tomb."

She arched a challenging eyebrow at him. "Then what's your concern?"

What was bothering him about her?

That he had yet to figure out what she was doing in Atlanta and his gut kept screaming at him that it was a mistake to gain her help this way.

He had no other option and lowered the pendant to her eye level, warning, "Don't try to pull any tricks. You won't like what happens to anyone who interferes with my finding this tomb."

CHAPTER 21

The pendant turned slowly in front of Reese's face.

Could she break his hold and escape with it?

Maybe she could from other beings, but she'd seen this one use his mind to kill a demon and doubted she could outrun that mind before he latched onto hers.

Bad gamble if she lost and Quinn saw what she hid in her thoughts.

Evidently, since he hadn't intruded earlier, this man had a personal code for using his mind lock ability, which was the only thing protecting her from an unexpected mental invasion.

Before she reached for the medallion, she said, "I need it lower so that my arms stay relaxed."

He tied a knot in one end of the broken cord, preventing the medallion from falling off, and lowered it another few inches.

Getting settled, she instructed him, "You can ask me questions while I'm under, but don't touch me or you'll break my trance."

"Understood." Quinn squatted in front of her and allowed enough slack for the medallion to drop into her open hand.

She closed her fingers around the disk, and felt her energy surge toward that hand. Now what? She had no true second sight gift, not like her mother's. Reese's remote viewing had happened when she least expected it. If Yáahl expected her to bring Kizira's body back, this medallion had better do its part now.

Shutting her eyes, Reese fell into the native language of her mother's people, the one that Yáahl spoke. He'd hear. He was too much of a busybody not to, but the question was, would he help or choose to ignore her?

"With open heart, I call to you, O Great Spirit
Hear these words, my humble voice.
As the raven soars to touch the heavens
I seek your vision to guide my own."

She kept calling out to Yáahl, asking for his help in locating the body of Kizira. As she did, she fell into a trance, her body swaying back and forth on its own.

Did that mean she was doing this right?

Then why couldn't she see anything but a blurry image?

She tried to focus in her inner vision. Light grew in the middle of a foggy place, then an opening burned away in the center of the mist to show ... a tent in the woods.

What the heck?

Someone said, "Any word from the woman's son yet?"

"No."

Reese strained to see who spoke and what was positioned around the tent. Her mind pulled back to see more and a fire pit came into view, the logs blackened from burning. This was not helping.

Was Yáahl jerking her around again?

She turned her head and ... her scope of vision shifted to show two men facing each other.

First guy was tall and strong looking. Short, black hair, square chin, and mean eyes. He grabbed his neck. "We can't stay here after tonight."

"We'll be gone before daylight, Lor."

"Not if we don't find how to open that tomb in time."

Her heart raced. The tomb.

The second guy was average height, dark complexion, and not in the best shape. His dull gray eyes shifted to the right.

Reese moved her head in the same direction.

There was a structure that looked like a tomb to her. It sat on the other side of the campfire. Unless taking one of those on a camping trip was standard, that tomb had to be Kizira's. Reese studied the ornate carving on the corners and the estimated size so Quinn could confirm this was the correct one.

Wait a minute. Why would she tell Quinn where it is when

she needed to deliver that body to Yáahl?

Her conscience niggled at her that she didn't know Quinn's reason for wanting this tomb and she'd given her word to help him find it. Just because he hadn't invaded her mind didn't mean his plans took precedence over hers.

He might have just as mercenary a reason for wanting Kizira's body as the men who now possessed it.

The one called Lor jerked her attention back to him when he shouted, "That damn thing is useless unless we figure out how to open it."

His sidekick tried to calm him. "Don't worry. When they find the note, they'll bring that Belador and we'll be set."

She stuck her head forward and forced the image to open wider to show two tents and the tomb positioned around the cold fire pit.

She pulled back to widen the view even more and saw men who reminded her of the four she'd encountered with Quinn's people this morning. There looked to be at least twenty at the camp.

Someone standing to the side suggested, "Why can't you crack it open?"

"It's a sealed tomb. I was told not to let anyone touch it. The damned thing is believed to be rigged. Might kill anyone who tries to open it except the person who closed it."

"I say we capitalize on this opportunity."

"I don't have time for harebrained plans," the rough voice of Lor argued. "I need that body in hand before the Belador Quinn has to hand it over at the Tribunal. We have until four in the morning. It can't leave this realm unsealed. I want that body."

"We'll be fine. We—"

Someone outside of her range of vision shouted something about Caldwell.

What?

Lor looked straight at her.

Shit. Had she said that out loud?

He yelled, "Shut up everyone! I sense something."

Reese froze, holding her breath. They couldn't see her, right?

Lor watched someone out of her view and said, "Someone is watching us."

Out of nowhere, spikes of pain attacked her head and her vision went black.

The pain shot through her like hot pokers in her eyes.

She grabbed her head and rolled over, screaming.

All at once, a soothing balm flushed through her mind and Reese let go of her head, letting her arms flop to each side of where she lay on her back.

She opened her eyes and stared up into worried, crystal-blue ones. Yes, she could breathe again, but at what cost? Had Quinn entered her mind? "What'd you do?"

"I put my hands over yours and blocked anything from touching your head."

"Oh."

"I don't enter anyone's mind without permission unless there is a life on the line."

"Ok. Thanks. Again." She took the hand he offered to get to her feet. He had some kind of crazy power when it came to minds. She dusted herself off, stalling for time more than anything.

"Are you alright?" he asked.

"I'm good." Not really, but she'd shake it off and get a grip any minute now. What should she tell him?

Might as well tell him the truth since she had no idea how to find the body and needed his resources.

"I saw a tomb-like structure eight feet tall and ten feet wide." She described the carved corners.

"That's the one." His face brightened with hope again.

She didn't want to see that. It made her feel like she was stealing from him. How could that be when the body didn't belong to him? But the guys in the vision said something about Quinn taking the body to a Tribunal to hand it off.

The Medb weren't allowed to be in VIPER the last time Reese had been here, so it sounded like Quinn was handing off Kizira to people who had no claim to her.

Okay, feeling better now.

But if she told Quinn everything, he'd leave without her to go find it.

What'd I ever do to the universe to get this life?
Stop blaming the world for your past, Reese.

Get out of my head, Yáahl.

She wouldn't admit it to Yáahl, but he was right. She'd given Quinn a hard time since meeting him and he'd been nothing but polite. Okay, surly at times, but mostly that was her own doing.

He asked, "What else did you figure out?"

"Trees. Mountains. Nothing distinct. A campsite with two tents and the tomb." She sorted through the rest of her information and said, "There were at least twenty of those men like you fought this morning."

He stared off as if lost in thought.

Did this mean the ongoing Belador-Medb fight was tied to this missing tomb? Yáahl could have told her there was a *war* in progress for Kizira's body.

But no, he'd just dropped her in the middle of it.

She'd like to assign a noble reason for his action, such as the Raven giving a helping hand by putting her in the best place for information, but come on. When she'd considered that earlier, it had to have been the demon poison turning her mind to mush. She was fairly sure Yáahl found it entertaining to dump her ass in the middle of this mess.

"Anything else?" Quinn asked.

"Two men were talking." She described what they looked like. "They're waiting on someone to show up and open the tomb."

Ah, he showed a flicker of interest at that.

She kept explaining, "It sounded like the tomb might be booby trapped." She waited, but he said nothing, which made her think he wasn't surprised. "Aren't you concerned about them opening that tomb?"

"No."

Okay, that meant he either knew how to open it or knew the person who could, which just complicated her world. She might need Quinn with her when she found the tomb. That would also complicate her escape plan with the body, which she had yet to formulate.

Just to make sure he didn't leave her locked up while he went hunting, she said, "I'll give this another try and see if I can find out more."

"No."

"Why not?" She debated sharing more, but said, "I think they said something about a Belador having to take Kizira to a Tribunal." She was not admitting that she'd heard Quinn's name unless he started giving up more info. "Is there some deadline coming up?"

"Yes."

"Don't you care about the Belador who needs the body?"

"I'm the one who has to produce it, and very soon." He completely threw her out of step when he said, "I'm not going to put you at additional risk for my gain. It doesn't work that way."

"It normally does with the men I know." She snapped her lips shut. She hadn't intended to say so much.

"Perhaps you should choose your men more wisely. Let's go."

He turned to leave. She called out, "Hey."

The face he turned on her said how little he thought of someone yelling "Hey" at him. "What?"

"You still don't know where the tomb is. We had a deal and I need my medallion. I'm still willing to stick to my part, but I can't do this if you don't help."

Rain ran in streaks down his perfect face, which had lost some of the cold emptiness from when she'd first met him. Instead he watched her as if conflicted over his thoughts.

That was different.

Usually by now she would've managed to annoy someone to the point they were too irritated to hide their thoughts from her.

Quinn might just be a master of facial expressions.

His eyes hardly moved from her, but she had no doubt he'd been constantly sweeping his surroundings since the demon attacks. He finally said, "I do need to find the tomb, but remaining here longer would not be prudent."

"Where'd you learn to talk with your head up your ass?" That should make this guy lose that icy control and put them back on equal footing as adversaries. She could not allow herself to like the enemy.

"Does that work for you?" he asked.

"What?"

"Insulting people to keep them at a distance?" He glanced around once and said, "I'm not putting you at further risk. You got what you could. We're done here."

She felt like one of Gibbons's fertilizer piles.

Perhaps you should choose your men more wisely.

Quinn's words struck deep. She'd chosen poorly and now she was taking it out on Quinn, who was being pretty decent to her.

He was making her regret what she'd have to do, which was stick with him to track down the tomb, then vanish.

With the tomb.

CHAPTER 22

Tristan crept through southeast Atlanta mud, up toward a hangar structure forty yards away. It should be empty, based on the overgrown five acres for sale around the building. He could think of a lot of better ways to spend a Saturday night, but at least the nonstop rain had done the unbelievable and, *finally*, stopped. He welcomed the chill in the air.

He muttered, "Your buddy Grady better be right about this."

Evalle slogged through the muddy grass next to him. "Have you ever met a Nightstalker with intel as dependable as what I get from Grady?"

"Can't say that I have, but the benchmark isn't that high to begin with when it comes to ghouls."

"That's not fair. Grady is very intelligent and you know it. If not for him we'd have no idea where Ixxter disappeared to when you lost him."

"If he's here." Tristan would not face Daegan and admit he'd lost the trail. He'd find Ixxter if it took shaking hands with Nightstalkers all night long.

"Let's circle the building to see how many doors there are and if we can find a window," she suggested.

Tristan stepped ahead, walking to the right. On the backside, the first thing he spotted was a white van. "Someone's here."

"It's a bad sign that we haven't gotten a telepathic message from Ixxter."

"Yep. If he was in trouble, he'd be calling out." Tristan had hoped Ixxter was just a pain in his ass and not a traitor.

"There are three skylights on top. They look pretty old and

dirty."

Tristan had noticed them too. The metal building was a half-round quonset hut shape. He could teleport up, but he might slide off.

Evalle must have figured out the same thing. She said, "Let me push you up with my kinetics and you look in."

"Good idea."

"What was that?" she asked. "I'm sure I didn't hear you clearly."

He glowered at her and moved over next to the building. "You're stomping all over my last good nerve. Let's move it before they come out."

She chuckled and said, "Ready?"

When he nodded, she lifted him in the air until he could lean over with his hands on the curved top of the building. He eased sideways for a look through the dingy skylight.

Ixxter was definitely there, but he was chained to the floor, and his neck was locked in a two-inch-thick, steel collar. His hands were in similar two-inch-thick cuffs, also chained to the floor.

Just Ixxter and two men.

One guy turned a small, handheld stun gun on Ixxter, hitting him with a steady stream of electricity.

Ixxter shook and yelled, though Tristan couldn't hear him. The Alterant's face twisted out of shape. His hands lengthened, claws curled from the tips. His legs shook and muscles ripped the sides of his jeans.

He was trying to shift.

What was shielding the sound? A spell or ward?

Tristan spoke to Evalle telepathically. *Ixxter is in there, but he's a prisoner. Let me down. We have to go get him.*

His feet touched on the ground.

Evalle had her game face on. "How many?"

"Two. They may have the inside warded. I couldn't hear Ixxter but they were shocking him and have him bound so that he can't shift."

A sick look in her eyes mirrored the feeling in Tristan's chest. He told her, "We have a better chance of rescuing him if we can get the men out of the building."

She looked around. "Get ready. This should get them out."

Walking over to the nearest tree, a maple maybe twenty-five feet tall, she stepped back and hit it with a kinetic blast.

With the ground saturated from too much rain, it didn't take much to topple the tree onto the van sitting by the door to the hangar. Evalle hid behind a tree with a giant trunk.

Tristan stepped in beside her.

The door flew open and one man stuck his head out. He took in the tree and van, started cursing and called to his buddy. Then he stepped out to walk around their damaged ride.

Bad guy number two joined him.

Tristan told Evalle telepathically, *I'll teleport us behind them.*

She jerked her head in a "let's do it" motion.

He called up his teleporting and they were behind the goons in a blink. Tristan slammed his guy with a fist powered by kinetics, knocking him into the van.

The guy rolled away and flipped his hand to shove the van at Tristan. It pinned him to the building. Damn, that hurt.

He lifted the bumper and sent the van flipping end over end until it crashed against trees. Then he called up his Alterant power that packed a lot more punch than a regular Belador.

His opponent stared at the van, then back at Tristan just as Tristan drove a pile-driver fist at the guy's chest. It caved in, which meant his heart should explode.

Blood ran from the guy's mouth, then he hit the ground clutching his chest.

Tristan murmured, "As Beetlejuice would say, dead, dead, deadski."

Tristan spun, looking for Evalle who was swapping kinetic strikes with her guy. She hit him with a hard one-two punch, then did one of her ninja moves to dash in fast and kick him backwards. He hit the building. She was on him in a flash, and broke his neck with one twist.

Tristan hurried inside.

Ixxter opened his mouth, which had returned to normal shape, but he could only say, "Key."

"Be right back." Tristan ran back out to Evalle. "Look for a key."

She frisked the guy she'd killed, and in ten seconds, she said,

"Found a ring of keys."

Back inside, they unlocked the bindings on Ixxter. He wobbled as he stood, but he could walk. He said, "Gotta go. Shift change coming soon."

"I've got a car a half mile away," Tristan told him. "Can you make it that far?"

"Can I fly?"

"No."

Ixxter said, "Shit. Won't be fast."

Tristan had stepped outside and rounded the building when headlights from a vehicle coming down the dirt road lit them up. He shouted, "Evalle, link with me and grab Ixxter's arm."

He felt Evalle's energy surge as she linked just in time. A streak of power shot out of the vehicle as Tristan teleported them away.

Teleporting was tough with one more person. He'd found out he *could* handle two without linking for extra power, and he was pretty sure that was due to Daegan showing up.

Treoir was the Belador power center and having that dragon on the island packed more punch than anything Tristan had ever seen. Macha had used and fed on the Belador power, but she hadn't actually *been* Belador. They'd gained nothing extra by having her in control.

Daegan was a total game changer.

Evalle mumbled something as they came out of the teleporting.

The last time he'd linked and teleported multiple bodies, Tristan had been jumping from point to point and between realms to outrun the enemy. He'd ended up with blood coming out of every orifice.

Yeah, not in a hurry to do that again. The link with Evalle made it way easier, but it still took a lot of his juice.

Evalle stepped away from Tristan and Ixxter as soon as they reached the rooftop in downtown Atlanta. He'd found it to be a safe spot in the past, and it was close to where he stayed in a hotel where a friend kept a room for him.

Wind swirled over the dark rooftop, bringing a promise of more cold weather with it.

He felt the link evaporate, and Evalle had her hand over her stomach.

"You're not going to barf are you?"

She swung around with an evil threat in her gaze. Earlier rain had stuck loose hairs to her face and neck. "Daegan is so much better at that."

"Well, he was born with it and he's had that power for two thousand years. I got mine as a side effect of a witch highball and I haven't had mine for even *two* years."

Ixxter said, "Sure you two aren't siblings? You sure as hell argue like you came from the same womb."

Tristan and Evalle both shouted, "No!"

Holding up his hands in defeat, Ixxter said, "Chill. I didn't think it was such a bad ride."

Tristan grinned, but then Ixxter added, "Sort of like flying in a cement mixer."

"You two suck," Tristan muttered and sat down on an air conditioning unit. "I save your ass and that's the thanks I get?"

He couldn't give Ixxter too much grief. The guy was hobbling around after not-so-delicate handling at someone's hands.

Ixxter hadn't used his Alterant beast power to heal yet.

Evalle said, "Now that you're free and we're not in danger of being captured, what's going on?"

Tristan wouldn't call Ixxter homely, but the guy was a bruiser and his nose had been broken so many times, there was no telling what it originally looked like. The other injuries were new, though. His skin had been burned and cut all over. He limped over to the other side of the large commercial unit Tristan sat on and parked his butt.

Ixxter expelled a tired breath. Torture was exhausting business. "Those people approached me with a deal to help them hunt stuff."

"Who are those people and what kind of stuff are they hunting?" Tristan asked.

Ixxter scratched his head. "I know you won't believe this, but they're Beladors. They have kinetics, telepathy and their power feels just like ours. Well, not like ours. We're Alterants, but you know what I mean."

"We believe you," Evalle said in a reassuring voice. "But did they *say* they were Beladors?"

"I asked and they said they were better than Beladors."

Evalle scoffed. "That sounds like testosterone talking. We need whatever you can give us, Ixxter. What are they hunting?"

"Alterants for one, but they're more interested in trying to get their hands on a body. They need someone who can get it out of a tomb."

Tristan looked at Evalle, who perked up. She asked, "Did they give you a name for this body?"

"No."

Evalle came into Tristan's mind, saying, *It might be Kizira.*

We need to know for sure.

What are the odds that a group who attacked an Alterant are looking for another body in a tomb they can't open?

Hey, I'm just sayin'.

She nodded. "What else can you tell us about the body they want, Ixxter?"

"Nothing really. They just can't get inside the little building."

Tristan asked, "Why not?"

Ixxter sounded exasperated as if he expected them to understand his roundabout way of explaining. "They talked to Nightstalkers at cemeteries until they found this body. Then they stole a ... little building, you know, a tomb with the body inside. They're afraid to open it 'cause they tried with a Medb witch, then a warlock. Both got hurt. That tomb didn't get sealed by a human."

Tristan traded a look of confirmation with Evalle. Her shoulders relaxed in a moment of relief. The thieves couldn't get to Kizira. Yet.

Tristan coaxed Ixxter, "Do you know where the tomb is?"

"Uh, maybe. They took me up to a camp they're using as their headquarters. I didn't know where it was until after we'd left there though. The guys you killed were bitching on the drive down through Atlanta. They were complaining about having to go so far away because their boss didn't want to risk having me nearby when they ... questioned me."

What Ixxter meant was they wanted to keep an Alterant that shifted into a gryphon far from their headquarters in case torturing him got out of hand.

"Where's the camp?" Tristan had to keep Ixxter on track.

"It might be Athens or Blairsville. They were talking about both places, and I couldn't see out the van when we left."

Evalle's face fell at having two different locations. She asked, "What are they doing about opening the tomb?"

"They need the person who booby-trapped it to open the thing."

Snorting at that, Tristan asked, "They really expect the person who put that kind of security in place to just show up and pop the body out?"

"No." Ixxter shrugged as if none of this mattered to him, which it wouldn't since he had no knowledge of Quinn's involvement or Kizira's missing body.

Frustration pouring off Tristan would drown them soon. He asked, "Did they kidnap you to see if you could open it?"

Wiping perspiration off his forehead, Ixxter said, "No. They have hostages they're gonna kill if the tomb isn't opened before some meeting."

Evalle jumped up. "What? Who did they take as hostages?"

Ixxter stood and looked like he was a second from shifting.

Tristan barked out, "Don't, Ixxter!"

Ixxter turned a deadly glare on Tristan, who met it and let Ixxter see what he'd be up against if he made the wrong move.

For someone who took forever to give up intel, Ixxter was quick to accept who was top alpha right now. He grumbled, "You don't want me shifting, then don't yell at me. I just had enough electricity shot through me to light up this damn city. I didn't cause any of this."

"You're right," Evalle said, lifting her hand in surrender. "I'm sorry I shouted. I'm not upset with you. I just need to know who the hostages are and where the tomb is."

"Okay, okay. Chill for a second and I'll tell you what I know."

Tristan rolled his eyes. Hadn't they been asking that since this started? He calmly asked, "Can you give us a run down in order of how it happened?"

Ixxter's brow creased with concentration. "I saw you tailing me so I dumped you." He peeked up at Tristan then continued. "I just need some time to do what I wanted to do. I put on sunglasses and went to a strip bar near downtown." He paused, eyebrows drawing together. "Bastards broke my glasses. Anyhow, I shook your tail, but not two guys who had been following me since I showed up in Piedmont Park."

Tristan had Daegan intentionally drop Ixxter in the park. Based on all the attacks in that area, Tristan and Daegan figured their enemy would have eyes on the park. Ixxter had been put right in their hands. Tristan felt bad about that after how he'd found the Alterant.

Ixxter said, "I knew those two stalking me were Beladors so I figured I was busted. Wearing sunglasses in a dark bar pretty much screams Alterant to any nonhuman aware of us. But nothing happened until I walked out of the strip joint. They cornered me and offered me an opportunity. Said I could make a lot of money if I helped them. Be set forever."

Had Ixxter believed that? Tristan hoped not. "What did they want you to do?"

"Convince Beladors to join them. They knew Macha was gone and Queen Maeve is pissed at us. They said if I helped them find the Belador who sealed that tomb, I could ask for anything I wanted. Sounded pretty good, but I didn't have any idea who buried a body in it."

"What'd you do then?" Tristan asked, wondering if Ixxter had considered swapping sides.

"I told them to show me what they had. They put me in that white van where I couldn't see anything and took me to their camp."

"But you could have escaped at that point," Evalle pointed out.

"Oh, sure. They were just Beladors. They couldn't stop me if I wanted out," he boasted.

Tristan pushed them back on track, needing to figure out where this Alterant stood. "So why'd you go with them?"

Ixxter looked at him with hard green eyes. "How'd you find me in that hangar?"

No point in lying to him. Tristan explained, "We were following you."

"Why? I mean, I'm glad, but why?"

Tristan exchanged a look with Evalle. She said, "We're running out of time on that body."

He sighed and laid it out for Ixxter. "We suspected Beladors were being recruited by an enemy. Some have played a role in recent killings. We had to be proactive about being sure who is on our side or not."

"Huh." Ixxter didn't look pleased. "So you thought I was going to the other side? A traitor. Why? Because I hate being on Treoir? I admit that, but it doesn't mean I'm the enemy."

Evalle raked her hand over her wet hair. "We know. I'm sorry we had to doubt you, but you've proven yourself today and we'll be the first to tell Daegan that you held firm."

"I didn't say I was going back to Treoir," Ixxter countered, still not happy with them.

At one time, Tristan had sounded much like Ixxter, and the bottom line was, he'd been disillusioned by everyone and everything. He wouldn't have lifted a finger to help a Belador, but Evalle had stepped in to save his bacon more than once.

Now Daegan was ready to face off against every power out there for his people.

Tristan had found a home and, by the gods, he was not allowing anyone to destroy it without a fight. But fighting Ixxter was not going to move this along.

"Listen, Ixxter, I know it sucks to have people not trust you. Having people doubt you is the pits. I've been there. But think about it. You didn't give us a lot of reason to believe in you. Consider this a test that you passed. You can piss and moan about the injustice of it, but we live in a world where nothing is as it seems. We have to know who we can depend on."

Evalle blinked in surprise then she said, "Uh, what he said. I can understand if you're angry, but we're glad to know you're on our side. Right now though, we need to know who they have for hostages. What else can you tell us?"

"Not much." Ixxter sounded weary, as if the fight had drained out of him. "They took me to this camp. The man in charge was not Belador."

"Really?" Evalle looked ready to leap. "Who or what was he?"

"They called him sir, so I don't have a name, and I can't tell you what he was. He didn't have the powers that the Beladors had, but every one of them jumped to do what he said. Big guy, but not as big as me. More like Tristan's size." Ixxter's eyes laughed in Tristan's direction.

"Whatever." Tristan waved him on. "Keep going."

"They took me to this tomb and told me to give it a go. To see if I could open it. I tried to hammer a kinetic hit on it. I chipped the marble. Gave me a freaking headache from hell for about ten minutes. I told them that was it, the only trick I had in my bag. The head guy demanded the name of the Belador who could open it and I told them I didn't know. He got pissed and told his men to take me to where they could get the answers he needed."

"Why didn't you leave then?" Evalle asked.

"Hell, I thought I'd stay with them until I had no choice but to go, then I'd have something to tell the Beladors." Ixxter turned his blazing gaze on Tristan. "I was thinking I could use it to prove I've got more value than using me as a drone on an island. I hate living there, but I'm not human and I'm also not stupid. I wanted a way to work here in the human world. That was a no-brainer. Just convince everyone I could do what you and Evalle do."

Man, this new job sucked, but Tristan couldn't go backwards now. "I hear you. Now's not the time, but we'll talk."

"If you knew Tristan was following you, why didn't you use telepathy at the hangar, Ixxter?"

"I tried. They had a spell hanging over that space and had to use mobile phones themselves."

Evalle huffed out a sound that let everyone know she was out of patience. "What about the hostages? Were they Beladors? What'd they look like?"

Ixxter stared off, thinking. "Two young guys."

"Anything else? Tall, short, hair color?"

"Good looking, about seventeen or eighteen. Identical twins. One in a black pullover and the other in a red one."

Evalle grabbed Ixxter's shoulder. "Blond twins?"

"Yeah. One of them called the other one Karlo or Kardo, something like that."

"Kardos?"

"That's it. The other one was Kellman. That Kardos gave the men lip and got a busted lip in return."

Evalle mumbled to herself, "Why would they take those

boys?"

Ixxter said, "They said they wanted a gryphon, but they had me so I didn't understand that."

Her head popped up. "They were looking for me. Those boys are friends of mine. They live in my house. That's it. I'm contacting Trey."

"Wait." Tristan grabbed her arm. He told Ixxter, "Give us a minute." Then he led her to the side.

When they had privacy, Tristan said, "Why call Trey?"

"To tell him to get in touch with Daegan. We have to go get those boys. He's our leader. We need him to help with this."

Tristan couldn't tell Evalle what Daegan had shared with him about the ring that would protect Daegan and his family. Neither would Tristan put Daegan's life in jeopardy by bringing him to the human realm when it might not be necessary.

He suggested, "Let's not do that."

She got up in his face. "I'm not letting those boys die because of getting caught up in our Belador conflicts."

"When did I say to let them die?" Tristan argued.

That stopped her short. She seemed at a loss for what to say in reply so Tristan explained, "We can't just go to Daegan without solid intel. They could be in Athens or Blairsville and we don't have it narrowed down any more than that yet. What would be faster? Me and you pinning down the location or bringing in a bunch of Beladors who might alert the enemy and cause them to move?"

She scrunched her face, working on her answer. "I can't believe I'm going to say this, but you're right. What's your plan?"

"First we find them and scout the situation so we'll know what we need before we call in support. That way, we'll know how to cover all the exits."

"How do we find them?"

Tristan called over to Ixxter, "You know anything else about the camp?"

"No."

Tristan asked Evalle, "Did you see a phone laying around where we found Ixxter?"

"No, why would I if everyone has telepathy?"

"I gave him a phone."

She looked incredulous. "Why didn't you say so? We could have had Trey triangulate his location."

"For one thing, Trey wasn't part of our roundtable meeting. For another, I tried calling Ixxter a couple times after he shook me off his trail, but he didn't answer so I don't know if he still has the phone. But if we hadn't found him when we did, contacting Trey was my next move."

Tristan walked back over to Ixxter with Evalle right behind him. "You got the phone I gave you before you left Treoir, Ixxter?"

"Yes. It's in my boot. They weren't smart enough to take my boots off." He grinned as if that was some major accomplishment.

"Give me the phone."

Ixxter's face fell from amused to suspicious. "Why?"

"I set it up so it could track your movements. It has a tracking program that should show any spots the satellite was able to pick up to form a route of where you've been. We might be able to narrow down the camp's location with it."

Ixxter puffed up. "You son of a bitch."

Tristan said, "What? I told you I'd been following you. First off, if we can't find you, we can't pull you out of trouble, which we just did. But didn't I just explain how we had to confirm that you were on our team?"

"I guess."

"Damn, Ixxter. You just want to fight all the time."

Ixxter scratched his bristly beard. "That's actually true."

"You need counseling."

Ixxter's green eyes glowed, which meant he was one wrong word away from breaking out gryphon whoop-ass.

Tristan suggested, "Or maybe we need to set up some boxing or wrestling matches so you and the others can burn off some aggression." When Ixxter settled down, Tristan returned to the problem at hand. He had a chance to regain the tomb and find out who was behind all of this, but he couldn't do it alone.

He told Evalle, "Let's get Ixxter somewhere safe so he can heal, then you and I can confirm the exact location of the tomb and hostages. Once we know that, we'll have something to work with."

When she hesitated, he said, "Change your mind, Evalle?"

She let out a sound of pure frustration. "Hell, no. I'm going after those boys, but the minute we find them we have to call in the cavalry. I promised Storm I wouldn't go racing into danger."

Tristan did not see her issue. She was one of the deadliest warriors he'd ever met. He kept it simple by saying, "Where's the danger in confirming intel? Besides, you told everyone you'd take a partner. Daegan put us together, so I'm your partner. Besides, when'd you become so fragile?"

She snarled at that.

Heh. He'd hit that nail dead-square and went for his closing argument. "There's always a potential for danger when we deal with preternaturals, but if you and I run into any trouble, I'll teleport us away."

That must have been all she needed to hear. She said, "I'll text him what we're doing. He won't get it until he shifts back from his jaguar form. Let's go."

Tristan kept his smile hidden inside. He did like getting his way, and his way included watching Daegan's back. He'd been honest about teleporting away from trouble, but he might have shaded the truth a little about his intentions.

He and Evalle had fought together in the past. They'd been a tough team to beat. Where was the problem?

He'd get Ixxter dropped off somewhere safe, then he'd handle this issue himself.

If Daegan was going to trust Tristan with being his right hand man, then Tristan was going to step up and show Daegan that his trust had not been misplaced.

Tristan was not about to take this problem to Daegan and put the dragon in a dangerous situation by asking him to come to the human world.

Not when two of Treoir's gryphons could handle this.

Storm knew what he was getting into when he mated Evalle. She was nobody's little woman. Storm had to trust her Belador teammates to watch her back just as she watched theirs.

Tristan gave Ixxter his phone back. "I'm going to let you use a hotel room I keep in town. It's not far so we can walk."

Ixxter's face widened with a full grin. "Now we're talking."

Tristan warned, "Keep your head down and out of sight once you get there. The hotel belongs to a troll. We're friends. Screw that up and you'll end up troll dinner."

Ixxter grumbled to himself and limped for the roof access door.

Evalle said, "Let's do this. Storm will totally understand me going after the boys."

"But is he going to ground you if you stay out past your curfew?" Tristan teased.

She shook her head, following Ixxter out, but sent a last shot over her shoulder. "You wish you had what we have. They say jealousy is an illness. Get well soon."

Tristan hated when Evalle had a point.

A human woman who held Tristan's heart in her hands came to mind. She even knew he was not human. He had to carve out time for Mac soon and he would, once Daegan's security was in place.

He smiled to himself. He couldn't wait to see Storm's face when they returned from this *recon* trip.

CHAPTER 23

Adrianna had been holding her umbrella against the drizzle, but in the last few minutes the freaky weather had taken a sudden turn. The cool change finally seemed more like winter. The rain had stopped and the temperature now felt closer to fifty. She pulled her umbrella down and closed the spines.

Hard enough to see at night without still having to dodge water puddles, but she'd take that over being wet from head to toe.

She walked up to her house in the quiet, reserved area around Emory University. She'd chosen this stone-and-brick home built sixty years ago because it had hummed with happiness when she'd first walked in to view it. She'd purchased it just this year.

She distinctly remembered the front porch being just as cozy looking when she left this morning, but without the man sitting on her porch swing.

That was new.

Isak had a streak of determination a mile wide.

"What are you doing here?" she asked as she climbed the steps.

He stood. "My men refuse to snatch you off the street again, after you turned their tires into stone. I almost had a mutiny."

She'd wanted to send Isak a message that she was not someone to kidnap and to remind him she belonged to the club of other, strange, nonhuman, *it*.

After all that, she should have found a way to squash this attraction—on her part at least.

When she said nothing to his explanation for not sending a

black ops team out for her, he walked over with his usual swagger. He had a confident stride and, to her detriment, she was drawn to that.

He touched her face with his fingers, gently moving them to push her hair over her shoulder. "Why are you avoiding me? I only want to take you to dinner."

She wanted to have dinner with a man. She'd like to do a lot more with this one, but deep down she knew this could be the one who would destroy her.

Not because he would stray. Isak would never be a man who cheated on a woman.

He would bring flowers and romance her.

She had the feeling that his focus would reach a new level while making love.

No, she couldn't fault him for his moral character or his attention, but he was human.

One day, he would look at her as a person on the wrong side of the human-not-human continuum.

"Isak, I don't live in your world."

"You could."

Those fingers of his were slowly severing every reason she had for staying away from him. If she didn't stop him soon, this would end up in the wrong place.

Her bed.

Taking a side step, she offered, "Would you like to come in for tea?"

"Sure."

She unlocked the door, then cleared a ward that he couldn't see, but would notice when it threw him backwards. She left the umbrella on the porch and dropped her purse on the side table.

He closed the door and said, "This fits you."

She'd just crossed the living room to the kitchen. The remodeling had turned this part of the downstairs into one large great room. "What do you mean this *fits* me?" If he said it was strange and unusual, she'd boot him out the door on her own, no majik needed.

"It's feminine without being frilly. It's attractive and has a sincere air to it." He placed his phone on the side table and strode across the room as he spoke, pausing only inches from her.

That was nice. He was nice. That wasn't the issue.

Toying with her hair, he asked, "Why are you so opposed to spending time with me?"

He was killing her the longer he touched her so tenderly. She had to put a stop to this. The best way to do that was by addressing their issue head on.

"Isak, you will never get over your prejudice against nonhumans, so we have nowhere to go. I don't want to get involved with someone who is—"

"Closed-minded?"

Those had been the next words she planned to say. Now, she wanted to smooth it over. But that would be counterproductive so she said, "Yes."

He argued, "I'm not running around killing all nonhumans anymore and you have to admit not all are good ones. I didn't kill Evalle the first time I found out she was an Alterant and I was actively hunting them."

"The way I heard the story, she used her kinetics to save Kit's life and still, Kit had to stop you from shooting Evalle with your blaster."

"Okay, that might have been a bad example," he admitted.

She found his honesty under fire adorable, but telling him so would not help her case. Since he'd brought up Evalle, Adrianna pointed out, "You were also attracted to Evalle. Now you want me to believe you're attracted to me?"

He pulled her to him and lowered his head until they almost touched noses.

She had trouble breathing.

Isak explained, "I'd never met anyone like Evalle who knew about demons. Sure, I found her intriguing, but ... you're different. If I had really wanted to be with Evalle, I wouldn't have given Storm a chance to get in the picture. I think about you day and night. If a man looks at you, I can't think about anything except bundling you off to keep you away from all of them. I want to get to know you, to find out what makes you happy, what movies you watch, where you'd like to go for a vacation, anything and everything. From the minute I saw you, I admit that I tried not to pay attention."

She'd been mesmerized until then. He lost points admitting

that he hadn't wanted anything to do with a witch.

"But you aren't someone to be ignored. You draw my eyes the minute you're in a room. You're a woman that appeals to me in every way. I'll never meet anyone else like you and I know it."

Okay, his points were going back up.

But there was still the issue that would never go away. She sighed and said, "We can't—"

He moved with stealth and kissed her, tasting her and sending his tongue in for a hello.

Unfair tactics.

How was she supposed to think and maintain her control when he ... his hand scooped her up to him. She gripped his arms, strictly for support since he had her off balance.

Very off balance.

His mouth would not give up, but then who liked a quitter?

Isak snaked his other arm around her and lifted. That brought her up against him and left zero confusion about how much he wanted her.

Her body was not helping one bit. Her breasts ached. She rubbed against his chest. Nice, but not exactly what she needed.

He moved a hand to the closest breast and cupped her.

She felt that touch in her womb.

This wasn't her first rodeo with a man, but it felt like the first time one had made it past the surface of her emotions. Touching Isak wasn't in the same category as touching other men. She loved his strength and she'd always found confidence in a man a huge turn-on.

Was she really going to take this step?

Breaking the kiss, she watched his face when he pulled back. She touched his lips with a finger, drawing it across the perfect shape. "This is not something I can do lightly, Isak."

"I know that without you saying so."

Still, she hesitated. "My friends are always going to include nonhumans."

"That's probably a good thing since it seems I now have a few myself." He smiled and her heart did a spin.

How could she deny him when he'd removed the one real barrier between them? She didn't expect a commitment of love before sleeping with him, but she was not frivolous with her body, or her emotions.

Maybe over the years she'd been forced to keep her emotions locked down while she channeled the pain of her twin sister who'd been in captivity, she'd forgotten how to open up. Her sister was no longer in pain, no longer of this world.

Adrianna took a breath and stepped off the cliff. "Yes."

"Yes, as in yes we can have dinner?"

"Yes, as in we can ... do more than that."

He picked her up and carried her to the sofa.

She said, "Are you going to go caveman on me?"

"Depends. Do you like it?"

He lowered her to the sofa and eased down next to her. His hands pulled her blouse from her pants. "I love how you dress so prim and proper." He smiled at her with so much warmth. "It's like a live fantasy, because I can feel the passion you hide beneath that pristine look."

When his fingers reached her breasts, she had to catch her breath.

"You're beautiful, but that's not what makes you special." He leaned down and kissed the mound of breast pushed up by her red lace bra.

She let her breath out on a sigh. That felt *so* good.

He kept kissing her, pausing only to say, "You're special because no other woman is your equal. No other woman can hold a candle to your bright light."

His fingers had unzipped her pants and eased in.

She had to be careful or her majik would slip from her grip.

"I want to see you let go of all that control you hold close."

Maybe not if he knew what it would be like if she did let go.

His phone buzzed.

Isak didn't so much as look toward the phone. He was too busy reaching inside her lace panties to touch her ... oh, yes. Right there.

He kissed her breasts through the bra and she thought about using majik to get rid of the barrier.

His phone played an announcement *"Isak, Code Red. Repeat, this is Code Red."*

CHAPTER 24

Evalle silently cursed Tristan as she clawed her way down the mud-slick wall of a hundred-foot-deep, abandoned open-pit mine in north Georgia. Close to Blairsville, which confirmed some of Ixxter's information. The endless rain had stopped in Atlanta, but not here. Rain came down in earnest, cutting little rivers into the dirt and clay sides of this wall. She'd need two showers to get all the mud off of her.

Teleporting meant they had arrived in Blairsville by midnight, but she took points off for navigation.

Tristan had landed them five miles away.

The relentless rain had been drizzling there, but the closer the closer they got to this chasm, the more the rain seemed localized to this spot.

She paused to catch her breath and scope out the dirt chasm below them. There were grooves cut into it from strip mining, but trees had clearly been growing since excavation work had ceased. Fifteen or twenty years old now, the trees had sprouted along rutted pathways that ran into a fog covering all but this end.

How could fog hang there with the rain still falling?

Maybe because none of this was natural.

Any other time, she might enjoy visiting this area of north Georgia with Storm, but right now she wanted to choke Tristan for doing the man thing. Once he'd downloaded information from Ixxter's phone onto a computer at the hotel, Evalle suggested they consult a map for the best place to teleport in.

Tristan had snapped the device shut and declared, "No, I've

got this."

Oh, yes, he had this.

"Stop thinking so loud," Tristan muttered, ten feet to her left.

"You can't hear my thoughts unless we use telepathy."

"I don't need telepathy to know you're thinking of ways to dismantle my body," he smarted back.

"True, but I'll add that to my list of payback. Your teleporting navigation needs work."

"Hey. This part of Georgia is a new area for me. What are you complaining about? I landed us in a baseball field. Wouldn't you rather have that than a grove of trees or *on* the side of this hill?"

"Did you consider that if the field hadn't been a giant soggy mess, we probably would have landed in the middle of a live baseball game?"

Silence was the same as a no in her book.

Her hand slipped. She sucked in a fast breath and her heart had its own little cardio workout.

She immediately thought about almost falling off another mountain, and not that long ago.

Storm hadn't been happy the night he'd found her dangling off the side of Stone Mountain. She hated heights and hadn't been any happier about it herself after a demon had knocked her out of a cable car. But she and Storm were learning how to live together, which meant communicating.

Not her strong point.

Her uber-protective mate had agreed not to interfere when she had a job to do and she'd agreed not to take unnecessary risks.

Technically, this was still a recon trip, but showing up at home without significant damage would mean not having to explain any of this.

To do that, she needed to hang on, climb down and avoid getting bloody.

She could heal broken bones, but investigating unknown beings with powers meant she'd be at the mercy of the enemy if they walked up while she was healing.

If not for Tristan convincing her they needed to conserve their power, she'd have used kinetics to flip her way down this slope.

Speaking of Tristan, he'd watch her back, but he had his own limits.

She'd only agreed to gain the intel they needed for formulating a plan to rescue the hostages. The minute they had a plan, she'd call in Quinn and let him run the show. Trey or Quinn would reach out to Tzader, since those were the only two who now had a direct telepathic line to him in the Treoir realm.

That was better than in the past, when trying to contact someone there meant sending Tzader in holographic form. Or going through Brina, which meant Macha might have been privy to the conversation.

The angle of descent changed so she could put more weight on her feet. As soon as she managed to stand up straight, she turned to figure out how close they were to the bottom of the mining pit.

Rain dumped harder now, streaking the lenses of her special sunglasses.

Lightning and thunder rocked the skies.

Huh, that was the first time there'd been any of *that* with the rain, which made it feel a little more natural.

Was this four straight days of rain now?

No, it was actually closer to five. She'd dismiss it as one of those unexplained Georgia weather events, but her noisy instincts kept saying that the unnatural fog below had to be tied to the rain.

Those instincts had been right too many times to dismiss.

The only positive was that the inclement weather could be confirmation that they were in the right place.

Sidestepping to reach a spot where they could almost stand, Tristan whispered, "That wasn't so bad."

She didn't look at him. "You don't want me to answer that."

"Give me a break."

"Give *you* a break?" She arched her neck to look him in the face. "You have no sense of direction. You landed us five miles away and way the hell up there." She pointed above her head. "You know I hate heights."

"Don't be a baby. Not like you wouldn't survive a fall. I got us close."

"Teleporting down here would have been close."

"To do it again so soon would have required linking. Thought we agreed to save that for an emergency." When she waved off his comment, Tristan looked to the skies as if he were begging for patience.

Good luck with that.

He wiped a hand over his mouth and returned to business. "It's all good. We'll have to be quiet in case we walk up on someone." Then he switched to telepathy. *In fact, why are we talking when we can be silent?*

She glared at him and answered in an audible whisper. "Because the men we fought in Atlanta have telepathy, and it wasn't private when it should have been. We have no idea if they can pick up our conversation or if the person behind all this can. Don't you remember the first time Daegan heard a private telepathic conversation between you and me?"

"Well, sure, but ... that was Daegan."

"Does that mean he's the only special snowflake who can do that?"

Clearly short on comebacks, he looked around. "Let's get moving and find the tomb."

Typical Tristan.

Then he said, "Yes, he is a special snowflake."

Evalle had spent a lot of time in tight situations with Tristan. He wasn't acting like the person she'd known for so long. Don't get her wrong. This was a huge improvement over the Tristan who'd hated anything to do with Beladors at one time.

She prodded him. "What's going on with you, Tristan? I'm not complaining, but you've changed."

He kept walking, leaving her question behind.

"Let me put it this way. I need to know why you're doing this."

That got to him, because he stopped. "What are you asking me, Evalle?"

"Something is off about all this. Why the change in attitude? We're all glad to have Daegan, but you've done a complete about-face. I feel like you're hiding something from me and I'm trying to trust you. Flip that freaking chip off your shoulder and talk to me. Tell me what you really plan to do."

He muttered a nasty curse. "You want the truth? Fine. I was shunted around like yesterday's leftovers as a kid, then my mother sold me to a fucking witch who tried to kill me and my foster sister. Petrina and I managed to escape that, only for me to end up captured by the Beladors and locked away in a jungle prison for four years just because I was born an Alterant."

Other than the jungle imprisonment, she hadn't known any of that and waited silently to see where he was going with this.

"I don't fault you for the times you tried to bring me in to join up with the Beladors. I know your heart was in the right place, but the next thing I know I'm a Medb prisoner who's compelled to do freaking Queen Flaevynn's bidding. When you asked me to help free a dragon throne from TÅµr Medb, I'd made my mind up to do that, then I was done. I had intended to leave with Petrina and my two friends."

He meant two Rías, beings who were similar to Alterants, but not as powerful and, as far as she knew, they wouldn't evolve into gryphons.

She shouldn't be surprised, but hearing him say he'd been ready to cut and run still bothered her. She'd gotten a sucky start to life. Tristan's hadn't been any better.

He breathed in and out while studying the trees around them. After a moment he said, "Then Daegan shifted into a dragon larger than any of our gryphon forms and stepped up to defend us. That ... hell, that shocked me. Next thing I know, he boots that bitch, Macha, off Treoir. He kicked a freaking goddess off the island. I didn't think that was even possible."

"Me either," she admitted.

"But damn if he didn't," Tristan said with no small amount of admiration in his voice. "Daegan flew around the island with me like we were equal or something."

Evalle couldn't stop her smile. It was good to see Tristan being shown his worth.

"I wasn't sure what to think or what I was going to do at that point," Tristan admitted. "Before Macha left, when she threatened Alterants with withdrawing her support for us to be treated as a recognized race, I thought, *here we go again*. But then Daegan laughed in her face and said we didn't need her or some spineless Tribunal to grant us the freedom we were born with." He shook his head at some inner thought.

"That hit home. It felt incredible," Evalle agreed, understanding exactly what he was feeling. She'd felt truly free at that moment.

"It did. I stuck around more out of curiosity at that point than anything." He chuckled softly, "Well, that and because I wasn't sure Daegan wouldn't torch my ass the minute I tried to leave. You want to know why I'm doing this? This is what he sent me to do. I am not going back to Daegan without solid information on what's going on. Okay? Now can we get this done or not?"

Something niggled at her that Tristan was still not telling her everything.

Pushing Tristan too hard would get her nowhere. She said, "I didn't see any lights down there when we were up top, but since we're depending on your infallible sense of direction, lead away, Mr. *Rí Dtús.*"

Ignoring her jab, Tristan took off.

She followed his steps, except his steps were quieter than her trudging. She was not meant for the woods. Give her an urban setting any time. She checked around them constantly and behind to protect their backs. In this miserable weather, the area was as black as the hole it truly was. If not for her sensitive eyesight she'd be blind here.

After a few minutes, they entered the fog-covered area. It was damp, but no rain fell. The whole area hummed, not loudly, but steadily. Not exactly like the buzzing in Atlanta. This was...heavier. Different.

Continuing on, she'd walked a hundred yards through narrow patches of trees when a flicker of light came into view. She touched Tristan's shoulder.

He turned halfway, whispering, "Saw it."

Letting go, she followed as he moved in closer. As the woods thinned, she split away from Tristan to find a tree thick enough to hide behind. She'd stopped too far back to get a good read on the barren area beyond their skimpy woods.

Even though the rain had ended, mist from the fog coated her sunglasses. While she removed them to clean the lenses, she squinted at the scene taking shape with two tents. The glow on the other side probably came from a fire pit.

Ambient night lighting didn't bother her sensitive eyes, but staring straight at any bright light without protection would practically blind her.

Tristan would be able to see just as well at night, but he'd gotten lucky. He didn't have to wear specially made sunglasses nor would he turn into a crispy critter if he stepped into the sun.

Guess I'm just special like that.

Still, this life was far better than the one she'd lived locked in a basement for the first eighteen years of her life.

She moved to another tree. The corner of a marble structure came into view in a gap between the tents. That could only be the tomb. It sat on the far side of the camp, but she could tell the base was out of shape. She needed a better vantage point for a clear view of the tomb and the rest of the camp.

Squatting down, she worked over to her left, moving to where Tristan had taken up a position. When she got to him, Evalle stood up and whispered, "See the tomb?"

When he nodded yes, she asked, "Can you get a good look at the bottom half? It looks like they've padded it with something."

"Looks to me like hostages are tied to the tomb."

Shit. Evalle stared at it again and realized one blob was moving. Tristan was right. "Oh, hell. That's Kit, a friend of mine, with the boys. What's she doing here?"

"Have no idea. I say we go get them while we can."

She felt the same way, but did this qualify as rushing into danger? Probably.

How could she go in there and face Storm later?

How could she walk away and risk losing her friends, and face *herself* later?

She suggested, "Maybe we should keep an eye on them and contact Quinn. That's what the plan was when we came here."

"I'm surprised we didn't run into a patrol of some sort already. If too many people show up, that group will scatter. If that happens, they might have someone teleport the tomb, and the hostages, to another location. Then where will we be?"

She suffered another wave of suspicion that she'd been unable to shake even after Tristan answered her earlier questions.

This gung-ho drive to take on the enemy now without waiting for backup was beginning to sound as if it had been Tristan's plan all along. She'd battled alongside Tristan. He could hold up his end of a fight, but this charging forward attitude had never been his MO.

She asked, "Why are you willing to go in there for three humans you don't know?"

Tristan didn't look her way. "Now I *am* insulted."

If she knew one thing about Tristan, it was the way he'd deflect when he didn't want to answer something.

Not this time. She asked, "Why, Tristan?"

He glared at her. "Why does it surprise you when I do the right thing?"

He had her there, but suspicion still ran rampant in her gut. She kept her voice quiet, but persisted in finding out what was driving him. Why wasn't he ready to call in their badass dragon?

Evalle watched for any movement in the camp, but nothing stirred. They needed to wait long enough to know what they were up against.

Tristan rarely spoke his mind. He'd shared more about himself earlier than she'd ever gotten from him.

She wanted to trust his ideas, but she couldn't risk the safety of those three hostages on some ulterior motive driving her partner.

"Come on, Tristan. If this is insulting, I'm sorry, because that's not my intention, but in the past you would have said we got the intel, our job's done, let's go. I like this side of you, but—"

"You don't trust it," he said in a tone that dumped a load of guilt on her.

She was jeopardizing the agreement she'd made with Storm this morning and had three lives hinging on what she and Tristan did. Tough shit if it pissed him off. She needed to get rid of this suspicion grinding at her.

Trying again, she said, "I've learned that you always have a reason for your actions. In the past, your reasons leaned more toward self-preservation than sacrifice."

He leaned against a tree, watching the camp. "You may have a point."

"Is this about the position Daegan gave you? He doesn't expect you to fight these battles without him."

The struggle to explain ravaged his face. He finally let out a deep breath. "Like I said earlier, things *have* changed. I flew with Daegan his first day on the island," Tristan said. "We landed at one point and he told me he meant what he'd said. That I was free to leave whenever I wanted. He said he needed dependable and capable warriors like me, but he'd understand if I couldn't stay." His Adam's apple bobbed with a hard swallow. Tristan lifted his head and met her gaze. "No one had ever given me a choice. Not once in my life. Daegan did that, then he made me his right hand man. I ... "

Evalle smiled at him. "That kind of faith is humbling."

"I guess so."

"I hear you, Tristan, and I get where you're at, but now I'm even more concerned with why you aren't bringing Daegan in on this. He sees you as his general and would expect you to confer with him."

Turning to lean his shoulder against the tree, he said, "Here's the deal. I can't betray his trust so I'm not going to tell you what he told me, but you'll have to trust me when I say that our first duty is to protect the Treoirs. That being the case, we'd be putting Daegan in a seriously bad situation if we call him here to help."

Whoa. That was not what she expected.

Tristan quieted, clearly waiting to see if she'd give him that blanket trust.

Hadn't she asked him for similar trust at one time when she'd been trying to do right by the Alterants? After he'd escaped the jungle, she'd once asked Tristan to walk into a meeting with Macha, the same person responsible for locking him away for four long years.

Now was the time for her to show she could give what Tristan needed from her if she had any hope for this new look being a permanent change for Tristan.

But she had to stick to her agreement with Storm, too. "Here's my deal, Tristan, and I'm in no mood for wisecracks. If you can't work with me, then I'm calling in everyone, which means Daegan will end up here."

Tristan stood away from the tree. "I'm listening."

"Storm and I have a relationship built on respect. He isn't comfortable with the work I do, but he knows it's part of me and I need freedom to make my own decisions. That being said, we both agreed not to race into danger. I want to get Kit and the boys out of there. Give me a workable plan. If I agree, we'll do it."

"We have to get to a better position to execute it, but my plan is so simple and foolproof you're going to be disappointed you didn't come up with it yourself."

Famous last words.

CHAPTER 25

Witchlock energy churned happily in Adrianna's hand, which she kept hidden inside the deep sleeve of her black rain poncho. She'd almost grabbed a leather jacket instead, but something told her not to trust the weather even though the night had been clear and was getting cooler when she left home.

Good thing she'd worn the poncho, since rain was falling again up here south of Blairsville. Her sixth sense now warned her that the thunderstorm meant they were getting closer to the enemy.

Gently calling up her Witchlock power allowed her to see at night without special gear.

That was a new trick she'd figured out just a week ago.

She'd taken possession of the ancient energy a while back, but she couldn't say it was entirely under her control, which was why she had serious concerns about wielding much of it for anything less than a critical situation.

But if the lummox leading her through the woods pissed her off one more time, she might just find out how far she could send him into another realm.

Covered in enough muscle to carry a car on his back, Isak *still* managed to move through the dark woods as silently as a predator natural to this terrain. She did her best, but every so often she'd step on a twig and Isak would freeze. He was a bundle of raw anger, and looking for a place to unleash it.

In fact, if he didn't need her, she wouldn't be on this field trip.

He stopped so quickly she had to slap her hands on his back to keep from ramming into him.

She mumbled, "Sorry."

Backing up a step was out of the question, because she'd repeat whatever noise she'd just made that only he could hear. Doing it twice would be illogical.

They'd hiked in from where he'd left his Hummer near a lake, then walked north toward a mining ravine geographically between them and the city of Blairsville. Hiking she could take, but this climbed down a muddy, waterlogged descent had strained her team spirit. She'd suggested they take the nice wide paths left from some machine that had cleared away trees.

He'd dismissed that suggestion without a second thought and told her to stick to the wooded areas. So much for team spirit on his part.

Isak took a step forward and turned, smooth as butter, blast his sexy hide.

She looked up at him through the water drizzling off the brim of her floppy rain cap. Also all in black, he looked like Rambo on steroids. He flipped up the monocular that gave him a cyborg appearance.

When he spoke, he kept his voice low, but the anger from an hour ago was still there. "If they hear us first, we're dead. That's how it works in *my* world."

And there it was again.

He just had to poke at her for not being human. She'd avoided using any overt majik around him to avoid setting him off, but she was tired of tiptoeing around the giant issue that sat between them. The one she'd warned him about and he'd declared they could get past.

Her heart had pulled in on itself, trying to heal the wound he'd caused the minute he discovered what had happened to his mother. He'd started shouting obscenities about nonhumans and how he'd kill them all if anything happened to Kit.

Traveling after that had been awkward. Adrianna had attempted to calm him and he'd ducked away from her hands. Cold had settled in her chest.

She reminded him, "I said I could cloak us."

"Don't use that shit on me."

She didn't flinch, but that stung. "Fine. I'll use it on me. Will that make you happy?"

"Getting my mother safely out of this crapfest is the only thing that's going to make me anywhere close to happy."

She would not allow him to see how much his attitude cut her to the bone. She hadn't been behind the kidnapping, but that didn't matter in Isak's mind.

He saw anyone who had any nonhuman ability as the other team. Not his team.

Why had she let him convince her they could be together?

Because deep down she'd wanted to believe she could have one normal thing in her life. That she could date a man who saw only her and had no interest in her power. Well, she'd gotten the *no interest in her power* part right.

He wiped a rough hand over his face, removing a layer of water.

If the supernatural quality of this incessant rain continued after tonight, she'd spend time researching how to stop it. Even better if she could figure out how to use Witchlock to send it west for the people in drought-stricken states who were desperate for any rain.

Lighting sparked in the sky. That was different.

Looking around, anywhere but at her, Isak asked, "How am I going to find you if you go invisible?"

"I won't be invisible. I'll be cloaking myself from view."

He rolled his hand in a "whatever" motion for her to finish explaining.

"I'll be able to see you. All you have to do is lift your hand to motion me to you, or speak. I can hear everything."

He dug into his vest and pulled out a comm unit, which he handed her. "If I have to speak to you, I can't raise my voice."

If I have to speak to you.

She would not think too hard on that or it would punch her heart again. Taking the comm unit, she slid it into place and called up her cloaking.

He took a step back in surprise at her disappearance, but said nothing.

You hardheaded man. Drawing a calming breath so that she sounded in control, she said, "This is me talking to you."

Isak might have tried to hide it, but she caught how he tensed at her softly spoken words. She held her breath, waiting to see if there was a crack in that granite expression.

Nope. He said, "Copy that. Let's move out." He turned and started making tracks again.

After covering another fifty yards, they entered a smoky fog, where the rain stopped. No rain broke through. How could the fog be blocking rain? Humming filled the trees and air. Different from the buzzing that had cloaked a few men in Midtown, and this was a much larger area.

Isak lifted a hand, signaling her to stop. Since she was the queen of quiet right now, she moved up close to see what had caught his attention.

It took a moment to catch the sliver of light dancing through a break in the trees.

That hadn't been obvious from the cliff above the ravine.

In spite of his anger and issues with nonhumans, at least Isak had listened to her warning that the fog hanging over the ravine had an odd quality. She'd suggested scouting the area before he brought in his men and he'd surprised her by agreeing.

Isak's men had contacted him as soon as they'd received a call about someone holding his mother hostage. He'd roared orders rapid fire, telling his men to triangulate Kit's mobile phone and find her.

By the time Adrianna had straightened her clothes and climbed into his truck, his men had triangulated the location of Kit's campsite. They'd found it intact but empty of people, and a note explaining that the kidnappers would negotiate only with an Alterant-gryphon who could unseal a tomb from Oakland Cemetery. Adrianna had withheld as much as she could about Quinn's private situation with Kizira's body, which that tomb had to hold, but she did tell Isak there was a missing body of a witch involved. The kidnappers stipulated that Isak had until three in the morning to contact them or they'd start killing hostages.

One of the twin male witches would be first.

The minute Isak realized this was not a human kidnapper, he'd flat refused to contact anyone with the Beladors except Evalle.

Adrianna hadn't been able to raise Evalle by phone and Isak's men couldn't find her anywhere. Isak wouldn't budge on bringing any of the others in and warned Adrianna against going behind his back.

In his shoes, she'd feel the same way since she trusted few nonhumans, but she would have enough faith in her supernatural friends to figure a way to rescue the hostages.

Isak lacked that faith.

She knew without asking that he believed any nonhumans would put their own interests ahead of humans.

Since Adrianna had no idea where Kit and the twins were being held, she had nothing to share with Quinn. The minute she knew for sure what they were facing, she was calling the Belador leader.

How much more pissed could Isak be with her at that point?

He'd allowed Adrianna to join him only after she'd reminded him that his massive firepower could end up getting Kit and the boys killed, where a spell might be safer.

Oh, he'd wanted to refuse her help, but they both knew he couldn't allow his prejudice and mistrust of all things preternatural to color his decision.

Isak had finally located Kit by a secondary tracking system he'd put in her favorite hiking boots, but the signal stopped at the edge of this ravine. His mother would probably rip him a new one for daring to tag her with a tracking device, but as Isak had said, "She'll be alive to do it."

His men remained half a mile out in a perimeter circling the ravine. Isak headed into what could be a supernatural conflict with the same single-minded determination he'd used against walls Adrianna had tried to keep in place between them.

Those walls had changed now. With every action and comment, he was building them taller and stronger than hers had ever been.

She allowed her senses to roam as she walked, sweeping the area for any scouts the kidnappers might have planted out here to intercept someone who tried to sneak past them.

If the kidnappers were expecting Beladors, their scouts might kill all others.

But did that stop Isak from striding straight into a majik war zone? No.

Adrianna sighed and asked, "What now?"

"We move in slowly and survey the situation," he said, his deep voice barely registering in her ear. The sound raised a longing for something that she should never have allowed herself to believe could happen.

Isak's temper burned fast and hot, but generally dissipated just as quickly. If they managed to get Kit and the boys back to safety, Isak would probably settle down and realize the damage he'd done.

One could hope.

But this changed things for her. He'd disappoint her when he did the same thing again, and he *would* do the same thing again, the next time an issue arose involving nonhumans.

Adrianna stayed even with his progress, but off to the side.

A shadow moved right to left across her vision between where she stood and the light peeking through the woods.

Isak must have seen it too, because he stilled, his only movement a subtle change in position of his demon blaster.

She warned him, "If you shoot anything out here, you'll alert the camp."

He nodded and headed in the direction the shadow had been heading. What did he think he'd do when he faced one of the kidnapper's scouts?

She suggested, "If you'll let me take the lead, I might be able to contain whatever that being is."

His reply was a sharp, "No."

Stupid alpha male.

He wouldn't speak to her during the long drive here, but he still had to play the protector.

She needed her head examined for trying to keep him alive, but Adrianna swept past Isak without him realizing it. She hurried ahead to find out what else was out here.

When she estimated herself to be fifty feet ahead of him, only because she'd practically run and he was gliding slowly in black-ops mode, a sound on her left pulled her up short.

She turned that way.

There were two figures and they'd stopped moving.

What were they doing? Setting a trap?

Following them had drawn her closer to the camp. She took a moment to assess her surroundings. Off to her right, she caught a glimpse of what might be the backside of a tomb positioned next to a tent.

Would that be Kizira's tomb? Evalle had mentioned it when she called Adrianna to update her on the meeting at Treoir. Why had the kidnapper's message referenced a Belador bringing an Alterant?

Or did the kidnappers think just any Belador could open the tomb?

They really needed Quinn here if the negotiation required freeing Kizira's body, which is what Adrianna would bet on if she were one to risk money.

Somehow, she had to convince Isak to rethink this plan or he was going to lose all the hostages, and possibly die at the same time.

She hadn't realized how quickly Isak could move.

He passed her with his blaster raised to eye level, preparing to discharge it.

Adrianna looked at where the two figures were standing and caught the flash of bright green glowing spots. At eye level. Like the eyes of an Alterant.

She ran forward, breaking out of her cloaking as she reached Isak, which startled him.

He swung the weapon on her and she held her hands up. "It's me."

"What the hell, Adrianna?"

"I'm stopping you from killing my friends," Adrianna hissed at him just loud enough to be heard by Tristan and Evalle, who stepped into view.

Isak cursed low but it came through Adrianna's comm unit. He lowered his blaster, letting it hang from the cord on his vest. Flipping up his monocular, he glared at everyone.

Before his control snapped completely, Adrianna whispered a quick spell that cloaked all four of them. She told Isak, "I've cloaked us so we can talk. If you start complaining about majik, I'll boot you out of here and talk to Evalle and Tristan by myself."

His cold eyes could cut her in half, but he nodded.

Evalle gave her a what-the-heck-is-going-on-with-you-two look that Adrianna answered with a brief headshake and mouthed, "Later."

Evalle said, "Isak, this is Tristan. Tristan, this is Isak."

Adrianna had thought they all knew each other, then remembered what Evalle had once told her. Back when Evalle hadn't known Isak long, he'd turned his demon blaster on her, Tristan and two of Tristan's friends.

Isak wouldn't recall that incident because Sen had wiped his memory.

Adrianna would thank Evalle later for not sharing that and saving Isak an aneurysm.

Evalle asked Isak and Adrianna, "Who told you about this?"

Adrianna grimaced. That was not going to help.

Isak's voice turned harder than she'd ever heard it. "You knew about Kit being kidnapped and said nothing?"

"No. One of our people heard about hostages that sounded like the twins who stay at my place. We came out to investigate," Evalle explained. "I saw Kit less than five minutes ago, *after* we got here."

"Kit took them camping. Didn't it occur to you that *she* might be a hostage, too?"

"No one told me about the camping trip," Evalle snapped right back at him. "So no, I didn't consider that possibility. But I'll bet there's a note at home."

When Isak didn't seem placated, Tristan quickly explained, "We just got down here, found the location and determined they do have three hostages, but there's no way to get a message out telepathically or electronically. We can argue over who knew what or we can act."

Adrianna gave Evalle a return look of who-is-this-guy-and-what-happened-to-Tristan.

Evalle muttered, "Later."

A conversation about what was going on with these two men would require copious amounts of wine.

It wasn't clear if Isak agreed with anyone, but he did start talking logistics. "I have a team circling this area. One call and they'll converge."

Adrianna started to argue, but Tristan stepped in again. "Bad idea."

"This is my mission," Isak stated with no room for argument.

Tristan shifted toward Isak and Evalle stepped between them. "I am not standing by and allowing his mother and my boys to be harmed because you two are having a testosterone battle."

"His mother?" Tristan questioned.

"Yes. Kit is Isak's mother, which is why he's close to losing his mind over this."

"I am not," Isak grumbled.

"Yes you are, and I understand," she told him. "But when it comes to battling nonhumans, you're in *our* territory, Isak. If you go in there balls to the wall, you'll get all of them killed."

That failed to break the tension.

Adrianna commented, "Why try to stop him, Evalle? I've always wondered what balls-to-the-wall would look like. It sounds chaotic and disorganized, but hey, I'm not the black-ops, expert soldier here. I'm just one of those nonhumans he's ready to mow down."

Evalle hit Adrianna with an impatient look. "Not helping."

"That's the point. He doesn't want us to help. He doesn't accept that saving Kit and those boys is just as important to us as it is to him. Or maybe he only cares about saving Kit since in his eyes she's the only pure human at risk."

Evalle stepped back, face rocked with disappointment. "Isak?"

CHAPTER 26

Isak glared at Adrianna, but he didn't have supersonic eyes or whatever the hell this bunch had. How was it that she could make him feel lower than a slug when all he wanted to do was get his mother to safety?

He took in Evalle and Tristan.

The looks those two were giving him dropped him down another notch on the food chain. Catching Adrianna's eye first, he said for everyone's benefit, "I want to save *all three* of them. I'm not putting anyone's life above the others."

Even if he was the kind of asshole who would leave two young boys in danger, which he wasn't, Kit would disown him for allowing any harm to come to the pair of street teens she'd taken under her wing.

Adrianna picked a hell of a time to drag their argument out in the open.

"Okay, we're all on the same team," Evalle announced. "Let's form a plan."

Breaking away from Adrianna's frigid gaze, Isak said, "Agreed. I have an idea."

Tristan piped up, "You haven't heard ours yet."

"But I have the ransom note."

"What ransom note?" Evalle asked.

Isak pulled it out for her to read since she had the equivalent of night vision even with her sunglasses on. She told Tristan, "They're demanding a gryphon to open the tomb in exchange for the hostages." Then Evalle turned to Adrianna. "You knew about this?"

Adrianna said, "Before you get upset, I tried to call you but you probably aren't getting cell reception out here."

"Did you call Quinn?"

"No." Adrianna pushed up a hand to stall any further discussion on this. "I agreed not to tell anyone except you when I joined Isak and his team to rescue the hostages. He asked me not to and I would not betray his trust."

Isak heard her unspoken words rattle in his head. *Even though you betrayed mine.*

Damn. Knife right through the gut with that one.

Isak looked at Adrianna, who ignored him. If she'd just risk a peek his way, she'd see the apology sitting on his face.

Not happening. She was doing a great job of pretending he didn't exist.

They'd talk later.

Obviously, his head had climbed up his ass the minute his mother landed in danger, but she was all he had. Protecting her was his job and he'd gotten lax by letting her interact with the supernatural community. He'd let her go off with two witches to camp in the woods and she ended up a hostage of some crazy person with powers that Isak couldn't begin to imagine.

Evalle waved her hands. "I'm good. Let's call a truce on all arguing for now. Agreed?"

"Yes," and two grunts answered her.

Isak looked at his watch. "I have to make contact by oh-three-hundred or they're killing one of the boys.

That sucked the blood from Evalle's face. "Less than two hours from now? No. That's not happening."

"They think I'm getting in touch with Beladors right now so we need to get this plan laid out and in motion."

Tristan said, "That simplifies everything. Let me try my plan first with you two as backup so if it doesn't work they won't know you were a part of it. That still gives you a chance to come in behind us with everything you have in mind. But if you go in first with firepower there's a good chance they'll kill the hostages the minute a shot is fired. They don't want hostages. They want that tomb opened."

Isak frowned. "What's the deal about the tomb?"

Evalle interjected, "You know how you kept radio silence on

us when you were coming here? Well, this is Belador business that we're not discussing with anyone else."

"Damn," Isak groused. "Negotiating a peace treaty between world powers has to be easier than this. Okay, what's your plan, Tristan?"

CHAPTER 27

The damn clock ticked off minutes faster than sand falling through an hourglass.

Quinn had two hours until Sen came to drag his butt to the Tribunal, which he had figured for three this morning. Hard to say what time down to the exact minute when the damn deities were burning the entire length of five-foot-tall candles as a time marker.

He'd dragged Reese around with him while he first tapped his resources, then that of the Beladors and finally Nightstalkers.

He hadn't found the person behind the killings in Atlanta, and he hadn't found the tomb. Out of ideas, he'd brought Reese to an office in a building he owned downtown. He kept one floor just for Belador business and since the rain had stopped earlier in the evening, the temps had dropped. He'd caught her shivering.

He was quickly running out of options for how to protect everyone from family to friends to the entire Belador tribe and their leader.

If he went into the Tribunal meeting with no body, the Tribunal leaders would give Queen Maeve the go-ahead to do with Quinn as she chose. He had no problem with facing her as long as Kizira's body was out of her reach.

He didn't fear dying, but he did fear the possibility of someone with her power accessing his mind and gaining the information he wouldn't give up willingly. Once Queen Maeve had him in her realm, she held the upper hand. She'd strip him of conscious thought and would compel him to turn on his own people.

He shuddered at that possibility.

If the person with the tomb had stolen it to trade with the queen, Quinn would end up opening it and very likely end up forced to watch Kizira stripped of her secrets.

He accepted what he had to do, which was to first retrieve Kizira's tomb from the group that had stolen it before they figured out how to open it then disappear with the body.

That wouldn't happen unless he found the tomb.

He contacted Trey by mobile phone and told him to put Devon in charge of the teams patrolling Midtown.

Trey said, "I'll do that, but I have some news I was about to send telepathically to you."

"Has someone found the tomb?"

"Possibly. Evalle sent me a message to let Storm know that she and Tristan were doing recon in the Blairsville area on a tip about the tomb and possible hostages. She said they were only going to confirm the intel then call in the troops."

Quinn asked, "Did she say anything about a campsite?"

"No, but something must be going down up in that area. That guy Isak and his men are up there. I got word from Beladors who noticed Hummers rolling toward Blairsville and parking near a mining ravine."

"Have you reached Storm?"

"Not yet. He must still be in jaguar form."

Hell. Quinn would feel better if Storm knew about this. He'd abandon anything he was doing and head to Blairsville. Quinn asked, "Why didn't Evalle contact me?"

"I asked her if she wanted me to tell you. She said Tristan wanted to be sure first before involving anyone higher up, especially Daegan. I haven't been able to raise her telepathically since she contacted me. I can't reach Tristan either."

"Not good."

"Nope. Have you been outside, Quinn? You know it quit raining?"

"Yes. We just got to one of my buildings here in town. Why?" Low-level accent lighting cast the room in a twilight glow. He walked over to look out at the clear dark night.

Trey said, "Might be coincidence, but weather radar shows only one storm still in the area. It's near Blairsville."

Reese had been sitting in one of the plush chairs in the meeting room. She walked over to the window to stand beside him and said, "I've been thinking about the rain stopping tonight. Something significant has changed. Might be good." She looked at him with doubt showing and added, "Might be bad."

Trey asked, "Where will you be if I need to reach you?"

A polite way of trying to figure out what the hell was going on without asking outright.

Quinn said, "I'll be out-of-pocket for a bit." That might be a gross understatement. "I have something important to discuss with Daegan, then I'll know more. Please let me know the minute you hear from Evalle."

"Ten four."

Using his direct access to Tzader, Quinn telepathically called to his friend in the Treoir realm.

Tzader came back quickly. *What's going on, Quinn? Any luck on finding the body?*

We have a lead, but I'm running out of time before the Tribunal orders Sen to bring me in. I need to speak to Daegan.

The lull on Tzader's end turned into a long, drawn-out sigh before he said, *I need to come back to Atlanta.*

No, Quinn argued. *Daegan laid out the reasons we all have responsibilities in the meeting this morning. You've been handed the protection of Brina, which includes protecting all Beladors. Leave this to me, Daegan and the others. Do what he asked ... for all of us.*

I'll get him, Tzader said. *But I'm telling you right now I will not stand by if the Tribunal locks you up.*

Understood. Quinn didn't want to point out that being locked up wasn't his greatest concern at the moment. The Tribunal had said only that Queen Maeve would be able to pursue Kizira's body without fear of retribution from the Beladors, but Quinn had been around for too long to think it would be that simple.

He suspected he'd be handed over to Maeve right there in the Tribunal meeting.

His gaze slid to Reese, who still looked out the window.

She had to be the most irreverent female he'd ever met, a warrior to the end, and that mouth ... she had one on her. She challenged everything he said and criticized him constantly.

Evalle had been surprised when Reese called Quinn a surly bastard and asked if his dog had died. Reese had cut him no slack since then either.

It had taken being jarred by this frenetic woman to realize he'd been keeping everyone on edge around him, afraid to say or do anything that would stress him. It was time to stop making his friends feel they had to tiptoe around. He had to find a way past the guilt drowning him.

Reese knew nothing of his history. She had no idea why Quinn wanted Kizira's body and he couldn't allow her to know. She was still an unknown. He had no idea where her loyalties lay, but she hadn't acted with aggression against his people so she could go once they located the tomb.

If Sen came for Quinn before that happened, Quinn would hand over her medallion. He would not leave her unprotected.

Quinn had been expecting Daegan's voice to flow into his mind once Tzader found the dragon, but a holographic image of Daegan wavered into view in front of Quinn.

"Daegan, I'm not alone," Quinn warned him.

Daegan gave Reese a brief look and said, "She can't see or hear me."

"What about her hearing me?" Quinn checked to see Reese's reaction to his question, but oddly enough, it appeared she hadn't heard it.

Quinn turned back to Daegan who explained, "Now that you're one of my Council of Seven, I can conceal this conversation on both sides. She'll see your mouth move but will hear no sound. Tzader and Brina don't have the ability to shield their holographic images from others, but my majik is very old."

"Interesting." Quinn got right to the point. "I think we may have located the tomb."

"Where is it?"

"That's the problem. Trey got a message from Evalle that she and Tristan were searching around Blairsville, which is a small town north of Atlanta. They received a tip that someone had the tomb and hostages. Evalle said they were going to confirm the intel then call in backup."

"Have they?" Daegan asked.

"Trey hasn't been able to reach either one of them since that initial contact and that's a bad sign. He's a far more powerful telepath than anyone else I've ever met. That's why he coordinates our people."

"Why do you think there's a problem, Quinn?"

"My first guess is that Evalle and Tristan are somewhere that is blocking their telepathy."

"That happens sometimes."

"True, but they have mobile phones and Trey can't reach them on those either." Quinn might as well give Daegan all the bad news. "I intend to go find them, but I have a time sensitive issue due to the Tribunal meeting and need your agreement on something."

"What is it?"

Quinn had hoped to have time to go see Lanna before this point, but she was still healing from a vicious attack that bordered on sexual assault and didn't need the stress of knowing any of this. "Do you recall briefly seeing Lanna with the witches in that basement while everyone was trying to break the curse on you? Tzader said the Fae woman brought Lanna back to the building before the Fae teleported the rest of you to Treoir."

"I do. Lanna was a young, blond woman injured by the crazy mage. Is she okay?"

"She will be. She's strong and she's healing with a white witch. I need to know that she'll be brought under Belador protection once I leave."

"Why would you leave? I thought we discussed this."

"At that time, I had hopes of a better outcome today. If I don't find a way to put Kizira's body somewhere safe by the Tribunal meeting deadline, they're supposed to give Queen Maeve approval to obtain the body through any means she chooses. I can't be sure the Tribunal won't hand me over to her right then, which would end with me being taken to TÅµr Medb. If that happens, she could very possibly compel me to do her bidding. I might be able to prevent it, but she may be too powerful, especially in her own realm. If she does compel me, she'll be in a position to do far more damage to the Beladors than has ever been done, even before she eventually gets her hands on Kizira's body."

"That is a situation we have to avoid." Daegan looked down,

his face thoughtful. He shook his head at some thought. "Tristan should have come to me as soon as he discovered who had the body. I don't understand why he didn't. I see so much potential in him. I still believe he's capable of being a strong leader."

"I don't think he wants you here."

Daegan's dark gaze lifted to Quinn. "Why?"

"No one has ever given Tristan a chance to prove he can be a part of the Beladors. You did that and more. I think he's taken it on himself to deal with this and not involve you."

Daegan made a disgusted grunt. "That's foolish thinking when I'm the strongest among us."

Quinn hadn't seen Daegan in action, but based on what Tzader had told him, Daegan was only stating a fact, not boasting. "I honestly think Tristan believes it's his job to protect *all* the Treoirs, starting with you."

Daegan cursed then muttered, "This is my fault, but I will fix it."

Quinn wanted to ask what that meant, but Daegan was talking again.

"We need a plan. Why do you think Tristan and Evalle can't reach Trey telepathically?"

"I don't know. Devon and Evalle had trouble with their telepathy last night when we were in the presence of the buzzing energy field during the nonstop rain Atlanta has been experiencing." He told Daegan about the rain that Trey had said was now near Blairsville, then said, "If she and Tristan have encountered that strange cloaking energy again, their inability to communicate could be related to that. Who knows? I'm purely guessing at this point. If anyone can find Evalle, it's Storm."

"Call in Storm."

"Trey is trying to locate him, but Storm found a subtle scent at the cemetery this evening. He can track best in his jaguar form, so he doesn't have a mobile phone handy. Right now, I need to know if there's any way for you to teleport the tomb from where you are in Treoir."

"No, but if Tristan is available, he can do it."

"That depends on how much he's been teleporting today. He's not like you in that regard." Quinn considered something Daegan had admitted in the meeting. "Is there a valid reason

Tristan doesn't want you to be here?"

That turned Daegan's already vicious mood downright ugly.

Quinn added, "I'm not questioning you as a leader, Daegan. I just want to know why it appears that Tristan is trying to handle this himself. He's not a bad chap, but I think his new position might be driving his decision making."

"I think you're correct."

"Does he have reason to think you'd be in danger coming to this realm?"

Instead of answering Quinn's question, Daegan said, "Send everyone you have to find Storm, then report back to me."

"I will, but about Kizira's body—"

"I know what we're going to do. Follow through on my orders and I'll explain everything when we talk next."

The hologram disappeared. Quinn contacted Trey with Daegan's request to pull out all the stops to find Storm, then stepped over to Reese.

When she turned to him, she smiled as if she'd found the answer to the universe. "Remember the súile marbh demons I told you about?"

"Yes."

"I know why it's not raining anymore."

CHAPTER 28

"You sure you can do this, Tristan?" Evalle asked as she stepped out into the opening between the narrow strip of woods and the camp with the tomb.

Tristan's idea was to walk in offering a trade to the kidnappers to release Kit and the boys. Once those three were out of sight, Evalle would pretend to use her powers to open the tomb.

At that point, Tristan would teleport away with Evalle and the tomb. If he couldn't move the tomb, he'd just get the two of them out of there.

He'd said it was a simple plan and she couldn't argue with that. Plus, now they had Isak with his demon blaster and Adrianna with Witchlock backing them up.

Why did she feel like she was breaking Storm's trust?

Because I am. She'd ended up in this position unintentionally and couldn't walk away with one of the boys facing death, but knowing all of that didn't erase the sick feeling she had in her chest.

Tristan said, "To answer you, I'm as sure about this plan as you are about doing your part."

Wrong answer. Her stomach hit her feet. She had no idea if she could bluff her way through this.

Six men converged on them with their hands raised to use kinetic power. She murmured, "Those are the bad Beladors."

"Bad Beladors?"

"That's my name for them to differentiate the Beladors I know from this pack of traitors."

He asked, "You don't recognize any of them?"

"No."

Tristan called out, "Who's in charge?"

The bad Beladors opened a path for a man who stepped out from between the tents. He was an easy six feet tall and had a build that could put a hurt on anyone who crossed him. Short black hair, harsh eyes, a narrow nose and pursed lips had been arranged in a decent way, almost attractive.

But not to Evalle. This man was evil incarnate to drag Kit and the boys into this.

He said, "I am Lorwerth."

Tristan acknowledged him. "Then you're the man I'm looking for. We got a call from Isak Nyght that you're holding hostages to trade for a gryphon who can open a sealed tomb. We're here to trade."

"Did one of you seal this tomb?"

"No." Evalle brought all the arrogance she could dig up. "But this is your lucky day. That tomb was sealed by a friend of mine and I happen to have the secret to cracking it open." When they'd gotten back to Atlanta from the Treoir meeting, Quinn said he meant to show her and Tzader how to open it, but that never happened. This Lorwerth didn't know that.

Lorwerth asked, "Why are there two of you?"

Tristan answered, "Because we don't trust you. No one would in our shoes. I'm here to make sure everything goes down nice and smooth."

"Have the woman open the tomb."

What century had this piece of work come from?

Evalle crossed her arms. "I'm not opening anything until you hand over the hostages and explain why it had to be a gryphon."

"Doesn't work that way," Lorwerth countered. "You give me what I want first."

"Let me make this simple for you," Evalle said, loading condescension in her voice. "There are only three people who know how to open that tomb. Vladimir Quinn and his two best friends. I'm one of them. Quinn and our other friend who can open it are in a different realm. I have no idea when they'll be back so I'm it or nothing. I came in good faith because Isak Nyght is a friend of mine, but I'm not lifting a finger until I see the hostages walk out of here under their own power."

She'd given them Quinn's name for the simple reason that calling Quinn in meant calling in an army of Beladors. Quinn would expect no less of her in this situation.

Lorwerth turned to one of his men and whispered something. The guy ran into the camp.

Evalle tried to look confident in spite of her anxiety spiking into the ozone. If any of the bad Beladors had empathic ability, she was screwed.

The runner came back leading three hostages.

Relief swamped her for a lightheaded moment then she added, "I want your word they'll be safe once they leave here."

Lorwerth smiled. "You have my word."

Like I'd trust you.

Isak and Adrianna had Evalle and Tristan's back. They would get Kit and the boys to safety.

The twins emerged first, with Kit right behind them. Kit kept her eyes on the twins as if she'd tackle anyone who tried to touch them. But when she lifted her gaze to see who had come for her, Evalle's throat tightened at the vulnerability she'd never before seen in that woman's face.

She hated that anyone had proven Kit's strength could be shaken.

Evalle shifted her stance as Kit and the boys approached her and Tristan. She needed to be able to see the trio all the way until they were out of sight, where Isak and Adrianna would take over.

Just as the three of them reached Evalle, Kellman slowed his step. His face had been changing into more of a man's recently. For all that he was the conservative one of the pair, he wouldn't hesitate to step into trouble with her.

She gave a tiny shake of her head without looking at him, hoping he understood that she needed them safely out of her way.

He kept moving, which meant Kardos would, too.

Message received.

She waited through a tense twenty seconds until the woods swallowed the trio.

Lorwerth lifted his hand.

More bad Beladors emerged from the woods, bringing the

total standing with Lorwerth to twenty.

Evalle and Tristan were surrounded immediately.

Unwilling to stretch this out any longer, Evalle demanded, "Show me the tomb and let's get this done."

"So you agree to open it, gryphon?"

Tristan asked, "Why did you ask for a gryphon if you didn't know she could open it?"

Lorwerth seemed amused at the question. "I know that Quinn sealed the tomb. Nightstalkers in Oakland Cemetery are full of information and my men had plenty of power to trade through handshakes. The Nightstalkers observed Quinn sealing the tomb, then Queen Maeve and Cathbad trying to figure out how it opened after Quinn was gone. They couldn't do it. My superior saw an opportunity when Queen Maeve demanded that a Tribunal force Quinn to return Kizira's body. He handed me an army to do what the rogue units had failed to accomplish. Acquiring a gryphon for my army from all of this was *my* idea. Kizira's body is so important to Queen Maeve that she'll be happy to include compelling a gryphon to follow my orders as part of the trade."

Evalle wanted to get one answer before Tristan teleported them away. "Where'd these Beladors come from, Lorwerth?"

He cocked his head in amusement, then looked at his men. "These aren't Beladors. They weary of pretending to be. Well, that's not entirely true. They were given equivalent powers at the same time as the original Beladors thousands of year ago. But when Belatucadros endowed Belador warriors with powers, he kept a contingent to do his bidding. These are some of his Laochra Fola. Now that you know, don't insult them again by calling them mere Beladors."

The Laochra Fola opened a path that led to the tomb. The humming shifted into the weird buzzing like what they'd experienced in Midtown.

Not good.

Afraid to risk telepathy so close to this bunch, Evalle strolled forward slowly and whispered to Tristan, "I've got a bad feeling. Forget the tomb. Let's go with plan B and get the hell out of here. You ready?"

"Yep. Link with me."

She opened up her energy to link with him ... but she couldn't push the energy out from her body to connect.

He murmured a concerned, "Evalle?"

She fought a growing sense of panic. "I'm trying. Can you force a link with me?"

The muscles in his jaws flexed from obvious strain. He couldn't do it.

She said, "Get out of here, Tristan."

"Not leaving you."

"You have to go for help. Bring Storm, Quinn, everyone you can find while I stall them."

"Shit."

Tristan said that so loudly she jerked around to him. He shook his head. "Screwed."

He couldn't teleport himself.

Lorwerth didn't even turn around when he said, "Are you two having difficulties? We've activated our dome of energy. It allows only our powers to function." He continued to the tomb and stopped, turning to her. "I kept my word and released the humans, now it's time for you to keep yours. I warn you not to attempt to play me, Evalle, because while I won't harm you, my army will make life extremely painful for Tristan."

This guy knew exactly who—and what—they were, which meant he wasn't bluffing about what he could do.

CHAPTER 29

Adrianna kept an eye on Evalle and Tristan as Isak handed throwaway ponchos to his mother and the boys, more for warmth now than rain. He was acting calm, but Adrianna hadn't missed the sick look of worry in his eyes as he assessed his mother's condition.

Kit was tough, but playing foster mom to a pair of teenage witches had not prepared her for being held hostage by preternaturals.

They were a whole different level of predator.

Still, she and the boys seemed to be okay.

Adrianna turned back to observe Evalle and Tristan walking through the group toward the tomb. Those men were clearly connected to the ones who'd attacked Beladors and Medb in Midtown.

How did she know that?

From the familiar buzzing that had begun vibrating overhead. She would tell Isak that, once he realized his mother was going to survive.

The twin known as Kellman walked over to Adrianna. He said "We have to get them out of there."

She gave him what she hoped was a reassuring look. "I know, but they have a plan. We're waiting here for them."

"It won't work."

Isak, his mother and the other twin walked up. Isak asked, "What makes you think it won't work when you don't know what it is?"

Kellman asked, "Do Evalle and Tristan plan to teleport out of there?"

"Yes."

"You hear that buzzing?"

Adrianna closed her eyes. "Yes. It's the fog dome."

"What's buzzing?" Isak asked. Kit's eyebrows were drawn in question as well.

Kardos, the usually cocky twin who had been uncharacteristically quiet, joined them. "I doubt humans can hear it, but Kellman's right. Lorwerth says only his Laochra Fola can use power inside their dome."

Before Isak asked another question, Kellman intuitively explained, "Laochra Fola are the men with Lorwerth, that tall, black-haired guy. I've never seen anyone use kinetics and talk telepathically the way Beladors do, but those Laochra Fola can do it."

Adrianna added, "We fought them yesterday in Atlanta. Now some things make sense. I think they can link their powers like Beladors do as well."

"What dome?" Isak still couldn't figure out what the nonhumans were talking about.

Adrianna took mercy on him. "It appears those men have some form of energy field. It was cloaking them this morning in Midtown and the only indication we had of where they were when the cloaking worked was a buzzing, like a bunch of bees. The minute the energy fell apart, the buzzing stopped and they were exposed." She snapped her fingers. "The rain!"

Her sixth sense had been spot on.

The boys were nodding. Kellman said, "They need the rain to control the energy domes. That's why it's foggy in this area even though we can hear a thunderstorm going on outside of it."

Adrianna exchanged a look with Isak that said they might just be on the same page for once.

They couldn't leave Evalle and Tristan.

Isak touched his ear. "Alpha Tiger to Romeo, come back." He repeated it.

Adrianna didn't have to ask to know Isak had lost communication with his team. She'd already discovered her mobile phone had no signal even though they weren't that far from local towers.

She suggested, "Why don't you take these three to your truck and contact Quinn. He'll bring in an army of Beladors."

"What about you?"

Now he was concerned about her? The strange nonhuman?

She waved him off. "I'll be fine. I need to stay in case I can help Evalle and Tristan."

Isak looked like he wanted to say something, but not with an audience. She couldn't help him with that, but she wanted to allow for a future conversation to clear up some bad feelings. "Once you get them to the truck and call in reinforcements, why don't you and your cavalry come back here, Isak?"

Her mouth curved up on one side in the start of a smile to let him know all was not lost after all.

Not unless he said something supremely stupid.

"I can't leave you."

That jump-started her deflated heart, but she wanted the humans out of this mess. The boys were more human than supernatural at this point, because they weren't trained. "I have cloaking. I can hide in the middle of an army. Go. Really. I'll be fine."

Not entirely convinced, he offered his blaster to her. "Keep this."

"I'm no good with that." She shook her head and pulled out her hand, opening her fingers to expose the ball of Witchlock energy. "But I'm deadly with this."

The twins were duly impressed. She feared they might bow down to her any minute.

Kit cocked an eyebrow. "Fascinating."

Still clearly torn over leaving her, he ran a hand over his soaked hair, pushing water out, and muttered, "Shit."

She shouldn't feel happy over his moment of worry about her after the way he'd acted earlier, but the more she was around him the more she realized he wouldn't intentionally hurt her.

He just didn't realize the damage he was capable of doing with nothing more than his words and attitude after she'd opened her heart to him.

Feeling charitable now that Kit and the boys were safe, Adrianna could give Isak a chance to make up for how he'd behaved earlier. That chance would require time and heavy groveling, but hey, an alpha male should be up to the task.

Tilting her head in the direction of the truck, she hurried them along. "You better get going."

He hesitated once more, earning him another point for caring, then he looked at his mother. She'd not uttered a word of complaint in spite of looking as if she'd been put through a wringer. The boys didn't look much better, but they were young and witches.

Didn't matter.

Untrained witches and a human had been cornered prey in the middle of preternaturals who had almost killed Quinn. That was a sobering thought to keep with her as she waited alone.

Isak led his flock into the woods and had been gone only a few minutes when she heard bodies crashing through evergreen bushes, heading her way.

The strange sound of Isak's blaster zoomed over and over.

Adrianna turned, holding her Witchlock energy in front of her, prepared to meet the enemy. She told her power, "I know you can handle this. I just don't know about my part."

Isak's deep voice yelled out, "Cloak yourself now!"

The humming overhead cranked up until the sound of a thousand bees buzzed around her, but there wasn't an insect in sight. She could feel the vibration racing over her skin, fighting against her majik.

She lost a half a second in surprise, but lifted a hand to toss up her cloaking ... that didn't happen. She looked at the spinning ball of energy and ordered, "Cloak me now!"

The buzzing dulled, the sound warping in and out like a bad radio connection. She whispered, "Witchlock?"

Kit and the boys raced toward Adrianna with Isak at their backs, shooting his blaster in every direction. Kit skidded to a stop, sucking air in and out as hard as she could. She and the boys stared at Adrianna with open-mouthed shock.

Adrianna wasn't sure if her powers would work in this buzzing if she stayed hidden, and from the looks on their faces, the cloaking couldn't be working. That was on her for lack of experience with the ancient power. If she survived this, she'd devote even more time to forming a bond with Witchlock and learning the intricacies of wielding it.

Isak stumbled backwards into their area. He turned to her. "We can't make it out past those things."

She was too busy trying to figure out how they could escape to take offense at his calling nonhumans 'things.' "I'll try cloaking all of us, then we can walk out."

Kardos popped off. "If that was your cloaking a minute ago, it only made you translucent. It didn't hide you."

Just as she'd thought.

But if she couldn't hide herself, she couldn't hide all five of them for sure. "Then we're going to have to fight our way out."

Isak was heaving deep breaths from his run back. "I don't think that's a good idea. I had to dive out of the way when the blaster bounced back at me."

Kellman shoved a hand past Adrianna, pointing at the camp. "Look."

She turned around to see Tristan stretched between two trees. From the look on his face, they were doing something painful to him.

Adrianna said, "Everyone stay here. I'm going after them."

"No."

She turned to Isak and narrowed her eyes. "Don't ever think to tell me what I can and can't do. As you stated so clearly earlier, I'm a nonhuman. This is not your area, but mine."

He sighed. "I'm not doubting you, Adrianna, but what will happen if you use that power and it boomerangs?"

She felt energy moving toward them.

Those *things*, as Isak put it, were coming at them from the woods. They were herding the five of them toward the camp and she had no way to stop them without harming everyone inside the energy field.

She had one more idea for cloaking them, but she'd have to use what she'd learned as a Sterling witch and they wouldn't be able to move undetected.

And she had sworn never to tap the dark majik.

CHAPTER 30

Quinn stood at the edge of the dirt cliff overhanging a giant hole left behind from a strip mine no longer in operation. He'd made the trip from Atlanta to Blairsville in record time. The gulley was probably three hundred yards long, half as wide and at least a hundred feet deep.

A fog floated across the majority of the hole. It hummed.

Lighting streaked overhead, followed by booming thunder. That was close, based on his count of time between the lightning and the thunder.

The rain and warm temperature here were too similar to what he'd experienced in Midtown this morning. Reese might just be right.

"That's one heck of a big energy canopy," Reese said, drawing his gaze to where she stood next to him. Not that he'd forgotten about her. She was impossible to disregard.

She had her own energy as a supernatural being, and as a woman, though he'd tried not to notice.

He could feel her vibrating with the need to do something. She wore a gray poncho now, longer than the convenience-store model the demon had shredded. Trey had been eyeing the weather radar, and had given her this poncho when Quinn stopped by briefly to go over the plan for tonight's event. He'd call it an operation, but that would suggest there had been actual strategic planning involved as opposed to terse orders from Daegan and chaotic rushing around to make it this far so quickly.

Only preternaturals could've bypassed Isak's men waiting nearby for word from their leader.

The fact that Isak's men were still here probably meant Isak couldn't get word out either, if he was in the energy field.

When Reese moved, it drew his gaze to her jeans, which were soaked below the poncho. Thankfully, Trey's sister-in-law had dug up a pair of boots that fit Reese.

She stared in fascination. "The rain coming down now is different."

He agreed, thinking out loud. "Even the national meteorologists are flummoxed over the odd weather phenomena, and up here it's more intense."

She cut her eyes at Quinn. "That sounds like a commode cleaner. Flummox once a week for a tidy bowl."

He was sick with worry over Tristan and Evalle. He had to face the Tribunal in just over an hour, and Kizira's body was still beyond his reach.

How could he possibly find anything humorous?

He had no idea, but the mouthy human tornado who had dogged his steps today managed to do the impossible. He suppressed what would have been a real grin, but couldn't quite keep the smile off of his face. He covered his chuckle with a cough.

She'd pushed every button she could find and at times had been entertaining.

There was no explanation for his reaction to her other than the fact that she stomped around him when others tiptoed. She'd forced him to take a look at who he was and how he was affecting others.

At the cemetery, he'd gone from irritated to confused to protective in a matter of seconds, the last of which he chalked up to nothing more than an ingrained drive to shield a woman from harm.

That was the only explanation, but who was he to protect anyone after failing Kizira? The ache in his chest drove deeper at remembering Kizira dying in his arms.

He deserved no woman.

Reese lifted her thumbnail to nibble on. She didn't actually chew her nails, but seemed to be deliberating on what she was going to do next.

Without turning to look at him, she said, "You're staring a

hole through my head, Quinn. Cut it out. Your staring that is, not my head."

Crazy vixen. He'd like to take a look inside that head and find a few answers, but since that wasn't going to happen, he asked, "Why are you doing this?"

Lifting her chin in his direction, she said, "You know why. I want my medallion back. Not to mention that I'm the one who figured out someone is using súile marbh demons to power the energy field and that the rain is needed for a massive cloaking spell."

"If you are correct."

"I'm right." No hesitation on her part. "And you need me to get through that field. What are you waiting for?"

The truth behind why she was in the middle of all this. Coincidences were for romantic comedies, not real life. "You're willing to dangle your energy in front of who-knows-how-many demons that want to rip you apart to get it, just to have your medallion returned?"

She shrugged. "Yes."

He didn't believe her. He could absolutely understand wanting whatever allowed him use of his powers, but she had yet to explain why someone had locked her powers down.

He'd offered to enter her mind and see if he could unlock them. How could that be more risky than the low odds of survival that waited below with demons and other powerful beings?

Quinn had survived many near-death situations by trusting his gut. He reached inside his pocket and pulled out the medallion still hooked on the cord. Reese was his only hope for regaining Kizira's tomb when he'd thought no hope existed.

She might be his only hope for finding Evalle and Tristan if they'd gotten into a scrape.

If Reese got this power ignition key back, would she race away and leave him to muddle his way through this rescue, or would she still be willing to face all those demons?

Did he really want her to stay and face getting injured ... or dying?

No.

He coiled the cord in his hand and dropped the medallion on

top, then offered it to her on an open palm. "Take it."

Her eyes flicked from his hand to his face and back again. She licked her lips, want shining in her gaze. Then the wary woman from earlier returned. "What's the catch?"

"Are you always so difficult?"

"Pretty much."

He felt a smile push at his lips, but to smile would say he enjoyed her spark. What man would do that while trying to locate the cold body of the woman who had made the ultimate sacrifice for him?

A very confused one.

Shaking off the strange reaction, he repeated, "Take it."

She held his gaze as she took her possession from him. Once she had a grasp on the cord ends, she immediately tied it around her neck. Her sigh of deep relief confirmed how much that meant to her.

He got a muttered, "Thank you," and for the second time in two days, had a feeling those weren't words she said very often. Not because she didn't genuinely appreciate getting her medallion back.

That wasn't it.

She'd sounded as though she couldn't believe he hadn't wanted her soul in exchange.

He'd had no intention of keeping her power device from her beyond today, but she trusted no one and for some damn reason he wanted her to trust him.

She deserved a choice in this.

In fact, now that he thought about it, she needed to just leave. She'd stumbled into this and miserable dog that he was, he had taken advantage of her situation. Sure, she was holding secrets, but had she harmed any of his people? No. Was she working with this group who apparently used demons to power the rain shields? Didn't look that way.

Would she survive being used as a demon magnet?

Probably not.

Don't I have enough blood on my hands?

Yes. Quinn expected Trey to contact him any time now with a green light to put the next steps in motion.

Reese had made the deal all on her own and he believed she

had powers she had yet to reveal, but she was not immortal. He was fairly certain of that.

"Reese?"

She'd been holding the medallion and staring out over the buzzing cloud below them. "Hmm?"

"You can go."

Ever so slowly, she turned a face to him covered with an expression that questioned his intelligence. "What? Have you come up with another way to break through that canopy, but failed to mention it until now?"

Smart mouth. "No, but I'm not putting you at further risk. This is our fight, not yours. It was wrong of me to press you for that agreement. You were right in the cemetery when you said my head was up my ass."

Her lips parted.

Well, damn. He'd managed to render her speechless. He'd bet that didn't happen often.

She started shaking her head slowly at first then adamantly. "No. We made a deal. I'm sticking to my part."

"I appreciate your honoring our original agreement, but I'd rather you stayed out of this."

"What about that Daegan guy? He sounds like your boss. What's he going to say?"

"It doesn't matter. This our battle, not yours."

She looked so torn you'd think she had a stake in this. After silently deliberating on something, she released a long breath. "Why is this so important to you, Quinn? What are you going to do with that woman's body?"

His hair lifted at the censure in her voice.

Who the hell did she think she was? "What I do with that body is none of your business."

"See, that's where I'm going to disagree."

"You need to get going before I change my mind," he warned.

"Not until I find out what you plan for that body."

He drilled a look at her that had made warriors cringe. Damn little pistol just stood there defying him. "You didn't know anything about this body until you stumbled into the battle this morning, right?"

"Right."

If she hadn't blinked and glanced away, he might have believed her. His suspicions jumped up ready to pursue the truth, so he fed her rope to see if she'd hang herself. "If that's so, why would you care about a body to which you have no tie?"

Her passive expression remained, but her eyes gave her away. Fire blazed in them. What drove that passion?

She said, "I have an issue with a body being used by preternaturals. I'm not leaving until I know it's safe."

Quinn couldn't decide whether to shout at her that she had some nerve dictating morality to him or thank her for not being yet another preternatural looking to take advantage of the body.

But, that still left the question of her interest unanswered.

In the end, he held his ear as if he were receiving a telepathic call, which had not happened. In truth, it was still a few minutes too soon. He stared off, nodding as if he was agreeing to something he heard.

After a moment, he lowered his hand and said, "I will ease your conscience. The Beladors down inside that buzzing fog are there to rescue the tomb and bring that body back. We are keeping it from beings who would use necromancy on Kizira. As for me, I have a personal stake in protecting that body. We now have enough people in place that your expertise is no longer needed. The sooner you get going, the sooner my people can move on this. Thank you for your offer of help. It will be remembered should you ever need aid from the Beladors."

"I don't believe anyone just contacted you. Why are you lying to me? And before you try to yank my chain again, keep in mind that you have not seen *all* my powers."

CHAPTER 31

Reese hated to admit the truth, so she wouldn't.

At least not out loud where one of Yáahl's snooping crows might hear, but she'd realized she was mentally defective.

There was no other reason for her failure to take the medallion and leave. All she had to do was find a place nearby to watch the battle, wait for one side to disrupt the energy canopy, then she'd slide in through the battle lines and find the tomb.

That wouldn't help Quinn, but she wasn't convinced that the Beladors had honorable reasons for getting the tomb back. From what she'd heard, Macha had been kicked out of their gang and a guy named Daegan had inserted himself.

What did that say about the Beladors?

They had once been known as the most honorable of preternaturals. Now some of them even used demons for dark reasons. So who knew?

She had the medallion and no intention of throwing herself to demons like fresh meat to piranhas, but she was not leaving Kizira's body at risk, even if she had to kill someone.

Yáahl was a roaring pain in her backside, but he was considered a benevolent being who would do no harm. If it came down to a safe place for Kizira's body, Yáahl topped the list at the moment.

Quinn's normally calm demeanor went through a pissed-off overhaul. "Are you threatening me?"

"Not specifically. I only warned you not to lie to me again because you don't know what else I'm capable of, should I take offense to your lies." That sounded reasonable to her.

He stepped forward, bringing all that powerful male up close and personal. She had the crazy desire to feel him right up against her, but that took her from being mentally defective right into just plain stupid.

Men are bad, remember?

Okay, got it.

Her body, however, had the memory of a toadstool when it came to the opposite sex.

"What the hell is it going to take to get you out of here?" Quinn growled.

Underneath all that anger was a layer of concern that permeated every breath he drew. Concern and pain. She'd seen both today. She was walking a tightrope through her conscience right now and needed to decide one way or the other if she was going to get involved.

"The truth."

He lost his homicidal look. "Come again?"

"Tell me the truth if you want me to leave." She wasn't saying she *would* leave, but a man this aggravating would assume it meant the same.

"About what?"

"Why do you feel so responsible for Kizira's body?" This would tell her if he had a nefarious reason for possessing it. Nefarious was a good word to use with this snob. She should have worked that into a comment. "Come on, Quinn. Put up or shut up. I'm tired of you feeding me crap."

A muscle in his neck stood out, but in the next second his shoulders lost their tightness. He said, "Her death was my fault."

Hmm. Reese wasn't sure what to do with that. "Did you kill Kizira?"

His mouth dropped open, appalled. "No, I didn't kill her."

"Did you pay someone to do it or make someone kill her?"

"Hell, no."

She didn't get this at all. "Then how was her death your fault?"

Misery flooded his eyes. A deep misery unlike anything she'd ever seen in a man.

Reese regretted bringing that to the surface.

Quinn looked into the distance. "During a battle between the

Medb and Beladors, Kizira stepped in front of me when a gryphon attacked. He gutted her and she'd been compelled not to heal herself by that bitch Flaevynn, who birthed her."

Reese reeled from the shock. From that little bit he'd shared, she figured out Kizira had cared for Quinn, maybe loved him, to have made such a selfless sacrifice.

But Kizira's death wasn't Quinn's fault.

Reese wanted to smooth that pain from his face. "Who controlled the gryphons?"

"The Medb did at the time. The gryphons are now with us, the Beladors. What's your point?"

Reese had no idea why she wanted to help Quinn through his grief, when no one had eased the pain she'd suffered over losing her child.

That was it. No one had been there for her.

How could she have explained losing a baby because of a preternatural energy that lived inside her? She couldn't. Just as Quinn had to feel isolated in his guilt over an enemy who obviously cared for him.

Had he cared for Kizira?

What had gone down between those two for him to put his life on the line to protect her body?

It didn't matter. Reese understood that part, if there had been some relationship between the two.

She'd lay her life down to protect the body of the baby she'd lost if it was under threat from preternatural predators.

Her tone was unusually gentle when she said, "You feel guilty because Kizira chose to save you. That doesn't make her death your fault, Quinn. She made a decision, knowing she couldn't heal. Why are you beating yourself up over it?"

"There are things you don't know, and that I can't tell you."

Reese tamped down on her exasperation. "Tell me one thing and I'll let it go."

Quinn said nothing, looking like he might toss her over the edge if she didn't drop this topic soon.

She asked the same question as earlier, but this time without condemnation. "What do you plan to do with her body if you get it back? There must be a reason you didn't cremate her, spread the ashes and so forth, which would have prevented all this."

Quinn took a while to answer and in that moment he seemed to be pulled inside out. "I shouldn't have put her in that tomb, but I ... had a valid reason, or so it seemed to me at the time. Now I see that my thinking was unrealistic for the world in which we live. If I get her back, I'm going to make sure no one can ever touch her body and use it for dark majik, but I'm running out of time."

Reese still didn't know everything, but she figured out something in listening to his voice as much as his words.

Quinn *had* cared for Kizira. He'd had some type of relationship with Kizira. No man, especially not a Belador, would put his life at risk to save the body of a dead Medb.

She suffered a moment of jealousy that Kizira had earned the dedication of such a man. Reese hadn't believed it possible. She'd never seen that level of caring before.

Who was this man? He'd given back her medallion, no strings attached.

She still had to face Yáahl. How had everything gotten so turned around?

She needed to know more about the Tribunal. "You've got a meeting tonight. I heard you mention it. Does that involve her body?"

He nodded. "I'm expected to deliver her body to a Tribunal just over an hour from now. If I don't, the Medb can come after me and the body without repercussion."

Crap. *Now he tells me this?*

Quinn rubbed his forehead. "Just go, Reese. Whatever interest you have in this is not going to supersede mine."

She mentally stuttered at that.

Had Quinn figured out she did have a personal stake in finding Kizira's body?

She did.

If she showed up empty-handed, Yáahl would never return her power. He wouldn't perform necromancy, which seemed to make this all better, but not really.

She needed her powers now that *jötnar* demons had found her.

Quinn crossed his arms. "Get moving, Reese."

"How do you intend to disrupt the energy field without me?"

"You mean without dragging you in there like a sacrificial lamb?" he snapped.

"Yeah, that's about right, but you need me to kill demons, too."

He replied in a droll voice. "I've killed a few demons in my time. The ones today will wish they'd met me on other battlefields. I'm not in a merciful mood. I'm done. Go now and stay out trouble. I know that's a difficult task for you—"

"Was that a joke?"

Quinn sighed hard and lifted his phone. It must have vibrated. She hadn't heard it.

He confirmed, "I'm ready." Pause. "No. I told Daegan everything. He trusts us to get this done. If you're still not reaching the others telepathically or through their mobile phones, you may not get through to me either once I go in there. I'm watching a fog below me that's buzzing and—"

Quinn listened with a stern expression. "Tell Storm to wait." Another pause. "No, that resource didn't work out. Tell him I'm working on another way to breach the energy field."

Reese had heard enough.

This medallion had only so much juice left.

She should take Quinn's advice and leave, but stay close enough to come in once the tomb was revealed.

That would be the wise thing to do in her situation.

Only an idiot would think about anyone but herself right now.

She turned to look down the side of the ravine and jumped, dropping as quickly as her IQ obviously had. The medallion had felt weaker each time she'd drawn on it. She clutched the disk tightly, hoping it wouldn't fade on her before she had to return to Yáahl.

CHAPTER 32

Quinn watched Reese disappear over the edge of the drop-off. That woman was insane.

He jammed the phone in his pocket and backed up two steps, then took a running start. He leaped into a dive then flipped in the air and shoved his kinetic power down before the last twenty feet, slowing his fall to land on the ground at the bottom of the incline.

Just in time.

Reese came barreling down the mudslide, all legs and arms. Fifteen feet up from him, her foot caught.

She pitched forward off the hill.

Quinn caught her arms, pulling her to him. He wheeled around to keep her momentum from carrying them both to the ground.

She clung to him for all of a second, then fought against his hold. "Let me go, dammit."

Don't bite her head off. He refused her order and shook her. "What do you think you're doing? I tell you to leave and you jump off a ledge?"

"I had it under control."

"It didn't look like you were using your power just now. What was the point in giving that medallion back to you if you're not going to use it? If you want to kill yourself, do it somewhere else."

Her face lost its spark. "I was not trying to kill myself. Don't you dare accuse me of that."

Why did she look hurt?

He said, "You're joking, right? I give you the chance to walk away and you're down here? Listen closely. I don't want you here. Stay out of this." He calmed his voice and gave her the truth. "I can't live with your death on my conscience too."

She did a quick maneuver of pushing her arms inside his and breaking his hold, then backed up. "You listen to me, Mr. Know It All. I understand your pain. Someone died on my watch, too. I've spent ten years torturing myself with guilt. I've finally realized that ... I was no more at fault than you were with Kizira. I understand grief and that you have to do it in your own way and in your own time, but you have to ask yourself if you're doing this for her or for your guilt."

His chest ached with a physical pain every time he relived Kizira's death, but Reese had just ripped open a wound he'd never heal. "I owe it to her to protect her secrets from those who would steal them."

Reese took another step back, looking at him as if she finally understood why this mattered so much. "Okay, I understand."

What did she think she understood?

Swiping wet hair off her face, she said, "I'll make you a deal. I'll help you get to her tomb, but if you want to do right by Kizira, you have to live. Cremate her body and send the ashes where no one can ever abuse her death. I plan to survive this too. The dead do not want us wasting our lives."

He was done with this conversation. "We can talk later—"

"No, we can't. You're not listening to me." She sounded anxious. "You want to get to that tomb? This medallion is getting drained every time I use it. This is the only time I'm helping. If you keep holding me up, I might just change my mind. Whether you believe me or not, I'm the only one who can help you right now. Kizira cared for you and you're wasting the gift of life she gave you by allowing this to end yours."

That knocked him back a step and squeezed his lungs tight.

Reese wasn't done. "I've been told for years by an irritating advisor that everything happens for a reason. I'm supposedly still alive today for a reason. If that is true, then I've wasted years not caring whether I lived or died. I could have been figuring out my purpose. No more. I've learned you should let go of guilt over something that was out of your control. If you do that, you just might discover why you're standing here today and she isn't. Why Kizira needed *you* to live."

Quinn knew why. His heart twisted and flipped around.

Phoedra.

Kizira depended on him to find their daughter and protect her. How was he going to do that if he ended up locked away by the Tribunal or handed over to Queen Maeve?

Reese was right.

He was entitled to mourn Kizira, but he had a giant responsibility that she'd entrusted to him and spending his life like an angry walking dead was not getting it done.

Kizira would never have agreed to be buried in a tomb where preternaturals could get their hands on her. She sure as hell wouldn't have supported putting his future and life at risk to protect a cold corpse when he should be hunting for their daughter.

I've been such a fool.

Reese stared up into his eyes with an understanding that amazed him. Real understanding from the real person inside her.

Who had she lost?

He wanted to know her story. To find out what made this outrageous woman tick, but now wasn't the time.

Her eyes flared wide. She jerked around. "I feel them. We need to find your people and get closer to the tomb before we let the demons near me."

"Reese."

She held up a hand. "I'm going after the tomb with or without you. Are you ready to do this or not?"

He was done arguing and he couldn't leave Reese here knowing she would interfere no matter what.

Looking around to get his bearings, he said, "I have no idea where anyone is so let's run through the center from this end to the other. That should put us close enough for me to hear or see something."

Her gaze jumped around. "We need to go. *Now!*"

"Got it." He turned to run down one of the chewed up paths, intending to keep his Belador speed down so that she could stay with him. The buzzing was stronger down here, and the canopy held off the thunderstorm.

He could feel the energy brush over his skin like tiny bugs climbing on him.

His speed slowed to that of a human.

"Keep going," she urged, running past him.

He got moving again, but ... where was his preternatural speed? On a thought, he flicked a hand at a branch.

His kinetics should have slapped the branch hard.

The leaves didn't even move.

Shit.

"What's wrong?" she asked, not slowing a step.

He must have cursed out loud. "My powers aren't working in here. That's why no one has been able to raise Evalle and Tristan via telepathy. That also means I'm going to be limited in my ability to keep demons away from you."

She nodded.

This was going to end badly, but he'd failed to shove her away. That left figuring out how to keep Reese alive.

He now sensed the demonic energy rushing toward them.

The buzzing canopy changed vibration, going from loud to quieter then back to loud again.

Between breaths, Reese called out, "It's working."

"What is?"

"The demons powering this energy shield are being distracted like I thought they would if they sensed me. Coming after me is dividing their attention. Any sign of your people yet?"

"No. We can't be that far from the other end of this ravine. If they aren't there, you and I will have to get out of here."

"I doubt we can just run off."

"Why not?"

She heaved a couple of deep breaths, still pumping her arms and diving over fallen trees. "Because this is a trap. The demons, and whoever controls them, let us in. They won't let us escape. The person behind these demons has to be waiting for something to have set up this energy field like a spider web, but for what? If your people are here and the tomb is here, what else could they want?"

"The thieves can't open the tomb without triggering security devices built into the tomb's majik that will kill them."

She stumbled, caught her balance and kept running. "Then

they're waiting on someone who can open it." She glanced over as he kept step with her. "Who's that?"

"Me."

❧

Reese was so shocked by Quinn's admission about being the only one who could open the tomb, she said nothing.

All this time, she'd been chasing a body that only one person actually possessed. She finally pulled her thoughts together. "Why have these people stolen the tomb if they can't open it?"

"Because in a little over an hour I'm due to face the Tribunal with Kizira's body to hand over to Queen Maeve. These people who stole the tomb believe I'll come looking for the it. My guess is they think I'll unseal it because they rightly assume I have no choice, at which time they probably plan to trade me along with the body to Queen Maeve for something like a Noirre spell. Or the VIPER liaison will show up about the time I find the tomb, then he'll teleport me to the Tribunal meeting where I'll be forced to open the tomb and give Queen Maeve the body or the Tribunal will gift *me* to the queen, along with the tomb. Either way, Queen Maeve will be smiling like the Cheshire Cat in the end."

Reese got it. "She'll take you to her realm where your powers won't hold up against hers."

"Right."

Her head spun at how messed up all this had become.

Not to mention having her ass tossed into the middle of it with no rulebook. *Thanks, Yáahl.*

Quinn said, "The good news about no one being able to open the tomb might mean Evalle and Tristan are still here and this bunch is waiting for me to show up, since they have to know I'm coming to get my friends back. The bad news is that if Evalle and Tristan haven't fought their way out because of not using their powers then it might not be possible for anyone to get out. We need a plan."

She had one, but he probably wouldn't like it.

The truth was that he'd hate it.

A pinpoint of light caught her eye.

"You see that?" Reese said, pointing ahead.

Quinn dodged a low branch and looked up.

Light that she hadn't seen from the cliff began to show up through breaks in the trees.

He warned, "Let's not run straight in there."

"We won't. I've got a plan of what to do before we reach that point."

"Want to share it?"

"No."

He gave her an incredulous look. "This is the time to work together."

Oh, he had this coming. She said, "We will. You do what I say, when I say, and it will go easier for everyone."

When he didn't reply, she pointed out, "I'm guessing that probably sounded a lot better in your head when you said it to me in the cemetery."

She'd called him a dickhead.

He must've finally seen himself through her eyes, because he sighed. "You have a point, but no plan works without everyone knowing what—"

"*There!*" Reese shouted and pointed at a tree, because she could feel the demons coming toward them. She peeled off to the left.

He stayed on her heels until she skidded to a stop and swung to face him.

Now she could hear footsteps pounding. The demons weren't far away. They were coming in from behind and each side. Maybe they should have run toward the light since she felt nothing from that direction.

No, she had to get as close as possible to the energy field above them for her idea to work. The medallion's energy had felt diminished when she'd taken it back.

That meant her power would be weaker.

Yáahl had told her the medallion would only function as long as she had a chance at gaining the body. How could it be acting as if she was running out of time herself?

"Give me a boost," Reese demanded from where she'd stopped by a substantial pine tree.

Quinn opened his mouth as if to ask what she intended to do.

She said, "This is where we work together. I have a plan. Every microsecond we squander lowers our potential for success."

Closing his mouth, he stepped over and cupped his hands.

She stepped up and he shoved her into the air. She caught a branch and used her athletic ability to swing her feet up and over the branch, landing on her stomach.

Thank you, Wiley, for making me practice chin ups, tumbles and rolls along with kickboxing.

She started climbing and noticed Quinn still on the ground.

"Get your ass up here, Quinn, or you're gonna be demon dinner in about twenty seconds."

CHAPTER 33

Quinn trusted Reese's assessment about demons closing in on them and hooked his hands around the tree to start climbing. He'd reached the second set of branches when three men came out of the trees around them.

All three looked up.

Not men. Black eyes flipped to red. They were all dressed in the same black coveralls as the one Reese had killed in Midtown. If they hid their eyes, they could move through human areas undetected until they attacked some innocent person.

He scurried up two more levels, which was as far as he could go. Anything higher wouldn't hold his weight. He checked on Reese. She'd made it six feet above his position.

He paused at the image of wild hair flying all around her face. Bright blue eyes full of intelligence and determination.

But they had no backup.

More demons were coming in by the minute and the first three were climbing up.

Quinn's powers were nonexistent.

Still, Reese moved with a confidence and excitement that spoke to her experience in this.

Whatever demons she carried inside her were of the human variety. She claimed she'd made a decision to no longer live on a knife's edge between life and death, but Quinn wasn't convinced.

Growling and scratching pulled his attention back down to the threat that had now climbed halfway to where he was. The demons would have reached him if a fight hadn't broken out, knocking them back to the ground. He didn't even have mind lock to use on them, but that was just as well. He wouldn't survive entering that many demon minds at once.

That left him with just eight triquetras hooked to his belt, the minimum that he carried into any fight. He might stop four demons with those, maybe five or six if he got a couple of damn good shots.

Quinn called up, "Reese, what do you need me to do?"

"Keep them busy for about a minute."

Another eight, no, make that twelve, filled in the space at the bottom of the tree. One started climbing over the top of the two that were making their way up again.

They snarled and fought, but the first one paused to lift his head. His red eyes stared at Quinn as if judging the distance.

Quinn eased two triquetras free. His pulse throbbed in his head. He heard Reese climbing even higher.

When the demon reached for Quinn's foot, the thing's gaze was focused on one spot. Holding on to a branch, Quinn swung down and sliced across the demon's neck. It reached for its neck and gurgled, sliding down into the next one's face.

The second demon yanked the first one out of the way, tossing him to the ground, but the dead demon burst into gray dust even before his body hit.

Quinn threw the two triquetras, taking out the next demon, which also turned into dust.

He chanced a look up. "Reese? I'm only going to be able to stop about four to six. We can't stop all of them. This isn't going to work."

She leaned over and lifted the medallion with her free hand. "See this? I'm the baddest bitch on the planet right now. Just keep them back for a few more seconds. That's all I need. Be ready when I shout at you."

He didn't know what she thought would happen in so little time, but he nodded and turned back as the second demon lurched up.

Quinn threw another triquetra. The three-sided blade struck between the demon's eyes, burying deep into his head.

He howled and kept coming.

Dammit. Quinn threw another triangular blade that hit the same demon in his neck. He fell. That left four throwing blades.

But even more demons showed up below.

Who controlled these things?

The buzzing fog surrounding Quinn got louder.

He'd thought drawing in the demons was supposed to weaken that field. Even if Reese managed to rip a hole in the energy field, they still had ... over forty demons to go through to get off this tree.

Quinn threw his last four triquetras. They hit true, but now what?

One of the faster demons scrambled over the others and leaped up.

Quinn braced for the hit, but the demon looked up at Reese with a feral hunger. Then it swung under Quinn and did a crazy flip to shove his booted feet into Quinn's chest.

Shit, that hurt.

It knocked Quinn's footing loose.

He dangled from one hand.

The only good news was the demon's momentum sent it sliding backwards, then it clawed a hold and kicked off the next demon heading up.

During the split second that Quinn dangled, he saw Reese above him with the medallion sandwiched between her hands. She called out words that sounded tribal, like something Storm would chant.

Power burst from her fingers. A hundred lightning bolts shot up then split out into a fiery flower of electricity.

The energy field rocked and rolled like waves on an ocean.

Reese's skin glowed white hot.

A claw slashed at Quinn's leg. He hissed and yanked himself back up to a standing position before the demon had a chance to climb over him for Reese.

The demon's unholy eyes were locked on Reese.

He wanted only her.

Quinn shook his head. "Not while I'm alive you bloody son of a bitch."

That jerked the demon back to him.

Buzzing turned into the screeching sound of something being ripped apart. Rain poured down on Quinn suddenly, as though someone had dumped a giant bucket. The demon hissed, furious about something.

Quinn blinked away the water in his eyes and risked another quick look at Reese. She was shaking so hard he feared she would fall.

Her arms dropped to her sides. She yelled, *"Now, Quinn!"*

That's when he realized he could feel his power again. He lashed out at the demons on the tree, knocking each off with a kinetic hit. He could do this all day.

The tree swayed hard.

Quinn grabbed the trunk to hang on, looking up for Reese, who had started down.

She lost her grip.

She fell, yelling as she hit branches.

He shot an arm out and grabbed her wrist as she came by.

Her weight yanked them both to the side, because the freaking demons were pushing the small tree over.

Some were starting the climb back up.

Quinn couldn't use his kinetics with both hands tied up. After entering the demon's head in the cemetery, he'd rather not dive into another one's mind unless it was a last resort. Jumping in a nuclear sewage dump full of razors would feel better. His mind was still raw even all these hours later.

Reese looked at him with an expression he'd not seen in her face before. Terror. Demons were drawn to her energy like piranhas to fresh meat.

They wanted her energy.

To get it, they'd have to kill her.

She whispered, "It's okay, Quinn. Let me go. You can get to the others while I distract them."

His heart tried to crawl out of his chest.

She thought he'd hand her over to them?

Quinn gripped tighter and yanked her up to him. "Hold on to me or you'll face something worse than demons."

"What?"

"Me, pissed off. Understood?"

"Sir! Yes, Sir!" she answered with her signature sarcastic tone. The only thing missing was a salute.

He almost smiled, glad to hear her confidence back.

The tree creaked and leaned further over, but it was heading for another tree. Quinn pulled Reese around to his back. "Hold on tight. We're going flying. Ready?"

"I guess."

"Ready?" he shouted louder.

"Yes, just do something dammit."

He pushed off and throwing his kinetics downward, he maneuvered them over to a bigger tree. When he reached it, he grabbed a branch, twisting to put his back to the trunk, sandwiching her in.

"Hold my sides so I don't slide off. I need both hands."

She said something that might have been yes, if he could have dug that word out of the curses. He kept his back to her while she clutched him, and not gently.

Good woman.

Demons had made it up the first tree and leaped toward where he perched with Reese. Quinn batted those away with kinetics. He pointed his hands at thick trees, shoving them over. Solid trunks slammed demon bodies to the ground, breaking necks and backs. He dropped more trees, pinning down the flailing bodies.

The howling turned into groans and cries, but demons still crawled around on top of all that.

Rain pounded them and thunder beat across the skies.

Lightning bolts far bigger than Reese's shot down to the ground.

As the demons died, the canopy of energy kept ripping in different directions.

But more demons were coming. How many were there?

Reese said, "The energy field isn't completely gone. It's affecting my power, because I don't have much left."

Everything had a limit, even supernatural powers.

Quinn was stronger than most, but he'd started wearing down after using his power nonstop today. He should have more battle endurance, but the lingering field still fueled by demons that hadn't died was draining him, too.

It didn't take a rocket scientist to calculate that they wouldn't get past these demons without more muscle.

Reese said, "If I had my sword, I could mow them down, but I don't and we have no other way out."

Quinn considered what he could do.

He pulled out his mobile phone. No service.

He shouldn't use telepathy after they'd determined the traitor Beladors might pick up their telepathic thoughts, but this was a hopeless situation. If he didn't get Reese out of here and find the others, avoiding telepathy would mean nothing.

He opened his mind and called to Trey, *This is Quinn. Can you hear me?*

Trey's voice said, *We ... don't ...*

Quinn couldn't get anything intelligible out of that, but Trey was powerful so Quinn decided to transmit and hope Trey heard him. *Find Daegan. Tell him we're pinned down inside the abandoned mining hole near Blairsville. We need help. When our warriors get close, they should hear the buzzing, but we broke through the energy field. I'm stuck above a mass of demons with no way out. I think the others might be here, but I can't get to them.*

Trey's voice came through broken again. *lost ... help ... time ...*

Quinn's heart sank. They were out of time.

Demons were scaling trees all around them.

Reese wrapped her arms around him and put her head down against his back. He patted her arm, letting her know he was still with her.

He had enough energy to fight them hand to hand, but that would last only until too many attacked.

CHAPTER 34

Evalle's hands were shaking.

She'd rather be the one being tortured than listen to the sounds coming from Tristan every time they stuck him with a hot poker. If he could shift into a gryphon, he'd make them sorry they ever drew their first breath.

But if he could shift, then he could teleport.

His scream pierced the air.

Bile ran up her throat. If only Quinn had been able to tell her how to open this thing, she'd have some hope of sparing Tristan.

It wasn't Quinn's fault.

None of them had expected to be in this position trying to open a tomb he'd sealed, least of all her.

She couldn't use her kinetics, but she'd been pounding a rock against one spot and a crack had snaked open. Her head throbbed, just like Ixxter had said. She'd suffer anything for this thing to open and free Tristan.

"Come on," she begged the thin crack, gritting her teeth against the throbbing pain at her temples, but there was no way that crack was going to open the tomb.

Didn't matter. She called out as if she'd made progress. "I found an opening. I'm getting into it."

Big lie, but Tristan groaned and she took that to mean they were leaving him alone for a moment.

When no one replied, she turned to yell at Lorwerth again to come look.

Lorwerth smiled as if he'd won the lottery. "Very well, we can give Tristan a break. I don't want to kill him, especially when it's not necessary ... yet."

Evalle's knees tried to buckle with relief.

"However, we can't afford to waste time," Lorwerth continued in a relaxed tone. "I was good for my word in allowing your humans to leave, but they encountered our scouts. They're being held until I call to have them brought to the camp."

She might get sick after all.

If his men had contained Adrianna's Witchlock and Isak's demon blaster, there was no way out.

Lorwerth said, "Now, what were you saying, Evalle? Do you have that tomb open?"

"Uh, not exactly, but I did manage to—"

He made a tsking sound. "I only want to know when you have reached the body. Anything other than that is not acceptable." He turned to his men and jerked his head toward Tristan.

She had to finally look and regretted it.

Tristan had been stretched between two trees, six feet off the ground. Blood ran down his face where he'd fought them before the Laochra Fola had used kinetics to hit him with everything handy from logs to metal cans from their food storage.

When Lorwerth's man cut Tristan loose, he dropped to his knees. They'd stripped him to his jeans and had been using a branding iron all over his chest and back.

She bit down on her lip to keep from crying out. She couldn't allow Tristan to be touched again.

"I have no choice but to bring down one of the boys," Lorwerth said. "They won't last as long as Tristan, but that's the great thing about twins."

There was no way she'd let them hurt those boys, Kit, Adrianna, Isak or keep on hurting Tristan.

If she couldn't open the damn tomb, it was time to fight.

She tried bluffing first. "I'm having a hard time, but I know the person who can absolutely open this tomb."

Lorwerth lifted his eyebrows at that, unimpressed. "Quinn, right?"

"Yes. I'll take you to him, but only if the rest of them go free."

He laughed. "You think I'd do that? Besides, as long as I have you, he'll come to me. I have an hour to open that tomb. That means Tristan and your friends have an hour to live. If Quinn doesn't show up and I don't get the tomb open, it's still of value to me, just not as much. By that point, all of your friends will look worse than your Alterant here."

Tristan had been kneeling on the ground. He lifted a head and looked at Evalle. They had no telepathy, but his eyes echoed her thoughts.

They would die no matter what, so they would fight.

She gave a tiny nod the others would take to mean she was just lowering her chin to see him.

Clapping his hands once, Lorwerth said, "Okay, who will be next?"

Evalle said, "Me."

"What? You're the one who's going to open it."

"I tried. I can't. If you'll let me use telepathy, I can find the person who can. If not, I'm next."

Tristan growled, "No."

She ignored him.

Evalle walked over to where they'd stretched Tristan between the trees and lifted her arms.

Tristan gritted his teeth. "Evalle, don't."

"You can't go again."

"It's my duty."

Daegan had really gotten through to Tristan, but she wasn't standing by while they turned him into charred hamburger. A change in the buzzing sound pulled her gaze up.

Lorwerth chuckled, a sleazy sound. "I'll grant your wish, Evalle, if for no other reason than to entertain us while we wait. Based on the intel I've been given, Quinn and your Belador friends will come for you. If they don't arrive in time, then I'll keep Tristan and trade you with the tomb to Queen Maeve. Either way, I get what I want."

The energy field began undulating.

Lorwerth hadn't noticed yet, and said to Tristan, "Oh well. Looks like you get a chance to open the tomb, Alterant."

Two of his men walked over and each took an arm from Tristan. As Tristan got to his feet, he pushed out of their hands and turned to Evalle.

She looked at him and looked up.

His gaze followed hers.

Lorwerth must have noticed their silent exchange. He tipped his head back. "What the fuck?"

A crackling sound preceded rips tearing through the energy field, running in all directions like a cracked window. Water poured in streams from the thunderstorm raging outside the buzzing canopy.

Evalle felt a tiny hum of energy spike in her body. She called telepathically to Tristan. *Do you feel it?*

Tristan jerked his attention to her. *Yes. I don't think I'm strong enough to teleport.*

She warned, *I don't know what powers we have, but...*

He finished her sentence, *We have the power of surprise if we do it now.* Then he turned and whipped a kinetic strike at the two closest soldiers. Their heads snapped to the side, but that hadn't been enough kinetic power to take this group down.

Evalle tried to link with him. Nothing happened.

She dashed over next to Tristan as Lorwerth realized he was losing control of his little party. He had only six men in the camp and the rest spread around the perimeter outside.

He snarled, "Everyone in here now!"

If only that power grid waving wildly above them would just explode.

Evalle zapped kinetic hits, popping Lorwerth's men all around their faces. Tristan shouted, "Lower." He was hitting them in the groin. She changed her hits.

Lorwerth's men yanked their hands down and turned away, trying to protect their family jewels.

She told Tristan telepathically, *Lorwerth's back is exposed.*

Let's get him, Tristan agreed.

They rushed around behind Lorwerth, but he yanked one of his men in front of him at the last second, then turned and backed away.

Evalle and Tristan ran up against the first kinetic field, hitting it with what power they had, but another had joined the first to shield Lorwerth. Now they had two men with linked powers to face. Evalle and Tristan deflected the return hits, slapping as hard as possible, but they were being knocked back.

More men were pouring into the camp.

To lose now would be death. There were no more second chances.

Evalle had a quarter of her energy level and Tristan was still injured. Any minute now, Lorwerth would regain control and the fallout would be hideous.

A roar of fury cut through the noise.

Few things can reach deep inside someone to unlock a primal fear in even the strongest. That ferocious sound came from one of the most dangerous supernatural predators she knew of and he was running top speed toward the camp.

Mouths dropped open and eyes turned toward the black jaguar bigger than any found in a jungle. This one would annihilate everything between him and his mate.

"Storm!" Evalle cried out with joy.

The jaguar snarled a roar in answer that shook the ground. He bared fangs the length of her finger. His next roar warned that blood would spill.

The Laochra Fola that had been racing toward the camp now rushed out and formed a shoulder-to-shoulder shield.

Another roar boomed. Any person with a lick of sense would know to protect their throats, but it would do them no good.

Storm hit a wall of kinetics and got tossed back fifty feet.

Tristan said, "Shit. For once, I was glad to see him."

Evalle thought about warning him to keep his distance from Storm until she could calm down her mate. She'd have her hands full as it was, keeping Storm from going after Tristan, because Storm would blame this mess on him.

She wouldn't let him, since she'd partnered with Tristan of her own free will.

But that argument wouldn't happen if they didn't get out of here.

She and Tristan used a kinetic barrier against the hits from the four men guarding Lorwerth. That worked only because they were distracted by the greater threat on four legs trying to get through the shield Lorwerth's army had formed by linking their powers.

Evalle snapped her fingers. "Those Laochra Fola are linked."

"That means they're even stronger than us," Tristan said in grim acceptance.

"It also should mean that if we can kill one, they all die. The entire line would fall."

"How are we going to do that when the four protecting Lorwerth won't let us get past them?"

"I didn't say I had all the answers," she griped at him. "I'm just pointing out a weakness if we can find a way to exploit it."

Storm leaped at the kinetic force field again and again.

Lorwerth told his men, "Stand strong. The demons will take care of him."

With no kinetic power, Evalle couldn't get to Storm and he couldn't get past a forty-man wall of powerful kinetics holding him off.

Maybe she and Tristan could create a diversion that would allow them to reach just one of the linked soldiers. They could...

Demons raced in from the woods and Storm spun to face them. Alone.

Her heart sank. She'd seen Storm fight off dozens of demons, but he'd been a full demon himself at the time and she'd almost lost him.

She couldn't watch him give up the humanity he'd battled for and won.

They were all going to die.

CHAPTER 35

Quinn had never faced worse odds.

Uprooted trees were now connected like a pile of scattered logs propped up against one another. Demons, new arrivals, were climbing toward them from all directions, foaming at the mouth to reach the prize—Reese.

Her weight shifted behind him where she still hugged his body. He felt her stretch to look past him.

She said, "You need to help me move in front. I have what they want. There's no point in both of us dying when they'll ignore you as long as the energy inside me is ... available."

Translation: Until they drained her and left an empty shell.

That made him so angry he couldn't come up with a civil reply. "What the fuck, Reese? Do you really think I'm going to step aside and let them turn you into a demon buffet?"

She sniffled and his heart twisted at the sound.

She was afraid and offering herself as a sacrifice.

No, no, and hell fucking no.

Gripping his sides tighter, she said, "Why can't you be logical about this?"

"That's not the issue here." He kept his eyes on the demons, who thankfully were fighting among themselves below, but that wouldn't last long. If Quinn was going to die here, he wanted to know something. "What man treated you so badly that you think all of us are self-serving jerks who would allow a woman to die just so we can survive?"

The fight slowed below. Bad news.

Two demons leaped over the tangle of bodies to start climbing quickly up nearby trees.

Reese's breath started coming in fast gasps. "I don't think we have time for me to answer your question. Just move, dammit, and let me do one good thing with my life before I die."

"No. Keep your ass back there and out of my way. If we get out of this, you and I are going to have a talk."

She dropped her head to his back again. "Yeah, that's never going to happen."

Quinn had no desire to give up his life now and he sure as hell didn't want anything to happen to her, but if this was it for both of them they wouldn't die alone.

He sent out another telepathic shout for help. *Trey, this is Quinn. We've created a rip in the energy field, but we're pinned down near the west end of the mining ravine by more demons than we can—*

Fire burst through a break in the canopy, spewing fury in a seventy-foot stream and torching demons all over the ground. They turned into fireballs, then clouds of gray dust that puffed out of existence.

A red dragon thirty-five feet long from head to tail burst through the hole above and incinerated everything in its path. He blew trees out of the way and arched up, breaking the energy field apart even more.

Reese screeched. "What the hell is that?"

Quinn smiled. "My boss."

"He's a dragon? They don't exist."

"Some people would think the same about us. He's two thousand years old and I'm damned glad to see him."

In less than a minute, Daegan had swooped in and out, killing enough demons that Quinn could feel himself powering up as the energy field weakened and sputtered.

Bodies of half-dead demons flopped around below, but they were no longer a force.

Daegan's voice boomed in Quinn's head. *Can you get down from that tree?*

Absolutely.

Good. Let's go get our people.

We're up against an army of those warriors with Belador-like powers, which is probably why Evalle and Tristan haven't made it out.

Yeah, well, the enemy doesn't have a dragon. Let's go.

Quinn rolled his eyes at the arrogant shifter, but the saying went that it wasn't bragging if you could back it up. He hoped like hell Daegan's power was half as strong as his ego.

Patting Reese's hand, he said, "Jump on my back and hold on."

"What are you going to do?"

"It'll be easier to show you."

CHAPTER 36

Evalle couldn't stand there and watch Storm face a swarm of attacking demons by himself.

She took a step and Tristan grabbed her. "You can't get to him."

"Let go so I can help my mate or I will hurt you."

"Ah, shit. Let's go." He released her.

There was no time for convincing him not to join her, so they raced forward, slapping kinetic hits at Lorwerth's few men in the camp, but Evalle's strikes were falling as short as Tristan's.

Lorwerth shouted at his four guards, "Give me an alley!"

Evalle swiveled her head at the same moment Tristan looked at the threat.

Lorwerth sent a ball of flame at them.

Tristan slapped at it with his kinetics and Evalle stepped in front of him to take the hit. Tristan couldn't stand much more at this point. She shoved her hands in front of her and fire raced over the wimpy kinetic field she put up. The flash of heat seared her arms and burned half her shirt away.

Thankfully, it only singed her bra.

Evalle, I'm close.

She searched all around. *Quinn? Is that you?*

Yes. Where are you? Quinn shouted in her mind.

In the middle of the camp. Do you see it?

Yes. You and Tristan find somewhere out of the way.

Why?

An explosion of noise hit her at the same moment that Quinn said, *We've got air support.*

She grabbed her head to cover her ears. Tristan did the same. It was as if the sound barrier had been broken.

Fire rained down on the demons, yet managed to miss Storm, who was taking on three.

Evalle had her first taste of hope at the sight of a giant red dragon dive-bombing the camp. She called out telepathically, *Good to see you, Daegan.*

You as well, Evalle. Have you got your powers back?

She murmured, "My powers are getting stronger, Tristan. What about yours?"

Tristan nodded and answered Daegan. *Yes. We could help if we have permission to shift.*

Granted. Get your asses up here.

Tristan turned to her. "You first. I'll cover you."

Rather than argue that they were breaking a VIPER rule, Evalle backed up and forced the shift into her gryphon form as fast as she could. It hurt like hell, but the quicker she did this, the sooner Tristan could shift and give his healing a huge boost.

She stretched and stood as the wings took shape, towering over those puny Laochra Fola who didn't look so tough now. She stretched her wings, showing off her aqua feathers. She raised her golden head and screeched out a war cry.

When Lorwerth and his personal guards turned to her, the shock riding their faces made her day.

When Lorwerth saw Tristan shifting, he shouted at his men to kill Tristan.

Evalle swatted the four guards with one kinetic hit of her lion-shaped paws and they went flying thirty feet, landing next to the line of soldiers still holding a wall between her and Storm.

With her, Tristan and Daegan on the same telepathic channel, Evalle said, *Daegan, that line of men blocking Storm are linked. Take out one and they all fall.*

The dragon had just made a fiery pass over the open area and flapped faster, rushing out then banking hard to come back in. He burned a wide path through the middle of everything, but every other guard in the line quickly lifted his field of energy like a shield to protect their heads.

Tristan finished fully shifting. He told Evalle and Daegan, *Fire isn't making a dent. Too many of them linked.*

Isak stepped out of the woods at the top of a hill with his blaster in hand. He advanced toward Storm, plowing through the demons that were still rushing in.

Storm had killed ten, but he was bleeding all over.

Evalle had an idea and decided that dragon could multi-task the best right now. She told Daegan, *We'll handle this side. Adrianna has to be somewhere behind the human with the blaster. Don't kill him. That's Isak. Have Quinn find her and see if she can get under that wall of kinetics.*

I'm going now.

Daegan scorched the ground, turning demon after demon to gray dust so quickly it sizzled before the rain washed it away.

Isak worked his way toward Storm, who ripped the head off of a demon, but three more took its place.

You got this, Tristan? Evalle asked.

Oh, yes, this bunch and Lorwerth are mine. Go get your tomcat.

Evalle took to the air as Tristan turned to Lorwerth, who was getting up off the ground.

Tristan used his kinetics to lift a steel rod that had been left heating in the fire. He sent it flying like a spear that hit Lorwerth, lifting him off the ground and staking him to a tree. He screamed.

Way to go, Tristan.

Evalle flapped her wings, gaining air. Isak had never seen any of them fly, but she hoped he'd seen her and Tristan shifting into gryphons just now. Surely by now, Isak had guessed that the red dragon providing air support was the man she'd told Isak had spent thousands of years cursed as a dragon throne.

She circled once and swept down, knocking demons every which way with her kinetics. With no immediate demons to fight, her jaguar turned right and left, looking for a target.

Then he lifted his head.

She'd never get over the awe and pride in Storm's jaguar gaze. She'd seen the firelight glimmer across Tristan's blue skin and translucent scales. Her own golden head and aqua feathers with blue skin would be just as spectacular. A glow of pleasure filled her.

Storm was finally seeing her gryphon form. He roared a sound of possession. She was his and he was hers.

The minute she shifted back to human, he would be furious at her for being in danger. She'd suffer his irritation as long as they both lived.

Adrianna ran out of the woods and stopped with her palm open. Witchlock power spun into a sphere the size of a basketball.

Wow. That was larger than anything Evalle had witnessed to date. Adrianna had said she was still learning to control the power. Evalle hoped she knew enough to not turn them all into dust.

The Sterling witch sent a comet-shaped blast of energy airborne. It flew high above, so high it crossed over the top of the trees around the camp. Using the same hand that wielded Witchlock, Adrianna directed the flight path of the fiery comet.

It landed behind the guards.

When the energy struck the ground, the earth opened and swallowed it.

Heads turned from the linked line.

Evalle held her breath.

Tristan murmured telepathically, *Come on, witch.*

In the next second, a sizzle of power shot up at the guard in the middle of the pack. He screamed and jumped around, then arched his back. His body shook viciously as if he were being electrocuted.

The entire line of men started screaming in pain, then the first one went limp and fell, his back hitting the ground.

Quinn came racing in behind Adrianna with Reese at his side.

Five demons were still alive, because their corporeal forms remained on the ground. Two struggled to lift their heads, both turning in Reese's direction.

Evalle sent a quick message to Quinn. *Those demons are still alive, Quinn.*

I can handle them.

If Evalle could see them, so could everyone else, including Storm who had a ground-level view.

Three demons pushed to their feet and headed toward Quinn and Reese. Quinn pushed Reese behind him and took out three with his kinetic power.

Huh. That was interesting.

Storm made quick work of the fourth, ripping off its head even before the dust released.

Daegan came soaring in over the top of the ravine that was now drenched everywhere with rain. Evalle couldn't see any remnant of fog left, which meant the buzzing field had to be gone.

The fire pit had continued to burn through all of it. That would take more than dirt to douse at some point.

Cold air swept over her wings. Evalle looked up at the skies where the storm was diminishing. No lightning or thunder. The clouds had thinned and were no longer spewing rain.

Daegan slowed and landed in the clearing right in front of a demon that clawed the ground, scrambling on all fours. It was crawling toward Quinn and Reese.

The scary dragon stared at the demon as if he studied a bug, then Daegan punted the body forty feet into the air.

The demon burst into dust mid-flight.

Daegan's face twisted into what Evalle took to be a toothy dragon grin, enjoying his soccer goal moment. Did he even know what soccer was? Doubtful.

Evalle landed next to Daegan, dwarfed by his huge, red body, and she was no small potatoes.

Isak and Adrianna walked toward her and Daegan.

Evalle felt a rough tongue lick her leg.

She looked down to find Storm rubbing against her and giving her a look she easily read as "I love you, but you're in deep trouble."

She sighed, which came out sounding like a snort in her gryphon form. Oops. She hoped Storm didn't take it as a challenge.

Swiping his tail slowly back and forth, Daegan stomped into the camp with Evalle and Storm following. He sent a telepathic order to Evalle and Tristan. *Shift back into your human forms.*

Uh, Daegan, Evalle started. *My mate will lose his mind if I shift into a nude woman.*

The dragon swung his massive body around. His tail whacked Lorwerth's drooped body. The man groaned.

Storm stood in front of Evalle as if he intended to protect her from Lorwerth, even though she was a giant gryphon.

Go ahead and shift, Evalle. I will take care of clothing.

At that, Evalle called up the change, noticing that Tristan was doing the same. As her legs and arms formed, she felt cloth drape over her body. He'd put her in ... a shift-type dress.

Really?

She never wore dresses.

That choice probably made sense for a man who had lived two thousand years ago and didn't know enough about modern clothes to majik up the right thing, but a *dress*?

Tristan, however, ended up in jeans and a T-shirt.

She looked up at Daegan and snapped, "Sexist much?"

Storm shifted. When he stood behind her, put his hands on her shoulders. "I don't give a damn as long as you're covered."

The dragon grinned again.

Men.

Tristan complained, "Can't you cover him up?"

A puff of smoke blew out of Daegan's nostrils. He was getting impatient, but he put Storm in a pair of jeans.

Quinn and Reese joined them as Isak and Adrianna walked up to stand beside Evalle and Storm. Quinn asked, "Are you okay, Evalle?"

"I'm fine. Tristan's the one they tortured."

Storm muttered, "Those are love taps compared to what I'm going to do to him for dragging you into this."

Evalle spun around in his arms and whispered in his ear, "I need to feel you as soon as we get out of here. Can we skip the argument and go right to makeup sex?"

He answered her by pulling her around and giving her a kiss that ranked right up there with sex against the wall.

Tristan grumbled, "Give me a break."

That drew everyone's attention to him. Evalle turned in Storm's arms again, but this time he wrapped his around her front where she'd wanted them.

Daegan whipped his big dragon head down to face Tristan.

Evalle caught their telepathic discussion since Daegan must have decided to keep her privy.

Daegan asked, *Why didn't you come to me, Tristan?*

Tristan, probably not realizing Evalle was listening said, *You trusted me with the knowledge that they can kill you in another realm. We need you to lead. I was trying to handle this without putting you at risk.*

When Daegan replied, his tone was soft. *I do trust you without question, but that does not mean I expect you to battle our enemies without me. I will continue to share things with you, but you cannot decide to protect me without my knowledge. We must always show a strong front by joining together against any enemy. Understood?*

Yes. I'm sorry.

No, never be sorry for doing your duty. Be proud, because I am. I couldn't ask for a better second.

Tristan nodded, clearly humbled.

Daegan shifted to his human form in the next instant. He must've had a reason for choosing leather boots this time, along with clothing that came right out of medieval times. He wore a huge sword strapped across his back in a sheath. She had no doubt a body that size could swing that sword with one hand.

He was one magnificent warrior, someone Evalle could follow into battle.

Evalle heard a low curse from her left. It was Isak. Evalle looked over her shoulder. "Thanks for the backup."

"You're welcome," Isak said, but he never took his eyes off Daegan. Isak didn't sound happy at all.

Adrianna gave Evalle a half smile. "Your turn to pick up lunch."

"You got it."

When Evalle turned back, Daegan was heading for Lorwerth.

She wanted to be there for that conversation, to find out who had been behind all of this and just who *was* Lorwerth.

Daegan called out to Quinn, "I may need your mind lock ability."

Quinn walked past Evalle.

She caught his arm and when he turned she said, "Daegan may not have understood that it's actually against your *moral* code to enter a mind without permission."

"That's not an issue this time. I would open up this enemy's mind with a sword and dip out what I needed if I thought that would work."

Whoa. That was more fire in Quinn's eyes than she'd seen since Kizira had died. Evalle glanced at Reese, who had nothing to say to anyone.

She wore her medallion again.

Why hadn't she left once she realized they'd found the tomb?

The small building was pretty damn obvious standing in the middle of the camp, still unopened.

CHAPTER 37

Quinn strode past the burned tents and into the center of the camp, sparing a brief glance for the silent tomb.

I'm sorry Kizira. I will find a way to keep you and our secret safe from our enemies.

When Reese left his side, wandering over to look at the tomb, he held his breath.

What powers, yet unseen, did she possess with that medallion?

She must have felt his eyes on her, because she turned around. She said, "Go. This is safe ... from everyone."

He had to trust her.

If she could spirit it away, she would have, right?

"Quinn?" Daegan called sharply.

Quinn stepped over to where Tristan and Daegan hovered near the person Tristan had identified as Lorwerth, who was no longer stuck to the tree. Quinn stopped short at the sight of a steel rod sticking out his back.

The tip jutted from his chest. "Can he be saved?"

Daegan shook his head. "I tried once and the wound ripped open. That is his doing."

Rain faded to a light drizzle as Daegan asked, "Where have you been since I last saw you, Lorwerth?"

Tristan looked as surprised as Quinn. Daegan knew Lorwerth?

The dying man snickered in a nasty way. "I can't believe you're still alive. I get sent to Anwynn and you end up living like a king. Literally. Again." He coughed and blood ran from the corner of his mouth.

"You don't deserve any life, not after what you did to help Maeve capture me. My sisters died because of you and Maeve. Did you kill my father, too?"

Again, Quinn exchanged a look with Tristan at this new information on Daegan's past.

Lorwerth twisted up his face in disgust. "The three of you deserved what you got. I didn't kill the king. Miserable brother that he was, he left me nothing."

Daegan lifted an eyebrow. "You weren't even blood related. My father took you in as one of *his* father's bastards, then treated you as a full brother, and we respected you as our uncle. You inherited the crown. Were you so greedy that not even *that* was enough?"

"A crown is nothing but decoration. Your father hid the fortunes he'd amassed. I was left with enough to feed the castle each month. Nothing more. It was his fault I made the deal that landed me in Anwynn to begin with and your fault your sisters died. Not mine."

The man had to be insane to say such a thing to Daegan at this point.

Surprisingly, Daegan agreed. "Aye, it was as much my fault. My arrogance as much as your betrayal, but you acted in hate and I acted in love. I don't care why you ended up in Anwynn, but who pulled you from that place and for what reason? Was it Macha?"

"That goddess still around? I have nothing to do with her."

Storm had joined them and announced, "Truth."

Daegan nodded his thanks and asked, "What about Queen Maeve?"

"I was to deliver the body to her."

"Truth," Storm confirmed then added, "but he's holding something back."

"Who else is involved?" Daegan pressed.

Lorwerth stared at him with bold defiance.

Daegan told the dying man, "This ends here and now. You tell me who is behind this."

Lorwerth laughed hysterically, which turned into racking coughs.

Everyone looked to Daegan, who stared at Lorwerth with

hate that was palpable.

Quinn asked, "Is he so far gone that he doesn't realize he's about to die?"

Lorwerth breathed in and out, his lungs gurgling. The smell of his blood tinged air left fresh by the rain. "I know exactly what will happen, but you don't, Daegan. This is not the end. This is the tip of what's coming. I've wanted to die for thousands of years. I'm ... I'm getting the best of the deal. I finally get to rest."

Daegan turned a dark face on Quinn.

Quinn warned, "If the same person who shielded the minds of these guards protected his as well, his mind may disintegrate as soon as I break through that layer. I can try, but I'll very likely just kill him when the shield implodes."

"You can't get through," Lorwerth rasped with smug authority. "My mind is more secure than any of the guards. I can control my own protective layer."

Quinn checked Storm, who nodded.

Standing up, Quinn said, "Well, that answers that. But ... I can try, if you wish for me to finish this."

Evalle said, "Quinn?"

He lifted a hand to silence her.

If Lorwerth died because of refusing to allow Quinn to enter when the man knew who was killing innocent people at will, then so be it.

Daegan shook his head. "I will never ask you to do a task that is mine alone."

Lorwerth looked confused. "What are you saying?"

Daegan reached over his head and withdrew a sword from the sheath on his back. "As the last of the dragon kings, I declare you guilty. You shall die by the sword, as that is the punishment as decreed during the time of dragons." Daegan lifted the sword.

Fear flushed color into Lorwerth's pale face, then a thought lit his eyes with mean amusement. "You don't know, do you?"

The sword hesitated in midair. "What are you talking about, Lorwerth?"

The crazy guy cackled a dead man's laugh. He coughed up more blood and spoke in a ragged voice. "I love it. You don't even know about the others."

Quinn watched Daegan's face lose its calm determination and

turn into the face of one who looked like he'd been given unexpected hope.

Daegan ordered, "Who are you talking about?"

The sickening sounds coming from Lorwerth were getting softer. "Blood kin ... she ... "

Daegan lowered the sword and dropped to a knee. "Tell me. Of whom do you speak?"

Lorwerth's eyes rolled up.

Cursing the man, Daegan stood and shoved the sword into its scabbard.

Quinn would have liked to find out more about that exchange, but he had to make sure no one had tampered with the tomb. He needed a plan for what to do about the Tribunal meeting breathing down his neck.

So little time left to make such a big decision.

He told Daegan. "Give me a minute to check the tomb."

Daegan waved him off, then the dragon king turned to Evalle and Storm, talking about cleanup.

Quinn's gaze went straight to where he'd last seen Reese.

Where was she?

CHAPTER 38

After a last check to see that Storm and Daegan could handle cleanup, Adrianna returned to where Isak had his mother in a bear hug. The woman was rock solid and hadn't whimpered or complained, even for a second. Adrianna respected Kit for the front she'd shown, but tonight Kit had faced real monsters that were a whole different level of terrifying.

The sooner Isak got her out of here, the better for Kit, who would not want to break down around the boys.

Adrianna checked on the twins, since Evalle would expect her to do that. She had to be careful not to wound their young manly pride.

She asked Kellman, the always calm and levelheaded of the two, "You guys going to be okay?"

"We're good." His wary gaze drifted to Isak. "I don't think he's ever going to let us near Kit again."

Talk about a heart wrenching sound in Kellman's sad voice. That ripped Adrianna's own heart, which hadn't had the best of days already.

But Isak had shown signs that he might be rethinking his harsh reaction when he'd first learned of his mother's kidnapping.

He's only human, Adrianna reminded herself with a chuckle at the truth.

She told the boys, "Give me a minute to find out the travel arrangements since I came here with Isak. I'm fairly certain he had all your camping gear and his mother's SUV picked up by his men. There should be plenty of room for all of us in his

Hummer."

At least the rain had quit, but now the night air was turning cool. Her body was tired of the bouncing weather changes.

When she walked up to Isak, Adrianna asked, "How are you doing, Kit?"

Kit unfolded herself from her overprotective son's embrace. "I've had better days, but I count that we're all safe as a blessing."

Evalle came running up to the group, really fast with the return of her super Belador speed. First she grabbed the boys and hugged them.

The relief on their faces warmed Adrianna's heart.

Seeing Evalle hug anyone was quite a change from when Adrianna had first met her.

Technically, the boys were legally adults. They'd grown up on the streets of Atlanta, but from what Evalle had shared with Adrianna, they'd gotten mothering from Kit that they'd never experienced. Clearly it had been good for them.

Kellman and Kardos might need a touch of that mothering now.

Evalle left the pair off to the side and walked up to Isak. "I'm glad everyone is okay."

He said nothing. The man had a head as hard as granite.

Kit told Evalle, "Thank you for coming to get us and please thank Tristan."

"I will." Evalle looked at Isak then Adrianna during the uncomfortable silence.

Kit cleared her throat and announced, "I need to talk to the boys."

Isak said in a firm but gentle voice, "Kit."

All Kit did was lift a finger, pointing straight up, and Isak gave up his argument.

That small woman had some kind of power in that one finger. Impressive.

Adrianna might have to ask Kit for lessons.

Walking away on shaking legs, Kit might be still rattled, but she was not one to cross.

"Stay away from her," Isak said in a quiet voice that Kit wouldn't hear, but Evalle and Adrianna couldn't miss the order he'd issued.

Evalle didn't even try to hide her shock. "What?"

Adrianna didn't want to believe he'd act this way now. Not right after everyone had risked their lives to save Kit and the boys. She asked Isak, "What is it you think I'm going to do to her?"

"Nothing, because you're never going to be around her again."

That was as final as it got.

Swallowing the lump that formed in her throat, Adrianna reminded herself she'd faced worse in her life without showing any crack in her mask.

She wasn't about to give him the benefit of knowing how deeply his words cut. She reminded him, "Staying away from Kit might be hard to accomplish since you made me come here in your truck."

"Not a problem. One of my men will be waiting for you and the boys."

She had survived years of poor treatment from her Sterling witch family and missed her sister desperately since her twin had died so that Witchlock would not land in the wrong hands.

If Isak thought he could break her, he was wrong, but he'd done a damn good job of knocking the foundation out from under her heart.

She gave an abrupt nod and started to leave, but Evalle grabbed her arm. "Wait a minute."

Then Evalle took Isak to task. "How can you be that way to her?"

He was just as cold to Evalle. "I'm done with you people."

"*You* people?" Evalle asked in a tone of warning.

Isak made it clear he was unwilling to say more than, "She can take the boys home or you can. Kit's going with me."

Evalle sounded ready for another throwdown. "*She* has a name. It's Adrianna."

He ignored her and said, "I don't want Kit around witches, demons or any other *things* again."

Looking over at Kit and the boys, who thankfully weren't listening, Evalle said, "Why are you being an ass, Isak? Bad enough that you treat Adrianna this way, but Kit loves those boys and they love her."

Adrianna sighed. "Give it up, Evalle. We'll never be more than strange *things* to him."

That must have pushed Isak's pissed-off button harder. "Kit is all I have. I don't want anyone to ever put her in that kind of situation again. The best way for me to ensure that never happens is to keep her away from ... nonhumans."

Evalle gave him an incredulous look and huffed. "Now I understand why Adrianna said she can't be with someone who can't meet her halfway."

"That's no longer an issue."

Staring holes through him, Adrianna waited until Isak finally looked her in the eyes. She said, "Would have been nice if you'd just listened to me when I tried to tell you we wouldn't work. Would have been even nicer if you'd never come by my house last night. Just so we're clear, don't *ever* come near me again or send your men. I won't play the good witch next time."

Bitter? Yes. She'd opened her heart and her body to this man and he'd stomped on her trust.

Spewing curses under her breath, Evalle shoved her hands on her hips. "Your loss, Isak. Big loss."

For a moment, he looked at Adrianna as if he agreed with Evalle, but Adrianna forced herself to stand stoically. She'd learned to manage her facial reactions many years ago and right now she had stone-cold bitch face firmly in place.

Isak called to Kit, "You ready, Kit?"

Kit hugged each of the twins, whispering to them. Then she joined Isak. As he stepped away, he said over his shoulder, "The second Hummer will be waiting for you."

Evalle replied, "She doesn't need it and neither do the boys. We take care of our people."

Still, Adrianna said nothing so he continued on with his mother.

The twins walked over and Evalle asked them, "Did you power up your hearing and eavesdrop?"

They didn't even look embarrassed when they both said, "Yes."

"Shoot. I'm sorry."

Kardos shrugged. "Don't worry about it. We're not

concerned. Kit said she'd have a talk with Isak."

Adrianna didn't have the heart to tell them that wasn't going to fix it. Isak was now firmly on the opposite side of the line drawn between humans and nonhumans.

She'd stay on her side, far away from the man who had mangled her heart. He'd never get that close to it again.

CHAPTER 39

Frogs were singing a chirping chorus, probably celebrating the end of the monsoon that had hit Atlanta.

A soft, chilly breeze stirred the night air as Quinn found Reese standing back, staring at the tomb with a face covered in worry.

"Thank you for staying, Reese."

She turned and the sadness in her eyes tore at him.

What was so awful in her world? He asked, "What's wrong?"

"Nothing."

He'd figured out that she had an interest in Kizira's body and was damned glad she hadn't done anything to make him regret letting her stay around. Not yet.

"Reese, I don't know who sent you here, but I don't think your interest in Kizira's body is personal. Am I right?"

"Yes."

He waited, hoping she'd give him more, but Reese was not someone who gave up anything without a fight. He actually admired that about her. "What did you want with Kizira's body?"

"Nothing really. Coming here was a means to an end. I was offered something significant for delivering her to another interested party," she explained, stepping carefully with her words. "But ... I now realize the only place Kizira belongs is wherever you place her."

After battling for this tomb, Quinn was humbled that this person who had no investment in him or his life would understand what this meant to him. He'd told Reese nothing about how he had to protect his daughter and that Kizira held the key to finding her, but this woman understood the emotional connection that he had anyhow.

She'd also seen what he hadn't been able to admit—that he'd have to let the body go at some point.

He'd come to terms with that today.

His friends were just as understanding, but this little pistol of a female had been the only one to force him out of the dark place where he'd been living for too long.

She'd made him take stock of what really mattered.

His daughter.

Now that he thought about it, maybe he could make good on what she was doing for him. He could replace Reese's loss by offering her a better deal. No matter what someone else had offered, Quinn would top that as a thank you and offer her more if she could help him find his daughter.

"It was nice meeting you, Quinn, and I wish you luck with all this." She was holding her medallion in a white-knuckled grip.

That sounded like goodbye. "I'm glad I met you, too, Reese, and I'll have someone give you a ride wherever you want to go, but first I have an idea—"

Evalle shouted, "*Quinn!*"

Shit. "I'll be right back." Quinn stepped over and looked around the corner of the tomb. "What?"

"You don't have much time left."

"I know. Give me a minute." He turned around and ... Reese wasn't there. He raced around the structure even though he knew this time she was really gone.

She couldn't have walked out of here that quickly.

That medallion. Had she teleported away?

He trudged back to where Daegan and Storm had returned most of the ravine to its natural state.

Tristan asked Daegan, "If Queen Maeve isn't behind this, then who is?"

"I don't know, but Lorwerth ..."

"Who was that guy?" Quinn asked.

"He comes from my time. He was my uncle, but he wasn't born with powers. I have no idea who gave him Laochra Fola warriors."

"Good thing they're all dead," Quinn pointed out.

"These may be dead, but the god who created them has more.

Rumors flowed about them years ago." Daegan scratched his head and seemed to catch himself. "When we're back on Treoir we'll talk more. I need time to think on what he was saying and what he didn't say."

All of that was clear as mud.

Evalle gave Quinn a worried glance.

Yes, it was almost time for the Tribunal. Quinn told Daegan, "You should probably teleport out of here pretty soon."

"And why is that?"

"The time draws near for me to go to the Tribunal. I apologize again for putting us all in a difficult situation. If I had it to do over, I would have handled her body differently. I had never heard of the Blood Law until Queen Maeve called it into force and demanded the Tribunal act upon it."

"I didn't get the whole run down on the Blood Law," Tristan said. "What is it exactly?"

Daegan stood silently with his arms crossed over his chest as Quinn explained it with specifics.

He wrapped it up by saying, "I did have an honorable reason, but that's not important now." He paused to look at the tomb.

Tristan said, "Daegan hasn't met Sen."

"No big loss there," Evalle offered. "Sen's a boil on the ass of humanity."

Daegan tossed an eyebrow up at that. "Friendly, are you?"

"No. He hates me. He's tried every way possible to have me locked away forever. He came close more than once. That I'm still walking around free is something he probably considers a personal failure."

Quinn noted that Daegan was taking it all in.

Tristan said, "Basically Sen is VIPER's and the Tribunal's messenger boy and enforcer."

"True," Quinn confirmed. "That's why he can find me anywhere in this realm. The minute they realize we are no longer loyal to Macha, they'll expect you to come and meet the Tribunal. The only reason it hasn't happened yet is because none of us have said a word about you taking over Treoir, but no point in putting you in that situation today. If being in the human realm is not a safe place for you, then I seriously doubt going to a realm with three non-ally entities would be any better an idea."

Daegan asked, "What will happen at this Tribunal?"

"They'll demand Kizira's body and for me to hand it over to Queen Maeve. I can open the tomb, but it's a slow process. I had wanted you to teleport it away, but at this point the only safe place for me, or the tomb, would be Treoir. Sending me there would put the Beladors in conflict with VIPER. The Tribunal would lash out. Our people would die."

Daegan listened as if he weighed every word Quinn spoke. The dragon king said, "What other options are there?"

"Not many. I will not open the tomb, so they'll want to hand me over to Queen Maeve as compensation. If I create a disturbance first, they may decide to lock me up instead. That's my best option right now."

"What kind of disturbance?"

Quinn rubbed his chin. "I might try to dive into Sen's head and see if there's anything in there besides hate."

Evalle said, "Quinn! You're kidding, right? Sen would kill you on the spot."

Exactly what he was thinking. "Of course, I'm joking."

Storm had walked up at that moment and his mouth dropped open with shock. He knew Quinn was lying. Quinn held his gaze, hoping Storm understood what Quinn was doing.

Storm's face darkened with anger, but he held Quinn's confidence. Good man.

"I see," Daegan announced. "And you think to rush me off so I'm not harmed when this Sen shows up?" Daegan's words held a touch of amusement.

"To be honest, yes. The Beladors need you. They need your leadership, and in particular, they need you because you care about them as more than an army to feed your power. We can't afford for anything to happen to you."

Tristan let out a long sigh. "Trust me when I say Daegan's not going to listen to you."

Evalle put in her two cents worth. "What's the deal, Daegan? If you have a vulnerability, you should let us know so we can watch your back."

Daegan bristled. "You expect me to admit a weakness? We already went over that."

"Good grief. You men just kill me." She crossed her arms,

looking just as deadly as the dragon king. "We have to build a cohesive army. If we know where someone will attack, we can defend against it, but if you don't tell us, then we're of no use to you, the Treoir family or the Beladors."

Storm watched with a grin that said, *my woman.*

"You've made a valid point," Daegan admitted. "I don't wish to speak of this further outside of Treoir, but I'll admit it's the truth that I'm at greater risk from a god or goddess if I'm in a realm other than Treoir or my mother's."

Before Quinn could ask just who his mother was, power flooded the area and Sen appeared between their group and the tomb.

The liaison took one look around and asked, "What happened here?"

"It does not involve you," Daegan answered.

Sen arched an arrogant eyebrow at Daegan. "Who are you?"

"I might ask the same of you."

Tension crept higher. Any minute now the air would combust from it.

Since there was no way to hide their new leader, Quinn nodded at Daegan and said, "This is Daegan Treoir, the new ruler of the Beladors." He didn't want to share the part about Daegan being a dragon since less was always better in these situations. "And this is Sen, the VIPER liaison I told you about."

Both of Sen's eyebrows lifted. "What happened to Macha?"

Tristan replied, "She didn't work out. We had to let her go."

Daegan found that amusing.

Quinn gave up all hope of saving their dragon king.

"How long has she been gone?" Sen asked, now sounding like he was the goddess police.

That was a question Quinn might have to answer in the Tribunal, which meant he couldn't lie or he'd light up like a red beacon. "Five days."

"And VIPER is just now being informed?"

"No," Daegan said. "*You're* being informed. Anyone else will be informed as I get around to it. If you have an issue with a Belador, you bring it to me."

Sen's chuckle had an evil kick. "No. If I have an issue with anyone, I take it to the Tribunal. I don't answer to anyone else.

I've heard nothing about you taking over the Beladors, which means you've failed to inform VIPER and the Tribunal. They aren't going to be happy to find out the Beladors aren't under a pantheon."

Shrugging, Daegan said, "I don't care what they think."

Quinn silently groaned.

Evalle chewed on her lip and Storm now stood with his hand on her shoulder.

Tristan frowned, flipping his gaze from Daegan to Sen and back.

Sen laughed out loud. "You aren't going to be around for long." Then Sen addressed Quinn, "Time for you to open that tomb and pull out Kizira's body." He'd pointed his thumb over his shoulder.

When Evalle sucked in a breath, Quinn leaned over to look at what caused her reaction.

Sen finally turned. "What happened to the tomb?"

Quinn told him, "I have no idea." But if Tristan or Daegan had teleported it away, Kizira was still not safe from Queen Maeve.

Angry now, Sen said, "Let's go."

Daegan said, "I believe I'll join you."

Quinn sent Daegan a telepathic message. *You can't go there, Daegan. Those three entities in the Tribunal can do whatever they want. You'd be facing triple a god's power.*

Daegan replied in the same silent way. *I will not have my people standing alone to face any threat.*

Quinn had to tell Evalle how to open the tomb and what to do with Kizira's body. He said to Sen for everyone's benefit, "I have two minutes before I'm due at the meeting. I'd like to talk with my team—"

The bastard smiled and waved his hands, sending them teleporting.

CHAPTER 40

Realm of Tuatha Dé Danann

Dakkar found Macha stretched out on a lounger covered in white and gold fur. She stared out into an endless dimension that appeared to be an infinite sky.

In reality, the view was whatever she dreamed up in her home realm of Tuatha Dé Danann.

He'd spent years running a bounty operation, even cutting a deal with VIPER to allow him space to function in North America of the human world as long as his people performed the occasional operation for the coalition. He'd built quite an empire and most of the preternaturals had no idea just how large it was or how far his reach extended.

But Macha knew.

She and Dakkar went back, way back.

One day, he would have almost as much power as she did. Almost.

He couldn't travel here unless she teleported him.

For now.

She'd been sullen since leaving Treoir Island. *Let's not sugarcoat it. She was tossed out.*

Without moving a muscle to face him, she asked, "Do you bring good news, Dakkar?"

"Yes, and no."

She moved a muscle this time and changed locations faster than he could blink. She had him up in the air with his throat gripped so tightly in one hand, he gasped for air. The goddess could not be harmed here.

He wouldn't dare use power against her in this realm, not if he wanted to live another day.

Energy flashed around her in golden sparks.

He stroked her arm with his hand, trying to calm her.

After several long seconds of watching stars fly through his gaze, she released him. His feet hit the ground, but he had preternatural agility that he'd been born with, just another perk for a mage of his power.

He straightened his suit jacket and smoothed back his hair. Macha had once enjoyed running her hands through his black hair. He'd have her back in his bed again, but not until she saw him as an equal. His muscular body had served him well under the rule of Genghis Khan, but the majik he'd been born with and a keen intelligence had made the difference between dying in that era or becoming immortal.

All he had to do was hand Macha what she wanted and she would give him what *he* wanted, with a smile. He cleared his throat and explained, "I was successful in my campaign with Lorwerth."

"Oh?"

Now he had her attention. "Yes, the Laochra Fola performed as expected. We even had Kizira's body in hand at one time."

"*At one time* is the same as saying you failed to gain possession of it. I had a purpose for that body." She floated away, ignoring him.

Actually, he wanted to thrash Lorwerth for costing him Kizira's body *and* the gryphons, but all of them were expendable in view of the greater goal. "I understand my dove, but that body has too many people vying for it. Besides, that's hardly the good news."

Turning on a loud sigh, she said, "Then enlighten me."

"We had Evalle and Tristan captive along with the tomb."

She flew back to him. "And?"

"Daegan came for them himself."

Now he had her attention. Her eyes glowed with excitement. "Did you kill that dragon?"

"Not yet."

She flew away, screaming in rage.

Gorgeous female minions came running in. "What do you require of us, goddess?"

"Nothing. Go away."

They were gone just as quickly.

Macha swept around in a flurry of sparkling gold and red. Her entire gown moved as a light display. "How is any of this good news?"

"Because now I know for sure I can bring Daegan out of Treoir. He's arrogant in thinking he's safe."

She didn't praise him, but neither did she blast him. "How many of my Beladors did you kill?"

"None actually. When you take control of Treoir again, you'll still have an army."

"*If* I take control again," she said, floating down to settle on the lounger again with an exquisite but glum face.

Now that the atmosphere had improved, Dakkar strolled over. "Not if, but when. I told you. We both have goals. I'm here to help with yours, then you can help with mine."

"I want that dragon dead. The minute he's dead that island is mine again."

"Soon, but not yet. You need the Beladors to want to follow you again. That isn't going to happen right now and definitely not if you are blamed for killing their new pet dragon. Everything will happen in its own time. At the right time. I would have preferred to deliver the body and gryphons to you as well as kill Daegan. Were that within my power, it would have happened," he pointed out to remind her she could have given him additional juice for facing Daegan. "I was not in a position to kill the dragon, but the additional good news is that he now thinks Maeve was behind all of this."

The energy that had been firing around her calmed.

She smiled, which was the same as high praise from this goddess.

Finally, the time Dakkar had spent dealing with that miserable Lorwerth and his heinous Laochra Fola was going to pay dividends.

He eased down next to her, taking Macha's slender hand in his. He kissed the soft skin, looking forward to gaining more than her good graces. "You are too beautiful to be kept tucked away in this realm. You are too powerful to be denied. You are too intelligent to allow anyone to outplay you. I am your servant in all things."

"Very well. What do you have in mind, Dakkar?"

Here was the woman he could play like a finely-tuned instrument.

CHAPTER 41

Tribunal meeting, Nether Realm

Quinn blinked his eyes as the teleporting ended. He checked the raised dais first to see if there was any chance Loki had passed on this meeting.

Nope. There stood the trickster god who created turmoil just to be entertained. Today he had brilliant blue eyes, black hair slicked back, and was wearing a suit Armani would be proud to sell.

To the side of that annoying god stood another one.

Hermes always appeared as bored. He played a happy little tune on his tortoiseshell lyre, which was basically a U-shaped harp the size of a ukulele. The chap was into wings. He had them on his skull-shaped hat and his funky leather boots. He had the usual beyond-perfect face of a deity, but with a long narrow nose and thin eyes. His scraggly golden brown curls poking out from his hat needed a trim, as did his beard.

Daegan leaned over. "Anything I need to know?"

Quinn was glad his dragon king hadn't used telepathy here since nothing was private in this place. "No matter which three gods and/or goddesses rule a Tribunal, their word is final. All deities with VIPER take a turn, but Loki must enjoy other people's misery. He's here often. Lying will make your body glow red and the Tribunal is judge, jury and executioner. Actually, Sen is their executioner and enforcer. We're waiting for the Medb contingent to show up."

"I know who Loki and Hermes are, but not the woman."

Quinn eyed her golden hair, shapely body and creamy skin. He shuddered. "Based on the white dress and black lips, I'm thinking that must be Laima, one of the Baltic goddesses of destiny. It's said that if she kisses you, that's your last one ever. She's like a black widow spider, but with more of a punch."

Daegan drew back in disgust.

Cathbad appeared to the side of the dais where the accusers generally stood. Little had changed with him from the last time Quinn had been forced to look at his cocky expression.

Loki nodded to each of his partners in judgment, then made a show of looking around as though there were more than seven beings present. He asked, "Where is Macha?"

Quinn whispered, "He knows the answer. Sen would have informed him while we teleported."

The subtle movement of Quinn's head indicated the dragon king should speak now. Quinn hoped his leader understood the dynamics.

Daegan replied, "Macha is gone. I am the rightful ruler of Treoir."

Loki's eyebrows lifted. "How do you intend to rule a force as large as the Beladors, plus the Alterant-gryphons, without a pantheon to back you up?"

Cathbad interrupted. "Pardon me, Loki, but we've made it clear that at least half of that herd of Alterant-gryphons belongs to the Medb. If Macha is gone, who's going to give us our part of the stock?"

Waiting for silence, Daegan said, "I have no need for a pantheon to aid me in ruling Treoir and leading the Beladors. As for Alterants, gryphons or anyone else beneath my rule, they are my loyal followers, and therefore, protected from scavengers like the Medb. I will hand over none."

Cathbad looked like he was going to blow a gasket.

Quinn could do nothing to help Daegan with this, but he was fist pumping the guy for the way he stood strong for his people.

Loki moved a hand, requesting silence and told Cathbad, "The Tribunal must settle the Blood Law issue first." Then he told Daegan, "Since you claim responsibility for the Beladors, the Maistir on your right has been found guilty of withholding a possession of Queen Maeve's. Where is Kizira's body?"

The goddess Laima asked, "Is it time for sentencing? I'd like to kiss someone and return to my realm."

Loki gave her a look reserved for idiots. "Not yet."

"Very well. Carry on," she said, lifting a mirror to study her mouth full of pointed teeth.

Sen got them back on track when he called out to Loki, "The tomb holding the body was at the site where I went to retrieve the Belador, but it vanished. Someone teleported it away." Sen finished that statement by glaring at Daegan.

Quinn started to explain that the missing tomb was his fault, but Daegan softly ordered, "Let me handle this."

Then the dragon king asked, "Who requests the body?"

Loki didn't like that one bit. "We covered all of that when Quinn was last here. I have no intention of spending time repeating our past meeting."

"If that's the case, the Medb messenger will leave here empty-handed."

Cathbad turned a deep red, struggling to keep from spewing his thoughts.

Quinn wondered how the Beladors would move forward once the Tribunal killed Daegan. This was turning out worse than even Quinn had imagined.

Sen offered to Loki, "Would you like this imposter placed in lockup where he can't continue to interfere?"

Quinn glanced at Daegan, who seemed unperturbed by the threat.

"Yes, Sen. That would simplify this meeting."

Sen made a tiny move toward Daegan.

Without even looking at Sen, Daegan swung a hand out and made a slight pushing motion.

Sen slid backwards thirty feet, hunched over as if a massive fist had shoved him. He hugged his middle, trying to breathe.

Quinn's eyes practically jumped out of his head. *Are you kidding me?*

Sen's shocked face was worth gold.

Quinn couldn't form a word. Everyone suspected Sen of being a demigod based on his powers and attitude, but that dis would make Evalle's day if Quinn survived to tell her about it. Sen had treated her badly for years whenever Tzader or Quinn weren't around to call him on it.

Then again, Evalle hadn't backed away from Sen in Blairsville today.

Sen lifted his hands, clearly intending to teleport.

Daegan spared him a brief look. "I'm not ready to go anywhere. You might as well put your arms down. No point in continuing to look a fool."

That earned him a death glare, which drew a chuckle from the dragon king.

Quinn stifled the urge to warn Daegan that while he clearly had an upper hand with Sen, the three deities were not only powerful alone, they could combine their powers to act as one. If Quinn survived this, and that was a big if, he would corner Daegan for answers.

Every moment around this man opened up new questions.

Returning to face forward, Daegan folded his arms again, completely relaxed. He continued talking to Loki as if nothing significant had happened. "We were discussing the body. Who wants it?"

Jaw dropped in shock, Cathbad gaped, then he snapped his mouth closed and replied in a sharp voice, "'Tis very simple. Queen Maeve demands the return of Kizira's body, a former Medb priestess. It's all in the rules of *Dlí Fola*, the Blood Law."

Angling his head toward Quinn, Daegan asked in a firm voice, "What exactly did you tell me about Blood Law?"

Daegan could not have forgotten what Quinn had just spelled out for everyone at the campsite. That meant he wanted the details of the Blood Law spoken for everyone present.

More than happy to do anything to help Daegan, Quinn repeated the terms clearly for everyone to hear. He summed it up as, "Evidently after a battle, the bodies of significant members of either leader's family can be claimed and the opposing group is to return those remains."

Daegan crossed his arms and took his time responding. "I think I understand now, but where is the queen? Doesn't she have to claim the body herself?"

Cathbad argued, "I am her emissary."

Daegan told him, "I don't care who you are, you're not her. According to the rules, Queen Maeve must make the claim herself."

"She did the first time, damn you," Cathbad shouted.

"I was not present when that happened."

"Macha was, and agreed the body belonged to Maeve."

Quinn kept track of everyone's reactions to Daegan. Laima ignored the entire proceeding. As Hermes gently strummed his lyre, his gaze flicked from person to person, but he showed no sign of anger. So far.

Loki seemed intrigued by the volley of discussion between Daegan and Cathbad. That could be a good or a bad sign.

More often than not, it was a bad sign.

Daegan lifted his shoulders. "I cannot be held responsible for what Macha did prior to my taking over."

"Are you crazy?" Cathbad shouted. Recovering his composure, he asked Loki, "Are you going to let him challenge what was already decided?"

Daegan quickly countered with, "I'd like to remind everyone of a precedent Cathbad the Druid and Queen Maeve set upon waking from their long slumber. As I understand it, those two argued successfully in a Tribunal meeting that they should not be held responsible for any action taken by the Medb, which occurred prior to their reincarnating to take over the coven. If that ruling no longer holds true, then those two should be held responsible for every wrong committed by the Medb at any time in history."

Hermes stopped playing to ask Cathbad, "What say you?"

Cathbad spoke through clenched teeth. "We will not hold him to Macha's agreement."

Quinn wanted to applaud Daegan on that maneuver. No deity would support the use of Noirre majik, which the Medb had used to commit crimes many times.

Daegan calmly nodded, and addressed the deities. "In that case, the only issue left to settle before we move forward is whether you intend to set yet another precedent by allowing a second-in-command to call the Blood Law on another house."

All three deities sent blatant looks of contempt to Cathbad. Loki didn't hesitate when he said, "Nay, we will set no such precedent."

Cathbad conceded, "I will call Queen Maeve to join us."

Queen Maeve had just had the game board spun around on her.

Quinn let out the breath he'd been holding while Daegan negotiated that position, but he realized bringing in Queen Maeve added one more powerful being who could harm Daegan.

The dragon king had made no political allies here.

He was beginning to question whether this dragon king had any sense of self-preservation.

CHAPTER 42

Quinn would kill for this to be a human court where he could request a five-minute recess to talk to Daegan, but Tribunals were meant to be efficient for the deities, and without possibility of appeal.

Queen Maeve appeared in a flurry of flashing black. Hard to imagine black actually flashing, but it did. Her hair was wrapped up in a black and blue weave of jewels. Her gown molded to her shapely body.

She leaned toward Cathbad, who whispered to her, then she nodded, pulling her shoulders back, ready to do battle.

One look at Daegan told Quinn all he needed to know about the dragon king's relationship with that queen.

Daegan wanted her dead. His face was chiseled from cold fury.

The queen watched him the way a person would observe a rabid T-rex. That might not be far off the mark if Daegan lost his iron control.

Loki asked Cathbad, "Have you explained what has transpired?"

"Yes."

"What do you have to say, Queen Maeve?"

She lifted her nose in Daegan's direction and demanded, "Give me Kizira's body. Where is it?"

Daegan said nothing at first, staring at Maeve for a long moment, then he said, "Are you claiming something you feel belongs to you?"

"Of course it belongs to me."

Addressing Loki and company, Daegan asked, "How old is this Blood Law?"

Quinn watched Cathbad for a sign of how things were going. That druid might bust an artery if this went on very long, but he currently seemed confident.

Loki smiled. "It's as old as any god or goddess who attends Tribunals."

"I see," Daegan said, giving a casual nod. "Would claiming something you lost, Maeve, be similar to holding me as a prisoner for thousands of years? If so, that means I would be due compensation."

She ignored most of his comment. "I was told the Blood Law was explained to you. Don't waste my time with drivel."

All the entities had taken an interest at Daegan exposing what the queen had done to him.

"Do you deny having captured me two thousand years ago?" Daegan repeated slowly, daring her to lie to the Tribunal.

She lifted her chin to Loki. "That is not what we are here to discuss. I have a grievance on the table. I'm not addressing anything else but that grievance at this moment."

Loki said, "She has a point. We can't have multiple issues popping up or these meetings would never end. You've brought no formal grievance to the Tribunal, Daegan Treoir. In fact, we didn't know you existed until now. We see this issue between the two of you as something that we are not in a position to rule on since you are, as yet, not part of the coalition. Due to that and the fact that you are now free from any imprisonment, we will not open this for discussion."

Quinn growled low. Damn gods and goddesses played with words and situations. No one ever knew which way they would lean.

"I understand," Daegan replied in a nonchalant voice.

Queen Maeve looked ready to chew rocks. "The body. Where is it?"

"You can't have Kizira's body."

Pointing at Daegan, Queen Maeve ordered Loki, "He defies the court and he is not even a member of the coalition. Strike him down now."

Loki scratched his nose, thinking. Then he informed Daegan,

"We do not allow anyone to refuse the Tribunal decisions. There are only two options for those with supernatural powers. You either join the coalition or you and all who follow you become our enemy."

Daegan's mouth twitched with a smile. "You just said you would not allow multiple issues to be brought up. I haven't decided whether the coalition deserves Belador support."

That drew a gasp from Laima and Hermes.

Unbothered by the reaction, Daegan said, "If I decide in favor, then my warriors will join the coalition. I will let you know."

At this rate, the Tribunal would make an example of Quinn and Daegan before ordering their deaths. Yeah, this was going south fast, but Quinn had no way to guide them out of trouble.

Cathbad accused Daegan, "You're not powerful enough to rule a force the size of the Beladors. One of our Tribunal deities should lead them."

Loki's face took on a happy expression, as if that idea intrigued him.

Daegan chuckled, clearly not recognizing the threat hanging in the air. "You think to take what is mine, Maeve? Have you and Cathbad not learned anything yet?"

The queen sneered, "You are nothing more than the son of King Gruffyn. When he died, he left you nothing."

Loki lost his enthusiasm over leading the Beladors upon hearing that. "King Gruffyn of Treoir? The dragon king? You have dragon blood?"

"Yes."

That one word echoed around the realm.

Quinn finally identified the look in Queen Maeve's eyes. Fear. Whatever she knew about Daegan frightened her and from a being as powerful as she was, fear was saying something.

Flapping her arms and hands wildly, Queen Maeve warned the Tribunal, "You do know what happens when two dragons mate or have you forgotten history?"

"I remember," Loki acknowledged. "I recall King Gruffyn and the destruction that followed his death. There were rumors about his children's deaths after that, but those faded with time. I do recall that two mated dragons could possibly kill a god, *possibly*," he stressed. "But one alone in an unfamiliar realm would be at the mercy of those same gods and goddesses."

Maeve broke out the smile of a conquering queen.

Quinn would die here the minute he used his powers, but he would not stand by and allow them to kill Daegan, who had wronged no one. He whispered, "Say when. I'm ready."

Speaking out of the side of his mouth, Daegan said, "Do nothing unless I ask it of you."

Shit. This bloody sucked.

Cathbad grinned with more confidence than before.

Queen Maeve purred, "Give me Kizira's body now or ... you'll find out just how powerful a Tribunal can be."

Undeterred by the level of menace permeating the air, Daegan said in a bold voice, "I call the Blood Law first. I demand you return the body of my sister, whom you killed long before Kizira died. Do you deny it? Go ahead. I would like to see how a person who lies to a Tribunal glows red."

Everyone froze.

The three deities turned to Queen Maeve, who lowered her arms and stared back during the stretched silence. Cathbad shook her from her state when he whispered to her.

She said, "You ... you can't ... I demand Kizira. I'm not talking about anything else. You've refused the Tribunal and you're a threat to our kind." She swung her attention to Loki. "This is the best chance you'll ever have to rid the world of a deadly threat to gods and goddesses."

Now the Tribunal turned to Daegan.

Hermes stopped playing the music.

Laima perked up as if scenting prey.

Loki studied Daegan with deep consideration.

Quinn said under his breath, "We may have to ... give up the body."

"No." Daegan spoke with the measured sounds of someone instructing a jury. "Yes, I am of dragon blood. And there is always a threat from our kind, just as there is a threat from deities who misuse their powers." He glared at the queen then continued. "You may try to harm or kill me, and you *might* just succeed."

Every god and goddess bristled at that subtle slap.

Daegan said, "Then again, you might not survive the battle. If, however, you did survive, keep in mind that you all know who my father was, but what do you know of my mother?"

Questions popped up in every face Quinn searched, including Sen's.

Daegan told Maeve, "You don't even know how I was created, do you?"

She hissed at him.

"I'll explain. Until I was born, dragons were the product of mating two descendants of dragon blood, but my father's wife died birthing my sisters. He asked the gods for a son and he got me. To breed a dragon shifter with no female of dragon blood required intervention from *higher* powers."

Quinn had to lock his jaws to keep his lips closed. Holy gods. Daegan was a demigod? No wonder he'd blown off Sen.

Daegan wasn't through holding court. "If any of you feels confident you can survive my mother, then by all means come for me. But I doubt you have lived this long by attacking the children of an unknown deity. As we all know, mothers can be deadly when crossed, and I ... am my mother's *favorite*." He smiled. "We can finish our business here by exchanging bodies or we can battle. Which will it be?"

Loki's eyebrows bounced up and it didn't take long to figure out why. Daegan had given him an out. The trickster said, "If Queen Maeve delivers the body of your sister, then will you agree to produce Kizira's?"

"If we can do this immediately, then yes," Daegan agreed.

Disappointment registered in Quinn's chest for just a moment before he scolded himself. He and Daegan had to get out of here to live to fight another day, but his skin had turned cold at the thought of Queen Maeve using Kizira's body. He cursed himself a thousand times over for not cremating the remains.

The queen yelled, "You miserable dragon!" She looked up at Loki. "Don't you realize that if you fail to kill him now while you can, you may never get another chance?"

"I realize what you are saying," Loki told her. "But I find this situation too amusing to take sides. Is his claim that you killed his sister true? If so, you must hand over her body. Now."

Queen Maeve began growing in size, something Quinn was fairly certain would get a deity banned from the coalition.

Loki warned her, "This is unacceptable behavior, Maeve."

Her hair exploded from the perfectly styled look of moments ago and flew all around her head.

The dress burst into flames.

Cathbad shouted, "No, Maeve. Come down here. Don't do this."

"Shut up, all of you," she roared in a deep, evil voice. "You had a chance to kill that miserable dragon, but none of you has the nerve. I want no part of this spineless group if you aren't capable of carrying out a judgment."

Loki snarled, "We have always dealt out our judgments and at this moment, you are in contempt of our court." He lifted his hand, but a flash of red flared into a giant fireworks explosion that sucked into itself and disappeared.

Cathbad vanished a second later.

Well, hell. Quinn would never have bet on that happening.

Loki conferred with the other two deities then turned to Daegan. "We have no argument with you, dragon king, but where do you stand regarding the coalition?"

No longer adversarial, Daegan said, "I believe there is a need for a form of government among the preternaturals. I have no desire to govern any except those who follow me. I'll support VIPER as long as *all* of my people, including Beladors, Alterants, gryphons or any other beings who have sworn, or in future swear, allegiance to me, are treated fairly." He paused to address Sen when he added, "*No one* is to touch any of my people without coming to me first."

Returning to face the dais, Daegan continued. "Am I correct in assuming that after the queen's exit that the Medb are no longer members of the coalition?"

Loki studied on that a moment and said, "Yes. Her action is unacceptable. Henceforth, the Medb are no longer members of the coalition."

"I want to make one more thing clear," Daegan added. "Quinn who stands with me now, Evalle Kincaid, her mate Storm, Tzader Burke, Brina Treoir, Adrianna Lafontaine and Tristan the gryphon are my high council. In fact, Tristan is my second-in-command."

Quinn caught a noise of surprise from Sen, but didn't want to move and distract anyone from Daegan while he held the floor.

"My Beladors will continue to protect humanity and not engage in conflict with any other preternaturals unless given reason. If we don't do this, chaos will rule the human world, deities will form alliances, then we'll be spending our time battling each other. I possess the largest army, but they have families who are human. Their families are under my protection as well. Are we agreed?"

The deities exchanged a silent communication then Loki nodded. "Agreed." Then the smart mouth added, "I look forward to discovering who your mother is ... or was."

Daegan said, "You do that."

Then Quinn's body spun out of shape as Daegan teleported them away.

CHAPTER 43

Treoir Island

The fire caught quickly and flames engulfed the body.

An hour after the Tribunal meeting, Quinn stood straight, hands at his sides, thinking of the last time he'd held Kizira. What he would give to touch her one more time and part on better terms than they had, but that was never going to happen.

Tears pooled in his eyes, but he held them back. He'd shed enough over losing her.

He'd never really possessed her.

She'd come into his life for two weeks when he was a very young man, just long enough to discover that the warm young woman with too much heart was a Medb priestess.

But some things in life couldn't be avoided, like an unwanted Medb birthright.

Kizira had hated being a Medb, but when they went their separate ways more than thirteen years ago, she'd accepted her duty as he had his. He forgave her for not telling him sooner about their child. But he'd missed a child's lifetime with Phoedra.

He and Kizira had met a few times over the years since parting ways. They'd been sometimes lovers, and always enemies, but the last time he'd looked into her eyes was the one he'd carry with him for the rest of his life.

"How are you doing?" Evalle asked, stepping up beside him.

That broke his focus from the funeral pyre. "I'm fine."

Storm stepped up and said, "Lie."

When Quinn looked at him, he saw that Storm had been poking at him in a friendly way and Quinn answered with a shrug. "Let's say that I'm looking forward and the future will be fine."

"Truth."

Daegan had teleported Quinn to Treoir from the Tribunal, which probably really pissed off Sen, who now knew he wasn't so special after all. Then Daegan teleported the tomb from Evalle and Storm's garage, plus both of them and Tristan to Treoir, where Quinn explained what he wanted to do.

Brina stood in front of Tzader with his arms wrapped around her baby bump. They whispered between them in a sad tone.

Tristan had taken on the duty of creating the pyre once Quinn explained that he was going to cremate Kizira. Daegan actually suggested doing it here, which had surprised Quinn.

He would never have asked to have the funeral of a Medb priestess on Treoir Island.

Things were going to be different with Daegan, for sure. It sounded as if the Beladors were heading into a war, but thanks to Daegan's intervention, Quinn would be there for everyone, including Daegan.

Daegan walked over, arms crossed over his bulky chest. He was still dressed like a warrior from centuries ago, which must feel normal to him.

Once everyone had joined Quinn, he said, "First, I wish I hadn't put anyone in jeopardy because of my relationship with Kizira."

Evalle gently argued, "If not for that, Kizira would never have teamed up with me before the big battle here to help save our people. It wasn't all bad."

"No, it wasn't," he agreed. "But I want to thank all of you. This was more than I would have expected to have for her. I feel like this will be the closure I needed."

Daegan observed him with sharp eyes. "You must have had a reason for waiting to do this."

It was time to give Daegan the entire truth. "I did. When Kizira told me about our child at the last second before she died, I was ... wracked with guilt. I convinced myself that the one thing I could do was give Phoedra a body to grieve. If we were human, that wouldn't have been unusual, but we're not. I foolishly thought I could protect that body. I should have been thinking about protecting my child first and foremost."

Tristan said, "Now I understand more."

Tzader squeezed Quinn's shoulder, a sign of support, and Brina said, "We'll find her, Quinn."

"Yes we will," Evalle confirmed with a determination that surfaced anytime someone in her close circle of friends was in need.

Daegan said, "She must be found."

Quinn nodded, in total agreement. He had no idea where to start, but he would find his child.

"We have time, but there's no telling how much," Daegan said, confusing Quinn.

"Queen Maeve can't touch Kizira's body now," Evalle pointed out.

"That solves only one problem." Daegan took in every face, then said, "Cathbad and Queen Maeve had not discovered anything about this child before I left, but that doesn't mean they can't find out. The queen kept watching Kizira die on her scrying wall. She knew then that something was up and will suspect even more now that she's been denied the body."

Tzader said, "I'm pretty sure we wrecked that wall when we pulled you out of there, Daegan."

The dragon king nodded. "I hope so, but that will not prevent her from finding out through other ways. No secret remains hidden forever in our world. After today, she'll be even more determined to find out what Kizira was hiding."

"Can she?" Evalle asked. "I mean don't we plan to salt the ashes and spread them afterwards?"

"Yes," Quinn answered.

Daegan continued on his line of thought as he stared at the fire. "Queen Maeve did not manage to keep her coven growing over thousands of years and reincarnate by luck alone. She's a dangerous adversary who will not be stopped by a destroyed scrying wall." The dragon king finally dropped it by saying, "We still have to figure out who was behind Lorwerth. I'm not fully convinced that it was Maeve, or at least not Maeve alone. Not after seeing her at the Tribunal. That will wait for tomorrow. We'll meet to develop a strategy for hunting the girl then."

Quinn's heart had beaten faster with each declaration Daegan made. Where would Kizira have hidden their child to keep her from all this bloody insanity?

His gut twisted with worry for his daughter out there exposed to the predators of his world. Dark witches. Evil mages like the one who'd harmed Lanna. Demons, like the ones that hunted Reese.

Where had Reese gone? Was she safe?

He'd never find out.

If he'd gotten to know her better, he might have asked her to use her remote vision gift to help him find Phoedra, but she'd vanished into the ether. Whoever had sent her to Atlanta had very likely covered her tracks when she returned home.

What would that person say when Reese arrived empty-handed?

As the fire burned, he said his goodbye to Kizira and swore he'd find their daughter. Now he just had to figure out how to make good on that vow.

Yes, the Beladors had resources, but the world was a huge place and she was one small girl.

CHAPTER 44

Mosquito Mountain, Haida Gwaii Islands, British Columbia

When the crazy fog of colors caused by teleporting ended, Reese was standing on Yáahl's mountaintop.

His pedestal boulder in the middle of the pond was empty.

He had to know she was here.

I'm not in the mood for his crap. She called out, "Can we get this moving? I'm tired."

Way above, the giant raven flapped slowly, circling the strange dome that enclosed his realm here. Yáahl continued spiraling down slowly until his raven feet touched the stone and he turned into his human form, all decked out in black.

The guy needed some fashion tips.

Holding his arms out, he asked, "What, no greeting?"

She had little enthusiasm for playing his games, but in an effort to move this along she replied, "Hey, Yáahl."

This time she sounded like Paula Deen after a wedding cake had fallen.

"I don't see a body, Reese. Do you have Kizira tucked in a pocket?"

Jimmy Fallon, you're not.

This was the moment she had to face never getting her powers back. Her stomach ached and her heart was in full depression.

Ten years without her powers had been hard, but in the back of her mind she'd always had hope. Yáahl was a pain in her backside, but he was good for his word and ten years ago he'd said that when he thought she'd earned them back, he'd untether

her powers.

That was all in the past now.

"No, I don't have the body, Yáahl."

"Why not? What could possibly be more important than your powers?"

She'd be asking herself that for the rest of her life and her answer would always be the same. "It wasn't mine to give to you and it wasn't yours to have. A lot of bad people were after Kizira's body, but one man risked everything to protect her." Reese's eyes burned with tears she would not shed.

Not here.

She swallowed the disappointment and said, "It came down to a choice. I had to ask myself if I should take something important from someone else just to get what I wanted. A funny thing happened along the way. I realized I wouldn't be able to live with myself if I did that. So, really the choice was whether I could take what I'd been sent for and leave without a conscience or leave that body with the person it belonged to and look myself in the mirror forever. I'm a fan of mirrors."

What she would not share with Yáahl was that she wanted to remember that image of Quinn's face filled with the relief that he hadn't failed Kizira.

No man would ever care that much for Reese, but it was nice to know one man with a heart of gold existed. A man capable of putting the woman he cared for first.

"You do recall our agreement?"

"Yessss. If I did not return with Kizira's body, you would never unbind my powers."

He frowned and rolled his head from side to side as if considering her answer. "That's not exactly what I said."

She had to suffer being critiqued on a paraphrase?

"In fact," Yáahl went on explaining. "I said that if you allowed the body to fall into the wrong hands I would never release your powers."

She thought through that, trying to figure out his point. "And?"

"My minions tell me the body was kept from the wrong hands."

She brightened. "Does that mean you're going to free my

powers?"

"No."

She swallowed a curse, not in any mood to be punished by Yáahl's landscape. "I'm not following you. Is this good or bad?"

"Neither and both."

Did she mention how much she hated this crap? She stared at him, determined to make him explain, which he did.

"You failed to retrieve the body, but you succeeded in keeping it from the wrong people. More importantly, you have proven you can change and that there is hope for you."

Don't smart off. She kept repeating that in her head.

"For that reason, you may yet receive your powers back," Yáahl explained.

That was good, right?

So why did she still feel such loss after all that had happened? Maybe because she'd had a taste of her powers, just enough to miss them even more, plus ... she'd never see Quinn again.

That was a stupid thought. She wanted nothing to do with men.

But she had liked being with Quinn.

It didn't matter if she ever saw him again. She couldn't compete with a ghost. Kizira had been a Medb priestess and from all accounts she'd read on the dark net, a beautiful one. It didn't take much of a leap for Reese to realize Quinn had been in love with Kizira.

Reese had no powers, was not a beauty and demons would still be hunting her. Not exactly a catch.

She still wondered about something, though. It was like getting to the end of a story and finding the last pages blank. "One more thing. What about Kizira's body? Is it safe?"

Only an idiot would ask him about the body she'd failed to deliver, but she'd proven her lack of IQ back in Georgia when she'd gone into that demon-infested energy field.

She'd do it again ... if she had Quinn at her side.

"Kizira's body is finally at rest and no longer under threat from her family. That is enough for me."

That was that. Now to get back to her life, but that wasn't going to happen. Not in the same place she'd lived.

She stated, "I'll go somewhere far from my place in San

Diego, but please don't lift your protection from my neighborhood. It isn't their fault I moved there." Or that she'd made friends.

And found a dog.

Gibbons's happy fur face popped into her mind.

She struggled against tears again. Would she have to give up her dog? Of course she would, or some demon would kill him. Her friends would forget about her, but how could her sweet mutt understand why she'd abandoned him?

Yáahl said, "I will agree to that, but I have no wish to spend my energy watching over your friends and that beast. You can do that yourself."

Her head snapped up. Had she heard correctly? "What are you saying?"

"I'm sending you home and the area you consider your neighborhood will be repellent to demons. Step outside of that and you're on your own. Understood?"

"I get it. Thank you." She was thoroughly confused on what he was up to, because Yáahl made no decision lightly. But if that made him happy right now, then going home to a demon-free zone worked for her.

She lifted the medallion cord over her head and held it in her hand. A crow flew down, picked it up and flew away.

Okay, then.

"You're definitely different," Yáahl mused.

Reese considered his words, but had learned less was more with him. She gave a noncommittal, "Uh huh."

"I think you met someone who made an impression on you."

"You think? Didn't your minions report everything I did?"

"They observe and return with specific details, but they could not observe you late in your visit."

He'd sent her into the middle of a bloody battle and called it a visit. What was he saying? Ah, the crows couldn't keep track of her while she'd been inside the buzzing energy field.

Not surprising, since other powers hadn't worked while the energy field was active, but still ...

Interesting.

He suggested, "It's not a weakness to care for someone again, Reese."

"Doesn't matter. I don't care for anyone." She'd said that too quickly.

Yáahl couldn't possibly know that she'd had a momentary attraction to Quinn, and she would volunteer absolutely nothing.

"That beast you feed. You care for him."

"Okay, I'll admit that Gibbons matters to me."

"And your neighbors and dog sitter."

"Fine. Okay, my neighbors and dog sitter, too." Her neighbor *was* her dog sitter. "What's your point? I don't want anyone harmed just because I'm around. It's not fair to them."

He moved around on the boulder platform and even in human form he reminded her of a giant bird, stalking around as he thought.

"Remember one thing, Reese, it is always easier to lie to others than it is to yourself. Perhaps Atlanta offers something San Diego does not."

Her heart moved around, trying to find a happy place in her chest when she thought about Quinn. He'd been nice to her even when he knew she wanted Kizira's body, too.

There was no future in thinking about him.

She pushed off the silly attraction and said, "I have no interest in ever going back to Atlanta. I now have two reasons to avoid the place." That city was bad luck for her heart. The first man she'd met there had gotten her pregnant then tossed her and her baby aside. The second one would never be hers to consider.

"Then you have no desire to go back or to have anyone from there find you?"

"Correct on both accounts. I want to return to my safe little corner of the world." Besides, Quinn was never going to look for her. "Can I go home now? Are we done?"

"You may go home. However, we are not done. You did not satisfy my request, but I'm generous in heart so I will allow you another opportunity to make good on your debt."

Reese rolled her eyes, not even caring at this point if she got swatted. She laughed to herself. If she had to deal with him again to get her powers, it couldn't be as bad as this last trip, right?

The lights dimmed in the dome. Her eyelids grew heavy and dropped.

She tried to shake off the sluggish feeling, but she slept

deeply until a honking horn woke her.

Her eyes popped open.

She was standing inside her apartment in San Diego. At least Yáahl hadn't dumped her in the yard or the middle of the street. *Gibbons!*

She couldn't wait to get a big sloppy hug from her dog, but she was filthy and starving.

After racing through a shower and throwing on a pair of shorts and a T-shirt, she was making a sandwich when the door opened and Gibbons came barreling in. She turned just in time to catch his paws when he jumped on her, whining and licking. Dogs were a gift to humans.

They loved unconditionally and missed you when you were gone. Gibbons always knew when she needed a hug.

Right behind him, a sweet girl with pink hair—this week—and a dazzling smile walked in carrying his leash and laughing. A tiny diamond in her nose winked. "I saw your Jeep outside and figured you'd be ready for company."

Yáahl had returned her Jeep?

Without thinking, she glanced toward the corner by the sofa, where she normally kept her shotgun and short sword stashed. There sat the innocuous-looking backpack made of heavy, rip-proof canvas, with the lock fastened on the zipper.

Well, well.

Reese might just have to thank him next time they met if it wasn't another ten years down the road. She said, "Yeah, just got back. How's it going with your boyfriend, Snook?"

"He's an idiot. I'm on to the next one." Snook made herself at home and fixed a half sandwich, then started chomping on it.

Gibbons finally dropped down to stand shoved up against Reese's leg. She buried her fingers in his thick, curly hair, so damn happy to be home even if she didn't have her powers back.

Snook asked, "How was your trip? We missed you."

Reese smiled at the fact that people did care for her. Yáahl had told her when she first left his realm to live on her own that she couldn't have her powers back until she would respect them. He'd told her she was closed off from everyone and that a person didn't need powers to be alone. Last, he'd said that powers shouldn't be wasted on someone with a death wish.

She'd left ten years ago, angry and determined to hunt demons in spite of his accusation.

The burning anger had subsided.

She'd fight a demon if need be, but after this last trip, she had no desire to hunt them.

Maybe he'd been right and she'd had a death wish at one time, but now?

Things did feel different. She felt different.

She wanted more out of life than just existing. It had taken meeting Quinn and seeing herself in him for that to happen. He had so much life to live, but he was burying it under guilt.

So had she. No more.

Don't think about Quinn.

It hurt to put him behind her, but he was not part of her world now.

Reese answered, "My trip turned out better than I would have expected. I missed both of you, too." She was so damned glad to have her home and this neighborhood. "Want to have popcorn and a movie here tonight to celebrate my being home?"

"Yes! Let me tell Donella you're home so she'll know where I am. Be right back."

Donella was her foster mother. The woman could be a bit stern at times, but Reese liked her, recognizing her maternal instinct and that she cared deeply for the girl.

Gibbons barked at Snook.

Reese said, "Now he misses you more than me."

"That's only because I spoiled him at lunch." Then she was gone. Reese and Gibbons went into the living room, where she found a houseplant in a painted clay pot, one of Snook's signature creations.

It had a small card sitting in front of it.

Reese smiled. She'd been telling Snook that people spend too much time online and don't appreciate the value of a written note until they get one. For the two years Reese had lived here, she'd been writing Snook notes.

She always wrote a thank you note for watching Gibbons and sometimes included a gift card to Snook's favorite clothing store.

Opening the envelope, Reese warmed at the message from a young girl who was on her way to charming the world.

Reese –

Thanks for working so much this summer on my self-defense   skills. My ex-boyfriend wasn't thrilled when I made him sorry for trying to stick his hand down my pants. You'd have been proud of me. My new boyfriend saw what happened and was very impressed with me, so he's showing me a few more moves I'm practicing. Can't wait to show you.

Anyhow, please don't kill this plant. It just needs a little love.

Phoedra, aka Snook

❧

Watch for BELADOR COSAINT (book 9) in fall of 2017.

NOTE FROM DIANNA

Thank you for reading this series. If you'd like to keep up with my new book releases and find out about events I'll be attending, please join my newsletter at www.AuthorDiannaLove.com - I only send them about once a quarter and I NEVER give away emails, because that annoys me, too. ☺

Thanks so much!!
Dianna

Website: www.AuthorDiannaLove.com and www.Beladors.com
Facebook – "Dianna Love Fan Page"
Twitter @DiannaLove
"Dianna Love Reader Community" Facebook group page
(Readers invited)

BLOOD TRINITY – Belador Book 1

Atlanta has become the battlefield between human and demon.

As an outcast among her own people, Evalle Kincaid has walked the line between human and beast her whole life as a half-blood Belador. An Alterant. Her true origins unknown, she searches to learn more about her past before it kills her, but when a demon claims a young woman in a terrifying attack and there's no one else to blame, Evalle comes under suspicion.

The one person who can help her is Storm, the sexy new agent brought in to catch her in a lie, just one of his gifts besides being a Skinwalker. On a deadly quest for her own survival, Evalle is forced to work with the mysterious stranger who has the power to unravel her world. Through the sordid underbelly of an alternate Atlanta where nothing is as it seems to the front lines of the city where former allies now hunt her, Evalle must prove her innocence or pay the ultimate price. But saving herself is the least of her problems if she doesn't stop the coming apocalypse. The clock is ticking and Atlanta is about to ignite.

"BLOOD TRINITY is an ingenious urban fantasy … Book One in the Belador series will enthrall you during every compellingly entertaining scene." **Amelia Richards, Single Titles**

"…a well written book that will take you out of your everyday life and transport you to an exciting new world…" **Heated Steve**

ALTERANT: Belador Book 2

Evalle must hunt her own kind...or die with them.

In this explosive new world of betrayals and shaky alliances, as the only Alterant not incarcerated, Evalle faces an impossible task — recapture three dangerous, escaped creatures before they slaughter more humans…or her.

When words uttered in the heat of combat are twisted against her, Evalle is blamed for the prison break of three dangerous Alterants and forced to recapture the escapees. Deals with gods and goddesses are tricky at best, and now the lives of all Beladors, and the safety of innocent humans, rides on Evalle's success. Her Skinwalker partner, Storm, is determined to plant all four of his black jaguar paws in the middle of her world, but Evalle has no time for a love life. Not when a Tribunal sends her to the last place she wants to show her face.

The only person she can ask for help is the one man who wants to see her dead.

"There are SO many things in this series that I want to learn more about; there's no way I could list them all." **Lily, Romance Junkies Reviews**

∞

THE CURSE: Belador book 3

Troll powered gang wars explode in cemeteries and no one in Atlanta is safe.

Demonic Svart Trolls have invaded Atlanta and Evalle suddenly has little hope of fulfilling a promise with the freedom of an entire race hanging in the balance, even if she had more than two days. She takes a leap of faith, seeking help from Isak, the Black Ops specialist who recently put Evalle in his cross hairs and has a personal vendetta against Alterants who killed his best friend.

Bloody troll-led gang wars force Evalle into unwittingly exposing a secret that endangers all she holds dear, and complicates her already tumultuous love life with the mysterious Skinwalker, Storm. But it's when the entire Medb coven comes after her that Evalle is forced to make a game-changing decision with no time left on the clock.

"Evalle, continues to be one of my favorite female warriors in paranormal/urban fantasy... I loved The Curse... This was a great story from start to finish, super fun, lots of action, couples to root for, and a fantastic heroine." **Barb, The Reading Café**

⚮

RISE OF THE GRYPHON: Belador Book 4

If dying is the cost of protecting those you love… bring it.

Evalle has a chance to find out her true origin, and give all Alterants a place in the world. To do so, she'll have to take down the Belador traitor and bring home a captured friend, which means infiltrating the dangerous Medb coven. To do that, she'll have to turn her back on her vows and enter a vicious game to the death. What she does discover about Alterants is not good, especially for the Beladors.

Her best friends, Tzader and Quinn, face unthinkable choices, as relationships with the women they love grow twisted. With time ticking down on a decision that will compel allies to become deadly enemies, Evalle turns to Storm and takes a major step in their relationship, but the witchdoctor he's been hunting now stalks Evalle. Now Evalle is forced to embrace her destiny . . . but at what price?

"Longtime fans of the Belador series will have much to celebrate in the fearless Evalle Kincaid's fourth outing…with such heart and investment, each scene has an intensity that will quicken the pulse and capture the imagination..."

— RT Book Reviews

⚮

DEMON STORM: Belador book 5

We all have demons... some are more real than others.

With Treoir Island in shambles after a Medb attack that left the survival of the missing Belador warrior queen in question and

Belador powers compromised, there is one hope for her return and their future – Evalle Kincaid, whose recent transformation has turned her into an even more formidable warrior. First she has to locate Storm, the Skinwalker she's bonded with who she believes can find the Belador queen, but Storm stalks the witch doctor who's threatening Evalle's life. When he finally corners the witch doctor, she throws Storm a curve that may cost him everything, including Evalle. The hunter becomes the hunted, and Evalle must face her greatest nightmare to save Storm and the Beladors or watch the future of mankind fall to deadly preternatural predators.

DEMON STORM includes a BONUS SHORT STORY - DEADLY FIXATION, from the Belador world.

"There is so much action in this book I feel like I've burned calories just reading it." **D Antonio**

"...nonstop adventures overflowing with danger and heartfelt emotions. DEMON STORM leaves you breathless on countless occasions."

~~Amelia Richard, Single Titles

∞

WITCHLOCK: Belador Book 6

Witchlock vanished in the 13th century ... or did it?

If Atlanta falls, Witchlock will sweep the country in a bloodbath.

After finally earning her place among the Beladors, Evalle is navigating the ups and downs of her new life with Storm when she's sucked into a power play between her Belador tribe and the Medb coven. Both groups claim possession of the Alterant gryphons, especially Evalle, the gryphon leader. But an influx of demons and dark witches into Atlanta threatens to unleash war between covens, pitting allies against each other as a legendary majik known as Witchlock invades the city and attacks powerful beings. Evalle has one hope for stopping the invasion, but the cost may be her sanity and having to choose which friend to save.

"Evalle and friends are back in another high energy, pulse pounding adventure…Fans of Rachel Caine's Weather Warden series will enjoy this series. I surely do." **In My Humble Opinion Blogspot**

❧

ROGUE BELADOR: Belador Book 7

Immortals fear little … except a secret in the wrong hands.

While searching for a way to save Brina of Treoir's failing memories, Tzader Burke discovers someone who can help her if he is willing to sneak into the heart of his enemy's stronghold— TÅµr Medb. He'll do anything to protect the woman he loves from becoming a mindless empty shell, but his decision could be the catalyst for an apocalyptic war. The deeper he digs for the truth, the more lies he uncovers that shake the very foundation of being a Belador and the future of his clan.

With battles raging on every front, a secret is exposed that two immortal powers have spent thousands of years keeping buried. Tzader and his team have no choice but to fight for what they believe in, because the world as they know it is never going to be the same again.

❧

DRAGON KING OF TREOIR: Belador Book 8

The Treoir dragon holds the fate of the Beladors in one hand … and his own in the other.

The Beladors finally have a true leader in Daegan, their new dragon king, but life is far from secure now that they've inherited his enemies. As their Maistir, Vladimir Quinn played a risky role in freeing the dragon from the lair of their enemy, the Medb.

Quinn now faces a heavy price for his part. The Medb queen is out for blood. Vigilante killings erupt among Atlanta's secret preternatural community and all fingers point to the Beladors. The dragon king has his first real test as a ruler when he has to choose between protecting his people and entering a hostile realm full of deities capable of killing a dragon. But as a two-thousand-year-old warrior, Daegan has never shied away from any battle. Quinn, Evalle, Storm and friends race to discover who is trying to turn the entire VIPER coalition against the Beladors before war breaks out. With the clock also ticking down for Quinn, who has been ordered to hand over Kizira's body to the Medb queen, Daegan reveals an even greater reason the Beladors have to prevent the queen from any chance to use necromancy on that body than secrets Quinn protects.

Freedom is never free. Not when the powerful gods and goddesses poised to decide Quinn's fate see an opportunity to also destroy a threat to their existence – the last dragon shifter.

"When it comes to urban fantasy stories, Dianna Love is a master." ~~A. Richards, Always Reviewing

Watch for **BELADOR COSAINT** (book 9) in fall of 2017.

OTHER BOOKS BY DIANNA:

Complete Slye Temp romantic thriller Series
Last Chance To Run (free e-book for limited time)
Nowhere Safe
Honeymoon To Die For
Kiss The Enemy
Deceptive Treasures
Stolen Vengeance
Fatal Promise

Micah Caida young adult Trilogy
Time Trap (ebook free e-book for limited time)
Time Return
Time Lock

To read excerpts, go to http://www.MicahCaida.com

(Micah Caida is the collaboration of NYT bestseller Dianna Love
and USA Today bestseller Mary Buckham)

AUTHOR'S BIO

New York Times bestseller Dianna Love once dangled over a hundred feet in the air to create unusual marketing projects for Fortune 500 companies. She now writes high-octane romantic thrillers, young adult and urban fantasy. Fans of the bestselling Belador urban fantasy series will be thrilled to know more books are coming after Dragon King of Treoir. Dianna's Slye Temp sexy romantic thriller series wrapped up with Gage and Sabrina's book–Fatal Promise–in June 2016, but Dianna is working on a new spinoff series that will include some of the Slye Temp characters. Look for her books in print, e-book and audio. On the rare occasions Dianna is out of her writing cave, she tours the country on her BMW motorcycle searching for new story locations. Dianna lives in the Atlanta, GA area with her husband, who is a motorcycle instructor, and with a tank full of unruly saltwater critters.

Visit her website at **www.AuthorDiannaLove.com** or Join her **Dianna Love Reader Community** group page on Facebook and get in on the fun!

A WORD FROM DIANNA...

Thank you for reading *Dragon King Of Treoir*. As you can see, we have a lot of new developments happening and more coming down the road. I love these characters and this series so much – I hope it shows in the stories I share with you.

No book happens without the support and love of my amazing husband, Karl. He's my rock day and night, through all that pops up in my life.

The next person who is there to keep me on track from managing communications that I would miss when I'm deep in my writing cave to being the best first reader any author could ask for is Cassondra. A big hug and thank you to Joyce Ann McLaughlin who is one of my very early readers and also my audio editor. Super thank you also to Judy Carney, Steve Doyle, Kimber Mirabella, Jennifer Cazares and Sharon Livingston Griffiths, who all have fingerprints on the pages from early reading and/or copy editing book – thank you so much!!

Extra thanks to Xiamara Parathenopaeus and SSquared Productions for all the amazing art you've so generously created.

Kim Killion creates the awesome covers for all my books, plus other art I'm constantly needing, and Jennifer Litteken takes the pages I send her then waves her formatting wand over them to do her majik. Much appreciation to both of you.

Hugs and love to Karen Marie Moning, who is so generous in spirit. She's a sweet friend who I always enjoy seeing. Speaking of which, I'll be signing this book with her at Karen's FEVERSONG release event in New Orleans Jan 11-16, 2017. Go to my www.authordiannalove.com for details.

I want to also thank considerate people I run into when researching areas of Atlanta. We have a wonderful city full of welcoming people who will chat with a stranger or walk a few steps to show you how to find something. I'm originally from Florida and love that state as well, but I've been in the Atlanta area since the mid 70s. That's why it's the main setting for the Beladors – this is home for me.

Thank you also to my peeps on the Dianna Love Reader Community group page (Facebook). You give me a place to visit that brightens my day. I miss you when I'm gone and always look forward to coming back.

Dianna

CPSIA information can be obtained
at www.ICGtesting.com
Printed in the USA
LVOW13s1611020217
523022LV00012B/1383/P